TO DIE FOR

**Center Point
Large Print**

**This Large Print Book carries the
Seal of Approval of N.A.V.H.**

TO DIE FOR

A NOVEL OF ANNE BOLEYN

Sandra Byrd

CENTER POINT LARGE PRINT
THORNDIKE, MAINE

This Center Point Large Print edition is published
in the year 2012 by arrangement with Howard Books,
a division of Simon & Schuster, Inc.

The text of this Large Print edition is unabridged.
In other aspects, this book may
vary from the original edition.
Printed in the United States of America.
Set in 16-point Times New Roman type.

ISBN: 978-1-61173-301-3

Library of Congress Cataloging-in-Publication Data

Byrd, Sandra.
To die for : a novel of Anne Boleyn / Sandra Byrd.
p. cm.
ISBN 978-1-61173-301-3 (library binding : alk. paper)
1. Large type books. I. Title.
PS3552.Y678T6 2012
813'.54—dc23

2011037836

ad augusta per angusta

Wyatt Family Tree

Richard Wyatt ⟶ Margaret Clark
B. 1428   B. Unknown

1. Margaret Bailiff ⟶ Henry Wyatt ⟶ 2. Anne Skinner
B. Unknown   B. 1460   B. 1482

John ⟶ Margaret   Thomas ⟶ Elizabeth
Rogers   (Alice)   Wyatt   Brook
B. Unknown   Wyatt   B. 1500   B. 1503
       B. 1485

John Rogers   Anne / Mary   Thomas
B. 1501   (Meg)   Wyatt
                  Wyatt   The Younger
Margaret Rogers Lee   B. 1501   B. 1521
B. 1515

Other Issue   Henry
                  (Edmund)
                  Wyatt
                  B. 1503

Boleyn Family Tree

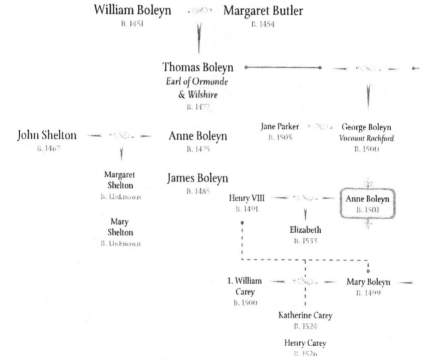

William Boleyn
B. 1451

Margaret Butler
B. 1454

Thomas Boleyn
Earl of Ormonde
& Wilshire
B. 1477

John Shelton
B. 1467

Anne Boleyn
B. 1475

Jane Parker
B. 1505

George Boleyn
Viscount Rochford
B. 1500

Margaret
Shelton
B. Unknown

James Boleyn
B. 1485

Henry VIII
B. 1491

Anne Boleyn
B. 1501

Mary
Shelton
B. Unknown

Elizabeth
B. 1533

1. William
Carey
B. 1500

Mary Boleyn
B. 1499

Katherine Carey
B. 1524

Henry Carey
B. 1526

Howard Family Tree

Thomas Howard		Elizabeth		Roger
Duke of Norfolk		Tilney		Bourchier
B. 1443		B. 1445		B. 1445

Elizabeth Howard
B. 1480

2. Elizabeth		Thomas		1. Anne
Stafford dau.		Howard		of York
Edward, Duke of		*Duke of Norfolk*		*Countess*
Buckingham		B. 1473		*of Surrey*
B. 1475				B. 1475

Henry Howard
Earl of Surrey
B. 1515

Mary Howard		Henry Fitzroy
B. 1519		*Duke of Richmond*
		B. 1519

2. William Stafford
B. 1500

| Thomas Bryan | | Margaret Bourchier |
| B. Unknown | | B. 1468 |

Francis Bryan
B. 1490

Nicholas Carewe		Elizabeth
B. 1496		Bryan Carewe
		B. 1500

Henry VIII Family Tree

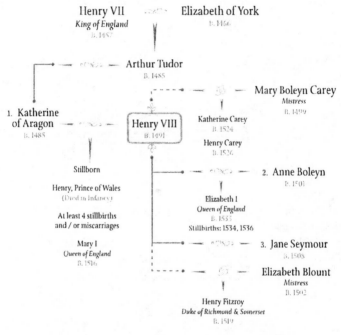

Henry VII
King of England
B. 1457

Elizabeth of York
B. 1466

Arthur Tudor
B. 1486

Mary Boleyn Carey
Mistress
B. 1499

1. Katherine of Aragon
B. 1485

Henry VIII
B. 1491

Katherine Carey
B. 1524

Henry Carey
B. 1526

Stillborn

Henry, Prince of Wales
(Died in Infancy)

At least 4 stillbirths
and / or miscarriages

Mary I
Queen of England
B. 1516

2. Anne Boleyn
B. 1501

Elizabeth I
Queen of England
B. 1533
Stillbirths: 1534, 1536

3. Jane Seymour
B. 1508

Elizabeth Blount
Mistress
B. 1502

Henry Fitzroy
Duke of Richmond & Somerset
B. 1519

1. **Louis XII**
King of France
B. 1462

Mary Tudor
B. 1496

2. **Charles Brandon**
Duke of Suffolk
B. 1484

Margaret Tudor
B. 1489

James IV
King of Scotland
B. 1473

Ogilvy Family Tree

William Ogilvy
Earl of Asquith
B. 1470

Rose Mayfew
B. Unknown

Walter Ogilvy
B. 1497

Martha Curlford
B. Unknown

William Ogilvy
B. 1499

Walter Ogilvy
The Younger
B. 1526

Philip Montague
Son of Earl Blenheim
B. Unknown

Rose Ogilvy
B. 1501

Philip
Montague
The Younger
B. 1525

Charlotte Denbigh
Ward of the Earl of Asquith
B. 1509

Matthew
Montague
B. 1530

PROLOGUE

There are many ways to arrive at the Tower of London, though there are few ways out. Kings and queens ride in before a coronation, retinue trailing like a train of ermine. Prisoners, however, arrive on foot, shoved through one cavernous gate or another by the wardens, who live, as all do, at the mercy of a merciless king. Some unfortunate few are delivered to the Tower by water.

The Thames lapped against our boat as it stopped to allow for the entry gate to be raised. The metal teeth lifted high enough for the oarsmen to row us into the Tower's maw, called Traitor's Gate. This beast never ate its fill and, like all beasts of prey, ate only flesh. It brought to mind the words of King David. *My soul is among lions: and I lie even among them that are set on fire, even the sons of men, whose teeth are spears and arrows, and their tongue a sharp sword.*

I glanced up as Lady Zouche caught a sob in her handkerchief. I then looked to my older sister, Alice, for comfort. She held my gaze with a somber shake of her head. Our falsely accused brother was even now waiting, being digested in the belly within. For the first time Alice had no comfort to offer me, no tonic of hope.

Momentarily we bumped up against the stone stairways leading out of the water and were commanded to quickly disembark.

ONE

=====

Year of Our Lord 1518
Allington Castle, Kent, England

"Come with me," I whispered to Anne. She turned to look at her older sister, Mary, busy flirting with our tutors—forbidden, and therefore enticing, conquests. After assessing the safety of our escape Anne turned back to me and nodded. She was up for an adventure, as I knew she would be. Rose Ogilvy sat in the corner, carefully plying her needle in and out of a stretch of muslin. She was seventeen years old, same as Anne and I, but I knew she would shy away from this particular exploit, any particular exploit, in fact. To save her embarrassment I didn't ask her along.

We slipped out the door, gathered the layers of skirts in our hands, and then raced down the long stone hallway. Recently painted portraits of my Wyatt ancestors were awkwardly affixed to the walls. When he bought the castle, my father, Henry Wyatt, had placed them there to make our family seem more ancient and noble than it was. We were not exactly pretenders but not exactly of Norman blood, either. They stared down at me, ill at ease, smiths and butchers and small-time landowners now forced into velvets and ruffs within a span of time no broader than the width of my hand. And yet we were gentry now. My father expected me to act like the lady he'd suffered to make me be.

We slid out the main entrance, one or two servants catching my eye and warning me back inside with a stern look. "No, Mistress Meg," one urged me. I disregarded them. They knew what might lie ahead for me—they'd borne the same fate, maybe worse. But I refused to be intimidated.

Anne and I linked arms and strolled toward the rows of unattended garden. Just beyond, on the neatly clipped field, our brothers play-jousted with long branches though all were training for real jousts as well. As we strolled by, my brother Thomas stopped, dipped into a bow, and flourished his hat in our direction. "What a polite young man," Anne said. "Mayhap you'll notice, *my* brother George isn't tipping his hat toward *me.*"

I grinned. "My brother isn't tipping his hat toward me, either. He'd as soon ignore me as do me good. It's you he's trying to impress, as well you know." A light flush of pleasure spread up

Anne's long neck and a little catlike mewl escaped her lips. She fully realized the effect she'd begun to have on men. Whilst she didn't court their praise, false modesty was not her besetting sin, either.

"I see another bow and this one is particularly in *your* direction," she said. I looked up and saw Will Ogilvy.

A year older than I, Will had brown hair that was long and tousled, his face slightly reddened from the joust. I couldn't help but notice that his arms and chest had thickened over the summer as he grew from a gangly boy into an assured young man. Even from this distance I could see his eyes had the same merry twinkle for me they always had. I nodded primly in his direction—after all, I was a lady, and we were in mixed company. He winked at me.

A wink! The audacity. Who else had seen it?

"Mayhap Lord Ogilvy's son should come out of the field. He seems to have dust in his eye," Anne teased. I turned toward her and grinned, thankful for her faithful friendship. She never trained her charm on Will. She knew I planned to have him for myself.

Rewardingly, he seemed completely uninterested in Anne.

We sat in the gardens, enveloped in the haze of the exotic scent of my mother's jasmine plants, gossiping about overheard conversations between

14

Anne's ambassador father and high-born mother; they had sent Anne and her sister, Mary, to apprentice at the French court when Princess Mary married some years back and they were to return shortly, after this visit home with their father. We talked about my sister, Alice, who had borne yet another child. I would soon go to stay with her for a few months, if my father allowed it. But as Alice was an obedient girl, marrying young and bearing quickly, my father favored nearly every request she made. Alas, the same could not be said for me.

"We've got new horses." I finally got the conversation around to its planned target. "My father's horsemaster brought them round last week."

"Ooh," Anne said. "Are they fast?"

"I don't know . . . ," I answered. We'd prided ourselves—unseemly, I suppose—on riding as fast and as well as any boy in our group.

"Should we see?" she asked me, as I knew she would. For me to suggest the idea would be disobedient, but for me to accommodate a friend would be hospitality indeed.

We ran to the stables and after petting old favorites we walked to the stalls where the new horses were housed. Our vanity guided our choices. Anne picked out her favorite, a raven mare, barely three years old with deep black eyes, like her own. I showed her the one I loved best, a tamed stallion with a thick auburn mane like my own. He glanced nervously about his stall till I gentled him with quiet words and touches.

"Should you have them saddled?"

"My father shouldn't be home from court till tomorrow morning." Then I called over a stable boy. "Saddle these two for us, please."

"If'n you say so, miss," he said, unable to disobey me but nervous nonetheless. I smiled kindly at him, hoping to gentle him as I'd done the stallion.

"I do," I said. And then Anne and I raced and rode.

The fields were thick and green, flowers clinging on the tips of the field grass, ready to fall forward into the late summer's heat. We slowed when we came to the woods and picked our way through the tangle of downed trees, their mossy shroud bringing a soft, dank smell.

"I've missed this," Anne said. "My father won't let me ride our horses unattended anymore."

"Mine says the same."

"Why did you not say anything when I suggested the ride?"

"I felt it would be our last time, as girls," I told her. "We're becoming women now and our lives are going to change."

We turned our horses around, back toward Allington.

And then.

I felt his eyes upon me afore I saw him from a

distance. My father stood in front of the stables. My first trembling urge was to turn my mount and gallop back into the woods, as far as he could carry me, and not return. If Anne hadn't been with me, I might have. But I couldn't leave her and anyway, where would I go?

"Your father . . . ," she said softly, though I heard her over the hoofbeats.

I nodded. "He's home early."

We rode the mounts into the stable. My father stood at the door, looking at me and no one else. My brothers, and Anne's brother, George, were there, and Will Ogilvy . . . as were all their sisters. *Like a bearbaiting,* I thought. Everyone come to witness the bloody violence, some there of their own will and pleasure, like my warped brother Edmund. The others dragged there by convention or lack of choice.

My father indicated that we girls should be lifted from our mounts—more to protect the horse than myself, I knew.

"I thought I told you not to ride alone. And you certainly understood not to lather my new mounts." He tapped his horsewhip against his riding boot.

"I'm sorry, Father." I felt a trickle of sweat course down my back; it felt like a spider scurrying away.

"It was really my fault." Anne nobly stepped in and tried to protect me. "I suggested it."

17

"And I could have told her no." I spoke up, not willing to let her shoulder the blame on her own. I needn't have bothered.

"Thank you, Mistress Boleyn," Father said. "But Mistress Wyatt knew not to ride out and chose to disobey me anyway." He cheerfully dismissed the Boleyn and Ogilvy children to the manor; their servants waited to take them back to their homes.

We Wyatt children knew to stand fast. My brother Edmund grinned. Thomas focused his eyes on the ground, as always. I knew my father would be softer on me if I cried, but I refused to.

I looked at my friends hastily retreating in the distance, and just as I locked eyes with Will, my father struck.

He backhanded me against the cheek and for a moment I felt nothing but my teeth chattering as if they would loosen in my heavy skull. I fell to the ground. He yanked me to my feet and then slapped me from another angle. Blood dripped out of my nose and I felt the tingle through the top of it and across the bridge above my eyes. In the distance, I saw George Boleyn restrain Will from coming back to the stable and I silently thanked him.

I stood up because I knew my father didn't want me to. I fixed my eyes on his, not blinking, willing myself not to be snuffed out, and forced out the words that we both knew were meaningless. "I'm sorry, Father. Would you forgive me?"

"You're to be a lady, do you hear me?" he roared. I stood still as he strode back to the house, Edmund nipping at his heels. Thomas waited behind for me.

At the end of the summer our tutors held a picnic for us on the grounds of Hever Castle, the Boleyns' home. Each of us was going a separate way, and though we would join again for social occasions and perhaps further instruction, we would not gather together weekly or monthly anymore. My brother Thomas would soon be sent to Cambridge and Edmund and I would continue at home with private tutors after my visit with Alice. My mother, ill again, could not be parted from me.

Anne, and her older sister, Mary, of course, were going back to the French court to serve Queen Claude. My father allowed a servant to take me to Hever Castle, the Boleyns' family seat, the day before the picnic so we could look through Anne's wardrobe trunks as girls are wont to do.

"Ooh, look at this!" I held up a skirt and stomacher of emerald green, perfect to set off her dark skin and eyes. "The waist is tightly fitted." I danced around the room with it and curtseyed to my imaginary suitor.

"Yes, I know," Anne said drily, rolling her eyes at me. It wasn't hard to see which of us was the refined friend and which the spontaneous one. Anne had a smart fashion sense and knew how to show off her best features.

She held up another gown, this one of navy satin, slashed to show a snowy white kirtle below with long French sleeves. "I think this would look good on you."

"I do, too. Shall you leave it here?" I teased.

"No, but sketch it quickly, if you want," she said. "They're in the French fashion, my father had them made for me in France. No one here will wear anything like them. Just you!"

I took a piece of paper from her study book and quickly drew a few of her dress designs. Our seamstress could do a rough copy, I thought. Perhaps not perfect, but still.

I ran my fingers through the treasures in her little jewel cabinet and then brushed my hand over the stack of her hose—silk, not cotton as we were used to. "I think your father has grand plans for you and your sister."

"He's the ambassador to France. Mayhap he wants England to be well represented," she answered evenly.

"Mayhap," I said. "Are you nervous?"

She nodded. "They have such big expectations for me and for Mary. And if we don't meet them, they'll set us aside. It's family advancement first . . . and last."

I nodded, wishing I could contradict her, but

our friendship had been built on honesty and I wasn't about to belittle it now with a soothing lie.

"I believe in you," I said. "And I'll pray for you every day."

She squeezed my arm. "I know you will. I am glad one of us has faith."

"You have faith!" I contradicted her.

"Not like yours."

After leaving her things for her maidservant to repack, we went down to the gardens outside.

The chairs and table were set up in neat little quartets on the Hever property, and Master Ridley, our music teacher, had recruited friends to play lutes. The notes wafted over the field, the sweetest of aural perfumes. The mood was one of love, of friendship, of pledge. We'd all been forged together and though circumstances might separate us for a time, we were somehow inextricably bound for life. I sat down alone at a table near the edge of the garden, a private spot, and wished it to remain so but for the company of one.

My wish was granted.

"May I join you?" Will approached. I remained seated, as a lady should.

"Of course." I gestured to the seat next to me with grace and dignity that would have made my father proud. I caught Anne out of the corner of my eye gently steering the others to different tables so Will and I might have some time alone.

"What's this?" He touched the wreath of daisies

I'd woven whilst waiting for the day to begin.

"A wreath of the last flowers clinging to summer," I said. "Something to both pass and mark the time."

"There is no flower here to contend with *you*. You believe they're dying off because it's the end of summer? Methinks they saw the competition and realized they must capitulate."

"Will Ogilvy, are you practicing courtly manners on me?" I teased.

"No," he said. "I mean it. May I have this wreath as a keepsake?" I wound it around his fingers and I wished it were my hand I was placing in his instead of that which my hand had created.

I nodded my agreement and kept my eyes lowered. For once, overcome by the moment, I had no smart retort.

We sat for a little while, intensely aware at the adult turn in our relationship. Will cheerfully turned the topic back to mathematics, and then horses, and finally Latin, which we both loved. We sparred over the rendering of a certain word, and in the end I believe I won.

"*Succumbo*," he admitted. "A rare victory, and one you will not soon duplicate."

"Is that a challenge?" I teased. But then his look turned somber. "Why not?" I asked, more subdued as I sipped from the goblet in front of me and tapped at the light sheen on my forehead with my kerchief.

"My father is sending me to Cambridge."

"Ah." I nodded. So now I knew why my brother Thomas was going to Cambridge. Not that my father couldn't have thought of it on his own, but he admired the Ogilvys and Boleyns as his betters in many ways. Feeling unsure of himself, he often imitated their choices. If only he would send me to France!

"I'll surely see you at pageants now and again," Will said. "And at the Christmas celebration at court."

"Surely," I agreed, knowing that those pageants and jousts would be infrequent, that my mother was often ill and required my companionship, and that the studies at Cambridge were demanding and could take up to eight years to complete.

"There are so many different teachers there." His voice rose with excitement. "I hope to learn more about our Lord too. What we have here is so . . ." He shrugged his shoulders. "Limited."

I nodded, happy for him but envious of his opportunity. Anne and I had many rigorous debates about holy things, too, which would have horrified my father and even Will, had they known. "You'll do well. I'm glad for you." I echoed the sentiment I'd given Anne just an hour before, and the words, whilst well-intentioned, felt as dry in my mouth as my oft-prattled apologies to my father.

"There are fine days ahead for you, too, Meg."

Will rested his hand on the table near mine, not able to take mine in his while others were around but showing me what was in his heart by his gesture. "I know it. *Omnino scire.*" He used the Latin word that meant "to know something without doubt, to be certain." Strangely enough, I believed he was right. I'd had the feeling that their ships were setting sail, leaving port perhaps a year or two afore my own, but that my ship would set sail, too, and it would be in the same direction. I looked at Will, suffused with happiness, and Anne, an already court-worthy hostess. Then I looked toward the sky, where the heavy gray clouds of late summer were already beginning to clot.

Lady Boleyn, ever the chaperone, made her way toward our table. As reluctant as I was to see her come, I understood she had my good name and Will's in mind.

"I'll send you a note sometimes through my sister, Rose," Will said, and I nodded.

"*Tui meminero,*" I said. *I will remember you.*

Perhaps because he was leaving and felt free to be candid, he answered me back more strongly. "*Te somniabo.*" *I will dream of you.*

Later in the afternoon, when the others had mostly returned home, I stayed to say my final good-bye to Anne. We walked in the garden and sat on a bench, carved gargoyles expressing silent horror over her departure. "I'll miss you," I said.

24

"Our constant companionship. Studying together."

"I'll be home soon. If Mary or George gets married or if someone dies . . ."

"Don't say that!" I told her, aghast. Even my jesting wouldn't go that far.

"No, no," she reassured me. "And then, soon, I'll be home to stay."

"Yes," I said. "And things will be as they ever were between us. We'll marry rich, titled, wonder-ful men, and have renowned parties and beautiful children." I looked at the gathering storm clouds and knew that if what I sensed was true then I was a liar and, worse, was breaking our friendship pledge of honesty. And yet I wasn't sure my impressions were true. They were wobbly things, jellies to roll out from under my thumb as soon as I tried to pin them down.

To make things even, I offered another oath. "You know how the boys, ah, relieve themselves together when they make a promise?"

Anne, mannered and discreet, looked at me, shocked. "Surely you can't be suggesting . . ."

I blushed. "No, no, I speak too fast." Oh my, what would my father think if he could overhear me now? "I just meant we could plight an oath too. Afore you leave."

She nodded and turned toward me on the bench before speaking. "A friendship oath. So you won't choose Rose Ogilvy as your dearest friend in my absence."

"As much as I like Rose, she's not the Ogilvy I desire to pledge an oath with," I teased, and we laughed. It was one of our friendship's better qualities, the ability to laugh together in the most difficult moments. "And make sure you don't find a French friend to replace me," I said.

"Never." She reached up and plucked one of the roses. She pricked her finger with its thorn till a little drop of blood oozed out. "It didn't hurt much . . ."

I looked at her hard, reminding her of the difficulties I faced with my father. "A poke to the finger is not going to harm me," I said, grinning. I pierced my finger too.

We held our fingers together and commingled our blood, friends to the end, never leaving one another's side, loyalty firmly pledged, come what may.

Two

Year of Our Lord 1520
Allington Castle, Kent, England

Two years had passed since my brother Thomas and Will had been sent to Cambridge to master rhetoric and Anne back to France to master the ways of their court.

But some things never change.

It began as it always did, Thomas begging me to do something against my better judgment, me wavering between my love for him and my misgivings toward the deed itself.

"Please, Meg." He dipped to bended knee, the incongruity of which made me laugh out loud. "I'll not ask you for anything else!"

Once again his charm pushed me toward an action I did not really want to take, though I teasingly waved him away like an errant bee.

"Just hand it to her privately. I cannot do so without drawing attention." He held out the parchment scroll. I took it in my hand and turned it over. *Mistress Anne* was carefully inked along the other side in his long, poetic hand and it was sealed with wax.

"What about *her?*" I asked, glancing toward our new marble terrace where his future wife held court. My father had arranged for Thomas to marry Baron Cobham's daughter, who, at twenty-one, was two years older than I. It was a great move forward for our family but would shackle Thomas to a woman he loathed. He'd already caught her in the arms of another man, and yet here she was, ready to celebrate Mary Boleyn's hasty wedding with us as if she were already family. No matter. She pushed us Wyatts forward and that's all that counted where my father was concerned.

"She's mine in name only," Thomas replied.

I nodded a grim agreement.

27

"I need my friends to keep my spirits up." He clasped my hands, smiling winsomely. Anne, polished to high shine during her years at the French court, had come home to celebrate her sister safely wed to Sir William Carey, a rich and obedient privy companion of King Henry.

"If you simply wanted to be the kind of friend to Anne that she is to me, I'd have had no qualms. But I know better."

"See, she likes me!"

"Her father has plans for her, Thomas, and now that her sister, Mary, has disgraced herself at the French court he's pinned all of his hopes on Anne. He's not likely to let her marry—nor dally—with the likes of you."

"It's only an innocent poem, Meg," he said, "I promise." He looked back over his shoulder at the grating sound of his future wife's laugh. "And besides, mayhap we can arrange a trade of sorts."

I spun around. "What do you mean?"

"You deliver a note from me to a girl I cannot have and I'll deliver a note to you from a man you cannot have."

"You have a note to me from Will?"

He nodded.

"Then what do you mean, 'a man I cannot have'?" I asked. My father would be thrilled if something could be arranged with Earl Ogilvy. He'd pay a huge dowry if need be.

"Oh, nothing." Thomas turned quiet.

"All right," I begrudgingly agreed, tucking Thomas's letter away. He pulled me close and danced a little jig right there in the ripe stable and I grinned along with him. *Keep his spirits up indeed.*

"You're my dearest sister, Meg." He kissed my cheek lightly. "The most affectionate. The kindest heart. Truly beautiful." And he meant it. For a woman who is often a highborn companion rather than the center of the swirl, the setting rather than the stone, this compliment was not held lightly. He knew it and used it to his advantage.

Our father called to us from the edge of his expensive new portico and we went to join him and our guests in the drawing room.

Mistress Cobham sat in a corner, demurely playing the virginals, looking for all the world like an angelic being, though, I thought to myself, an angel who dwelled in which realm I could not say. Her brother George, the future Baron Cobham, sat nearby and drank spirits. Where he got them I knew not, as most houses did not keep them. As the fathers withdrew from the room young Sir George patted the seat next to him proprietarily.

"Have a seat, Mistress Wyatt." He tried to keep his voice inviting but it sounded of a man speaking to his dogs. Nonetheless, trained well, I did as I was told.

"I hear you've been at court with your sister, Alice."

"Yes, though I can hardly call it at court. I stayed at her manor house in the city and attended to her children whilst she attended to the queen. Nevertheless, we did get to spend some days together and for that I am grateful."

"Did you like court?"

"I did," I said. "I much prefer it to . . . country life. Which one might equate with a slow death."

He snorted. "I will agree with you there. Country life holds impossible challenges, the largest of which is the management of the animals, and by that, I do not mean the beasts of the field. I mean the hands hired to tend them but who rather spend their days drinking ale at my expense. If they poorly manage the field and the barns I have no recourse but to reprimand them. For if they cannot be held to account for that which is given them to steward, why, then, who is to blame?"

Used to reasoning with my brother Thomas and with Will, I answered with the first thing that came to mind. "The same might be said of those who steward the field hands themselves, is that not so?"

He slowly drained his glass of its amber liquid and quietly set it down. "Good day, Mistress Wyatt," he said, and then he stood, curtly bowed, and left the room. I remained seated till his sister finished her ethereal song.

I didn't have to wait long to have the echo from

my observation return to me in full force. My father called me into his library shortly after a stiff and uneasy dinner with our guests. Edmund was already there, smirking in the background. Thomas idled by the window out of habit, well out of arm's reach of my father.

I knew Father would not scar my face days before the celebration of Mary Boleyn's wedding because the king was rumored to be coming. It's not that hitting your child, or your wife, was unacceptable. It was only unacceptable to leave marks to prove that it had happened because it would cause discomfort to those who must look upon them.

"My Lord Cobham tells me that you have many opinions on matters which concern you not at all and are not shy about sharing them with your betters."

"Father, I . . . I was trying to have a conversation with him. That's all."

"Lord Cobham took it as a rebuke, and, as such, says he has no desire to marry a woman who may scold him for the rest of his years."

I sat down in the chair next to me afore my knees buckled. "I, marry Lord Cobham?"

"Not any longer," my father said, his rage barely contained, the skin on his face taut and red like an infected boil.

"Perhaps a scold deserves a scold's punishment," Edmund offered. I turned around and

31

glared at him, not bothering to conceal the hatred in my eyes. A woman accused of being a scold would be tied to a clucking chair and publicly dunked in a nearby river, soaking her in humiliation to the general amusement of all who came to watch.

My father barked out a laugh. "Mayhap I should. But . . ." He came near my chair and towered over me. "You will marry whom I choose. You will be kind and quiet and submissive to the next man I bring to you. You will win him with your gentleness and you will prove your good breeding."

"And if not?" I dared whisper.

"Then you will get you, immediately, to the furthest abbey I can find. And not an abbey of high standing, either, for I'll not pay a dowry to the Lord when I've already paid your keep these many years. You'll work out your short years in poverty and dirt so far away that it won't matter what you say to whom. Do you understand?"

I nodded. He wouldn't tie me to a clucking chair for the shame it would bring upon him, but he would keep his word and send me to a vermin-ridden abbey, that much I knew. "Yes, sir," I said demurely, and I meant it this time. I was dismissed, and on my way back to my room I prayed, fervently, that I might speak to Will at Hever Castle and that his father would be in attendance to speak with mine.

The next day, as there were no stable boys in sight, my brother Thomas held my stirrup for me as I got on. Then he held the brood mare for our manservant so he could accompany me. No lady should travel alone, no matter how light the initial path, nor how dark it later grew.

"I expect my letter when I return home," I said. "Or I'll tell your intended about this innocent poem."

"You wouldn't dare!" Thomas looked at me, shocked, and then relaxed when he saw my smile.

"Don't test me," I teased. Then I pressed my heels into my mount and we headed toward Hever Castle.

When I arrived, the castle was already in an uproar. They'd just been told to expect the king at the next day's celebration and Sir Thomas, Anne's father, was unsure if the entertainment, the wine, or the food was of high enough quality. Lady Boleyn supervised the servants, one of whom let me in. I went upstairs to the girls' annex and found Anne with her hands on Mary's shoulders as Mary wept. Anne caught my eye in the mirror to let me know she'd be with me shortly and I withdrew to her chamber to wait.

Momentarily, she joined me. "Meg! I'm so glad to see you."

"Is Mary all right?" I asked.

She nodded. "You know Mary—always emotional, and on this day, when anyone would be emotional, she's more like overwrought. She didn't want to marry Sir William, though he's a nice enough man. She'd fallen in love with a man in France, at Francis's court, and won't put him out of her mind. She just asked me how he fared. I told her he was to be married."

"Oh dear," I said, my heart tender for Mary. "It's an awful thing to face a lifetime of being married to a man you don't want. But she can't chase a man she can't have," I pointed out. "It could be worse. At least Carey is handsome." I paused. "Is Will coming this night?"

Anne grinned. "Yes, I've not heard otherwise. I'm glad for you." She reached out, took my hand, and squeezed it as old friends do. But there was something more substantive, raised higher, a certain je ne sais quoi about her. She seemed sophisticated, and, well, French.

"I'd best get back to assisting Mary," she said. "We'll have a full week to talk and enjoy one another afore I must return to France to serve the good Queen Claude."

I hugged her quickly and pulled away. "I'm eager to hear all of your news."

"And there is news . . . ," she added tantalizingly.

"There's *always* news with you," I said, grinning. "Oh—I almost forgot. From Thomas." I pulled the scroll out of the sleeve I'd used to smuggle it in.

"Oh, Meg, he's still sending poems."

"Yes, I know. I've told him he must let you go."

"And so he must. He's a dear friend to me . . . but naught else."

"I know," I said. "Dance with him once at Mary's wedding feast and then tell him he must move on."

I took my leave and rode back home quickly with my manservant to beat the darkness. Once home I handed my wraps to my maid, Edithe, and then went upstairs to check on my mother.

Her chamber was darkened, as it almost always was these days. I'd spent a good amount of time with my sister, Alice, in the past year or two, staying at her household for months at a time and then returning to Allington to help my mother manage the household and her affairs, which I didn't mind at all, for her sake. But she'd purposefully placed more and more of the daily concerns into the hands of her trusted lady servant, who had been with my mother since she was a child.

I didn't know if it was her pain or her mood that made her desire the darkness. "Shall I open your tapestries a bit to let in the last light of the day, my lady?" I asked softly as I came into the room. She nodded weakly and I pulled them back. The effort released dust, and the motes floated to the ground in a gentle downward drift, symbolic of my mother's state of being. It was clear she was not going to make it to dine this evening.

"Tomorrow is Mary Boleyn's wedding celebration." The ceremony itself had been some months past but Sir Thomas wanted to show off his fine gardens while they were in bloom. I sat on the edge of her bed and stroked the hair by her temple. I waved to her lady servant, dismissing her to rest for a time. "And the king is coming!"

"I fear I shall not be able to attend," my mother answered. "This day I am too weak to sit aright in bed, much less dress to be seen."

I tried not to show my alarm. My sister was in London, her ninth baby due to arrive any day. Thomas would escort his intended, and if my mother didn't go, my father wouldn't, either. Which would leave me at home with the loathsome Edmund, who would amuse himself, I was sure, by lowering his boot on live insects to hear them crunch and then see them squirm and die.

"Are you certain?" I looked into her face, which, over the past months, had gone from mothlike white to a slowly hardening mask of wax gray.

"I am certain," she said. "But I will ask your father if he will allow Thomas and his wife to escort you to the wedding. I know you want to see your friends." She reached out and took my hand in hers; it was papery and dry, the skin pulling into folds that did not recover to smoothness. "I have a gift for you, Meg. Call Flora."

I kissed her hand before letting go of it and then rang the bell to indicate that we required a servant. When her servant came my mother sent her for the seamstress, who soon returned with a large dress box.

"Bring it here," my mother whispered, and then indicated for me to lift the lid. I did, and pulled out the most amazing gown of russet silk, the perfect color to set off my hair and eyes. It was trimmed in cord that I knew to be copper but glinted dangerously close to the gold only allowed to royalty. The kirtle underneath was ivory, as were the ruffs. It was cut in a French style but not a copy of one of Anne's.

"Oh, Madam!" I said. "This is too beautiful for me, for a simple country celebration. Thank you, thank you." I reached forward and hugged her, her skeletal frame somewhat cushioned by the layers of bedclothes.

" 'Tis no simple country affair when the king will attend," my mother replied, smiling. The first real joy I'd seen in her eyes for quite some time then dimmed. "I fear I shall not be here to see you wed and have *that* dress made." She coughed and I saw the brown phlegm though she tried to quickly fold the kerchief in half to hide it.

"Father wants me to marry soon."

"It will take time to arrange, but he will find someone highly placed and who owns vast properties," my mother said. "And who knows? Your husband may end up being kind."

"But Father is not!" I said, keeping a care not to let 'my voice rise too much but not tempering my frustration, either. "He beats me senseless and then, when I'm of some profit use to him, he marries me off to the highest bidder."

My mother flinched at that most impolite word, "profit." "Do you know why your father suffers so?"

We never discussed my father—any of us. "I'm unsure."

"As a young man, your father joined in a revolt against that pretender and murderer King Richard. They captured your father and put him in the Tower and tortured him, night and day, for two years. When Henry Tudor, father of our good king, came to the throne, he released your father and rewarded him with lands and titles for his loyalty. But the demons beat into your father never left."

I said nothing. I was sorry for his torture but failed to see how that left him free to beat me. If it were me, I'd have shied away from torture for having suffered it. Just then I caught the sound of my brother Edmund idling in the hallway, wait-ing to wish our rarely awake mother, whom he worshipped, a good eve.

It occurred to me that Edmund, like my father, responded to his torment by tormenting others.

Only whereas my father's fits of anger seemed like an ill-restrained impulse, Edmund's seemed a well-rehearsed pleasure.

My mother's feeble grasp on my wrist grew weaker. "Mayhap your father wants to marry you quickly for your own good."

"Mayhap by marrying I advance the Wyatt name."

My mother nodded. Pain had not clouded her vision. "It would be best for you to remain often with Alice until the time that you are married."

In other words, after her death, I should get away from my father. I kissed her cheek and a short time later she fell back into the laudanum of sleep. I left, taking my prized dress box back to my own chamber and thankful not to have met Edmund still skulking in some dark corner.

My servant, Edithe, made a show of smoothing my bed over and over, and just as I was about to remark on her odd behavior I saw the scroll. "Thank you, that will be all," I said softly, and she grinned at me as she left.

Meg was tenderly etched along the side, above the smooth wax that I knew had been sealed by Will. I slid my finger underneath, relishing the knowledge that his finger had touched this very same paper.

THREE

Year of Our Lord 1520
Hever Castle, Kent, England

My father had purchased a fine new litter, so even if he wasn't attending Mary's wedding party we arrived in style. Lord Cobham's sister—I must learn to speak of her as Elizabeth—sat close to Thomas. He recoiled slightly, as someone does when sitting near a sweating sickness victim, though she was perfectly healthy and hale. I understood. I kept a distance from my brother Edmund, who pressed his leg into mine in a menacing manner, taking two-thirds of the bench to my third. I dug my foot into the floor to brace myself from sliding into him.

We pulled in front of the castle and one of the Boleyns' men let us out. I held up the hem of my new dress so I wouldn't soil it in the mud and horse muck, both of which steamed into the cool evening air. We four navigated the crowd, quickly making our way on the cobblestone path. The yard was alight with torches and music escaped from the new upstairs great hall, which was very great indeed. Anne's father prided himself on his entertainment and it was justified.

The minute we got in the door Edmund headed

for the mead as he often, and noticeably, did. I scanned till I found Anne, busy acting the part of co-hostess with her mother. I stood to the side and observed her for a while. Her manners and conversation were now those of a French woman: smooth, subtle, wry, sophisticated. She made her way to me.

"Meg! I must attend to the guests with my mother, as Mary is the guest of honor and unable to assist."

"Of course," I reassured her. "We'll have the evening to talk after the party; our serving men are instructed to bring us home in the morning. Your father has kindly offered his hospitality."

"Marvelous!" She squeezed my arm.

"You look beautiful," I told her, and it was an understatement. She wore her hair long and free, as an unmarried woman is allowed to do, an overflow of black silk with teal string threaded through it to match the teal green of her gown. Her skin shone in the candlelight and when I looked more closely I could see she had powdered herself with something that glimmered.

"*You* look beautiful," she said. "I've never seen a gown that color before nor a cut quite so enticing and modest at the same time." She turned her head and I followed her gaze. "Rose Ogilvy has arrived. Why don't you go and talk with her?"

Then she slipped into the crowd effortlessly, like a swan floating on the Thames, moving yet seeming not to move, her long neck and graceful beauty drawing the eye of both men and women as she walked.

The tables had all been arranged, but of course the food could not be served till the king arrived. I made my way toward Rose and she greeted me warmly. "Good evening," she said. "My brothers are here, both of them. And my father. And my . . . intended."

"Rose!" I exclaimed. "I didn't know. Who is the fortunate soul?"

She turned her eyes downward but I saw a pleased smile cross her face afore she took cover in humility. "My Lord Blenheim's son."

She was too reserved to say it: the *heir* of Earl Blenheim, the *only son* of Earl Blenheim. But this was a coup indeed. Her father had noble aspirations for his family and he'd wasted no time, apparently, in placing Rose well. "Congratulations," I told her. "I wish you the most happiness."

She lifted her eyes, suddenly more adult-like now that her marriage was settled, and, if I wasn't mistaken, a bit more sure of herself. Mayhap a bit *too* sure of herself. Her nose had an upward tilt that I hadn't detected in the many years I'd known her, and without a word, she quickly took her leave of me to greet one of Queen Katherine's ladies-in-waiting. She seemed warmly welcomed.

I took a goblet of watered wine from a liveried servant and spoke with my mother's cousin. As I did, I caught sight of *him* as he entered the hall from the terraces outside.

Others may have been waiting all evening for the king to arrive, but I had been waiting for Will.

He stood there, a man now, with his brother, Walter, his father's heir and pride. I watched with, I'll admit it, relief as Lord Asquith, his father, forcefully steered Walter toward some of the highborn young ladies in attendance, but not Will. Will looked up, caught my eye, and grinned ere he could stop himself. I lifted my pomander to my nose to hide my smile. *Fortunatissima!*

"Look, Meg!" My cousin took my elbow and directed my attention to the courtyard. A great stomping of horses could be heard and the musicians stopped their songs. A loud herald of trumpets drowned out the clatter and clank of the carriage wheels.

"The king!" A general murmur went through the crowd. I first thought of my poor mother, who had so longed to see the king again, and then had the puniest of kind thoughts for my father, who had stayed home rather than attend without her. Those thoughts were soon gone, though, as I lifted my eyes and looked for the sovereign himself.

Of course I had been to court a time or two, for jousts and for pageants, but that had mostly been when I was younger. My sister, Alice, had taken me to court with her a few times as well but we'd mostly stayed in the ladies' quarters.

The king.

He strode in, a great, ruddy bear in wine-colored velvet trimmed in gold cord and slashed in gold silk. Sir Thomas, Anne's father, followed the king around in the most attentive way. I must say, the king didn't act as I'd expected he would, dignified and quiet. He threw his arm around Sir Thomas, took a great mug of ale and gulped it, threw his hand toward the musicians, and shouted, "Play on!"

He was the height of handsomeness, he emanated power, he completely dominated the room. One could not imagine him anyone but the king. My knees automatically dipped as he walked. He went to the dais, the table set up for himself and, at his insistence, for the bridal party.

Anne's father indicated that we should sit and eat, and we went to find our places.

Will came alongside me. "I have been looking forward to dancing with you," he said, and that sent a shiver of reassurance through me. I'd been worried, because the tone of the note he'd sent me through Thomas had been cooler than the others he'd sent, some of which had fairly singed the paper they'd been written on. In the most courtly, appropriate way, of course.

The servants brought out great platters of swan and eel—the king's favorite. Whole roasted hares were set on each table, as were minced loin of veal with great platters of fat to spread upon them.

Bowls of hard-boiled eggs were passed. Though I loved them, I did not take one, not wanting my breath to smell of egg after the evening's events, though my brother Thomas took three. I shot him a warning look and he popped one more in his mouth, to the dismay of one of our more proper cousins. I did take some spiced wafers, which I also loved. They'd been cunningly made in white and red, cut in the design of the Tudor rose. I heard the king voice his approval when he saw them.

Then I heard him express his appreciation for the bride in an overly familiar way. Mary and Sir William had been married months before but still the king drew near to Mary, beautiful and golden, as the king was known to prefer his paramours. Mary drew closer toward him too. Her new husband looked on in impotent horror. What could he do? Henry was law.

I heard a quiet comment from someone at the end of my table. " 'Twas not enough to shame herself with the French king, now she's going to shame herself with England's as well."

There was a mushrooming of approval from those who heard the comment, though I held my face still. *Oh, Mary. Please don't encourage this.*

At meal's end the king claimed the first dance with the bride, who willingly agreed. Sir William tried to look enthusiastic but his earnest face showed his pain. *Sir William, you have a steep and rocky path ahead of you.*

The servants removed the tables and the musicians began to play. Everyone partnered off quickly. My brother ignored his wife but she didn't seem bothered; she'd taken up with another man the moment we'd arrived. I could tell she'd had several goblets of wine—probably unwatered. My brother headed straight for Anne, who met him graciously, though a bit coolly.

She was a childhood flirtation, Thomas. I willed him to understand. But he would not.

A moment later I felt a hand on the small of my back. "Have you a partner yet, Mistress Wyatt?" Will asked.

"Do I now?" I responded a bit coyly, I admit, but then a girl is allowed.

"You do."

The musicians struck up a pavane, and we lightly touched fingers, as all the couples must. For that reason it was one of the favorite dances for those in love or who wished to be. My gowns swirled along the floor as we danced. Though we were close to others we were still able to carry on a private conversation.

"How does your sister?" Will asked, a bit formal. He seemed restrained somehow. Unusual. Maybe we needed to become accustomed to one another again. We'd never had to ere this, though.

"She's fine, the baby comes soon. How go your

studies?" I asked, maddeningly polite and distant.

"Wonderfully well. I have the opportunity to study abroad for a few months whilst my father is in Belgium for the king, and then I return home to . . . study more. And to the court, of course. I will often be at court."

"You'll do well at court, I'm certain."

We broke apart to dance a galliard with other partners, a quick, humorous dance that soon had the entire hall clapping, laughing, and making merry. I danced with my brother Thomas and then with another courtier whom I did not know but who looked at me appreciatively.

I prayed a prayer of thanksgiving for my mother and her gift of the dress. I confess that I was glad that Anne wasn't alone in drawing admiration.

The king called for a volte to be danced, and the room shifted uncomfortably. The volte was the only dance which allowed partners to embrace. I saw the king lead Mary Boleyn—ah, Mary Carey—to the dance floor. Will swooped in before my galliard partner could claim me again, though he tried.

I softened in Will's arms; I felt the heat of those many secret scrolls and their honest declarations as we danced. I sensed the momentum of our years of laughter and honest, heated disagreement and unspoken, deep affection.

"Meg," he finally said, intimacy and urgency in his voice now that he'd dropped the well-mannered, unwelcome mask of civility. And there was something else in his manner, though I could not tell what. "Can we speak together outside, alone?"

"Yes!" I said. It wouldn't be improper with so many strolling around.

"Good. Perhaps we should dance a few more songs first so as not to draw attention."

I agreed and then unwillingly let go of his hand as the dance ended. I could feel his reluctance to let go, too.

We met outside the main door and then walked, hand in hand, to a bench just outside in the close gardens. The rain of the earlier evening had dried to a mist on the petals of the flowers nearby; the sky had cleared to a cool, starry evening. Will picked a daisy and put it in my hair, a tender gesture of love and possession that I welcomed. "Do you remember your wreath of daisies?" he asked.

"I do, and I'm pleased that you do as well."

"I have news, Meg," he said after a moment. My back stiffened at the tone of his voice.

"You're to be married," I said, cutting directly to my worst fear.

"No . . . not exactly."

"Not exactly? Marriage is a clear thing. You're either married or you're not."

"My father has been spending a lot of time with the king," Will said.

"I'd heard."

"And the king spends a lot of time with Cardinal Wolsey."

"Indeed," I said. We all knew that the cardinal was the king's closest, most trusted advisor.

"Wolsey read some of my work at Cambridge and felt that I had promise as a priest. He approached Henry. The king approached my father, who thought it an excellent idea, or so he told the king. I am the second son, after all."

"A *priest?* Your father is not even devout! Not all second sons must go into the priesthood. It's not a law."

"It's a practice," Will said. "My father thinks it a good idea."

I drew back from him. "And you? What do *you* think?"

"Meg, above any person in this world, I value you. I trust you, I dream of you, I long for you. But there is someone I value still more. And I have become more and more aware, lately, that He is calling me to Himself. To service."

"You can serve Him whilst administering your father's lesser properties."

"I could," Will said softly, trying to take my hand in his own. "But I don't feel at leave to do that."

I moved it away without speaking but I was thinking, *Leave from our Lord or leave from your father?*

"I know that I am supposed to pursue this," he

finished. "I . . . love you, Meg. And I love God too. In fact, I only speak Latin with you and with Him. But I must obey."

Dolor.

A great sorrow overcame me because I could see the stark truth commingled with sorrow in his beautiful, honest face. He would not hurt me if he could help it, and yet I could not help but feel that he could stop this, and he was choosing not to.

I stood to take my leave, and he, a gentleman, stood as I did. The gardens had grown empty now; several litters from nearby estates took their leave. The lutist played a sweet and winsome tune that twisted and turned through the estate till it found and remained with us.

I could have asked him, *And I? What of me?* But we had no precontract, nothing declared, nothing finalized. Will stood next to me, looking at the ground, and I loved him to the point of anguish. I had nothing but searing pain and wanted to run away as fast as I could. In spite of it all, my heart broke for him, seeing the grief of the moment writ on his face. Unlike almost anyone else I knew, he put God first, a trait I'd admired when it had cost me nothing.

He impulsively reached over and pulled me close to him, a personal volte dance. His scent, like my favorite spiced wafers, was both faint and intoxicating. He pressed his lips against mine softly at first, and then more powerfully. My flesh failed my will and I kissed him back readily, longingly. My body willed him to move forward though my spirit knew he must stop.

I pulled away—far away. "Don't ever kiss me like that again until and unless you're ready to make good on the promise behind it," I said. I had never been kissed, but I knew that was the kind of kiss that should only be between a man and his wife.

I took to the castle as quickly as I could. Another woman I knew I would not lose to; no other woman could take my place with Will, of that I was as certain as I was that no other man could take his place with me. But God? How could I compete with God? I could not and therefore it was unjust of him to set up such a contest at all.

When I entered the room I saw my brother Edmund and he tipped his head toward me and smiled, if one could call it that.

He knew. And Thomas knew, too, which is why he'd told me earlier I wanted a man I could not have. Thomas had had too much to drink and was slumped in a chair in one far corner.

"Good-bye, Margaret," Rose Ogilvy called to me as she headed toward her fine litter. No one called me Margaret—it was my mother's name. They called me Meg to distinguish me from her.

I nodded politely, tears blinding my path, and hurried to Anne's chamber ere the tears spilled down my cheeks.

I didn't have to wait long. Anne arrived, dismissed her servants, and closed the door behind her.

"What ails you?" she asked, sitting beside me.

I fell into her arms and she held me as I poured out my story about Cardinal Wolsey and Lord Ogilvy and King Henry—the king who had his eyes and hands on the bride all evening!—talking about holy service.

"And so now Will's studying for the priesthood of his own accord, and then he'll take vows," I said. Anne picked up a brush and began to brush my hair, and I finally calmed.

She began to tell me tales of the French court, and how exciting it was, and what her life was like. I stilled then, listening to her, glad to discuss something new.

After a bit I stood up, and as I did, the daisy fell from my hair.

"What's this?"

I shook my head and let it fall to the ground. "Nothing important."

I went to the trunk I had brought with my nightshift and a few personal items for spending the night. I withdrew a small, well-worn book and walked back to Anne.

"I want you to have this—a souvenir to take with you as you return to France."

She held out her hand and took the book, then opened it and began to read a page here and there. "Meg, not your prayer book, your book of hours. Look here—you've added personal prayers and notes."

"Take it," I said.

"Surely it must be important to you—or you'd not have brought it tonight."

She was right. I'd read from or written in or prayed from it every night.

No longer.

"I don't need it anymore. I have no intention of praying to a God who has put me in the bloody hands of an evil father, who robs my kindhearted mother of her every breath, and who has stolen from me the only man I'll ever love as well as my hope."

Anne shook her head. "It's not like that. You don't know how this will end. Mayhap you and Will are not done yet."

I sensed that there were things ahead that I did not yet understand nor could I foresee. I knew that feeling was meant to be comforting.

I did not want this comfort. I pushed the thought, and him, far away, and fast-locked the gate behind them.

"And you've written in your beautifully rendered Latin," she said softly after reading a few pages, knowing that's how I often spoke with God, and with Will. She tried to hand the book to me.

I firmly pushed the book back into her hands. "I will never speak Latin again."

FOUR

Year of Our Lord 1522
Blickenham Manor, London, England

My mother had arranged for me to spend the
months following the Christmas celebrations with
my sister, Alice, at her home in Chelsea. So it was
with some surprise that, one evening whilst we
dined, a messenger arrived with a letter to my
sister from our father. She nodded to the servant
to set it aside till the meal was over, but her
concern showed in her face. Had my mother
passed away? Was my father in some kind of
trouble? It was rare for him to have a care for me,
so I wouldn't have suspected that it involved
me at all except for the burning feeling deep
beneath my corset that warned me, preternatu-
rally, that the tide was about to shift.

My nephew John Rogers was Alice's oldest son,
home from Cambridge; he paid no mind at all to
the messenger. Rather he kept talking even
whilst the serving girl ladled out his soup. "So
Cranmer, of course, began to gather a group of us
for late-night debates. He said he had been
mightily troubled by the discourse that Luther had
started and the longer he dwelled on the matter
the more troubled his spirit became. Perhaps, he

thought, Luther may be right on some points."

Because Alice was the daughter of my father's first wife she was much older than I, which meant that John and I were of an age, more like brother and sister than aunt and nephew. He turned directly toward me.

"A friend of yours was invited to the discussions," he said to me. "Will Ogilvy. Do you remember him?"

Alice shifted in her seat and sent a confidence-inspiring smile in my direction. She often nurtured me when my own mother slipped under the horizon and was unable to attend to the questions and concerns of young womanhood. Alice had mended my broken wings as best she could after Will's announcement that he would be a priest, reassuring me that she hadn't married for affection, either, but had grown to love Master Rogers well.

Amenable Alice. Always compliant, making the best of things, peaceful and settled. I could see why my father found me a grave disappointment.

"I do remember Sir William," I said. "Well."

"He's got quite a talent for languages," John continued, sensing nothing amiss, I was sure, as men often do not. "And for debate. I'm not sure with whom he's been sparring at rhetoric all of these years because it certainly wasn't his brother Walter." He turned to his mother. "I'd like to have Ogilvy to Blickenham sometime. You'll not mind?"

"Of course he's welcome," Alice murmured. I made my way through the soup course as, thankfully, the conversation turned to other matters, and then excused myself from the meal as soon as decently possible.

I wasn't in my room for long before there was a short knock on the door. "Come in," I called out, expecting it to be my servant, Edithe. Instead it was my sister. She had a letter in her hand and she came and sat next to me on the bed.

"It's from Father, as you know," she began. "He'd like for you to pack your things and return to Allington. He'll send a cart for you the day after tomorrow."

I abruptly stood up. "What? Why? I've only just arrived."

She reached up and folded my hand into her own. "It seems he's found a potential husband for you and they're coming to visit."

I arrived home two days hence to find my father in high spirits and my mother aright on her own two feet, which was rare. I knew she meant to wring every last bit of vitality out of her bones to ensure that this meeting went well for my sake and for Father's.

"Don't overextend yourself, Lady Wyatt," my father said, gesturing roughly for a manservant to bring a cushioned chair to the portico so my mother could sit in the sun whilst we waited for our guests to arrive. The manservant hefted a chair and my father had it arranged in the best possible spot before easing my mother into it. I had never seen my father be gentle with anyone or anything other than my mother and his horses. Alice never spoke of her mother; she'd died when Alice was young and Alice had been married off at fifteen—as soon as my own mother arrived at Allington. But I'd overheard the kitchen servants speak of my father's first wife and he had treated her as rudely as he'd treated me, so I suspected that when he'd given her his hand in marriage it had been often and with blunt force.

Not so with my mother. If I'd been in the frame of mind to thank God for small favors this was one I could have thanked Him for. But I didn't.

Within the hour we could see a traveling cloud of dust in the distance, winding up the village lane, past the priory, on the way to Allington Castle. The ground shuddered slightly with the force of the oncoming horses. As I stood, I smoothed my hair and my dress, which earned me a rare nod of approval from Father. Thomas was at court and Edmund upstairs with the tutors, so we three navigated our way down to the great hall in which we would shortly greet our guests.

They arrived preceded by a small clutch of attendants, across the brackish moat, and when the carriage door was opened, two men alighted. One was my father's old friend Lord Blackston, with whom he had fought Richard the Third many years back. The second was his nephew and, as Blackston had no children of his own, the baron's heir.

My father and Lord Blackston clapped one another on the back and chortled loudly about the gambling my father had arranged for that evening's entertainment after dinner, though the baron warned my father about cheating him—again. My father, notoriously tight with his money but honest, ignored him. I saw the flash in his eye.

"Lady Wyatt. It's a pleasure to see you again." The baron extended his hand toward my mother's, taking her hand in his and kissing it softly.

My mother lowered her eyes demurely as she withdrew her hand. "Thank you, My Lord. As always, it's a pleasure to have you as our guest. It's been too many years."

He grinned. As he did I could see that whilst he may have won his fortune at the Battle of Bosworth it was clear that he'd forfeited some teeth in exchange.

"And this jewel was naught but a girl at that time."

I curtseyed politely and heard the man to his side clear his throat.

Lord Blackston turned and urged forward the second man. "My nephew, Simon." Simon was a good Norman name. Norman blood. Titled. Moneyed. I held out my hand and cast my gaze downward, as gently bred girls are well taught to do.

Simon took my hand in his. My first instinct, which I checked, was to withdraw it immediately. His fingers were long and cool, like recently snuffed tapers. He brought my hand to his parched lips and kissed the back of it. He then let go. "Pleased to make your acquaintance, Mistress Wyatt. I've heard so much about you. But I find that what I've heard seems to be untrue." I looked up at that. Exactly what had he heard about me and from whom?

"You're far lovelier than I'd been expecting." With that, he bowed courteously and my mother led the way into Allington.

That evening all the servants were in their best liveries. My father had ordered an entire ox roasted—roasted meat being a sign of wealth—as it showed that we Wyatts had enough money to pay one or two men to do nothing but turn a burdened spit over a hellish inferno all day. There was stuffed swan and pale ale brought from Bruges. And of course, jellied eels. I tried hard not to compare Simon's fingers to the jellied eels but I found myself unable to enjoy them for the first time ever. Afterward there was music, though no dancing, as dinner was a smallish affair. My mother withdrew and my father and Baron Blackston retreated to a far corner of the great hall where tables had been set up. Several gentlemen from the neighboring properties had arrived to play cards and dice. I wasn't sure if I was gratified or disappointed when Simon politely declined to join them and instead asked me if I'd ask the musicians to continue to play whilst he and I sat by the fire and kept company.

What could I do? "I'd be pleased to," I answered, remembering my father's warning to be kind and submissive to the next man he brought to my side. Scraping hardened horse dung with my bare nails from between the cobbled stones on the path to a Scottish abbey didn't appeal to me. So Simon and I kept company.

"I've heard that your father has seen fit to educate you," Simon began. I dared to look up at his face. The fire had brought some color to it, which made him more pleasant to look at than he had been in the cool stone dining hall. His smile was not warm, but it was not cruel, either. I was glad of the fact that it would be impolite to look into his eyes for too long. The irises were blue but the whites around them slightly rheumy, perhaps a bit like eggs which had not been cooked quite long enough. They stared at me, however, intently. I became aware that he was expecting an answer.

Would he find my education to his liking? "Yes, my father found my mother's education pleasing to him and had me educated along with my brothers." I answered as safely as I knew how.

"What have you studied?" He folded his long fingers over his knee and used the movement as an excuse to move slightly closer to me on the covered bench. I held myself steady so as not to flinch. I looked into his eyes as I spoke, hoping that he wouldn't misread my desire to gauge his response as a desire for intimacy.

"I studied mathematics and rhetoric, Latin and letters," I began. His eyes held mine and betrayed no emotion but I thought I saw a slight downward dip in the corner of his mouth.

"And dancing, of course, and needlework. I can play the lute. And my mother has schooled me on household management." At that he smiled.

"Yes, yes, of course she would have. I am sure you play a fine lute. I'd like to hear it." He looked as though he were about to signal a musician. I quickly held up my hand.

"Perhaps tomorrow?" My voice was soft as carded wool. "I feel a bit tired now, the excitement of the day . . ."

"Of course," he said. He spoke at length about their property up north, which I knew to be extensive, their many castles and landholdings. Lord Blackston's sister had been his mother, and when she had died shortly after his father at the Bosworth Field the baron had taken him in and raised him. In spite of having married several times, the baron had sired no child of his own.

"I think you might like the north, mistress,"

he said after I'd admitted I've never been north of London. "It's very family-oriented for the lady of the manor. There are serfs and peasants to attend to and alms to give. Servants to attend to, birthings and the like, and quite a bit of needle-work, of course."

"Sounds . . . bucolic." I reached past the first three or four words that presented themselves to me to snatch one that might sound faintly praiseworthy.

He nodded. I wasn't entirely certain he knew what "bucolic" meant.

"If you'll excuse me, I must ensure that my mother is well settled for the evening, and then perhaps it is time to retire myself." I kept my voice soothing and pleasant. I hardly recognized myself. I sounded like Alice. It wasn't an entirely unpleasant sensation, but then again it reminded me of the times when I, as a girl, had slipped into her adult gowns. Mayhap it was time I grew into them. I smiled at him warmly because he truly had been a gentleman in every way. He was very . . . proper.

"Of course." He stood immediately and held out his hand to assist me as I stood. I took it, and he turned it over, kissing the inside of my palm this time, rather than the back of it, which gave me some discomfort. After a careful curtsey to my father and his friends, I made my way to my chamber.

● ● ●

Days later Lord Blackston and Simon led the dust cloud back the way they had come, down from Allington, past the priory, and toward the guesthouse many miles away that would be their first stay on the days' journey north. It had been no small feat, nor small honor, that they came to Allington to meet me. Of that I was aware. I suspected, however, that I had failed in my mission because from the second day forward Simon had noticeably cooled toward me.

My father called me into his study. Edmund was already there, thumbing through a book, trying to look scholarly, and I had to grant that he had a quick wit. Numbers and accounts, though, they were what he preferred. In that he was as far from my brother Thomas as two brothers could be. My father, now sharing responsibilities for the king's treasury with Anne's father, was as miserly with his money as Anne's father was generous. Edmund took after our father in that way, and our father applauded him for it.

"You've done well, mistress," my father said to me. He indicated that I was to sit in the chair next to him.

It was done then. I was to be married.

"Lord Blackston and I will be in negotiations for terms, and if we come to some that are agreeable to us both, and I expect we will, you will be betrothed to him anon."

In the front of my mind I thought that surely I had misheard, but the back of my mind heard Edmund breathing his peculiar stalking breath and it warned me that perhaps I had heard correctly after all.

"Sir, did I mishear you? Surely you meant to say that you are arranging for my possible betrothal to Simon, My Lord Blackston's heir?" I kept my breath steady and my gaze low. The carved wood of the arm of the chair became a focal point.

"You heard me correctly," Father answered. "At first, Blackston and I had expected to come to some kind of an arrangement for you and for young Simon. However, after laying eyes upon you he found you pleasing to look at and thought that perhaps a nubile young bride would bring him a son of his own after these many long years. His nephew had already reported to him that you have a pleasing manner. He's convinced that he should take you for himself."

A minute slipped by. Then another. "He is nearly of an age with you," I whispered.

"Yes."

That was all, *yes.* I had no say in the matter. Lord Cobham could repudiate me because I had rebuked him, which he found disagreeable; no matter if I found him agreeable or not. I had to prove myself pleasing to Simon, and Baron Blackston, but they did not have to prove anything to me. I had questions; my father was not required, nor inclined, to give me answers. I was to marry a man whose skin was as loose as his sputum.

"May I speak?"

My father nodded. I tried my very best to cloak myself with a quiet spirit of gentility.

"I do not think I can love him," I said. I hoped he would understand. After all, he so clearly loved my mother.

"Love!" He snorted. "Listen to what Thomas's cursed poetry has wrought in you. It's a plague upon the sensibilities of my house. You, Mistress Wyatt, will hold your tongue and be obedient as you have so recently learnt. And if God shall bless you with children by Lord Blackston, then you will thank God that through them your name will not be buried in the earth. Think no further of love."

He dismissed me with a wave of his hand. I curtseyed and fled the room.

I rushed to my chambers and then fast locked the door behind me. My maid, Edithe, was in my room preparing for my evening's dressing. I flung myself on the bed and she came and stood beside me. "Can I get something for you, mistress?"

I looked into her wear-worn face. Though she was perhaps only five years older than I, she had already borne two children who lived with her mother because she spent most days and nights here at Allington serving me well. Her husband was a field hand at Hever Castle. Disregarding social boundaries I let my horror spill out.

"I am not like my mother, bless her, to want to take purpose in life by the breeding of those who are to follow me. I do not yearn for meaningless ritual, not in worship, not in friendship, not in womanhood, not in marriage, nor in life. How can I live the life I desire?"

She handed me a kerchief to dry my eyes but she spoke to me honestly, not soothingly, woman to woman. "You cannot live a life you desire. Our destiny is not ours to choose. Even Mistress Boleyn must hie her to court because her father and His Grace the Duke of Norfolk ha' decided her expensive French education shall be put to their good use."

I took her coarse hands in mine for a moment, admonished by her harsh life, and then I went to bed and wept silent, angry tears of protest that I knew would profit me not at all. In the middle of the night I got up and looked in the trunk where I'd stored Will's letters. They were gone. I was devastated by the loss of the only physical tokens of our love—papers his hands and mine had touched, breathed upon, kissed. And further, my joints jellied at the thought of them in someone else's hands, but I dared not make inquiries lest I draw attention to their existence and bring down a rain of abuse.

But Edithe's comments *had* given me an idea. I would go to Anne. She would know what to do.

My father, of course, pleased with himself and with me in an odd way, gave me leave the very next day to ride out and visit her. I'd have a short stay and then return.

It was too cold for a walk in the gardens, so we sat in Sir Thomas's great hall and worked at wretched needlework near the fire for an excuse to talk. She had not been long home from France, having returned with her father after the king's great meeting at the Field of Cloth of Gold in Calais. I plied the needle whilst she wove the story.

"It was magnificent, Meg," she told me. "I had thought that perhaps our court was coarse and unsophisticated, missing a certain je ne sais quoi, and I was not looking forward to returning home from Queen Claude's court," she said—then she must have caught the look on my face. "Though I missed you, of course, and my lady mother." She had not mentioned her sister, Mary.

"But I tell you, the king was *formidable*. He wrestled with Francis and could have won, but he allowed Francis to prevail, which only endeared him to us more. His words were fine; he cut a better figure of a man. I knew, then, that I could come back to England and that, for certes, my fate is here."

"Mine is too," I said morosely. I'd poured my story out to her the moment my courtesies with her mother had concluded and we were in private.

Anne set down her needlework. "Come with me to court," she said.

"What?"

"Come with me to court. It will take some time for your betrothal negotiations to be completed—my father has been working on mine with Butler for years. In the meantime, I go to court with my father in March and you shall come with us!"

Now I set down *my* needlework. It would certainly appeal to my father—raise my family's stature for me to be at court in even a minor capacity in Queen Katherine's household. Sir Thomas rode high in the king's esteem since the success at Calais, so Baron Blackston could certainly have no objection. And I might never get another chance. When Anne married Piers Butler she'd be off to Ireland.

Anne settled the matter, as she often did, without waiting for my agreement. "I'll have my father write a letter to yours and you can take it with you upon your return."

The next day I returned to Allington, the letter from Sir Thomas clutched in my hand. I stilled my wrist as I held it out to my father. I was almost tempted to pray for a positive response, but no need. He agreed. I would leave for court in a little more than one month's time. My mother was overjoyed and we spent many hours together planning what I would pack in the trunks I'd bring. One day, after she'd left my chamber, Edmund appeared like a sudden onset of disease.

"The court nourishes itself on compromise, taking in the very people who like to pretend that they are good and then retching them out after they cede their alleged moral standards one by one."

"Pity you're not coming then," I retorted. "It sounds like someplace you would thrive."

"Oh, I'll get there, after I help Father negotiate your marriage portion," Edmund said. "I'll be there to watch as you are broken."

I dismissed him but couldn't dismiss his accusations as readily. Would the court bend me to its will too?

FIVE

Year of Our Lord 1522
York Place, London, England

It was the day before the beginning of Lent, Shrove Tuesday, and we'd been at court nigh on a fortnight. We'd settled into the queen's retinue, Anne as one of the queen's many maidens of honor and I as a highborn friend there to assist and to make friends that might help my father or my future husband. Our days thus far had consisted of going to Mass with the queen, playing cards in her chamber, sewing shirts for the poor, and, of course, providing modest feminine companionship at meals and jousts. For the most part our time had been a disappointment.

The queen did not enjoy high spirits, preferring to spend dark hours in her chapel on her knees and favoring those who did likewise, most of whom had come with her from Spain a lifetime ago. Ash Wednesday would mark a period of little merriment and no meat. The king desired to indulge so as to carry us through till the celebration of the Resurrection. Cardinal Wolsey had planned an extraordinary masque. Even to me, a woman comfortably estranged from God, it was unseemly that the cardinal spent more time preparing for Henry to gorge his senses than preparing for the forthcoming denial of those same pleasures in honor of our Lord the next day. I'd heard it said that his solicitor, Thomas Cromwell, attended to Christ's business while Wolsey attended to the more important matters of the king.

Somehow, someone had whispered a strong suggestion in an important ear and Anne was to be one of the principal players in the masque.

"How does the cardinal have enough money to entertain so lavishly?" I asked as I helped Anne into her shift and then went on to ensure that her gown sat perfectly. "There are legions of people to attend this evening and he is sure to serve dozens and dozens of courses to please the king. And he's got hundreds of servants!"

Anne nodded and then laughed. Her laugh was pleasant to hear but not filled with merriment as an ordinary woman's laugh might be. Rather it was a mix of joy and sophistication and maybe a little bit of challenge to the listener. It was compelling and altogether different since she'd returned from France. I'd seen the men at court respond to her laughter and to her presence, almost against their will, in a way unlike the manner in which they approached the other ladies in the queen's household.

"The cardinal's servants are better dressed than I," she teased. Although it was not exactly true, they were finely attired, for certes. Just then, another young woman burst into the chamber, her sickly strong jasmine perfume preceding her arrival.

"Do you know where Mary has gone?" she asked.

"Hello, Jane," Anne replied, reminding Jane Parker that she had forgone the civility of a greeting in order to bleat out a demand, as usual.

"Hello, sister," Jane replied impatiently. " 'Tis a short time till we're required in the dining hall. Have you seen our sister Mary?"

Anne looked at me and even though her expression did not change, I, who knew her well, could read her impatience with the woman soon to be betrothed to Anne's beloved brother, George.

71

"She left some time ago. Mayhap she's with the king."

"Indeed!" Jane's eyes lit up at the idea of inserting herself into the king's close orbit. "I'll see to her." She took her leave but not afore reminding us to hurry. It was a credit to Anne's discretion that she held her tongue.

"You'd wish better for George," I said. I understood. In spite of the fact that my brother Thomas had a sweet son by his wife, Elizabeth, they spoke not at all and I had already seen Elizabeth in a dark hallway with one of the king's privy counselors.

"I'd wish him happiness, in all ways, in great measure," Anne said. "And I fear he's not going to get that with Mistress Parker. But my father is sure to get a great dowry, and one that he supposes to use in part for my marriage portion, so he warns me to say nothing at all to my sister Jane but to welcome her into our family. For his sake, and for George's, I do." She stood and turned in her gown, her long black hair flowing majestically around her shoulders, her eyes played up with the tiniest bit of kohl in each corner. "How do I look?"

"There will not be an eye with the free will to look away from you," I said, suddenly feeling very dowdy in my sapphire gown.

"Don't fret, you look lovely, Meg," Anne said, reading my mind. "Let us go ere Mistress Parker brings herself to a fit."

We first went to dinner, the king and queen on a dais at the head of the room and the rest of us stratified according to rank outward from their position. Anne was several tables in front of me, and I sat with a group of happy young ladies-in-waiting, next to a table of the king's gentlemen, who laughed, and yes, we parried with one another, well out of the queen's earshot and gaze.

"I hear that there are to be sixteen women who are costumed for roles at the masque," one young courtier said. "And yet only eight men."

"Perhaps that is because it takes two women to subdue one man!" another courtier offered, to the general laughter of the rest of us.

"What think you, mistress?" The first young man trained his eyes on me and smiled flirtatiously. I was unused to courtly manners. Did he intend to pay me such intense attention? Or was this a part and parcel of the illusory world of the court, where nothing was as it seemed?

"I should rather not offer my opinion," I said. "I know that one of the maidens shall represent *malebouche*, a sharp tongue, and should she fall ill I'd not like to be pressed into service."

The tables erupted in laughter and I smiled.

"Never," the young man thrust back. "I find your *bouche* to be anything but sharp."

For him to comment on my mouth, especially implying that it was soft, was perhaps a step further in this game than I wished to go, so I nodded toward him. "Touché," I said, and left it at that. His eyes did not leave me for some time, and I allowed myself to suppose that my gown was not as dowdy as I had feared.

I glanced at Anne. She had been seated next to Henry Percy, the heir to the Earl of Northumberland. One glance at Percy's face told me that he was smitten with Anne, which was unsurprising. What was surprising, however, was the look on Anne's face. Underneath her practiced court luster I could spy honest interest. I made note of it because Anne did not waste her affections.

After dinner we made our way from the dining room into the large chamber in which the performance would be held. Each masque had a theme, and the theme that Cardinal Wolsey had determined for this celebration was that of unrequited love. How fitting! I scanned the room, both wishing for and hoping against Will's being in attendance, as he well might. When I saw that he was not, I relaxed and allowed myself to be transported, along with the other guests, by the story.

In one end of the hall had been built a replica of a castle, covered with green foil, which concealed the court musicians. Within were eight women, representing the feminine virtues to which we were supposed to aspire and to which, I admit, I did strive, though I often fell short. The king's sister Mary, as the highest-ranking of the masqued women, played Beauty. Jane Parker played Constancy, something I found difficult to believe, and I wondered if the choir master had known her well, or at all, when appointing her to the position. The Countess of Devonshire, wife of the king's cousin, who still had the smell of treason about him, was strangely nominated to be Honor. Anne's sister, Mary, played Kindness, and I agreed that was a suitable role. She had not much wit, nor principles, but she was kind.

Anne had been selected to play Perseverance.

The eight costumed men attacked the eight women dressed as unlovely feminine vices, throwing dates, fruits, and other sweetmeats at them till they yielded, allowing the eight feminine virtues, headed by Princess Mary, to escape into the willing arms of the men. At the victory, the queen stood and led the crowd in applause. After she had recognized the end of the performance she was free, by custom, to take her leave, and she did. When she left, the cool air of disapproval left with her, leaving behind a warm current of gaiety.

"Play on!" the king commanded the musicians, free, too, from Katherine's zeal and censure. "Something that will put us in a fine mood for a long night of dancing and revelry."

As the music struck up the king led out Mary Boleyn Carey as his first partner, but he did not limit himself to her. Henry was a man who liked a table laden with an uncountable number of fine delicacies, so many that he could not possibly eat them all at one sitting. But he enjoyed sampling them each with his eyes at every meal, and when he took a fancy to a particular dish, it had better be set afore him to be enjoyed at his exclusive pleasure. I watched as his eyes roved across the crowd, alighting here and there. They settled on Anne for a moment longer than on any other. I exhaled as soon as his gaze moved on.

'Twas no surprise that Anne was a much-requested dance partner all evening long. And yet, several times I looked at her returning a warm smile to the longing gaze of Henry Percy and she danced with him more than the others.

"Have a care," I warned her as we stood next to one another while the king danced a galliard. "He's the Earl of Northumberland's heir and roosts on a high perch."

"Even high-flying birds must come down to hunt," she responded, flushed and enjoying herself.

I grinned at her wit and banter. I enjoyed being young and in demand this evening too. We squeezed one another's hands in friendship ere parting when the dance opened up again to all.

And yet I must admit to a certain uneasiness when, later, I saw Henry Percy secure one of the dates that had been thrown in the earlier mock battle in order to win the affections of the virtuous maidens. At a pause in the music, Lord Percy offered the sweet to Anne.

She took it from him and enfolded it in her hand.

The months at court passed quickly, and early in springtime of 1523 my father sent my brother Thomas to court to assist with the king's finances. It was an attempt, which we were all sure would prove futile, to force verse out of Thomas's head, thus leaving room within for figures. I was glad of his company, though, and told him so as we strolled together in the gardens.

"How goes it at Allington?" I asked. While I enjoyed the festivities at court and even in the queen's household, such that they were, I missed home.

"Much the same." He took my hand and rested it in the crook of his elbow. The narcissus were just forcing their way out of the ground and Thomas bent down and plucked one. "Edmund is, as always, sure of himself and Father grows increasingly sure of him too. I think, truth be known, Father would prefer him here at court rather than I. But I am the eldest, alas, so none of the three of us will get what we desire." He held the flower to his nose and then held it out to me. "'Twould make a fine badge on Edmund's coat of armor, wouldn't it?"

"Indeed. I'm fairly certain that Narcissus is Edmund's patron saint," I replied. We giggled together and then sat down on a bench.

"Our mother?" I dared ask. Her letters had become further apart and shorter.

"Unwell," Thomas said, and then said nothing more. There was no need. In the distance I saw Anne and Henry Percy strolling together, her hand also in the crook of his arm, but the meaning much different, of course, than when it was one's brother.

As they approached Thomas stood and I remained seated.

"You look as beautiful as ever, Mistress Boleyn," Thomas said.

Anne laughed and the gaze of both men held rapt upon her face. "Oh, Thomas, no need for formalities. Things go well for me, and, I hear, for you. A new appointment at court?"

"Yes." Thomas appeared pleased to have his achievement recognized in front of Henry Percy. "And how are you, Lord Percy?"

Anyone with eyes could tell by looking upon Lord Percy's countenance that he was very well indeed.

"Well, thank you," he replied. No mention was made of his accomplishments. He needed none. He was rich and the heir of the Earl of Northumberland, ruler in all practicalities of the north. The look in his eye told me that he considered the distance between us Wyatts and himself an unbreachable gap. And it was, of course. But I counted it as a mark of weakness to have to intimate that to others by your manner. The king, after all, was known for his bonhomie. We discoursed for a time and then the two of them went on their way, a lady chaperone trailing discreetly behind. No one would mention the word "chaperone," but that was indeed the role she played that hour.

Thomas rejoined me on the bench and nodded toward the backs of the couple as they retreated from us. "How long has that been under way?"

"Since last spring," I said. No need to protest that nothing was under way. The court was the ultimate repository of open secrets.

"And his father?"

"Does not know, I am certain," I replied. The Boleyns were held in high regard by the king— Sir Thomas was even now away on a diplomatic mission on the king's behalf—but they were certainly not in the same drawer as the Percys.

Thomas sat on the bench, his poet's hands holding his head in a glum pose.

"Come now, Thomas. You are married. They are not."

He picked his head up. "Nor will they be," he said. "Mark my word. Wolsey will not let it happen."

"Who is Wolsey to say?" I asked.

"Wolsey is the king whilst the king plays," Thomas replied. Left unsaid was that the king was often at play.

We began our walk back to the palace, to his duties and mine, and that conversation was forgotten until one evening several months hence when Anne burst into our chamber. The suddenness of her action and the atypical loss of her composure shook me.

"What is it?"

She pulled me close. "Cardinal Wolsey approached Henry Percy and asked him what his intentions were toward me. Henry declared his love for me and indicated that he intended to marry me."

"And?"

"And Wolsey confronted Henry and told him that he would speak with him again and that he was not to see me for now. Also that he would get his father here anon to set things straight."

My brother Thomas was at York Place working on the king's figures with Thomas Cromwell when Cardinal Wolsey next spoke to Henry Percy. Thomas heard the cardinal call Anne a foolish girl and he marveled that Percy, heir to one of the noblest and most worthy earldoms on earth, would tangle himself with the likes of her.

Shortly after Thomas reported this to me I returned to my duties. After straightening and ordering the queen's gowns I asked and was granted dismissal. I threw Anne a look so she'd know to follow me.

Dear me. Anne had brought me here to be her

friend, and I had been so taken in with gladness that she had found love, and had so enjoyed late-night talks about him, that I had not advised her well. I needed to take off the cloak of a girlish friend and put on that of a womanly advisor. When she arrived, I recounted what Thomas had told me, but she already knew.

"Anne! What of Butler?" As far as I knew, her father was years into negotiations for a marriage between them.

She waved that away. "Who knows if that will come to pass? And my father would let go that proposal in a moment if he thought the Earl of Northumberland was in my reach."

This, I knew, was true.

"I have . . . corresponded with him." Ah. So Sir Thomas had given a tacit approval to this match and was letting Anne wrangle to win.

"Anne, think. Wolsey is the most powerful man in our world and he is implacably against you."

"Because he does not want to advance the Boleyns, see us reach too high beyond our grasp. Although why he, as a butcher's son, should be the judge of that I know not. And he's obsessively against my father's interests in the reformers' thoughts on faith. He removed my brother, George, from his position in the privy chamber, for example."

Please, please don't let Jane Parker be idling about.

"So what next?" I asked.

"Henry Percy will declare his love for me and my love for him and convince his father that we should be married."

"And if not?"

She shook her head. She never considered the possibility of losing. "I know how Percy loves me, and I believe that will give him the strength to do what needs to be done."

Shortly thereafter Anne had me deliver a letter to Henry Percy. She could not be seen with him, but I knew by her determined look that she had not given up. I knocked lightly on the door to his chamber and he opened it himself. His face was a bit crestfallen when he saw who it was—I suspected he'd hoped it would be Anne—but then recovered his graciousness and invited me in. I stepped in, to be polite, but had no intention of staying.

His chambers were large, the largest of any gentleman's chambers I'd been in, and richly appointed. We moved to the back of the large greeting room, toward a window, and I withdrew the letter from inside my deep French sleeve. "I'm to wait for a response, if you like," I said. He nodded, then left me standing by the window while he retired to his desk to read the letter and, I presumed, respond. I wandered to a further window, and then another, looking outside as I did. A large barge, one I didn't recognize, had been moored on the riverside alongside the palace grounds. It rivaled the king's for its ornamentation, though mayhap not Wolsey's.

I idled, but within a few minutes there was a sharp knock at the door. Percy's manservant answered and like a cloud clap a large man, emanating power, burst into the room.

"My Lord Northumberland," the servant stammered. The Earl of Northumberland approached his son, who had blanched.

"Sir!" he said in a menacing voice.

His son, who looked nothing so much as a just-weaned whelp, cowered as he turned before his father. I, tucked into a dark corner in the room, went unnoticed.

"I've always considered you an unthrifty wastrel, proud, disdainful, and certainly you should have been the runt of my pack rather than one of your nobler brothers. Now you've proved it to me and to all assembled. We shall discuss this, and the prospect of your disinheritance, with the cardinal's attorneys."

His father turned and as he did, Percy followed him out of the room and down the hall. Forgotten, I waited a moment and then took my leave. As I did, I knew Percy would never be the champion Anne hoped him to be.

Two days later Anne and I watched as our laden trunks were loaded into fine carts. She was banished to Kent to get her out of Percy's field of vision till his marriage to Mary Talbot, which had been ponderously negotiated for years, could be quickly consummated. I tried to make good conversation. "I will be glad to judge my mother's health on my own."

Anne remained silent as we rode our steeds.

"Was it the man or the title?" I finally asked what only the closest friend could.

"The title was important, of course. But I loved the man too." I'd never seen her defeated in position and in heart. A tear slid down her cheek and she abruptly brushed it away.

I picked at a sliver that lay just below the skin covering my own heart. "Through Wolsey, God has taken away both of our loves," I said.

She looked up. "No, that's where we disagree. You blame God for the deeds of men, I blame the men themselves. Mark me, this will return to Cardinal Wolsey. He's a gluttonous climber who has become a wolf in shepherd's cloth of gold. As a man sows, so shall he reap."

I was not sure if she was vowing revenge on Wolsey herself or quoting Scripture to remind God what should next follow.

"How can anyone truly respect a weak man?" she asked. I had no answer, because the truth was, you couldn't, and we both knew she didn't mean Wolsey.

"I do know this," Anne said after some miles of

silence. "I will never again pledge myself to a weak man."

I remained silent, pretending not to hear the word "pledge" in relation to Henry Percy. It was a dangerous, even perilous, word.

SIX

===

Year of Our Lord 1526
Allington Castle, Kent, England

I was an educated woman, not susceptible to superstition, so when old ladies waggled that bad things happened in sets of three I'd dismissed it as easily as one dismisses a gossipy servant. You can always look back on events past and find patterns in them, like seeing a tapestry after it's woven. And sometimes, by happenstance, bad did come in threes. Of course some events seemed bounteous at first sight but upon later reflection were clearly catastrophic.

"Mother is not well and will not be joining us for dinner," I announced to my father one evening as the whole family gathered for the evening meal. "I will remain with her, if it's agreeable to you."

He nodded, solemn. We all knew her time drew near and were reluctant to leave her alone. I had forgone joining my sister, Alice, for much of the past year, and my father had delayed my marriage negotiations so that my mother might have what comfort could be afforded her last days. I left Father, Thomas and his wife, and Edmund to the meal whilst I rejoined my mother.

"Flora, that will be all for now. I shall call upon you if the need arises." I dismissed my mother's servant and approached my mother in her bed. I brushed back her hair. " 'Tis unbound, as a bride's," I teased her lightly.

"I am a bride, the bride of Christ, shortly to join mine husband," she said. Her voice was lighter than it had sounded for some time, which concerned me.

"And you shall shortly be a bride too," she continued. "Your father will complete your negotiations with Lord Blackston, for certes, when I am gone."

"Hush, now," I said, not wanting the conversation to turn down that narrow path. We'd avoided it thus far and I feared that we would not find our way back once it was taken.

"In that trunk"—she pointed—"there is a portrait. I would have you bring it to me." I walked over to my mother's marriage trunk and opened the lid. There were folds of cloth and some of her fine gowns. I wondered if it had been with joy or trepidation that she had packed this as a girl, and unpacked it as a young woman come to Allington to take the bed of a dead woman. It was a fate that now, seemingly, was my own.

I lifted out what seemed to be a small wrapped portrait and my mother nodded her approval ere coughing into her linen. I brought the portrait to her bed and handed it to her.

She unwrapped it and handed it back to me. " 'Tis me!" I exclaimed.

She laughed, a beautiful sound, and I thanked God reflexively, begrudgingly, for the small gift of it, because I knew it would echo in my heart long after my mother had taken His hand. " 'Tis not you, darling, 'tis me."

Now that I looked harder at it, I could see there were some differences. She had not the dimple cleft in her chin as I did, and her brows were thicker than mine. But it was close.

"My father had this painted for me just before I left home to marry Sir Henry. He wanted me to remember my home and you can see, it's my girlhood chamber in the background."

I nodded.

"There I kept my treasures. My few jewels, my book of hours, hairpins my mother had given me. And my butterfly jar."

I looked up at her. "A butterfly jar? What is that, Madam?"

"Oh, I was a free-willed girl, the only girl in my family, as you know, indulged and overloved, perhaps, and I think your father would agree. I had very little responsibility so I ran among the fields—to the distress of my nurses and my lady mother, I fear. One favorite pastime was to catch butterflies in a netting, then let them go. I got an idea—I would catch the butterfly in a net and keep him in one of the physic jars in which leeches had been brought to help my ailing father. I waited till I caught the one I wanted most to keep—he would live with me, we would share secrets. He was beautiful and would adorn my chamber and fly out when I commanded and then return in like manner."

She took a moment and coughed so that I thought she might not be able to stop. After some minutes she regained her breath.

"Alas, one morning shortly after bringing him to my chamber I awoke to find that he was dead. He was not meant to live in a glass jar, even a beautiful, expensive glass jar. Instead of flying freely about he beat his wings against the jar, and try as he might he could not adapt. Thus trapped, he sickened and died. I think he gave up, because there were holes aplenty to let him breathe."

I had not taken my eyes off my mother. She now looked full into mine. "Do you understand, Meg?"

I nodded.

"Thomas is a dreamer, and Edmund is your father's son. But you, dear Meg, you are mine."

"I will not let you down, Madam. I promise you that." I leaned over and kissed her wan cheek.

Exhausted with the effort, she fell back in her pillow and I stayed by her till her shallow breathing grew regular. I then took the portrait with me and slipped back into my own chamber.

In the springtime, we buried my lady mother at the priory near Allington. I spent days going through her belongings, folding her linens, reading her letters, dabbing on her scented water, crying silently into her gowns after I folded them and before I laid them away. One afternoon I found Edmund sobbing behind the gatehouse. It reminded me of how, as a boy, he'd held on to my skirts to steady himself, how he and I had sat in the long hallway and rolled balls to one another. As we'd grown older, we'd grown apart. "Edmund," I said. He looked up, startled to see me and clearly not happy at having been caught at grief.

"I am sorry for, well, for whatever has driven us apart. Mayhap it was my fault as I spent more time with Thomas. I don't wish us to be distant any longer."

He brushed his riding gloves across his face and stared at me with not one scrap of warmth. "I have no use of, nor desire for, your affection or interest, now or at any time."

I looked into his flint-blue eyes. The boy Edmund was gone. The man Edmund was no one I cared to know, dangerous and ugly.

Some months later I was going over the kitchen accounts with the chamberlain when a messenger arrived from Hever Castle. As the lady of the house now, I took the correspondence and opened it. It was an invitation to a feast being held in the king's honor a fortnight hence. The whole family was invited, and Sir Thomas took special care to inform my father that my nephew John Rogers would attend along with some of the other fellows from Cambridge in advance of their priestly ordination.

Which other fellows? It had been several years since I had seen Will, and truthfully, he had probably forgotten me. We were, as I'd told Thomas, a long-passed youthful flirtation akin to his affection for Anne.

I brought the invitation to my father, who was home from court as the treasurer of the king's household for the time being, the better to allow my brother Thomas to become proficient at his job as clerk.

"Sir, this has just arrived from Sir Thomas and Lady Boleyn." I handed the invitation over to him, fully expecting him to instruct his secretary to write a polite note of refusal, as we were still a household in mourning. Still, I hoped he would allow us to go, as I was eager to see Anne again.

My father read it quickly. Then he turned to his secretary. "Please write Sir Thomas and thank him for the invitation. My sons and my daughter and I will attend, and my grandson John Rogers can return to stay here at Allington, as I know that the king is on progress and the other houses likely to be well occupied. Oh—and please inform Sir Thomas that My Lord Blackston will attend with our family. He will be here anon to complete his marriage with my daughter."

I swooned, but just slightly.

"That will be all." My father dismissed his secretary, and I remained for a few moments whilst he instructed me to prepare to be married shortly and return to my husband's home with him afterward.

I went up to my chamber. Edithe was there, mending one of my gowns. "We will find something for Flora to rework among your mother's gowns for the dance at Hever Castle," she said. "Flora may accompany you to Baron Blackston's, if it be a'right, lady. My Roger is here at the Boleyns'." I nodded mutely, knowing I'd miss her desperately.

The day before the ball, Baron Blackston's carriage arrived. I went to meet him, as was expected of me. But when the carriage door opened Simon came out and no one else.

"My Lord . . . I am pleased to see you," I said. "And"—I looked into the open carriage door—"Lord Blackston?"

"Is unwell," he said shortly. "I am come to talk with Sir Henry on his behalf."

I wanted to disallow my heart to hope, hope

having often been torn out by the roots in my life. *But perhaps,* I thought, *perhaps . . .*

On the night of the feast my father and Simon shared a cart with Edmund, and I rode with my nephew John Rogers.

"A priest," I said as we bumped along the hardened path to Hever Castle. "Was your father shocked?"

He nodded. "For a time, but I think he always knew I was thus inclined. He will train my brother to take my place in the family."

"And . . . no wife?" I pressed on.

He shook his head. "Not for lack of desire, I assure you. But in spite of the fact that Luther himself has taken a bride whilst serving God completely, I just do not feel able to part my heart thusly."

"Luther says priests can be married then." I was exultant.

"Not in England, they can't," John corrected me, and my heart fell. "They can't even read Tyndale's New Testament translation in England without risk of being burned alive."

I leaned forward and whispered, though there were only we two in the cart. "Have you read Tyndale's New Testament, John?"

He grinned at me and said nothing. His face was alight with passion. I envied him. I felt the desire to read the Scriptures in my own language kindle, but I quickly patted it out.

Anne must have had a hand in the seating arrangements as I was neatly placed at dinner next to my nephew, which meant that all of his friends rallied round our table to talk after the meal was complete. Try as I might to force my eyes away from the Ogilvys, I could not. Rose was there with her husband, the flush of new motherhood making her a bit fairer of face and thicker of waist. My own waist, fashionably thin underneath my corset, felt inadequate and unwomanly. Walter Ogilvy was there, coughing disruptively, and his wife was there, too, appreciably heavy with child. I envied her and felt the yearning in my own small waist. And then there was Will. He locked eyes with me each and every time I looked in his direction so I knew he must have been looking at me often.

The king roared his approval at a joke, commanded the musicians, and the dance began. Noticeably absent from his attention was the pregnant Mary Boleyn. I did not envy Mary her second child, certain, like her eldest, Katherine, to be a golden redhead unlike her husband, dark-haired Carey. The king threw nary a glance in her direction and all knew that his affections had, like the court, gone on progress for fresh lodging and novel fare.

"My lady, a dance?" George Boleyn came alongside me.

"Certainly," I said, and he swept me into his brotherly arms. I leaned forward and whispered, "Does not your new wife expect you to dance with her alone all evening?"

"If she'd quit of her harsh chattering I may, but alas, there is no hope for that, so I dutifully make the rounds with my father's guests," he said.

"Why hasn't the queen come?" I was certain that as the host's son he would know.

"She's angry because the king is considering naming the Duke of Richmond to the line of succession along with Princess Mary. No one other than a lawfully begot son of the king shall take precedence over Richmond."

"Ah." The Duke of Richmond was Henry's bastard son by Bessie Blount, whereas Princess Mary was the one surviving child of Henry's union with Katherine of Aragon.

"What is your opinion?" I whispered in his ear. As a courtier, George would have heard the murmurs in the king's privy council.

" 'Twas only one woman ever tried to rule England, the empress Maude, and Henry, as well as all of us, knows how that ended," he grimly replied. I nodded my agreement. Decades of bloodshed, political unrest, and civil war. "He must not let that happen again. And he knows it."

The music slowed, indicating a change in song. "And now I shall turn the conversation over to more pleasant matters, and the lady to a most pleasant partner." And, as if by happenstance but most likely by plan, Will came to claim the next dance.

He took my hand in his and pulled me near. I nearly closed my eyes in delight, but I was aware of Simon's gaze boring into my back. I dared not show my true feelings.

"You look well, Meg," Will said, his voice deep and thick with emotion. I allowed myself to look into his eyes briefly and then willed the look he returned imprinted upon my heart and mind.

"You, too, sir. I trust your studies have gone well? My nephew John tells me that you both shall graduate with your MA at Cambridge and are shortly to take your vows."

He sighed heavily. Well, I couldn't help it. What other were we to talk of, and in any case, I had never hidden my true heart from Will Ogilvy and I wasn't about to start now.

"Yes. My brother's wife will soon have a child and my father feels secure in allowing me to take my vows. I shall do so shortly. Will you attend the ceremony with Alice?"

We parted momentarily but remained partners for the next dance as well, a notable social indiscretion and sure to draw eyes. I held my voice aloof. "I shall be married soon so I shan't be close enough to attend. I wish you well."

"Meg, please don't put this barrier between us. Let us sit awhile and have a cup of wine, as friends, and I shall tell you about what I've been studying and where I plan to go."

The idea of an intelligent discourse that did not include what was remaining in the larder, or how much small beer had spoiled, drew me. And the man did too; I admit it. He put his hand in the hollow of my back and steered me to a table, where a servant delivered two cups of wine. I looked about me and, not seeing Simon, Baron Blackston's eyes and ears, breathed easier.

Will leaned in toward me in order to be better heard above the musicians. I had no place to look—not his eyes lest I be drawn in, not his lips lest I imagine what could not be. I affixed a firm, friendly, sisterly look to my face and tried to focus on his cheekbones. I'd traced them once and longed to do so again but a verse of Scripture came back to me, unbidden. *Touch not God's anointed. Noli tangere.* He was not mine to touch.

"I'm going to Antwerp, to be a chaplain to the cloth merchants. But also . . . there is printing going on there. And translating. Tyndale is there. And I have honed my gift for languages. I'm going to see if I can be of some help. Perhaps it was for this that our Lord called me. Imagine it, Meg, hundreds, thousands of people able to read what God says in their own language. German, French, English. Not dependent upon Latin any-more."

"I've done quite well without Latin myself," I

said, wanting to remain aloof in light of his enthusiasm, but I couldn't. I grinned.

"Still my stubborn girl," he said, unaware what the words "my girl" meant to me. Or maybe not.

I could see Simon making his way toward me. I drew my shoulders back to appear disinterested. "Be careful in Antwerp," I said. "I will pray for you."

"*Te somniabo.*" He quietly echoed his long-ago words spoken in the gardens just outside. *I will dream of you.*

"Don't," I urged him. "It's not fair to either of us."

He nodded but held my gaze. "You're right. I apologize. I love our Lord with all that I am, but I am still a weak man in at least one area. I . . . I will not reach out to you again."

At precisely that moment Simon arrived. "Meg," he said overfamiliarly, "a dance? You've been sitting here so long." He shot a look at Will.

"Thank you, yes," I said. "This is Will Ogilvy, a childhood friend. He's about to take his priestly vows with my nephew John."

At that Simon relaxed, but not completely. They made small talk for a few moments and then Simon led me onto the dance floor, holding me, if anything, even tighter than Will had. As we did I thought, *Unlike Anne, I could love a man with a weakness, so long as it was the right one.*

Will had left his seat and was talking with his

97

sister, Rose, and a demure friend of hers, auburn-haired like me. But I saw his face as I danced with Simon; it was tinted with jealousy.

My brother Edmund danced with Rose Ogilvy's young friend. Anne sat in a corner, attended by several young men. I joined them and we chattered for a moment. I was about to suggest a walk in the garden when the young men disappeared like ice on a summer pond. Anne—Anne!—grew demure and I looked behind me. It was the king. I quickly dropped to a curtsey, but I needn't have bothered as it wasn't me he was looking at.

"Do I know you?" the king asked Anne.

"I am Mistress Anne Boleyn," Anne said. I found it hard to believe that he did not remember Anne, having been to Hever Castle many times. But Henry was a man with a singular focus and it had been trained on another Boleyn girl for many years. And in the years since she'd left court Anne herself had blossomed from a somewhat cocky, self-sure girl to a young woman in complete command of her alluring repertoire.

"Why are you not at court?" Henry asked. "Surely such a lovely flower should not be hidden away in the countryside to blossom and die unheralded."

Ah yes, the master of courtly flirtation.

"I had the privilege of serving the queen for some time, sire, but Cardinal Wolsey thought perhaps the fields of Kent were better suited to me than the garden of Your Majesty's court." The words themselves were straightforward but Anne, too, had been well trained in court manners and there was a certain lure in her voice that men found irresistible. Henry, it need not be said, was a man.

"The cardinal has made a grievous error, I fear," Henry said. He bowed slightly, chivalrously. "A dance, mistress?" As if anyone would dare decline!

Although the king had been expected to return to Penshurst Castle that night he chose, instead, to accept Sir Thomas's offer of hospitality and dwell a little longer at Hever. Anne and I spent the night awake, nearly all night, giggling like young girls in front of her fireplace talking about women and their clothes and their prospects and Will and Simon. And the king, of course.

The next evening Sir Thomas put on another dinner, smaller, of course, but certain to bring him to the edge of bankruptcy, as visits from the king were often the financial ruin of the host. George Boleyn was the king's cupbearer, and as Anne and George sat idling, talking, the king beckoned to George. "I'm thirsty." I watched from some feet away as Anne let go of George's arm so he could assist the king with his wine. And then Henry spoke again, loud enough for all to hear.

"Bring your sister with you." The king looked directly at Anne, comely in a yellow gown that didn't fix her dark complexion as sallow so much as sun-kiss it. I wondered if anyone considered that he might have been asking for George's sister Mary instead. But she was nowhere to be seen.

All those present separated to two sides and Anne glided along the open path toward the king. She approached him, curtseyed deeply, and held his gaze. It was rare for anyone to hold the king's gaze, much less a woman. He reached out and took one of her hands in his own, and then took the other one. He held them for an exceptionally long time ere turning to speak to George.

"Methinks these hands are prettier than yours, Boleyn." The room roared with laughter. "I should rather be served by yon delicate fingers than by your hairy ones." George grinned, bowed, and handed the king's gold cup to Anne. She approached the king and lifted the cup to the king's lips, gaze never wavering. After a moment, she lowered the cup and stood fast. I realized, with a start, that I was not breathing and forced myself to do so.

The king spoke again. "I feel refreshed as I haven't in some time, mistress. Where have you learnt such comely manners?"

Anne spoke clearly, sweetly, with a well-cushioned barb. "Here in the house of my father, sire. And at the French court."

There was an audible gasp then, the implication being that etiquette was better learned in a French court than in an English one. But Henry seemed delighted by her forthrightness, becomingly coupled with her feminine charm. He laughed aloud.

"Well, then, mistress, I will depend upon you to share with us what you have learnt. The French court's loss is our gain." He indicated that she should take a seat next to him, and, in fact, fairly shoved the Duke of Suffolk out of the way to make room for her.

He never took his eyes off of her. It was as if he'd commissioned an expensive tapestry some months before and now, to his delight, it had been set before him. I suspected the musicians were going to have to play well beyond their commissioned hours in order to provide an extended, acceptable opportunity for Anne and the king to talk. She was bold but not bawdy as she paid him attention, a sophisticated flirt. I doubted he'd ever seen anyone like her.

Late that evening I spied someone in the tattle's corner, a dark corner to hear from but not be seen. It was Mary Boleyn Carey. Our eyes met and I saw that she knew her time with the king had ended. He had nary a further thought for her, but he had given her a husband, a fine manor, some baubles, and two children.

My heart reached out. I pitied her, and Sir William Carey as well.

One week hence Simon and I met in my father's chamber. The village priest was there, twitching in front of my father. I was to marry Baron Blackston by proxy. He was too ill to travel south to complete the marriage, but neither he, nor my father, wanted it delayed any further. Simon had told us that he'd argued against a hasty marriage but that the baron had pressed on. "I finally convinced him to do it by proxy, if he must," he said. "I insisted that he didn't want his young bride to come to him as a nursemaid and not as a wife, and he agreed."

Since my mother's death my father had grown less and less interested in the matters of our estate, so Edmund and Simon had completed the negotiation of my marriage portion. Neither shared the details with me. Simon would stand in for the baron and I would join him, at least for a time, within a year, for certes.

Edithe dressed me in a fine gown, merrily chattering as she did, though we both knew this had not been a wedding day any girl or woman should desire. As she spoke of the simple village wedding she herself had had, I wondered, for the first time, if perhaps simple folk had an easier life in some ways than the higher born. We made our way to my father's study, where Simon waited.

The proxy words were read and I numbly nodded and added my agreement, though of course 'twere no agreement at all. After the priest married us, Simon spoke up. "A marriage isn't complete till it's been consummated. To the bed-room."

Surely not . . . ! But my father insisted. Simon gleamed with malice.

We walked to my bedchamber, and, to my horror, the priest instructed us to get upon the bed. "Bare your lower legs," he said next, and, feeling somewhat immodest, I obeyed. "Touch them together," he continued.

We did, although Simon pressed his firmly into mine and kept them there, rather than a moderate and transient touch.

When he took his legs from mine he gave me a look that told me he'd rather have dismissed them all from the bedchamber and consummated it the traditional way. Thankfully, as he was not my husband, that would never be.

I tried not to think about when I *would* have to consummate my marriage the traditional way with Lord Blackston. But I was wed now and there was no turning back.

With a wicked grin, Simon bowed to me and then left the chamber. After dinner he played cards with Edmund late into the night and then, the next day, left for the north.

I was a married woman and yet I'd never felt emptier. I stayed my mind from the memories of dreaming of my wedding day to Will and sat quietly in my chamber that night so as not to give others acquaintance with my sorrow.

• • •

I idled for a month, reading my books and talking to the servants as they prepared to finish the chores that accompanied our property just before harvest time. One day a Boleyn retinue arrived at Allington on horseback. Anne dismounted, her black hair shimmering against a French hood. I went to meet her.

"The king sent me a stag he'd killed at hunt," she said. "And a letter."

"A letter?" All knew that Henry detested writing.

She nodded, and we headed toward the sitting chamber, where she pulled me close and then handed the letter to me. I scanned it, amazed at some of the words as I read them aloud. " 'My mistress and friend, I and my heart put ourselves in your hands, begging you to recommend us to your favor and to not let absence lessen your affection to us. For it were a great pity to increase our pain, which absence alone does sufficiently and more than I could ever thought.' "

I stopped reading and looked at her with alarm. "What does he mean by this?"

"One can speculate," Anne said. Her bemused expression told me she'd been doing just that. "He wrote to my father at the same time. I am commanded to court. At the very least, my father is sure to find a fine marriage match for me whilst I am there. After all, that's how I met Percy . . ." Her face grew suffused with excitement. She'd been worried since negotiations with James Butler had soured and little else had surfaced in the ensuing years. The king kept her father busy, perhaps too busy to find a good match for Anne. Truth be told, she was indeed a flower who thrived on the close heat of the court and not the whistling breeze of an empty countryside.

And then, a surprise. "Come with me," she said. "I need a friend. A true friend there, a trusted friend. I feel that it was my fault that you left court early last time and I'd like to make it up to you. I know the king would not take exception to my inviting you to join me in service to the queen again." Henry would certainly not take exception to anything she asked, judging by the tone of his letter. But I shook my head. "I am married and will go north as soon as my husband has recovered his health."

"Mayhap he'll pass on afore you can meet with him. God rest his soul."

"Anne!" I said, shocked that she'd speak aloud my shameful hope. She, who was not given to examining herself in shame, burst out laughing. I laughed with her.

"I jest. But come to court till he is well. He can summon you from there just as easily as from here. And . . . Edmund is not at court."

This was true.

Within the week Edithe and I finished packing. I was to join Anne at court.

SEVEN

Year of Our Lord 1526
Richmond Palace
and
Year of our Lord 1527
Allington Castle

And so we spent the autumn at court. I was now a member of the aristocracy, thanks to my as-yet-unkissed husband, and therefore entitled to better rooms. Anne certainly had better rooms; her chambers were draped with among the finest tapestries I'd ever seen. There were more than one hundred ladies waiting upon the queen in various capacities and those she kept closest were, naturally, Spanish women who had joined her when she came to England decades ago to marry Prince Arthur.

Alas, Katherine's marital bliss had lasted only a few short months ere Arthur succumbed to consumption. The new princess had to wait, her temper and gowns growing threadbare, till her knight in shining armor, Henry, rescued and married her just after his father died.

I studiously learnt many things from the busy lips of those hundred women as we dealt cards or sorted ribbons and silks, paying careful attention so that I could better guide Anne. I learnt that the king had not joined the queen in her bedchamber in many years and that she had not had a monthly flux for many years, either. I learnt that she spent long hours praying in Spanish in a chapel aflame with candles, beseeching the Lord for a miracle son. While I didn't share her zealous religious devotion, I admired her constancy to it. I learnt that though she was haughty to nearly all but her closest friends, when Henry did talk to her she was gentle, and perhaps too pleading to hold his respect or interest. I learnt that there were some principles she would not bend on—her marriage, her faith, and her daughter, Mary, even if it meant locking horns with Henry. I was shocked that a woman of such intelligence would not understand that locking horns with Henry on anything meant that she would lose, and lose badly. Anyone who had heard the king in temper, or had it spoken of, or remembered the death of poor Buckingham should have learnt that well.

I learnt through whispered conversations that although the queen would not cause direct harm to those in her path, there were others in her household who had no such scruples. They smelt blood, and as times became more desperate they would become bolder in protecting their mistress. Well, there were those of us who would protect Anne, too, though none, I dared say, would stoop to bloodshed.

Though the king attended to royal business during the day, Anne was the first one he sought for companionship during musical performances, his most frequent dance partner, the confidante he could be seen laughing with as the court made its way from gallery to gallery after dinner. I sensed nothing amiss for some time because, after all, courtly flirtation was the lingua franca and we were always among a crowd. Anne's high profile and clear favor with the king would allow her father to find a husband for her, something we'd oft discussed. But it eventually became clear to all, and they spoke of it in hushed tones at feasts and in darkened hallways, that Henry was besotted with Anne in a way he'd never been with either Bessie Blount or Mary Boleyn, the two ladies who had most publicly shared his attentions. The reason why was clear to me. Anne was Henry's equal, and he, the consummate jouster, relished her for her ability to parry. He'd styled his friend Charles Brandon the Duke of Suffolk for the same set of skills.

One of the joys of being at court was the pleasantries of spending time with my brother Thomas. I walked with him in the autumn gardens among the leaves tinted magenta and, yea, even purple, as this was a royal household after all. As he was unhappy in his marriage I had poured out my sorrow to him about my last meeting with Will, and how I felt, *noli tangere*, now that he belonged to our Lord. Thomas understood. Neither of us spoke of Baron Blackston. Anne joined us from time to time and one day, for a lark, Thomas snatched a jewel that Anne had on a knitted string, hanging from a pocket in her gown. After Anne had introduced the fashion I noticed several other ladies at court imitating it.

"Give that back!" she insisted. Thomas shook his head and instead plunged the jewel and its chain into his bosom.

" 'Tis mine now," he said. "I shall use it as an excuse to speak to you when I will—come to return your favor or ask one of you, you'll know not."

"Thomas," I said quietly. He looked at me, winked, and backed away. Anne waved him off with a laugh.

" 'Tis only a courtly banter," she said, relenting. "And a paste jewel. Let him have it." She linked arms with me and we strolled back to the palace, wind now picking up. A few days later, she burst into my chamber.

"Your brother," she said before closing the door, "is not to be trusted."

I sat her down next to me. "Edmund is here?"

She shook her head impatiently and dismissed Edithe from the room—really my prerogative, though I said nothing. "Thomas. Apparently he was playing bowls with the king and other gentlemen when the king hit a shot that he claimed had made the mark though it hadn't.

Thomas, fool that he is, disagreed with the king."

Oh no. Everyone knew that the king, once settled on a matter, would not be dissuaded. His opinion was always right, his assumptions and assertions the correct ones, and he never changed his mind because that would imply that, impossibly, he'd been wrong in the first place. To claim otherwise was foolhardy indeed.

"That's not the worst of it," Anne pressed on. "Thomas withdrew the jewel he stole from me and used the knitted chain to measure the distance from the king's bowl to the mark and his own bowl to the mark whence he claimed victory— showing the king my jewel as he so declared! The king, completely understanding that Thomas was claiming *me,* and not the bowl, replied that it might be true but then he had been deceived. Henry Norris had come to warn me of it and I am come to ask you—please tell Thomas to keep his distance from me. I dare not be seen telling him on my own."

I nodded and as I did heard Edithe quietly come into the room. "Mistress Boleyn's maid is here," she said, her voice sounding like one who suffered watery bowels. "The king has asked for her."

Anne left and I went to listen to some musicians that the queen had arranged to play in her room. She sat eating Seville oranges and tapping her toe to the melancholy refrain so different from the galliards Henry preferred. I peeled an orange

110

and worried about Anne. Later that night Anne appeared in the queen's chambers and, smiling, settled down next to me. Every eye was upon her and the queen's mouth grew pinched.

Later Anne snuck into my chamber and told me that she'd convinced the king that Thomas's actions were a playful gesture left over from childhood and that he meant nothing more to her, and perhaps a great deal less, than a true brother. The king was well pleased and asked her to stay with him for dinner in his chambers.

"What does he intend, Anne?" I asked.

"I know not," she said. "But the king is a huntsman and it seems, somehow, I am now his quarry and all others must back off."

"This will not do well for marriage negotiations on your behalf. How do you feel about it?"

"At first I had no feeling for the king other than pleasure at bantering with a learned man and my monarch. But now . . ."

"You don't want the life Mary lived," I reminded her. I would not be a good friend if I let her wander down that road.

She shook her head. "No. I do not. And I shall not have it, either."

She took her leave for the evening, and as she did, foreboding twinged deep within me. I thought to myself that she rather enjoyed the chase but perhaps, like any hind, did not expect to suffer an arrow through the heart. I shared my thoughts with my brother as I warned him away.

At the Christmas celebrations that year it became increasingly clear that the queen was isolated. No one but her Spanish ladies sought her company, but all sought Anne's. The king gave Anne a necklace of diamonds as a gift.

Thomas, to his credit, was writing poetry and staying out of Anne's way. One day he slipped a poem to me. "I've written it for both of us," he said. I raised my eyebrow expecting further explanation but he pressed it into my hand and said, "You'll see what I mean."

I took it to my chamber and read it.

Whoso list to hunt, I know where is an hind
But as for me, alas, I may no more.
The vain travail hath wearied me so sore,
I am of them that furthest come behind.
Yet may I by no means my wearied mind
Draw from the deer, but as she fleeth afore
Fainting I follow; I leave off therefore,
Since in a net I seek to hold the wind.
Who list her hunt, I put him out of doubt,
As well as I, may spend his time in vain.
And graven with diamonds in letters plain
There is written, her fair neck about:
Noli me tangere, for Caesar's I am,
And wild for to hold, though I seem tame.

Touch me not. *Noli me tangere.* I belong to Another.

In January the king sent Thomas on a diplomatic mission to Italy. I would miss him but understood it was best, and safest, for all.

My father, knowing nothing of the king's distrust of Thomas, celebrated Thomas's unexpected appointment as a diplomat with a dance at Allington Castle. Anne was unable to take leave of the court and, as this was a smallish affair, there would be no king nor many courtiers, mostly Kent gentry. My sister, Alice, was coming. My father had written to tell me that my husband, Baron Blackston, was well enough to attend.

Alice and I got ready in the same chamber though I would share the baron's chamber for sleep once he arrived. She shook out my gown and instructed Flora to go to another room to get some ribbon. "Are you . . . prepared?" she asked when Flora had taken her leave.

I nodded. "My mother talked to me of marriage afore she passed away, God rest her," I said. "Though I cannot say I am eager. I wish I could forgo this portion of my duty."

She nodded sympathetically. She'd told me once that although the act was for procreation, and that although she and Master Rogers had procreated quite enough, she also enjoyed it for the intimacy and pleasure. I am certain she had not confessed that to anyone but me, and perhaps her daughters, as conjugal enjoyment was frowned upon. But a sister was a sister, after all. I noticed she didn't suggest that I may enjoy the act with the baron. She knew I wouldn't. But she knew my duty as well as my station as a woman required me to follow through.

I was seated next to him at dinner and he was able to keep up a conversation about our home, Haverston Hall. We had exchanged some letters over the past few months, mainly impersonal letters of duty with small bits of news, court news from me, country news from him. He said he was not yet strong enough to dance and I noticed him breathing heavily.

"I confess a curiosity to see Haverston," I told him. And I did. It was my home and I was the lady of the manor and I wondered what it would be like to command and care for a staff in a home that was not my father's.

"I will be visiting my other properties for the spring, my lady Baroness, after my three days here are complete. It will be an arduous journey of many months, not fit for a lady, as there are a dozen or more of them I must attend to. Simon," he said, looking in the direction of his nephew, "contends that he is not able to undertake the journey for me this year as he has other duties to attend to. So I must undertake the task myself."

I accepted that. It wasn't odd for husbands and wives to be separated for long periods whilst one or the other was at court, or about the king's business, or attending to the vast holdings of the nobility or even the middling ones of the gentry.

"When my travels are completed," he continued, "I look forward to your joining me at Haverston, as indeed I look forward to your joining me tonight."

He gave me a look that told me he was talking about exactly what I suspected he was.

I stayed at dinner and dance longer than the baron, as Alice and I shared hostessing duties. Truth be told, I stayed as long as I reasonably could, delaying the inevitable. My brother's wife, Elizabeth, and his young son, Thomas, had not come for the event, which was noted by all. When I finally found the courage to shroud myself in a high-necked white shift and make my way to my husband's bedchamber, he was fast asleep. I could not wake him, and for a moment, I thought he was dead.

"Meredith!" I called down the hall to the lady servant who had come with him. "My Lord Blackston wakes not."

" 'Tis normal, My Lady," she said dismissively, the longtime servant to the short-time wife. "He sleeps deeply." I found it strange that she was still fully dressed at that hour. I shook my head, though grateful for the reprieve. He had seemed so determined to, ah, keep company.

The second night I steeled myself to do my duty and went to join him earlier and he was already asleep, again. He made no comment about it during the day and, in fact, seemed discomfited to discuss it when I mentioned his deep sleep. He made reference to being older and still recovering and brushed the topic aside and yielded to a wet, tight cough that plagued many each January. That night when I went to talk with the musicians I heard them discussing the baron's inabilities, so I knew the staff were gossiping.

On the third night, the night ere he was to return to Haverston, I made my way to my chamber to change when I saw Meredith slipping out of Baron Blackston's rooms, empty cup in hand. She made her way down the dark hall, opened the door not to her own room, but to Simon's, and slipped in. I heard laughter before the door was firmly shut. When I went to see the baron some short time later he was already firmly asleep.

If I had been praying still, I would have prayed a prayer of thanksgiving. As it was, I felt like a stubborn child not even offering a small token of appreciation to our Lord for helping me escape this unwelcome obligation for now. My attitude shamed me.

Lord Blackston prepared to take his leave the next day. He kissed me good-bye, once on each cheek. "I will call for you, My Lady, when I am done with my journeys . . . and when I am in better health and able to be a husband as I should." He would not look me in the eye as he took his leave.

I was still a maiden, though I did not speak of it to anyone so as not to shame my husband.

I suspect others knew, though. Servants always inspect the bed linens.

EIGHT

Year of Our Lord 1527
Greenwich Palace
Allington Castle
Hever Castle
Hampton Court Palace

When I returned to the court a week or more later it was immediately apparent that spring had arrived early. The court was humid with the bond between Anne and the king.

The court musicians began to play the composers she preferred.

The king was seen reading books written in French.

In March, when the king hunted, he ensured that the finest stag was cleaned, dressed, and roasted, and the tenderest portion sent to Anne. The season's first joust was held then too. We all gathered in the covered tiltyard, the ladies seated near one another in their finest dresses, the queen toward the center. I settled in next to Anne and raised my eyebrows at her ruby dress made of rare sarcenet with a square-cut bodice. The kirtle underneath, exposed by slashing, was shot through with royal gold thread. Either Sir Thomas had made the acquaintance of a generous clothier in Paris or there was another sponsor for these expensive gowns.

"A gift from the king," she answered my silent inquiry.

The Duke of Suffolk, the king's closest friend and brother-in-law, rode out first, the challenger. His wife, often ill, was not at court, and it was unknown whose favor he wore tied to his lance, though it was certainly not hers. I, the daughter of a dedicated horseman, recognized the appropriateness of each of their steeds. Suffolk's mount was a warm-blooded charger, bred for agility and speed. The king rode out onto the tilt field next to the roar of the men and the polite clapping of the assembled women. His horse was a cold-blooded destrier, a war horse, really, slower than a charger but twice as heavy and able to slam into an enemy with devastating force. The king cantered toward the crowd and all expected him to stop in front of the queen, as was his custom, in order for her to tie her favor onto his lance. He did stop in front of her and nod respectfully but he already had a favor tied to his lance. It was a knitted jewel string.

One night in April Anne and I dined together in her chambers, as we often did. Food that was served in private dining chambers was warm, while that brought from the kitchens to the hall often arrived stone cold due to the long distance it had to travel. After we were served, she dismissed the servants and then we closed the door to her chamber. The firelight burnished the carved wood panels in her apartments to a rich glow. She handed me a silver tray of sweetmeats that her maid had left out and then took one for herself.

"Henry's asked me to share his bed," she said simply.

"But you're not married," I said after she told me of their conversation.

"Your ability to state the obvious is noted, Baroness," she replied dryly.

"And just as important, he *is* married," I said. Well, if I was going to be chided for stating the obvious I might as well press forward.

She surprised me then. "No, he's not."

"No, he's not? The queen is a phantom, then?"

She laughed her singular feline laugh. "No, dearest Meg, she's not a phantom. First of all, I told him no, that I would not be his mistress." She reached for another date. "But be patient, and I shall explain it all to you as the king has explained it to me. Henry has long held the conclusion that our Lord is angry with him. Why else should he have withheld sons from Henry, sons that are necessary for Henry to fulfill the oath, the sacred oath, he made before God at his coronation to uphold the realm? This cannot be achieved by a woman, as we well know, and the king has but one daughter and no legitimate son."

I nodded. So far, she was correct.

"Henry had studied Scriptures in great detail as a young man, afore Arthur's death, and he felt compelled to go back and look at them anon to see from whence he might have turned from our Lord's affections. With some help, he settled upon a passage in Leviticus. Come." She stood and beckoned to me and we went to a further corner of her chamber where a great upright chest stood. She lifted the lid and I peeked in with her.

"Books. And . . . a Bible. In French. And other books by the reformers," I said. I had spoken of the reformers with my sister, Alice, who counted herself among them. I, thus far, had remained politely disinterested. I glanced at a book by Lefevre. "This is dangerous, Anne. Should someone uncover these . . . Where did you get them?"

Anne nodded but smiled, unworried, content in the hidey-hole of the king's protection. "Some I brought back with me from France, gifts from Marguerite, King Francis's sister, after we'd read them together. Some are from my father. And of course, George."

I'd heard rumors that George was a notorious religious book smuggler. It fit with his sense of charm and daring—not to mention his faith.

Anne lifted one of the French Bibles out and opened it to Leviticus and read aloud. *"Si un homme prend la femme de son frère, c'est une impureté; il a découvert la nudité de son frère: ils seront sans enfant."*

" 'And if a man shall take his brother's wife, it is an unclean thing: he hath uncovered his brother's nakedness; they shall be childless,' " I said. "But—the pope gave Henry a dispensation to marry Katherine."

Anne nodded. "But who is the pope, Meg, or any man, no matter how good he may be, to overrule Holy Scriptures, God's own word, to declare what God has said is impermissible, permissible? Why else would there need to be a dispensation, except to claim that something that was wrong wasn't?"

I opened my mouth, shocked at her heresy and boldness. And then I closed it again. Because what she said might well be true. I well remembered my father saying that the good people of England had been aghast at the near-incest when Henry chose to marry Katherine against his late father's desires. Henry the Seventh had loudly bemoaned that he'd sent his first son to his death by encouraging marriage, with its physical demands, upon a young man of ill health and never forgave Katherine for it, though it be upon his own head, for what could Katherine have done? It was not in her power to refuse, as I well knew.

"How long have you thought this way?" I asked. "About Scriptures being the highest authority?"

"Not Scripture, Meg, God, as he speaks through Scripture. A long while, since my last return from France," she said. "I hadn't voiced them before, but the convictions grew. And when God led Henry to me, I saw how it all fit together."

I opened my mouth to question whether or not God had led Henry to her, but that seemed beside the point at the moment. And then I felt betrayed in our friendship. "Why haven't you spoken of this with me? I rather thought that, well, that we had no secrets."

"I did not think that conversations about faith were welcome after the situation with Will. So you'd said."

So I'd said. I held my hand out and ran it over the delicate leather that bound the French translation of Scripture.

"Do you want to take it?" she asked.

I hesitated. Then I returned to my seat and shook my head.

She put the books back into the chest and rejoined me by the fire.

"So what will happen next?" I asked.

"The king has been speaking quietly and kindly to the queen for months. Years, actually, since he began considering the addition of the Duke of Richmond to the line of succession long ago, well afore he'd met me. He has asked her to have their marriage quietly annulled. He promised her a fine house and privileges for herself and Mary. Or to go to a highborn abbey, as she prefers to spend most of her time in prayer. She has rudely refused any and every suggestion." As there was no servant present, Anne poked the fire a bit to stir up some quiet embers.

"Which is understandable."

"On one level, yes. But we, as women, are always aware that our lives are not our own. The queen, even more, must realize that her own desires must be set aside for the good of the realm. If she is as devout as she professes to be, she will see the truth in the matter. But she will not. She is Spanish—now and always—and has not a care for England. She will marry her daughter to some Spaniard and England will be gobbled whole"—she snapped her fingers—"like that!"

"And now?"

"And now the king has asked Cardinal Wolsey to solve the matter."

I laughed softly. "Wolsey is no friend to you."

"You are right. But he is a friend to the king. And he has in mind for the king to marry a French princess and beget a son, so he is likely to be overeager to get the king's marriage annulled."

We sat for a while and then I asked, "Does the king have it in mind to marry a French princess?"

Anne smiled but admitted little. "The king has not yet shared his mind on that matter with me."

"Do you wish to bed him?" I asked.

She nodded. "But I will insist on being his wife first." She teased, "You, Meg, should understand the pleasures of married life." We'd discussed, with relief, of course, how I'd thus far escaped fulfilling my connubial duties with the baron.

I tossed a small stuffed cushion in her direction as we often had done as girls and she threw it right back at me.

After she left, though, I began to grow irritated that the man who loved her was willing to literally move heaven and earth for her while the one who loved me had his eyes solely trained on heaven. I pushed the thought away before that envy could burn the edges of my friendship.

In June Cardinal Wolsey arranged for a play to be held at Hampton Court Palace and, afterward, a feast. I stood beneath one of the tiers of stained glass windows at the far end of the great hall as the dimming day's light cast jeweled reflections across the room. Wolsey himself, a consummate host, circulated about the guests, a great red bird, preening himself as he pecked at others. It drew my attention, though, when I noticed him paying attention to Katherine's ladies-in-waiting, particularly those who had served the queen for many years. I was standing next to Anne, who conversed with her great-aunt, the Dowager Duchess of Norfolk, who had served the queen for many years and had been hand-somely rewarded for it.

"Good day, Mistress Boleyn." Wolsey nodded curtly in Anne's direction. "How does your sister, Mary? We miss her cheerfulness at the court."

Anne flinched at the open insult, the insinuation that Anne had taken Mary's place and was much less pleasant. It was true that Mary was accommodating but also was true that she accommodated too often and with too many. As Anne's friend I was tempted to ask the cardinal how did his mistress, the one hidden in the country with his two baseborn sons. But I did not, for it would not help my friend at all.

One of the king's men came up to Anne and pulled her away for a moment when Wolsey slipped in to talk with the duchess. I, of little import, went momentarily unnoticed by either of them.

"Good day, my lady," Wolsey said, his voice well trained as a social lubricant to coax secrets from among the unwilling. "I wonder, I wonder if you might help me help the king."

The duchess, always attentive to her own high status, smiled graciously. "Of course, Cardinal. Anything to assist His Majesty. How may I be of service?"

"Do you recall the night the queen was married to Prince Arthur?"

"Indeed," she said. "It was a time of great

celebration. The prince and princess enjoyed themselves, and one another, immensely. It set off a frenzy of romance among the courtiers." She dabbed a linen to her forehead, remembering her own youth, I supposed, as cloth sponged the fetid sweat from between the deep creases in her face.

Wolsey looked immensely pleased as he steered the duchess to a private corner to continue their chat. I heard no more.

It wasn't a week later when we ladies were in the queen's chamber sewing shirts for the poor when the king strode in. The queen's principal lady met him with a sweet greeting. But he would have none of it.

"Where is your mistress?" he demanded.

"She is at chapel, Your Majesty."

The king roughly strode past the woman and down the hall to the queen's private chapel. He opened the door with no care to what state her worship may be in. "Lady, methinks it is time for us to resolve this matter."

"Please, Your Majesty, join me in worship. And then we shall talk, and dine, and spend time together."

His reply was rough, certainly not that of a husband of two decades, or even a kind friend. "Our time for talk is over, my lady, and I fear that for us to worship together would be an abomination. I am sending a contingent to the pope to request an annulment of our marriage, which must be a stench before our Lord."

The queen stood and looked alarmed. She had a hard time regaining her balance on her feet after so long a time kneeling. I felt badly for her and wished for one of her other ladies to help her steady herself, but none dared. "Our marriage is true and pure!" she pleaded. Neither of them seemed to be aware of others listening, but that was the royal prerogative. We were to pretend not to notice, or repeat, what was said or done.

"We have never been honorably married. You were married to my brother, Arthur."

"Perhaps in name," she said, her Spanish accent getting even thicker with her fluster. "But not in truth."

Henry roared his disdain. "No, madam, you may convince others, or even yourself, of that lie, but who other than a husband would know if his wife was a maid at their marriage or not?"

I glanced into the chapel and looked at his face. He was telling the truth, or at the very least believed that he was.

He blew past us like a squall on the Thames and as soon as he left we lesser ladies hastened away.

I tiptoed away and raced to Anne's quarters to repeat the conversation to her.

In June Cardinal Wolsey left for France to discuss the king's annulment, or, at worst, divorce, with the pope. He'd told Henry he was convinced that the Holy Father would see the truth of the matter and set things right quickly. Shortly after, Anne came to my chambers.

"I leave for Hever," she said. "Will you come away with me?"

I nodded and replied, "Of course. But why? Will you risk losing the king's favor if you depart?"

She shrugged in that most French manner. "Mayhap. But I seek to retain my maidenhood and for that, I fear, I must take my leave. I've told the king that my mother requested my presence and he cannot refuse without good cause."

Our first weeks home I spent at Allington. My father seemed to have slipped into some kind of forgetfulness. I would ask him about accounts and he could not remember having told me the instructions he had given only hours before. I questioned the servants, but they offered little, seeming to be in fear of Edmund, and I suppose they were right. One night the three of us supped together.

"How is the king?" my father asked politely. Age had made him smaller and more frail. I'd seen him kick one of the hunting dogs earlier, hard, in the ribs, so I knew that whilst the outward man may have been changing in preparation to meet his Maker, the inward man had not.

"The king is in good health."

"And the queen?" Edmund asked with a wicked grin. I knew he went back and forth to the court on my father's business, and some of the king's as well, but we never sought out one another's company.

"It's pleasant to serve with her ladies," I said. Which was true, even though the queen never had a word for me herself, though I toiled long hours on her behalf.

"I was just telling Father how expensive it must be for Lord Blackston to keep you at court," Edmund said. "The dresses, the jewels, the gifts you're required to give."

"My husband has not complained," I answered, taking a bite of the roasted swan. I pushed the remainder around on my plate with a piece of bread.

"He has not the occasion, Simon tells me. He is too frail."

Edmund seemed to be particularly well informed on my life as well.

"Mayhap he's taking it out of the first installment of your dowry." He threw down the rest of his glass of wine and put the cup on the table.

Installment of my dowry? Hadn't it all been paid?

With relief, Edithe and I went to stay at Hever in July. I knew she was eager to be there for a long period of time, with her Roger and her children, and I was eager to get away from my brother and father though I missed being at my family home, which had been a warm and lovely place when my mother had been alive and in good health. Perhaps when Thomas inherited it would become more welcoming again.

We rode through the countryside and onto the long gardens that led to Hever Castle. The bushes were aflame with blossoms and the air heavy and ripe with their perfume. The grasses waved untended. I saw the priest just outside of St. Peter's, blessing what looked to be a field hand on the way to the property. The priest was a kindly man, a godly man, and Sir Thomas kept him on though he was perhaps too old to attend to his duties any longer. As I approached the castle itself I gave a start. There was a messenger there carrying the king's pennant, resplendent in the king's colors.

Anne showed me to a room just down the corridor from her own. She was wearing a rich sapphire bracelet, one I knew to be new.

"Is one of the king's men here?" I inquired.

She nodded. "The king has sent me a letter and his man has been instructed to await my reply." After I'd refreshed myself she drew me into her father's paneled library. Henry's letter claimed concern for her health and well-being and distress whilst not understanding what her intentions were toward him. He'd signed it, "Written by the hand of your entire servant."

I drew close to her. "Does your father know of this?"

"Nay," she responded. "Not this particular letter. But we've talked of how I should respond should the king write."

"How shall you respond, then?" I asked.

"Honestly." A few hours later, after a cheerful dinner with her mother, Anne showed me the letter she would return to Henry in the morn. In it she reiterated what she had already told him in person afore she'd left the court. She found him noble and worthy in every capacity and enjoyed his company above all others'. But she had given her maidenhead into her husband's hands, and there, by the grace of God, it should remain.

We spent the next days wandering the gardens, reading Erasmus together and making plans for our future children. Perhaps our daughters would be friends, too, I mused. Anne laughed. "I am much more concerned with my sons! But yes." She took my hand. "I would that our daughters would be friends too." We sat down on the stone bench where we had once made our blood pledge and talked of gowns and slippers.

Henry arrived at Hever Castle within a fortnight.

Lady Boleyn was not, I assume, given to entertaining the king without the commanding hand of her husband but alas, he was away on the king's business. "Lady, I require but simple fare and good company, and I know well that both can be found within your household," the king replied. His visit was ostensibly to take advantage of the hunting in the area. He was hunting for certes. I could scarce hold back my grin, but he was kindly to me as well. He inquired after my husband's health and thanked me for being a constant friend to Anne.

Anne appeared to be in high spirits. She rode out to the hunt with the king; 'twas a sport they both enjoyed, and being competitors, both of them, they passed the day in good pleasure. When they returned they rode side by side, her face flushed, her eyes shining; she looked beautiful in her velvet hunting outfit of forest green. Henry's men and her serving ladies bantered and laughed behind them. I met them at the bridge over the moat afore they dismounted.

"I see you were successful," I called out, indicating the stag.

"Aye, the lady beat me to the shot and carried the day," Henry called back, more a young man than the king. He looked at Anne, besotted, and what was even more concerning was that she looked back at him with genuine love and affection. The king stayed for three nights before returning to court and after he left, Anne told me that, although it must remain a secret, as he considered himself an unmarried man he would soon make her his wife.

"So Henry does not plan to marry Wolsey's French princess?" I said in shock.

"How wonderful! I am entirely satisfied in

your dignified match and future happiness!" She reprimanded me by quoting what a woman friend would have been expected to respond with rather than what I'd offered her.

"Your happiness is paramount to me, dear friend. But I fear for your safety too. There will be many who will not welcome you at court after this. The queen has many who are partial to her. And Wolsey wants the French."

"They can be partial to Katherine or to the French elsewhere," Anne said. "Katherine has tenses. Henry assured me. I have no desire to go awry of our Lord in this, so I looked fast into his eyes and determined that he was telling the truth. They are not truly married—and never have been. I have his word on that and the king, as you know, is the anointed of God and above deceit." She held out her hand, upon which was set a magnificent emerald ring. "I told the king I should answer him anon in a letter. But first— to write to my father."

At the end of the month she heard back from her father and then returned a letter to the king, along with a gift she commissioned, one that cost her dearly: a model of a ship with a woman on board wearing a diamond pendant. As a ship meant protection and a diamond a woman's heart, I knew, as Henry would, what her answer was. She was giving her heart to him and depending upon him, and not her father, to guard her henceforth.

She pulled me into her chamber and showed me his return letter upon its arrival. In it he obliged himself to forever honor, love, and serve her sincerely and asked her to do the same, out of loyalty of heart. I sighed as I read it. It would be hard not to as they were so deeply in love. She set the letters, with the others he'd sent to her, in a small trunk. I felt heartsick all over again at the loss of my letters from Will. But perhaps it would have been unbecoming for a married lady to keep them, and in any case, their contents were writ upon my heart.

Along with some gifts for Anne, Henry had sent another box. Anne held it out to me. " 'Tis for you."

I was taken aback. "Me?"

She nodded and smiled and I took it into my own hand. I opened the box and inside was a beautiful bracelet of gold and garnet. There was a small note thanking me for being "a faithful friend and true to my dear heart," along with an invitation to return with her to court. My sister, Alice, would join us there frequently, as would Jane, George's wife, and a few other of Anne's cousins.

An invitation from Henry was a command, and unless my husband decreed otherwise I would return with her. Henry was already looking to reinforce Anne from the factions into which he knew the women would divide.

NINE

Year of Our Lord 1528
Windsor Castle
Allington Castle
Hever Castle
Richmond Palace

The court, returned now to Windsor, was a happier place for the relative absence of the queen, who deplored frivolities as much as Henry adored them. We'd been recovering from a May Day masque, drinking small ale and talking over the next week's plans, when a new maid came in to tidy Anne's chambers. A small girl trailed behind the maid, hiding in a corner.

"Where is Bridget?" Anne asked the new woman.

"She's taken ill of a sudden, m'lady. I'm her cousin come to take her place if'n it's a'right with you."

Anne nodded her agreement and turned back to the conversation she was having with the court musicians. She was commissioning the pieces for a dinner in the king's honor to be held two weeks hence. I grinned at the little girl in the corner and crooked my finger to her, drawing her near to me. It was rare to see a child at court. Royal children were often set up in their own households, like twelve-year-old Princess Mary, and children of the nobility and gentry stayed at their own properties or were tutored with other noble families until such time that they were old enough to be introduced to court life.

The little girl came close to me. "And who are you?" I asked.

" 'Scuse me, ma'am, my name's Jess'ca," she squeaked out.

"And what are you doing in Mistress Boleyn's chambers, Jessica?" I asked.

"Me mum is helping with the cleaning, my lady," she said. She looked as though she were about to cry. I hadn't meant to put her on the spot. I suspected she'd had to tag along when Bridget had grown ill at the last minute.

"Would you like a sweet?" I asked, and held the silver tray in her direction. She nodded shyly and took one and then dipped a curtsy. She may have been a servant's child but she'd been taught manners. I took three more sweets and pressed them into her hand afore she fled.

The next day Anne rushed into my room. "Pack. Quickly. Henry is sending me to Hever. We are leaving the court."

I stood up, alarmed. "What is it?"

She held my eye for a moment before rushing out of the room. "The Sweat."

Anne went to her home and I to mine. My sister, Alice, arrived at Allington Court, too, with a few of her younger children in tow, avoiding London, where the Sweat dominated. Thomas, upon his arrival back from Italy, had immediately been appointed as the marshal of Calais. The king had sent him out of arm's reach, not of the Sweat, but of Anne.

Alice and I sat on the portico and talked. "Father has resigned his position as treasurer of the king's household," I said, noting how our roles had reversed. As a lady-in-waiting of long service to Queen Katherine, she had once shared court news with me; now I did with her. She nodded.

"Yes. His mind . . . wanders. So 'tis for the best, I believe. And Edmund has taken over the running of the property accounts?"

"Yes. Father has placed all family business in his hands now."

"Mayhap we should help find him a bride," Alice suggested, though her dour look revealed her doubts. "I shall endeavor to think upon it."

"I wish you success with that, sister," was all I said. I looked out at the grassy field between Allington and the river and tried to keep my face pleasant and impassive. "What do you hear from John?"

Alice's face broke into a broad grin. "He's to come back to London. Anne's 'friend' Cardinal Wolsey offered him a scholar's position at his new cardinal's college, at Oxford. Wolsey offered the same position to John's friend Matthew Parker, who is a friend of the Boleyns. A position was also offered to Will Ogilvy."

If John took a joint position with Will, in London, I was like as not to see him more often.

"Did John accept the cardinal's offer?"

Alice shook her head. "All three declined. The cardinal is set in the old ways, and John, Matthew, and Will are stoutly convinced that reform is necessary, mayhap even certain. What that reform should look like is something no one can yet agree upon. Most, myself included, believe it should include Holy Writ in the reader's own language, English, and a focus on salvation by grace, not by works."

"Anne told me that the pope had agreed to nearly all of Henry's requests. Mayhap he is open to the changes needed within Holy Church as well."

"I wish 'twere so, but I suspect not. There are many pure men in the church, but there are also many impure. The pure men are serving with the heart of Christ. The impure men clench power tightly in their fists. 'Tis not to their advantage to loose the yoke of works. We shall see."

From the corner of my eye I saw Edithe trying to get my attention. I excused myself from my sister and went to her. It was unusual for Edithe to interrupt me for any reason.

"Forgive the intrusion, my lady," she began.

" 'Tis no intrusion, Edithe. What ails you?"

"My husband, Roger, has sent word. The Sweat has come to Hever Castle. Many of the servants have it and there are few to care for the ill; Anne's servant Bridget has died. Master George is infected, as is the lady Anne. And I fear for my husband and children."

Anne. With the Sweat!

"Let us go," I declared.

"I shall, lady, if you give me leave. But surely not you!"

I suspected Anne needed me now, and, as I had no husband of my own nearby nor children to attend to, I was free to insist.

We rode to Hever within the day and when we arrived we were not greeted at all. Lady Boleyn was ill; Sir Thomas was away. Edithe and I parted ways, she to the servants' chambers, I to Anne.

She lay in bed, her black eyes deep in their sockets. Her skin looked not golden but yellow.

"How fare you?" I asked, kneeling beside her.

"Better, I think." Her voice was small.

I helped her from her nightshift, which was soaked and cold, and into one that was dry. I stripped the linens from her bed and replaced them with some from her cupboard nearby.

"Henry sent his second-best physician," she said. I tried not to frown. I'd heard that he'd taken his first-best physician with him—and the queen—to Waltham Abbey and then from safe house to safe house as he tried to flee the illness.

At each stop he was scrupulous in observing religious rituals, having special prayers composed in every church. All London was whispering that the Sweat was visited upon England due to sin, perhaps the king's. Henry, I am sure, would have agreed, though the sin he had in mind—his impure marriage—was most likely not the one the gossips would finger.

"Of course he did; he cares for you," I said.

As she recovered her strength she recounted to me how it had all transpired. "On the journey back from court I was hit with the certain, uncanny knowledge that something dreadful had befallen me," she said. "And then I began to tremble violently. By the time I arrived I could scarce keep my wits about me, I would laugh and cry without cause and my lady mother helped me to bed. I remember seeing fear in the face of my brother. George!" She looked up at me.

"He recovers," I reassured her, and she sank back into the bed. "As does your mother."

"I shall too," she declared imperiously. I relaxed. The Anne I knew and loved had survived.

We remained in Kent for much of the summer, waiting for the illness to sweep through and then out of the realm and allowing Anne to recover her health. I took her for walks and then short rides to get clean air into her. We let the horses walk across the pastures nearby and watched as Edithe's husband, Roger, directed the field hands to break up tough land more thickly studded with stones than one of Anne's new bracelets.

"Henry sent jewels and letters declaring his love and they, more than anything, cheered me," Anne said. "He tells me that Cardinal Campeggio will come anon to declare his marriage invalid and that we may move forth as we planned then. Wolsey reassures him this is so."

I watched as the field men pushed the oxen, oxen that threw their whole weight to the task under the whip. My sister, Alice, had told me that Henry had also recently asked for a dispensation to marry a woman who was a close relative to— perhaps even a sister to—someone he'd had relations with. His logic confused me. Sometimes dispensations were wrong in his eyes and sometimes required? "So you have hope," was all I said.

"I do," she said, turning her face to the sun and sighing at its warmth. "Both for our marriage and for the reforms in the church. Henry is sure to bring things to rights on both counts."

I hesitated ere speaking, knowing that there were certain topics we chose not to speak of for fear of damaging our friendship. "Henry does not strike me as particularly . . . passionate for church reform," I said. "Unless there is a clear benefit to His Majesty."

She smiled. "I know. But there is much there that he will champion for, and if other good is done in the process, then that is an even greater profit. I believe God has chosen Henry for this purpose."

I looked back at the oxen and spoke without thinking. "A good farmer uses the strongest beast to plow up the hardest fields, though that beast may not be the gentlest."

"Exactly," Anne said.

Word came shortly thereafter that Sir William Carey, Anne's sister Mary's husband, had died of the Sweat.

"Those two children are now left without their father," Anne said sorrowfully. "I shall write to my sister."

I looked at her face, steady and unyielding. Clarifying the true father of Mary's children was one of the topics we left unspoken, to spare her feelings and unwillingness to admit their sire. Anne was mainly honest and direct to a fault, but sometimes she allowed herself the unwelcome luxury of self-deceit to align reality with her desires. Then, too, till the king himself acknowledged a child as his own no one else dared say a word of it.

By August we had rejoined the court and those who had survived seemed all the merrier for having passed through the storm unscathed. Henry took his health, and Anne's recovery, as divine approval of their relationship and Anne became, in nearly all matters public, though not private, his wife. He could scarce keep his eyes or his hands off of her. She often sat beside him as he entertained courtiers and even occasionally for official business. I and Mistress Gainsford, another of her ladies, idled outside the king's presence chamber when Cardinal Wolsey arrived to conduct business with the king. One of the king's men ushered him into the presence chamber whilst we courtiers nearby could hear the entire conversation.

Wolsey approached the throne, and the comfortable seat nearby where Anne sat, splendidly arrayed. Henry knew Anne's appearance reflected on him and he delighted that she dressed accordingly. This was no hardship on Anne, for certes. Years in the French court had nurtured a healthy desire and natural talent for fine couture.

"Majesty," Wolsey began with a deep flourish. His bloodred gown had been expertly sewn and folded in all the right places.

"Thomas," the king said. "So glad you're back, old friend. There is a matter you wished to discuss with us?" Wolsey looked at Anne, who did not move, and then at the king, who did not indicate that he planned to dismiss Anne. Wolsey had no choice but to press on.

"I've come about the matter of the Abbess of Wilton, sire. May I inform Dame Isobel that she has your approval for the post?"

Anne spoke up then, before the king could

respond, definitely forbidden by protocol. "What about Dame Eleanor Carey, sir?" She turned toward the king. "The sister of Will Carey, so lately passed from the Sweat, God rest his soul." I dared not breathe so as not to call attention to the fact that I was listening. Dame Eleanor of Anne's suggestion was a known reformer.

The king did not reprimand Anne for speaking in his place, but he did not give way to her, either. "Mayhap you can find a third candidate, eh, Thomas?" It was not a request, it was a command, but one that allowed both his love and his friend to retain their dignity.

A week later I received a disturbing letter. I was on my way to Anne's chambers to discuss it with her when I heard the king inside, shouting. Something crashed to the floor and then there was a silence. I slipped back down the hall and hoped that my friend was all right. When I came back a short while later Anne was sitting in a chair, composed, serene. Jessica's mother was cleaning up some glass from a broken decanter. "What happened?" I asked.

"Wolsey directly disobeyed the king. He appointed Dame Isobel to Wilton. I'm afraid this is an infraction from which he will not recover unless he convinces Campeggio to annul Henry's marriage in short order. What is in your hand?" She motioned kindly, but perhaps a bit regally, too, to the letter I carried.

"A letter from My Lord Blackston. He commands me to Haverston."

Anne reached out and hugged me tightly. "Then you must go. But as your husband gives you leave, come back to me."

I promised that I would.

"Will you give this letter to my manservant on your way out?" she asked.

I took the letter from her. "Certainly." Cardinal Wolsey's name was inked along the outside.

She explained what was within though she certainly didn't need to. "I've asked the cardinal to remove the parson of Honey Lane, Dr. Forman, from the scrutiny of possible heresy, for my sake," she said. "Dr. Forman is a reformer."

I suspected Wolsey would hasten to act on that request. The tides had turned.

It was several days' journey to Haverston Hall, high in the north. Baron Blackston had arranged for me to be a guest at several houses along the way, with other members of the nobility who were his friends. I was shown every deference and comfort, beyond what I experienced at home, where I was the younger sister with little to offer, or even at court, where I was Anne's beloved friend but certainly consumed by her aura. I had to admit that I could acquire a taste for being treated thusly. In short order my fine litter arrived at Haverston. It was an imposing estate, many times larger than Allington or Hever Castle. In fact, it looked more like a royal residence, which I understood it had been at one time. Though he was unlike the Northumberlands, who ruled the north, fewer were richer or more powerful than Baron Blackston. I alighted and was greeted by a long line of servants outside of the imposing stone stairway that led within.

A man whom I assumed to be my husband's primary gentleman's servant greeted me and showed me inside. The reception hall was of marble, perhaps Italian marble, and there were large rooms branching off in every direction. The draperies, I noticed, were faded, and I suspected that there had not been much merriment in the great hall in some time. A lack of a woman's touch. And yet . . . it had potential.

"Good morrow, Meg." Simon crept up behind me and drew near to my side. I was in a mind to correct him with a "My Lady Blackston" but I was too tired for a fight. He was perfectly dressed and made pleasant conversation, asking about the court and my family and expressing appreciation that we had passed safely through the Sweat. "Meredith will show you to your rooms, wherein you might refresh yourself, and then, after dining, I'll escort you to My Lord."

"He won't be dining with us?" I had wondered why he hadn't been there to greet me but had sent Simon instead.

"No," was all Simon offered, and then he indicated that I should be shown to my chambers, which were marvelous indeed.

After we dined, on fine plate but in a lonely, vast dining hall, Simon brought me upstairs. He left me at a set of great oak doors, kissed my cheeks a bit too close to the lips, and departed. I pushed open the doors and there were no serving maids to be found.

"Sire," I called into the dark.

"Come here, wife." A feeble voice called from beyond. I made my way through the room, which smelt faintly of smoke, telling me that the baron's illness had been treated recently by filling the room with thick smoke from the fire whilst leaving the windows and draperies closed in hopes of overcoming whatever malady might reside in his lungs. I made my way toward his bed and took a chair nearby. I looked into his eyes, and they were even more deeply set than Anne's had been when she'd taken ill. Although he had on a nightshirt I could see his skin stretched tightly across the bones, like a thin linen across a corset.

"No, sit here." He patted the bed, and I obliged by sitting next to him. "Would that I could have you to bed in another way," he said before launching into a laugh broken by coughs. "Old King Louis took the king's sister as a pretty bride to warm his old bed. Killed him, like as not, but he died happy."

My horror must have shown on my face because

he took my hand and patted it. "Not to worry, I shan't make you an accessory to my death. Mayhap I should have let Simon take you in the first place, but a man can always hope. I hoped for a pretty bride and a young son. Alas, I got one but not the other."

I swallowed my gorge at the thought of either of them taking me and limited myself to a cheerful, "You are not well, then, sir?"

"I am sick unto death."

"Surely not!"

"Aye, my lady, 'tis true. But I wanted to see you again once afore I die, and to reassure you that you will be well provided for. I know not if I will last a week or a month or mayhap many months, but I see the angel of death about me from time to time, pursuing me closer and closer. My time draws near."

"I shall remain with you," I said. "For however long it takes."

He coughed again. "You're a good girl, but that is not necessary. The king has had his secretary write to me of the pleasure of having you at court, yea, has even given us a manor in the Marches as a wedding gift. A suggestion from your friend Mistress Boleyn, for certain."

Dear Anne, she'd never mentioned it. I'd like as not never visit it but would have an income from it now, to add to my own small stipend from the baron.

The baron sat up and I arranged his linens around him. "I shall ensure that the king's gift is included in your portion so that when I am gone you will be taken care of. Simon and your brother negotiated your marriage portion and it will go to you. As my heir, Simon will inherit my other properties and income. And title. He will see to the return of your portion after I am gone."

I was glad to hear that I would be well provided for but about to protest the macabre conversation when he held his hand up. His manner was strong and commanding and I imagined he'd been a much different man decades before. "No, lady wife, in this you will submit to me. Rest a few days and then, anon, get thee back to court. Simon will send you word when our Lord has come to collect me."

He was a kindly man after all, and though I could not say I would miss him I could have been situated much worse. As a dowager baroness, a widow, I would be free to remarry or not. I would have my jointure settled upon me and be independent of male control. It would not be the life I'd envisioned, but it would not be a bad life, either.

The kindest gift I could give then was to be humble before him, recognizing what manhood he had retained. "Yes, sir, as you wish." I stood to take my leave.

"Wife, a kiss," he said. He pointed at his cheek and I smiled before gently placing one on his lips. He grinned. "Thank you." Then he fell back into his bed and I pulled the tapestries around him to allow the warmth to remain well into the night.

TEN

═══

Year of Our Lord 1529
Richmond Palace
Hampton Court Palace

One late spring night a few months after I'd returned to court, Henry threw a masque. On the off chance that anyone at court had not realized the state of his heart and mind, he chose a Greek mythology theme to make that point clear, in particular, to Cardinal Campeggio and others of the delegation now here to decide his "great matter." Henry was cast as Eros.

There was a rare moment when Anne and I could talk alone. Normally a swarm of courtiers enveloped her in their cloud. The closer you were to the king, of course, the easier to imbibe of the royal nectar, and some used the excuse to intoxicate themselves. Not Anne, though he exalted her of his own accord. "Why does Henry insist that we pretend not to know who he is, thusly disguised?" I asked. It was ludicrous, really. There were few men as tall as he, nearly none with his mane, and his presence was unmistakably regal.

"I think he desires to be liked for himself and not his position," Anne said. "In masque, he's allowed that."

It was a rare glimpse into the heart of one whom we rarely acknowledged as having the needs any man may have, and perhaps one reason why he loved Anne remarkably. Some said he controlled his ardor because, as a master huntsman, he desired to close the chase. And whilst I suppose that was true, Anne was also the only woman who treated Henry as mere man, chiding him one moment then building him up the next, offering him new books and new thoughts, displaying her love for him in unadorned offerings as a simple country wife would to her husband.

Of course, he wasn't her husband yet.

The hearings to determine the validity of Henry's marriage were under way; the pope had determined that Cardinal Wolsey and Cardinal Campeggio, from Rome, should judge the matter. It was understandable that the pope did not want to rule on it himself. The queen's nephew, Charles the Fifth, had made his will plainly known by sacking Rome two years before and holding the pope hostage in part so he could not rule on the validity of his aunt's marriage. Hence, the pope had not ruled. We all knew what Wolsey, the king's lapdog through and through, would decree and he assured the king that Campeggio would find the marriage void as well. Back and forth the arguments went, with nearly all men, courtiers and priests, siding with the king, with a few notable exceptions. Women were not allowed at the Blackfriars hearings save one, on one fateful day.

The queen.

After each day's trial proceeding George rushed into Anne's apartments to give us the day's events. I told Jessica to help herself to a date afore she and her mother took their leave. Afterward, she curtseyed to me and backed away. "You're shameless with that girl," Anne said. "Encouraging her to come with her mother and then feeding her sweets. She will not know her place."

"She knows it well enough," I said, allowing my voice to show my irritation at Anne's rising imperiousness. So soon, already, she had forgotten what it was like to be a curious girl. " 'Tis not hard to give the child a few reprieves in a hard life."

George grabbed a goblet of wine and drew near to us. He was splendidly attired in blue silk sleeves slashed to show white linen beneath, silken hose like an aristocratic voice, and boots blacker than an ironsmith's forearms. I had watched many a woman at court, married and other, young and other, try to beguile him, and though he flirted, as we all did, he had not yielded.

"Where is your wife?" I asked him.

152

"I know not, nor care," he said. "She was kind-tongued to me for a fortnight after I was knighted, crowing about her title, and now she's back to chewing my ear whenever our paths cross. But I have news."

George's voice grew excited. "The queen was at court today to answer the charge that she was Arthur's true bride. She denied it, loudly, from the courtroom for all to hear. She declared herself a maid then and true now as she knelt at his feet. And, after doing so, she turned her back on Henry before he could answer her and departed from the court with her retinue."

"What did Henry do after she boldly lied to his face?" Anne asked, aghast as all would be that she would call the king a fraud, publicly, and then turn her back on him.

"His mouth opened, and then closed, and then opened again. Henry has his faults but his honor would not allow him to call the queen a liar in an open court full of men. But the look he gave Bishop Fisher, her defender . . ." George took another drink of his wine before continuing. "I should not care to sleep in his bed this night."

As for myself, I had never suspected the queen could lie. But Anne was no fool and Henry had made his assurances to her. If a queen could not lie, could God's anointed king? Surely one of them must have. I, like Fisher, slept uneasily that night.

By the end of May the court disbanded with no clear answer for Henry. Campeggio went back to Rome, stalling, as no doubt the pope had instructed him to do. Wolsey was undone and he knew it. Henry had run out of patience. Another solution to the great matter needed to be found.

Wolsey, in damage control, had new quarters fashioned for Anne at Hampton Court Palace, his magnificent Thames-side residence, and we stayed there first, on progress. The gardens were heady with tulips, lazily nodding like children tempted to a nap on a hot afternoon. The hedges had been cut in neat rows of lover's knots, and Anne and I strolled through them.

"Why was Henry apoplectic this morning?" I asked. All had seen his blood-infused face as he strode through the long hall.

"Thomas More," she answered, winding her way down through the roses.

"Truly?" Thomas More had been like a surrogate father to Henry; Henry admired him greatly and though More differed with the king on the great matter, he had mostly kept his peace and thus retained their friendship and his head.

"Sir Thomas has issued another book and in it he stridently defends the pope and comes out against all who question him." Anne looked at me over her shoulder. "Which would include Luther and Tyndale, mainly. But though it remains unspoken, all know he means Henry as well."

"What has he said?" I asked.

"Oh, everything. That Tyndale's a heretic. More ridicules them at every turn, including his marriage. You knew that Luther had married and yet still claims to remain a priest."

My heart was ensnared. "Mayhap . . . mayhap with reform that will be the case for priests here, as well," I said.

Anne reached out and twisted a lock of my hair in the sisterly fashion. "No, dearest. Henry himself has told me that there will be no married priests in England whilst he is the king. In most manners, Henry is a prim man with a desire to follow, not change, rules. His rules, of course, but he views his rules, rightly, I believe, as God's rules. He's the anointed king. Any priest in his realm will always remain unmarried. His idea for reform is to bring that which concerns the king into line with Holy Writ—as rendered in Latin."

Which would not include priests who could marry. I gently slid away from her and turned my face toward the river, ostensibly to look out over the gliding swans but also to hide my anger. It worked well enough for Henry to overthrow those canons that suited him but perhaps not those that might rightly benefit others. *Do not his subjects both great and low deserve to have reform in keeping with Holy Writ?* I surprised myself with my strong feelings on the matter. I turned back to her. "And, as we speak of marriage, Anne, does Henry still speak of marriage to you? Or only of bedding?"

Anne sat down on a stone bench under an arbor of curled roses, climbing for all they were worth like any ambitious gentry. She patted the seat beside her and indicated that I should sit down. I did.

"He does seek to bed me still, but I have persuaded him that we must wait. Not only for my own honor, but also for the sake of the legitimacy of our son. Another Fitzroy would do him no good."

"Nor you," I said, my voice not unkind. But I was aware that a shell of pretense now surrounded Anne at court and if she were ever to hear the truth it would only come from myself or George.

"Nor I," she admitted. "But do not fret. I will not chase a man I cannot have. I'll let the one I can have chase me."

"I'm no longer certain this is such a good idea," I said, foreboding rising up within me like bile. "There has been no annulment and a divorce does not look likely, either."

"I've not been polished by years in the French court to be sent to a backwater after a short time as Henry's bedmate. God did not create me to be any man's plaything. My father, for all his worldliness, has never taken a mistress, nor had he bedded my mother before marriage."

Anne stopped and faced me afore taking my hands in her own. "God has given clear instructions on how a man is to treat his wife. I require—and desire—that kind of treatment. I will not back down."

I had never been more aware that my own life and fortunes were so closely buttoned to those of Anne, especially as my husband was disabled by illness and shortly would no longer offer me any legal protection, though my finances would be well situated.

"Henry's ability to resolve his own marriage situation is his right, as it is any man's who claims that his bride was not a maid. As well, it's to vindicate his rule—his right to determine what happens in his own realm. He must be sovereign over his entire kingdom. Hence, his title: king."

This last one, of the king's superiority over even the pope, was a new thought, and I wondered where she'd come upon it.

"He's often recounted to me how he, as a boy, cried in the Tower as he and his mother took refuge there whilst his father defended his kingship. It could not have been defended by a woman. Henry cannot let that victory be nullified by his lack of a capable heir.

"His marriage is null and void before God," she continued. "We speak openly of it. He knows how I prize a true marriage and he would not lead me astray if one were not possible."

"That prize comes at a cost," I said pointedly, not backing away.

"Everything comes at a cost," she replied.

We often spent an evening in Anne's rooms, which were large and many; they had become a center for social gatherings of both sexes, but often just for us women as the men were hunting or at bowls. Sometimes when our numbers were few and trusted, Anne brought out her reformist books and started a discussion. She was interested in reform for its own sake, of course—her faith was true and vibrant and I could see it grow within her—but also, I believed, she enjoyed such discussions because they engendered risk and that fit with her personality. I knew she agitated for Scripture in English and for priests who spoke of salvation by grace and not by works. I sat nearby and listened but did not participate. Though I attended Mass with all, in my personal life God and I remained alienated. I oft felt like a stubborn child with crossed arms but a justified one who crossed said arms over her heart to protect it from an untrustworthy Father.

Anne Gainsford, soon to be Lady Zouche, had no such alienation. "May I see?" She reached out and touched a book from Anne's cache, William Tyndale's *Obedience of a Christian Man*. It had been published in Antwerp the year before and smuggled to Anne through George.

"Of course," Anne said. "I have marked a few passages to share with the king. Here, look."

Mistress Gainsford leaned over and paraphrased some passages aloud for us. "All men should obey God's law, not the law of the church, which is not the same." She scanned some more. "All men are subject to the earthly authority of a king and the king is not subject to the separate authority of the church but instead is the final authority in his own land." She looked up. "You know that More and Wolsey have burnt Tyndale's books. And men themselves have similarly been set ablaze for like cause."

"I know," Anne said. "Take it. Have a care, and return it to me when you are done."

A week later Mistress Gainsford raced into Anne's chambers in the most indelicate manner. "A terrible mishap has befallen me!" She fell on her knees before Anne and rested her head in Anne's lap. "And therefore you, mistress! Lord Zouche found Tyndale's book in my possession and was reading it when the dean spied him. The dean snatched the book, asked who it belonged to, and when he replied that it was yours he swore to take it to Wolsey to be your undoing."

Anne patted her head, and though I could spy a twist of concern between her eyes she kept her voice smooth and commanding. "Fear not. 'Twill be the dearest book that ever dean or cardinal took away."

Later that evening she returned to us, triumphant. Mistress Gainsford had worn her hands and eyes red with anticipation but she needn't have worried. "What did the king say, my lady?" she asked.

Anne grinned. "I showed him my marked passages, those declaring his supremacy in his own realm, and he said, 'This is a book for me and all kings to read.'"

Weeks later Henry set a zealous young priest of a reformist bent to find biblical cause for the resolution of his great matter. The priest, Cranmer, was a friend of my nephew John Rogers, and therefore of Will. Cranmer boarded at Hever Castle whilst he began to marshal the evidence.

On October ninth of that year Cardinal Wolsey was charged with praemunire, appealing to a foreign power, in this case, the pope, over his own king. Henry did not take Wolsey's life for treason but did demote him, allowing him only to keep the title and office of bishop of York. The cardinal had never been to York, but he commenced anon and he looked dressed for a long, cold journey.

As he and a small band of attendants pulled away from Hampton Court, I asked Anne, "Does it trouble you that Henry seems to show so little loyalty?" I was thinking of Wolsey, of course, but also Mary Boleyn and Henry's own children by her, of Henry's lawful daughter, Mary, and even the queen. She may have come to him under false pretense but she had served him well. Now she may as well have never existed.

"Perhaps Wolsey did not earn the king's loyalty. Thomas always and ever served himself first." Anne thought I spoke only of Wolsey. I did not disabuse her of the idea by bringing up the others, though perhaps I should have. Anne had her prize in sight. I had a care for the considerable cost she, and maybe I, might pay to achieve and keep it.

ELEVEN

Year of Our Lord 1530
Windsor Castle
Hampton Court Palace
Greenwich Palace

At the start of the year Henry raised Thomas Boleyn to the position of Lord Privy Seal, the third-highest position in the land and one normally reserved for clergy. Only a year before, Cardinal Wolsey would have received this honor, but Henry's affections, and motivations, had swiftly changed course. He was about to send Lord Boleyn off to Bologna, along with Cranmer, to argue one last time with the pope and Charles the Fifth, who was now Holy Roman Emperor, for a divorce from Katherine. I can't have been the only person who saw the irony, yea, perhaps the predestined failure, in sending Anne's father to Katherine's nephew to ask for a divorce. Mayhap it had been designed to fail.

In any case, Anne was now Lady Rochford, daughter of an earl. Not all of the nobility who had been raised high by the king for the comfort and pleasure they gave him were pleased with her elevation. One day, shortly after Anne's father left, I made my way down the great hall with Anne and my sister, Alice, talking of Alice's children—and now a grandchild—and other topics of general discourse among women. Without warning, Charles Brandon, the king's closest friend and brother-in-law, stepped to block my path. The king was with him. I stopped abruptly and curtseyed deeply, as did my sister. Anne left our side to slip her arm through the king's.

"Your Grace?" I addressed myself to the Duke of Suffolk, as it had been he who'd closed our path.

"Good day, My Lady," he said. "Mistress Rogers, Lady Rochford." He included Anne in the address but did not turn to face her. Instead, he looked at my sister and me. "I hear your brother shall be at court anon."

"Thomas?" Alice answered. "Oh no. He serves the king faithfully in Calais."

"Nay, I speak of your other brother, Edmund," Suffolk said.

This threw me. Edmund? Coming to court? And why would someone as highly placed as the Duke of Suffolk know, or care?

"Lady Rochford shall be glad of his company, for certes," Suffolk went on. "I hear they had quite a romance in their youth."

"Not Edmund," I blurted out. "Thomas." Alice's eyes grew wide and I saw Anne's face drain. I felt light of head at what I'd just been trapped into admitting. Fool! My tongue was my enemy. I looked at Suffolk and he grinned with glee. He turned to the king, triumph at hand.

Then Anne spoke. "Thomas and I were naught but childhood friends, no romance at all. Mayhap this is something that His Grace the Duke of Suffolk cannot grasp, as it seems to him that unseemly affection for a child is something that continues into adulthood?"

There came a titter of laughter from those gathered around us and a howl from the king, who enjoyed Anne's wit as it wasn't trained against him. Charles Brandon was widely believed to be romancing his young son's intended bride, twelve-year-old Katherine Willoughby, under his guardianship, though his own wife was very much alive.

"Good day, Your Grace," Anne said, and the king led her, chuckling, down the hall. Blood suffused Brandon's neck and the whites of his eyes as he bowed curtly to us and took his leave.

"Watch out for him," Alice whispered to me as we made our way to my quarters, which were more sumptuous than hers.

My mind was on the more pressing problem. Why was Edmund coming?

Late that night, after I'd already gone to bed, I heard a knock at my door. I'd already dismissed Edithe so I got up to open it myself. It was Anne, splendidly adorned.

"Come, come." I motioned her into my room. " 'Tis late. Is all well?" Afore she could answer I rushed out an apology. "I'm so sorry for what I said today to the duke. He trapped me. And I know this couldn't have come at a worse time."

She cocked her head at me. "How do you mean?"

I pressed on, wishing I'd said nothing at all, which was becoming a common sentiment. "Well, you know, people are . . . grumbling about your father being made Lord High Privy Seal. And the queen having been sent away. And . . . you," I finished lamely.

She waved an authoritative hand. "Let them grumble. That's how it's going to be. Listen, I have news for you. Edmund will arrive tomorrow to tell you that your husband has passed away."

I pulled my robe around me against the chill that the stone walls caught and kept before settling into a chair by the now-dead fire. Anne reached her arm around me. " 'Tis a shock, I know, but I thought it best come from me and not from

Edmund. He'd like as play your surprise to his advantage."

"Yes, yes, thank you," I said. " 'Twas not unexpected, of course. And I did not love him. But he was a kind man, in his own way."

Certain now that I was all right, she backed away. "Now you shall have your marriage stipend and that will allow you to live as you like, where you like. But of course you'll stay with me, for certain?"

It was phrased as a question but spoken as an order. I could settle on one of my properties, or in a town house near my sister. Although I wanted to right the balance in our friendship by stating I was not sure, truth be told, neither of those options appealed. But I was hardly going to let her over-power our friendship, queen-to-be or not.

"Is that a request or a command, my lady?" I asked coolly.

She locked eyes with me. "Touché," she said, and softened her voice. "It is a request from one friend to another."

I nodded. "Of course I shall stay with you."

Satisfied, she kissed my cheeks one by one, in the French style. "And now to get some sleep, dear Meg. I shall speak with you tomorrow, or mayhap the day after, as I am increasingly engaged in court matters."

Then she took her leave. Edmund would arrive within hours.

• • •

The next day I remained in my apartments waiting for Edmund to appear. Anne, the de facto queen, had given me leave to do so, and as I did not want to miss Edmund I pulled out some unwelcome stitchery to while away the hours. Anne had set all of her ladies upon sewing for the poor, which some took to be false concern on her part, but we close to her knew better. I had not long to wait. Shortly after midday Edithe came softly to my private chamber. "Edmund is here, my lady," she said.

"Show him to the sitting room," I instructed her. "And bring him ale and some sweet meats. I shall be there anon."

I waited a few minutes to let the ale calm his temper and then I went in to greet him. "You look wonderful, Edmund," I said. The way to deal with a devil, I'd learned, is to speak to him as magnanimously as he speaks to himself.

"Yes, thanks be. And so do you," he said more by way of custom than by belief. "Please, be seated." He nodded toward the chair next to him and I did as he told me to, thankful that Anne had brought me this news early and I was therefore not at a disadvantage. "I'm afraid I bring ill tidings," he began. "But also good."

My curiosity was piqued now. I knew the ill tidings. "Go on," I encouraged him.

"Sadly, Baron Blackston has passed away,

166

God rest his soul." He crossed himself. If ever there was a more blasphemous action than seeing Edmund claim the cross over himself I was not sure what it was. I crossed myself against him though I suspect he thought it was for the departed baron.

"He was a kind man," I said, feeling genuine remorse. "And yet this was not completely unexpected. His age, his ill health . . . he shared with me his certainty that he would soon depart this world at our last visit."

"Yes," Edmund said. "I am sorry for you. But along with these ill tidings I bring some that are glad. The new Baron Blackston, Simon, wishes to take you as a bride. So you'll not lose your title."

This was his glad tiding? I took a care not to show my shock and dismay. And then I remembered. I need not say yes.

"What a kind offer," I said, not bothering to conceal my sarcasm. I tried to gather my thoughts. "I shall think upon it."

Edmund's face turned stony. "What is there to think upon? The man has offered, I have agreed, and you have nowhere else to go."

"I am welcome at court," I said, nodding to Edithe to refill his mug of ale. "And I have my marriage portion to support me, and the manor the king granted me as a wedding gift."

So there. I am not dependent upon your lack of good graces.

167

A wicked grin stole across his face; he licked his lips and it put me in mind of a reptile. "Alas, there is no marriage portion for you." I scarce could breathe but he continued on. "A widow's third is only allocated if consummation can be sworn upon. Can you swear upon it?"

I indicated nothing but clearly he knew I'd remained a maiden. How?

"When your dowry was negotiated," he continued, "it was to be paid in portions over five years. If the baron was to die without issue within five years of the marriage, then half of the portion would be returned to Father, who would agree to care for you as a widow." He spread his hands in mock concern. "Alas, 'tis not yet five years and, as you have no issue by the baron, the monies shall return to Father for your care. The other half will remain with Simon, Baron Blackston. There is no jointure nor inheritance for you."

"And what does Father think of this?" I stood up and demanded.

"Father has slipped into twilight most days. He has left family matters in my charge."

"So you've agreed to all of this on my behalf?" I said.

"Not completely. The baron is not yet buried a fortnight. But I suspect that Simon and I shall come to some understanding after I return from France, where I go to attend to the king's business. Simon must visit all of his new properties and estates. But we shall come to an agreement anon."

"And if I disagree?"

"You have no dowry, sister. It has been spent. You have no marriage portion. Even the king won't keep you forever. What else will you do?" He stood up and I resisted the urge to slap him.

"Thank you, Brother. And give my thanks to My Lord Blackston, Simon, as well." My voice was thick with scorn.

Edmund pulled on his gloves and prepared to take his leave. "No need, Baroness. You can thank him yourself at the king's dinner two nights hence. He'll be here for the festivities."

The dining hall at Hampton Court Palace was ablaze with candles; light shone from every corner, at every table, and surrounded the king's table, at the head of the room, like the aura of the sun. We were to be seated in the front third of the room, and when Alice and I arrived at our table I was glad I had taken care to wear a finely wrought dress, in dark blue so as to recognize my husband's passing, and my diamond earrings. My hair was pulled back and up under a net, as a widow's should be, but I knew it was a becoming style on me. "It appears we're to sit in Kentish Corner," my sister whispered teasingly, her daughter Margaret, new at court and named for me, trailing along behind us. I raised my eyes to our seats and saw what she meant. At our table were already seated the Earl of Blenheim and his son and heir, Rose Ogilvy's husband. Rose was there again, large with the promise of another child. Her brother Walter and his wife both looked peaked. The Earl of Asquith ignored me entirely, so I greeted his daughter.

"I bid you good evening, Rose," I said.

"Margaret. 'Tis good to see you again," she responded coolly. I held my hand out to her husband, who kissed it. I then turned to greet her brother Walter. "How fares your family, My Lord?" At that I heard my sister clear her throat warningly.

"We grieve the loss of our son, but as my wife is young still we shall expect more soon," he said. Grief was fixed upon his thin face.

"I am so sorry for your loss," I said. I had not been aware that his young son had died. "I am acquainted with loss myself." He looked me in the eye and held it for a moment before speaking. He knew I meant my love for his brother.

"I was sorry to hear of your husband's death, Baroness," he said. My brother Edmund joined us, as did Simon, who let his eyes explore me disconcertingly. I noted that they lingered upon parts of myself that should be noted only by a husband or a seamstress and I turned to take my seat. As she sat with the king, we were missing Anne from our reunion.

And Will, of course.

My brother introduced Simon to the assembled guests at our table. He didn't mention the fact that Simon and I were to be betrothed, of course. It would not have been proper for at least a year. When he was introduced to Walter, Simon's eyes focused.

"Do you have a brother?" he asked.

"Yes," Walter responded. "My brother William. A *priest* soon home from Antwerp."

Unwillingly, unwittingly, I had to believe, nearly every eye at the table turned to me, including Simon's, whose bored into me. I could feel them. I met no glance and instead turned to quietly instruct my niece, who would need to display stamina for the five to seven hours dinner might take at Henry's court. Soon enough the servers brought the first of nigh on twenty courses: roast porpoise and salmon pie; figs stewed till they were tender; manchet of the finest, whitest wheat; roast goose with honey and almond paste. I ate but little and drank less, wanting to keep my wits about me. As soon as the meal was over, the king declared it time for dancing and we followed him into the great hall, which was grand indeed. Even the ceiling was intricately sculptured, though the faces carved within, the Gossips, sent a shiver through me.

Simon took my hand afore the first note was struck. I noticed my brother Edmund had pressed in to quickly take the hand of the young raven-haired Charlotte, who had been seated with the Ogilvys. She was their ward, I believed. I should have to ask Alice if Edmund and Charlotte had been her idea.

"Meg, I am sorry about the loss of your husband. You should know that I cared for him as I would care for a father." Simon drew me as near as was socially respectable.

"Thank you," I said. "I thought he was a kind man, though we didn't get to know one another well."

At this, a smirk crossed his face. Of a sudden, I knew he was thinking I meant in the way a man knows a woman. He knew!

"I am sorry for his loss," Simon said as we danced. "But glad for my gain."

"You mean because he died with no son of his own?" I said, having not a care if I offended Simon at this moment.

"Alas, 'twas not to be, through no fault of your own for certes, My Lady," he said. "Indeed, I am his heir and he left ample accounts. No, I was thinking on bounty of another sort. Mayhap that is conversation left for another time. I shall be back to court after I make the rounds of the properties. As soon as a . . . suitable time has passed."

I nodded and held his sleeve and kept a deceptively gentle smile on my face. "Thank you. It's been difficult to come to understand all of these changes, as you can well imagine. Why, I

172

have not even been able to sleep well these past days since Edmund brought me the news." I mocked dull feminine wiles.

He smiled down at me. "Have not another care. I shall have Meredith bring a draught to your lady maid which will aid you. I find it at a physic in London."

I put my head down demurely to conceal my response. *The Duke of Suffolk is not the only member of court able to coax an unwilling thought from an unguarded mind.* I watched Edmund, who appeared as near happy as I'd ever seen him, dance with the Ogilvys' young ward. His warning about how the court would change me rang in my ears.

Yes, Edmund, you were right. But here we must be wily as the serpent as well as gentle as the dove.

Serpents were not far from my mind throughout the remainder of the year. In October the king learned that the archbishop of York, Thomas Wolsey, so recently demoted, had been in secret negotiations with Charles the Fifth on behalf of the banished queen. There was no word for it other than treason, which Henry never brooked. The king summoned Wolsey to appear before him. Wolsey died, apparently in justifiable fright, en route. No mourning took place. When the king was told that the man who had served him selflessly for decades had died, he declined to interrupt his archery lessons to comment. I wondered if Anne felt vindicated in any way—over the Percy affair—but she, wisely, said nothing.

Rather than be buried in the fine black marble tomb Wolsey had prepared for himself, the king had him interred, without monument, in obscure Leicester Abbey.

One day I was with Anne and a gaggle of other ladies when the king strode into the Long Hall. He approached Anne and drew her near him as he went to the head of the room to take his throne in advance of a diplomatic meeting. She indicated I should come along with her; I suspected Henry had told her he wanted to share a word with me.

The king looked upon me. "We are sorry for your loss, Baroness."

I curtseyed and looked down for a moment before meeting his gaze. "Thank you, Your Majesty. The baron was a good man."

The king nodded. "That we know well. He fought with our father, and indeed, with yours, at Bosworth."

I said nothing, knowing that conversation was not required nor perhaps even welcome.

"Your father shall find you another husband anon," he said. "Or your brother. 'Tis not good to remain unmarried too long." At that he turned to Anne and grinned, his teeth wolflike behind his fair beard, and yet the sexuality and power of the man were almost unbearable. Anne smiled back but there was some strain that, having known her so long, was clear to me. I took my leave but not before watching as the king's eyes searched for and found a pretty young maid of honor. She smiled modestly, yet flirtatiously, and held his gaze.

I looked up at Anne. She'd seen it too. The look on her face told me that it had not been an unfamiliar sight.

TWELVE

Year of Our Lord 1531
York Place
Windsor Castle

We began the year at York Place for the simple reason that there were no separate lodgings for the queen. That made it unlikely that she would come, even if she had been invited, and made things less uncomfortable for Anne and her mother, who shared prime accommodations underneath what had been the archbishop's library. I did not believe in ghosts, of course, but of a sudden I could come around a corner and feel a cold, queer presence of Thomas Wolsey, whose house it had been. Henry set about refashioning it into his own image, as he did everything he touched. At a masque that year he styled himself as Midas and Anne was dressed in a magnificent gown of cloth of gold. Perhaps there would be a reverse Midas touch at play, later, wherein everything he turned to gold later disintegrated into ashes. But not York Place, or as it was to be known, Whitehall Palace. Henry spent a great deal of time there supervising the trans-formation and cavorting with Anne.

She, in her cloth of gold, was the sun, and all were drawn toward her. Anyone wanting to seek the king's favor—or a grant, or a property, or an office—sent gifts to Anne. She received jewels and cloth and hairpieces and sweets and rare fruits of all kinds. She did not have a taste for sweets or fruits, save dates, but accepted them graciously and noted the benefactors who sent them her way. Sir Nicolas Carewe, a lifelong friend of the king and Anne's cousin, brought her a monkey as a gift. Mayhap he did not realize that Anne hated monkeys above all other animals, finding them noisy and vulgar. I rather suspected that Sir Nicolas did know that Anne hated monkeys but that Katherine of Aragon loved them well. It was his way of drawing a comparison between Anne, whom he loved not, and Katherine, whom he did.

Often Anne passed along a good tiding to the king on the gift giver's behalf, but most often her favors were granted to reformer priests or simple gentry families, countless of whom had nothing with which to earn her pleasure. In spite of this, many of the king's men grumbled that she was too politic for a woman. I suspect they nursed injured egos after a bout with her tongue. But she used her skills well, to the advantage of those whom she loved, and one could hardly fault her for this. 'Twas the way of all at court.

We ladies were caring for her gowns, observing the throng in her apartments seeking to curry her favor. As we did, Lady Zouche noted with pride, "Those who thought Anne Boleyn would be a passing fancy were woefully wrong." As I tended one of Anne's hundred or so dresses I had to agree, but my spirit was nervously discomfited.

One day in March, as the rain wept down the high leaded windows, Thomas Cromwell escorted a small assembly of men toward the king, enthroned in his presence chamber, wearied by one request after another from obsequious courtiers. Except for Anne, who remained near the king, we ladies mingled toward the edge of the room with our chatter and our spaniels. When the king spied Cromwell, who had been a lawyer under Wolsey till the latter's death, he motioned him forward.

"Come forward, my good man," the king called out. "Have you a report for me?"

The court grew quiet then. Many loiterers looked about them for a quick escape route should the king unloose the stays that contained his temper if the report should ill serve him. I looked at Cromwell, who broke into a smile, and Cranmer's happy countenance, and knew all was well. The king summoned them forward. As we had not been dismissed to take our leave we stood fast and pretended to go about our business though every ear tilted forward.

"We've completed the final copy of the *Collectanea satis copiosa*, sire," Cromwell stated. His voice, usually calm and hard to hear, fairly boomed through the chamber. My mind translated the Latin as the "sufficiently abundant collections."

"Your findings?" Henry said. I watched his face, and Anne's. Neither showed surprise. I looked about the chamber. Nearly every courtier of import was present as the king planned a dinner that evening to which everyone of consequence had been invited—nay, commanded.

I glanced at Lady Zouche and saw that she had drawn the same conclusion. This announcement was not a surprise. It was staged, as one of Henry's great masques, for dramatic effect.

"Our findings, Your Majesty, have been reached after several years of studies by the finest minds here in England and also on the Continent. Learned men, dedicated to the truth and to Your Highness and to our Lord. We studied religious texts, primarily Holy Writ, and Latin texts, and Anglo-Saxon documents from the time of the establishment of our great land."

Cromwell undid a scroll with unusual flourish.

178

His habit was to be as dour a picture in muted black as Wolsey had been a preening red bird. But not today. As the king gave him leave he undid the ribbon wound round the scroll and read aloud.

We have conclusively established through an unbroken chain of documents and scriptures that the Church in England is autonomous. This matter has been examined many times over the years, including by your noble fore-bear and namesake, King Henry the Second, who also sought to assert ultimate control over his realm. For over which land, sire, did Saint Peter, the first to be claimed as pope, ever have say? Which sovereign did he overrule? None, sire. In Holy Writ he claimed for him-self only the titles of *servus et apostolus Jesu Christi*, slave and apostle. Therefore, we are fully convinced that the king has both secular *imperium* and spiritual supremacy in England.

There was an audible gasp in the room, and several of the queen's supporters, and also the religious conservatives, edged toward the door, slipping away, for certes, to strategize separately and apart.

"Therefore," Cranmer elucidated for the sake of the gathered listeners, "it is Your Majesty who exercises jurisdiction within your realm on all matters of state and religion."

Lady Zouche reached over and squeezed my hand. This was a victory for Anne, certainly, and also for reformists, of which Cromwell was perhaps the highest placed. Cromwell took nearly an hour to read out a number of the supporting documents and admittedly, they were legion, and credible, and not twisted to purpose. One had to believe that they had been lying comatose waiting to be summoned forth again to life. Cromwell's smugness, however, endeared him to me not at all.

"We thank you," the king said. "You've served king and country well."

By the end of February Henry demanded that the Church of Rome recognize him as the sole protector and supreme head of the English Church and clergy.

John Fisher, Katherine of Aragon's confessor and defender at her long-cooled Blackfriars trial, refused to accept this Act of Supremacy. For his honest opinion he was imprisoned in the Tower. The king's surrogate father, Sir Thomas More, offered to resign his chancellorship rather than acknowledge that anyone other than the pope was the supreme head in England. It was refused.

Meanwhile, Thomas Cromwell was made one of the king's most highly placed advisors.

Anne looked exultant, radiant, victorious. She had been passing along reformist books, not only to her ladies but to the king.

It was, as my lady mother might have said, too merry to persist.

In May Anne came down with a minor flux and kept to her bed. As her closest friend and confidante, as well as mistress of her robes, I visited each day, carrying tidbits of court news and lady chatter with me as well as broths and meals of plain oats I'd ordered from the kitchens to entice her to eat.

"I cannot take any food yet," she said weakly. "My innards will not tolerate it." I looked upon the desk in her reception chamber. There were boxes and baskets of gifts, all sent from those seeking her favor and, by the by, the king's. I opened one box to find a fine brush with a carved handle and took it in to her.

"Let me brush your hair. 'Twill make you feel better." She sat a bit and sipped the broth I brought to her as I did her hair and talked. I soon noticed a sickly sweet scent wending throughout the room and commented on it.

"Oh, 'tis George's wife Jane's perfume; she had been receiving guests and gifts for me earlier on. Her father, Lord Morley, purchased some from the Saracens present at Calais so many years ago and she's used it ever since. 'Tis jasmine or some such thing. But she applies it too strongly."

I rose and went to the servant in the outer chamber. "Please change the rushes in Mistress

181

Boleyn's rooms. And add some rosemary and lavender."

She curtseyed to me and went to obey.

Soon Anne looked tired again. "I shan't keep you any longer," I said. "I will be back tomorrow to see if you're well." She nodded sleepily and sank back into her bed. "What shall I do with those?" I nodded toward the foodstuffs in the gift baskets.

"Remove them, please," she said. "The smell nauseates me."

On my way out I pressed the baskets into the hand of her lady maid. "Please, take these to your family," I said. "There are dates and nuts and oranges and some fine cheeses."

"Thank you, ma'am," she said. "May our Lord reward your kindness and generosity."

I had caught the flux as well and had been unable to visit Anne for a week. When I did, I found her to be fully recovered physically but sick at heart.

"What is it?" I asked.

She nodded for me to sit down next to her. "I have ill tidings."

Edmund? Thomas? My father? Mayhap things had gone awry with the king. "Go on," I urged her.

"One of my lady maids—and her daughter—has perished."

"Perished? Who—and whatever do you mean?"

"Your charge, little Jessica, and her mother. One

of my ladies came to tell me. Apparently they had eaten of some oranges which had spoilt and took sick till they vomited blood. Talk in the servants' quarters was that the deaths were warranted as just rewards for stealing fruit. The fruit, they reason, must have been stolen, for where else would a plain maid get oranges?"

I ran from the room, down the hall to the close chamber, and was sick. Sweet Jessica and her mother dead of oranges I had given them. After I finished heaving into the open hole, which exhaled stench back upon me, I wiped my mouth with my linen and returned to Anne. It would have been unseemly for her to have chased after me, and she hadn't.

"Those oranges were not stolen," I said, my shoulders wracked with repressed sobs. "I gave them to the mother. Seville oranges," I said, "*Spanish* oranges. Sent to you by a well-wisher whilst you were ill. And they were not spoilt. I handled them myself."

She looked at me quietly. "Poison?"

I nodded. "Poison. From now on you mayn't eat anything except that which comes by the king." He, after all, had a taster to ensure that his food was untainted.

I took my leave of her as soon as I could. She hugged me tightly and wished me well and after I returned to my rooms I dismissed Edithe and took to my bed in the middle of the day. Later, after I'd recovered some sensibilities, I recalled that the year before the Duchess of Norfolk, Anne's double-minded aunt, had smuggled a note of support to the queen in a basket of oranges. I was sick again at the thought that Anne could have been poisoned, I could have been poisoned, as sweet little Jessica was.

Summer came and the king was restless, pacing on progress from property to property like a great beast on the prowl. In July he sent Anne, and a hunting party, ahead of him to a neighboring estate and then snuck out of Windsor Castle himself, leaving instructions that, upon his return, the queen was to have been removed to a smaller, dank estate. When he rejoined us he seemed merrier than I'd seen him in a long while, relieved of the burden of his sinful relationship with Katherine, he said, and content to leave the running of the realm in Thomas Cromwell's competent hands, as he'd done for years with Wolsey. Cromwell had handed him the thing he most wanted—an airtight legal and religious rationale for his divorce. Anne promised to give him what he needed most—a legitimate son.

"Is this wise?" I asked her one day whilst we strolled. "Offering something that only God Himself can ensure?"

She nodded, confident of her own abilities, I suspected.

"Have a care what you promise him," I said. "He always ensures his promises are collected upon."

I myself had believed that the king and Anne shared not only intellectual agreement on the sovereignty arguments that the reformers made, but also a religious understanding. Just a few days earlier Anne and Henry, both ignoring the priest, had passed her book of hours back and forth in chapel whilst the priest said Mass. Like children in church, Henry wrote in the book and then passed the book to Anne, who seemed to write a response afore passing it back to him. He grinned at her and came very close, I believe, to kissing her in the middle of the service, which would have been shocking indeed.

It would not have been fanciful, then, to believe that Henry would look kindly on reformers even as he set his jaw against religious conservatives.

But it would have been wrong.

In August George had his gentleman deliver a note to me asking to meet in my quarters later that night. I sent a note back agreeing. At the appointed hour he arrived, as did Anne. I showed them in and we three sat round the fire.

"Thank you, Meg, for allowing us to meet here," George said. "Anne's quarters, as you know, are the center of all things these days and mayhap not as private—or safe—as I'd like."

I nodded.

"And my own, well, my wife hangs round me listening, waiting, wanting, and nearly all hours of the day. She is scarce company at night, though, when a wife might be expected to be present. Who knows whom she might whisper to, and what."

I looked at him, alarmed. Was he suggesting that his own wife would betray him?

"In any case," he continued, "I trust you've not heard."

"Heard what?" Anne asked.

"About Thomas Bilney. He was dragged from his pulpit today, midsentence. Taken to Lollard pit and burned alive."

"Dear Lord," Anne said. "For . . . ?"

"Lutheran sympathies." George unrolled a small scroll that he withdrew from his sleeve. "He said, 'Scripture is more pleasant to me than the honey or the honeycomb; wherein I learnt that all my labors, my fasting and watching, all the redemption of masses and pardons, being done without truth in Christ, who alone saveth his people from their sins; these I say, I learnt to be nothing else but even, as St. Augustine saith, a hasty and swift running out of the right way.' He was a very good priest."

"Does the king know?" she asked.

George shrugged. "But I cannot believe this would be carried out if it were known that the king would strongly disagree."

Anne looked truly troubled. "But . . ." She

looked to be hard-pressed to place her thoughts into words. "I thought we were of a mind."

"Mayhap he is being advised from two opposite quarters," George said.

Later, Anne came to my chambers, cuddling her little dog Pourquoi, a gift from Lady Lisle, in her arms. "I have heard that there are secret meetings going on within the court. I need to know who attends—who is honest and true, who may be plants and spies. Since the king sent Katherine away all know that our marriage is nigh and it becomes dangerous to me . . . as you may imagine."

I nodded, thinking of Jessica, of the duchess, of Bilney.

"As your sister is a known reformer, no one will think it strange if you attend a meeting should you be found out. Especially as you are not known to be . . . devout. Will you cloak yourself and attend after the Christmas celebrations?"

"Will it help you?"

" 'Twill, or I wouldn't ask it of you," she said. She held my gaze. "But ere you agree I must confess. I have heard from George, who heard from Latimer and Parker, that Will Ogilvy is back from Antwerp and may be in attendance."

THIRTEEN

Year of Our Lord 1531
York Place
Richmond Castle
Greenwich Palace

My sister, Alice, was present at court and the day after my discussion I drew her aside in Anne's chambers. "I'd like to speak with you." I gave her a meaningful look. "Will you be at your rooms after dinner?"

"Yes, of course," she said. "I will wait for you."

Later that evening I made my way through the ravenish shadows of the ladies' courtyard chambers where my sister was quartered. She was not nobility, as I was as the widow of a baron, nor even as tightly connected with Anne, so her rooms were comfortable but meager. She served willingly in spite of that fact. I knocked sharply on her door and she opened it and let me in. "My dearest," she said, taking my shawl from me and patting the chair closest to the fire. "How fare you?"

I hugged her tightly before sitting down, the scent of her lightly perfumed hair evoking memories of my running into her arms when I'd been hurt or harrowed as a child. I wondered if I would ever outgrow the need for her comfort or have a child of my own to offer it to. "I have a favor to ask," I began.

"Anything." She drew near to me and offered a small platter of comfits.

After taking a bite of one as a courtesy I said, "I understand there are some reformer meetings going on at court. I'd like to attend one. Or more."

She cocked her head warily. "For yourself?"

These times, perhaps, would bring much good and yet could still make a beloved sister question another. "For Anne." I explained the situation briefly. She had, of course, heard about Bilney. "And mayhap for myself." I did not mention that it was a man I sought and not his God.

She nodded. "Of course." She let me know that the meetings were often held in rooms and chambers furthest out from the circle of courtiers, though not always; directed me to a few; and gave me a password to use if I should be questioned. "Romans eight," she said. "Do not forget that."

I had no idea what might be found at Romans eight, but of course I would remember it as if my life depended upon it, as well it might.

Nighttime at court was quiet. The halls echoed and amplified the softest of steps because most were safely behind doors. Some closed doors sheltered right and honest activities, sleep or reading; sewing; discussion or pleasant discourse of intimate sorts between husbands and wives.

Some doors hid corrupt activities, thieving and plotting and horrors upon which one didn't like to let the mind dwell. Some doors, like the one I crept toward, hid activities that were just but might not always be perceived thusly. I pulled my cape around me, left the hood up, and knocked lightly on the door. A young courtier I did not recognize opened it to me. "Romans eight," I whispered, and he nodded and let me in.

I admit to it. I immediately scanned the room looking for Will and was unsure if I was disappointed or relieved not to find him present. A priest whose name I did not know but recognized as a friend of Matthew Parker, whom Anne had helped install as a chaplain at court, was speaking from the front. I did not listen to him at first but continued to look about me. Most people were courtiers I recognized but had few dealings with. Few held copies of what seemed to be Holy Writ. I leaned over and glanced at the copy of the woman next to me. I could just see that it was written in English before she glanced at my hooded form. She closed the book and slipped away. After all, it had been just the year before that Henry had decreed an injunction against anyone owning an English Bible and Bilney's ashes were not yet cooled. Though there were a hundred or more people packed in the chamber, I only recognized one woman whom I knew to be a lady in the service of the Duchess of Norfolk,

Anne's highly placed aunt and sworn enemy.

She looked in my direction but could not recognize me, as my cloak was pulled tight about me and fell down from my forehead. *Is she here as a spy for her mistress, as even I am? Or does she have questions she cannot voice to her mistress and seeks answers here?*

It seemed I'd arrived late. The speaker was nearly done and I wanted to take my leave afore any could recognize me. "There are many good priests," he said, drawing his hand down over his priestly vestments. The crowd laughed. "But sadly the best of them cannot read Latin nor Hebrew nor Greek. We love the Church and all who serve within it. Let us seek reform from within so we may provide those good, simple priests, and the gentle souls they serve, Holy Writ in their own tongue. They, too, may then hear the voice of the Lord speaking to them directly and sweetly."

I slipped out, my spirits dampened a bit. I had hoped for more. To see Will. Perhaps, though I would not willingly admit this to another, to see God. I believed in the priest's good intentions, but I, who read Latin, and had read Holy Writ for myself, could not say that I'd ever heard from the Lord directly and sweetly, so it did not follow that making it available in English could help all.

I reported to Anne what I had seen and heard; naught to be of concern but perhaps the morsel about the Duchess of Norfolk.

I went back two nights hence and all was nearly the same as the first visit, except it were held in different chambers. In spite of my every attempt to locate those who might cause Anne some harm, there were no highly placed listeners other than those I knew to be her true friends. Some seemed to do nothing but grumble against all who kept to the old ways, and Rome, which impressed me not at all; many conservatives I knew to be good people with admirable motives. Some were there solely for political advancement. I'd seen them sidle up to Cromwell's lackeys. Some were genuine seekers, thirst writ across their faces, and nearly ecstatic joy at hearing Scripture spoken in English. I envied them. None seemed dangerous. I'd determined not to visit again, but when I was about to take my leave I caught the scent of something in the room. I could not locate its wearer but I recognized its source. It was jasmine perfume.

I determined to return to the next meeting, for I knew that sooner or later I would meet with Jane Rochford, who professed to be against reformers one and all, her husband included, one presumed. I slipped along the dark hallway, skirts swishing in the rushes, and stood outside yet another, larger chamber, and held my hand up to the door to knock. Ere I did, though, I heard the voice of the speaker.

A sweet voice, a deep voice, a voice that made me wish for all things that could not be and mayhap a willingness to throw away all things that must be in order to gain them. My flesh won—or was it my spirit? In any event, I knocked on the door, gave the new password, and entered.

It was Will speaking, of course. I pulled my cloak about me, which drew no notice because many present sought to keep their identities secret either by cloak or by downcast gaze.

I dared not go into the great room. Instead, I stood behind a stone wall that still had a sword slit in it, just large enough to allow my ear to hear everything that was said whilst revealing nothing of myself. His voice was filled with both fiery rhetoric and soothing reassurance, with logic and with passion. For the first fifteen minutes I heard nothing of the meaning of the words, only drank in the voice that caressed my ears and my heart. I risked peeking through the slit and took my breath when I saw him. The sweet boy had grown into a powerful and striking man. He emanated moral, intellectual, spiritual, physical strength. The Latin came to me, unbidden.

Vires. Fortitudo.

I went back again the next night and dared to come a bit closer though I did not uncloak myself. I listened to the words this time as well as the man. Lord and Lady Carlyle recognized me, I know, as Lady Carlyle came up and bid me good evening. As the meeting was being held in her apartments I had no fear of her making me known. " 'Tis because of your closeness with Anne that you must remain secret," she suggested, and I agreed with her. She took special care to place me where I could best see and hear but not be seen nor heard.

I went back again for a fourth night and a fifth. The court was about to leave York Place and move to Hampton Court shortly, and the meetings would, of necessity, stop for a while. I saw not Jane Rochford but, on the last night, someone even more treacherous. He did not bother to cloak himself, so certain was he in his own powers and being in the protection of Cromwell, for whom he now kept close accounts.

Edmund. Edmund, certainly, was no religious seeker. He worshipped no one save himself.

I hid myself back in the corner a bit more and listened whilst Will finished reading from the Epistle of Saint Paul to the Romans. "For we know not what to desire as we ought: but the spirit maketh intercession mightily for us with groanings which cannot be expressed with the tongue. And he that searchest the hearts, knoweth what is the meaning of the spirit." He closed Tyndale's English translation and finished from memory. "For we know that all things work for the best unto them that love God, which also are called of purpose."

I watched as Edmund took note of Will's English Bible and then snuck out of the room. The rest of the crowd began to disperse, and indeed, most of them did so in a quick manner. I did not wish to irritate the scar of a badly healed wound but I knew that I must. I slipped up to Will and, after he'd finished talking, Lady Carlyle.

"Meg," he said roughly. Lady Carlyle looked from him to me and back again. Then, in the way of women since the beginning of time, she nodded knowingly. "Mayhap you'd prefer to talk in my closet?" She indicated the small private room off to the side of the public chamber.

Will took my hand and I followed him in. "May I take your cloak?" he asked, and I nodded and shrugged it off. I was glad that I had taken a care to dress well that night; my dark blue gown showed off my russet hair to its best advantage, though some curls slipped disobediently from the hood casually holding it back. Though I could say in honesty that I hadn't dressed for the man, I must also be honest in admitting that I was glad that I still had an effect on him. He kept a modest distance from me as he pulled his chair alongside but never took his eyes from my face. "How are you?"

"I'm well," I said. "All goes well for Anne for the moment, and therefore for me."

"I'm sorry to hear of your husband," he said.

I looked up, startled. "Lord Blackston passed away some time ago," I said. "But he was ready to meet his Maker."

"I hear from my sister that your brother Edmund is negotiating to have you marry the baron's nephew and heir."

"Your sister is particularly well informed for someone who spends her time with child or languishing in a large household in Kent," I replied somewhat tartly.

He laughed. "She was always the one that heard everything. We called her 'hare-ears' as a child. Always twitching to listen to others."

I laughed with him. "And how do you?"

His face became infused with light. "I do well. I have been in Antwerp helping with translations, with printing. We have now moved some printing here, to England, and I am come to assist with the setup. I am passionate about my work. And about sharing it with others. It has the power to transform the mind, you know." He looked sheepish. "Epistle to the Romans. Chapter twelve. I've been studying it quite a bit."

I envied his study and his transformed mind. "Your rhetoric is as sharp as ever," I said. "I heard you speak from the Gospel of Saint Matthew last night, about our being the bride of Christ and He our bridegroom."

He blushed at the mention of the topic of brides and bridegrooms, as I'd intended him to do. I felt pleased, not in an unkind manner, that I could still provoke him thus.

"How many nights have you come?" he asked.

"All," I replied simply. I would not lie to save my pride.

"The test of a speaker is not in carefully chosen words nor in the fine rhetoric of delivery, but in the effect he has upon the hearts and minds of those listening."

I offered nothing, not willing to admit that there had been a tiny unclenching of my heart the past few nights. The irony of God in using Will thusly had not gone unrecognized. "I come to warn you," I said. "My brother Edmund was here. He paid particular attention to your English Bible and he knows you are no low-level simpleton. He works for Cromwell now. All know that Cromwell is a reformer, but also the king's man. The king's law decrees that no one shall own an English Bible. I urge you to have a care; do not let my brother see you, nor warm you with false words about his desire for church reform."

Will stood up, ran a hand through his dark hair, and sat down again. "He's already been to see me —to claim friendship and brotherhood. Knowing his facility with money, I was about to see if he could arrange funds here in England for printing. I am aware, of course, of Alice's inclinations, and your brother Thomas's. I thought maybe Edmund had grown kinder with time."

"Mortar sets with age," I said, "afore it crumbles. Be wary. Do not let your Bibles remain in your quarters."

He glanced down at the copy in his hands. "This is the only one I brought with me. Have you read it?"

I shook my head. "I don't even read the book by Father Erasmus any longer. The one you'd given me. 'Tis written in Latin."

He laughed. "You should still read *Handbook of a Christian Knight*, of course. Erasmus remains a scholar par excellence. But this." He tapped the cover. " 'Tis in English," he teased. "Hence, allowable."

I grinned. He reached out, took my hand in his own, and loosened my fingers from their self-protective fist. He placed his copy of Tyndale's Bible in my palm and closed my fingers around it. He held his hand over mine for a long while, longer than was necessary, longer than was wise as well. He seemed unwilling to remove it and I wished that he wouldn't. But of course, he did.

Tentatio.

"I have been directed back to Antwerp. I shall not share my plans with your brother Edmund, nor the names of those working here in England. But I will certainly return." He stood up and moved back to a safe distance. "Shall you . . . remain at court?"

I nodded. "I shall be where Anne is, till I am married, and perhaps even after."

"Mayhap I shall see you, then," he said. He took my hand, the one with the Bible clutched in it, and kissed the back of it before taking his leave.

The imprint of his lips burnt into my skin, and I held it near my cheek as I made my way back to my chamber. When I arrived, I set the Bible next to my bed, considering where to hide it, even from Edithe. I touched the cover, knowing that his hand had done so as well. And then, as I turned the pages, I came upon something. A fragile dried wreath of daisies. The one I'd made Will so many years before in the garden at Hever and that he had claimed as a keepsake. I pressed it to my lips, returned it to the Scriptures, and hid the book away next to my neglected, well-loved copy of Erasmus.

The next day Anne drew me into her sleeping chamber, the one place we could be certain to have privacy. We sat on the foot of her bed, cross-legged, and I recounted to her my entire evening. After telling her everything about Will I said, "Have a care with Jane Rochford. She will not be loyal to you, nor even George, I believe. She is only ever after loyalty to herself."

Anne nodded. "Yes. And you have a care with Edmund. Has he brought word of the new baron?"

"Yes. He says negotiations go well. Enough time is elapsing that as soon as they settle the financial matters, I can expect the baron to come to collect me. They seem to be at odds over the money, no surprise with Edmund, but I expect them to come to terms very soon." I did not say, *Because I grow older and it becomes more difficult to be assured of conceiving a child.* Anne and I were of an age and that was something, in her precarious position, she did not need to be reminded of.

I finished dressing her in layers of silk and cloth of silver and fastened about her graceful neck her finest pearls, which she loved. Anne and the king were entertaining diplomats that night at a quiet dinner in Henry's quarters. After she left, I straightened her wardrobe and dismissed the rest of the ladies. When I was certain that the last one was gone I went to the cabinet where Anne kept the reformist books she often read aloud from or loaned to her closest ladies. I opened the cabinet and saw the book of hours that I'd seen her writing in with Henry.

I took the book out and opened it, thumbing through the pages till I came upon some that had been written upon.

There it was. Henry had written, *If you remember my love in your prayers as strongly as I adore you, I shall hardly be forgotten, for I am yours. Henry R. forever.* He'd written it on the page under the Man of Sorrows, presumably representative of himself, a rather unsuitable comparison.

Anne had written back, *By daily proof you shall me find, To be to you both loving and kind.* She'd written it under an illustration of the angel telling the Virgin Mary she was about to have a son.

I closed the book. By this I knew, and Henry would too, that Anne was promising him a son.

Oh, Anne.

I was compelled to open the book back up again and when I did I stared at the Man of Sorrows. His skin was slashed from the top of his head to the bloody wounds on his feet. His face was writ with anguish. Blood dripped or ran across his entire body. And yet He still knelt in prayer and obedience. Underneath Him were written words from Isaiah: *He was a man of sorrows, acquainted with grief.*

I sank into a chair, the book still in my hand, and I gave free rein to the memories and feelings flooding forward. I felt anew the beatings at the hands of my father, whence blood had coursed down my face, too; recalled the unjust hardship of my mother's lifelong illness; anguished at the powerlessness of being chattel—sold in marriage for a price. I allowed myself to truly recognize the fears I felt for Anne, who had given herself wholly to a man I suspected would be true to none but himself. Finally, I grieved the utter despair of my relinquishment of Will, who remained, as our Lord must know, my heart of hearts.

And then, that for which I had yearned happened. Christ spoke to me in our common language, one I could understand. Not Latin. Not English. Distress.

I am a man of sorrows. I am acquainted with grief.

He understood and, therefore, could be trusted. I let Him wrap His arms around me and for the first time since my lady mother died, I cried myself dry.

FOURTEEN

Year of Our Lord 1532
Greenwich Palace
Richmond Castle
Woodstock

We were back at Greenwich for Christmas that year and in every way save name and body, Anne reigned over the celebrations as queen. Court etiquette demanded that courtiers give gifts to one another and, of course, to the sovereign. The boundaries of many relationships were narrowed or expanded by the value of the gifts given, the placement of the person understood by the significance of the gifts received.

That year Henry decided, as Katherine was no longer queen and also, because of her unwilling-ness to cooperate with his plans, no longer his friend, to give Katherine of Aragon nothing at all.

Furthermore, he decreed that all were to follow suit and that no presents were to be sent to her at Enfield, where she moldered. The whispers grew strident among the ladies that Anne had been behind this indignity. I failed to understand how any person with more than a Whitsunday's experience at court could imagine that Anne, or anyone, could steer Henry in a course not of his own plotting. His sailed by his own star alone.

I supposed the rumors were fueled by the fact that Katherine's loss was clearly Anne's gain. Not only was she the recipient of dozens of expensive gifts of plate, cloth, and jewelry from ambitious courtiers, she was the benefactress of Henry's wealth. He'd apparently kept his jeweler, Master Hayes, busily employed with, among other gifts, a girdled belt of crown gold. The gift I found to be the most perplexing was Henry's gift of a Katherine Wheel set with thirteen diamonds. It had a beautiful shape, of course, gold spokes enclosed in a delicate ring, much like a wedding ring. But all knew that the Katherine Wheel, also called a breaking wheel, was a device intended for execution of the condemned.

No one else seemed to note it, or if they did, they kept their peace.

My brother Thomas returned from Calais and was immediately appointed as commissioner of the peace in Essex, far from court. Mayhap the king had his hand in it. But the order was signed by Cromwell and initialed by Edmund Wyatt. We had barely time for dining together once or twice before he was whisked out of Anne's sight again.

Once the forced conviviality of Christmas had passed, the court again drew tense. The factions were clearly marked, and though Katherine was no longer present at court, some of her supporters were. They spoke mostly in whispers and in corners. Anne told me that the king grew intolerant of them. He had proved his point, legally and scripturally, and they were waking a dangerous impatience by their prodding.

We arrived at chapel on Easter Sunday. Anne and the king sat in the royal chamber, out of sight of the rest of the gathered courtiers, though we all heard the same message. I normally sat with Lady and Lord Zouche, but this day I had helped Anne a bit longer than usual and approached the chapel by myself. Most pews were filled. As I stood there, a man about my own age caught my eye.

"My lady?" He indicated the pew he'd just vacated. "Please."

I smiled at him. "Thank you, Sir . . ."

"Sir Anthony Litton," he said. "At your service." His smile was warm and, indeed, welcome. I saw him shove a friend over, as schoolboys do, to make way on the pew in front of me and I held back a giggle.

We had come, of course, expecting to hear of resurrection and new life and celebration after the bleak weeks of Lent. William Peto, one of Henry's favorite friars, of the Observants, began the message. He took his text from the Old Testament. Strange, for Easter Sunday. And then the court grew palpably ill at ease as he began to preach, energetically, about King Ahab.

"Ahab was a wicked king who had been handed a good kingdom and misspent it," he said. "He was selfishly willful. He was blessed and yet returned curses for blessing. And then he chose to marry Jezebel."

Friar Peto went on to indict Jezebel as a Baal-worshipping pagan, a domineering woman who ordered her weak-kneed husband around and would lead his kingdom to ruin.

Rivulets tracked down Father Peto's face though 'twere only the end of March. I dared not look up at the royal chamber, but in the stillness of the church we could hear Henry panting with anger. All knew Peto styled Henry as Ahab and Anne as Jezebel. Shortly after we sang the Te Deums and filed out.

Henry, to his credit, didn't have Friar Peto strung to a Katherine Wheel. Instead, he reasonably sent one of his chaplains to preach a rebuke the next Sunday. When the king's man arrived he was barracked and prevented from speaking. They followed that indignity up by hauling said chaplain before the ecclesiastical court for discipline.

George dined with Anne and me weeks later,

the night after Henry responded to all of this with stunning force. "He brought himself to his full height, was dressed in his richest robes, and had a wondrous fury on his face," George said. "He reminded all present that they had agreed, in principle, that a king has jurisdiction in his own realm. He recalled that he had proved his case for sovereignty, as well as against the legitimacy of his first marriage, legally and scripturally. And that they had agreed, in kind."

"Who spoke against him?" Anne refilled George's ale herself, though we knew as many maids as could stood just outside the chamber, listening.

"The Church in Rome elected the bishop of Winchester, Gardiner, to speak on its behalf. Before the assembled churchmen, courtiers, and government officials he told Henry, 'We, your most humble subjects, may not subject the execution of our charges and duty, certainly prescribed by God, to Your Highness's assent.' "

"In other words," Anne said, "the pope, who has never been to England, and who is under the sway of Charles the Fifth, shall be the ultimate law in our land."

George raised his eyebrows. "I'm not sure they would see it that way but . . . yes."

"Henry will not stand for it," I said. "Will he?"

They both shook their heads. "Indeed, Henry unmanned Gardiner in front of all assembled, raging that he, too, had a God-given appointment as anointed king and that he would defend it afore all comers. Few looked ready to pick up a lance and meet him in the tiltyard." He looked at Anne. "They blame you, you know."

She nodded. "It's not about me. It's about sovereignty. But they find me to be an easy scapegoat. A sacrificial lamb. However," she said, biting into a date, "I am safe. Henry's promised me."

It had come to a head. Within the month all had declared sides. Sir Thomas More, Henry's friend and the writer of the hopeful *Utopia*, but also the author of half a million sharp words against Tyndale and church reform, threw his weight against the king and tendered his resignation as chancellor. Henry accepted his resignation with cool civility.

By the end of April Henry had decided that since the Church in Rome would not do things by halves, neither would he. He had a bill presented to Parliament that would strip the Church in Rome of *all* its powers in England.

By June, King Francis of France had allied himself with Henry. Now not even Charles would agree to come against England lest he fight France as well. All seemed settled.

Till July.

We ladies had gathered in the court gardens of a sticky summer evening to play cards. The woody freshness of rosemary mingled with the nectar of the roses and the slight salt of feminine sweat—hot months did not excuse us from the cumbersome number of layers required for us to be properly dressed. I reposed with the Duchess of Norfolk and her daughter Mary, who had caught the eye of the king's baseborn son, at a table a few feet away from Anne. She sat with Lady Lisle and Lady Zouche. "Here comes the duke's manservant," Lady Norfolk's daughter teased her mother. "Mayhap he is come to bring funds with which to pay your debt."

The duchess, never known for a quick smile, puckered at her daughter, drawing her wrinkled skin round her mouth as purse strings. I grinned at Mary Howard and admired her wit. The duke's manservant did not stop next to the duchess, however; he went directly to Anne and handed her a note. She read it, folded it, and made her excuses to leave. As soon as I could reasonably do so I followed her. Once in her chambers I saw that she had dismissed all of her ladies save Jane Rochford, who was not so easily put out.

"What is it?" I asked.

"Henry Percy," she said.

"Henry Percy? Whatever can he want?"

"It's not what he wants. It's what his wife, Mary Talbot, wants. She claims that her marriage to Percy has been one sore grievance after the next and that the reason for that is that it is illegal

208

and ill conceived. She claims that Percy and I were precontracted and therefore her own marriage is null and void."

I opened my mouth to speak and just before I did, Jane Rochford's utter stillness caught my attention. I gathered my thoughts and then responded, "What will you do?"

"I shall take this to the king," she said, "and demand that he investigate it."

The breathtaking audacity of the action caught us all unaware. What would Percy say? He, as Anne knew, was not a man of strong will, and he'd been further broken since their ephemeral romance by a wife as icy and depressive as the north lands he ruled over.

And yet, mayhap Mary Talbot had reason for her coldness.

Expectedly, within the month Henry Percy was to be questioned under oath. Unexpectedly, the few of us who knew Anne during that time were also to be deposed. Her family spoke freely, of course, knowing little, and after the Sweat there was only myself remaining of those who had served her during that time.

I was called before one of the king's chaplains, a priest of the age one expects to be tending to abbey physic gardens rather than deposing young widows. He sat me down in his office.

"My lady, I've heard that you are a woman of honor and valor."

"Thank you, Father," I said. "I strive to be."

"I understand that you were a friend at court with Lady Anne during the time in question."

"Yes," I said. "I was here to serve her." I hoped to deemphasize that I'd been her friend and therefore a repository to her secret thoughts.

"Do you recall her relationship with Henry Percy?" Father Peter asked.

"I recall that they were affectionate toward one another," I said.

"Do you recall the moment that they became engaged? Surely that would stick out in your memory. Those kinds of things do, with young women."

Is he trying to entrap me? "I was not privy to any of their private conversations."

"So to the best of your knowledge, with all of your understanding, they were not precontracted. Nor had they pledged themselves to one another."

My conversation in the litter with Anne that year was crystal-clear. She'd promised never again to pledge herself to a weak man. Was there a difference between a pledge and a precontract? I had thought not. But I was not sufficiently sure and I could see a way round this.

"No. They were not precontracted."

"Nor pledged?"

I considered myself a poor liar. I had, I'd thought, little practice. So it was hard to keep my face from betraying me as I answered, "No."

I was almost certain he knew that I was lying but he pressed no more and dismissed me.

I scurried to my room, burdened with shame. I recalled Edmund's taunt about the court bending me to its will and my certainty that it would not happen. After the ladies' gathering that evening I drew aside my sister, Alice.

"I have something I need to confess. A sin."

She raised her eyebrows in question. "To me?"

I shook my head. "No. In fact, 'tis something I cannot confess to anyone. Not even a priest. And yet—my spirit within me needs relief."

She drew me near her and kissed my temple. "Dear Meg. Only our Lord can forgive your sins, so 'tis to Him you should bring your transgressions. As Master Tyndale pointed out, Holy Writ teaches that there is forgiveness for all that repent and believe therein. See now. If you do some harm to me, you do not go to Margaret or John and ask them to ask me to forgive you. You come direct to me. There need not be intercession by anyone on your behalf except by Christ, the High Priest. 'Tis one great reason we push for church reform. So go and confess to Him who tells no secrets."

"Just . . . tell Him? And then what? How shall I know 'tis taken hold?"

She laughed. " 'Twill take hold. But here's how you'll know. 'Twill be harder and harder to sin again likewise, of a willing spirit, and 'twill grow stronger and stronger in you to do right when tempted to wrong."

After allowing Edithe to help me dress for the evening, I dismissed her but kept my candle burning and took Will's New Testament out from the hiding place in the false bottom I'd fashioned in one of my drawers. I opened it up to read, looking for relief. I started at the beginning and kept reading through the Gospel of Saint Matthew. I admit to it: it was like hearing Him whisper in my ear, or shout in my chambers. I read till I reached the twenty-sixth chapter, wherein the Lord said, "For this is my blood of the new testament, that shall be shed for many, for the remission of sins."

His blood and I met again.

I closed my eyes, confessed my wrongdoing, and asked forgiveness for my lie. I felt a gentle peace settle around me and as it did, I could breathe easily. As I went to slip the New Testament back into its hiding place, I noticed something strange. The wreath of daisies had been moved from the place I'd put it, near Romans eight. That was where I'd left it, for certes.

It more than unsettled me to know that someone had been in my chamber, searching through my things. I could do naught but ask Edithe if I had had visitors, though, because to ask if any had seen my Bible would be to train the eye upon myself. I could have moved it to a different hiding place, but I doubted that would have protected me. I could have disposed of the Holy Writ, but that I would not do.

Within the week Henry Percy had been questioned under oath before two archbishops and then again in the presence of the Duke of Norfolk and the king's lawyer. He swore on the Blessed Sacrament that there had been no precontract with Anne. They did not ask him about a pledge and Anne was never questioned.

Henry set about refitting St. James's Palace, which he had bought the year before with the intent of preparing it to be the residence for the Prince of Wales he expected shortly to arrive.

Within days of the closing of the Percy hearings Anne came to share joyous news. She took my hands in her own. "I am to be married."

"Anne!" I said. "When and where?"

"In October. In France."

Of course. Where else would Anne be married but in France?

Henry immediately set about raising Anne to the highest levels so that she would be a fitting bride for him. As mistress of her wardrobe I had the responsibility to see that her clothing was well kept at all times and that Anne was stunningly prepared and presented for every occasion.

"Look!" She lifted the lid on a box that held an open-sleeved cloak of black satin. Next was a black satin nightgown, one I was certain Henry had intended to see in private sometime. My favorite was a French-cut gown in green damask, a dress suitable for a queen. I suspected that green damask would be slipping its way through the hands of most fashionable seamstresses for months after Anne debuted it.

The king came by her chambers, as he often did, that afternoon. He took her in his arms. They kissed for so long that the rest of us ladies in the room busied ourselves and pretended not to see or hear. I felt a small seed of jealousy shoot roots into my heart. My own body ached with the desire for someone to hold it, my lips for someone to require them. Instead, I busied myself with cloth and gowns.

"I bring good tidings, sweetheart," Henry said. "I have sent a request to Katherine to retrieve your jewels. I expect them to arrive ere long and then we will have them quickly reset afore your marquess ceremony next month."

All knew that a "request" from Henry was no request at all.

Anne leaned over and kissed his small mouth. "Thank you, Your Majesty. I want to do well by you." It may have looked like pure gratefulness, or even greediness, to an onlooker, but to me, who knew her heart, I knew it was a response of love. Anne remained deeply in love with the king. And he, apparently, with her.

"You will, sweetheart." He caressed her shoulder and, as we ladies were present, limited it to that.

A week later he stormed into his great presence chamber and shouted for his chamberlain. When the poor man arrived, the king threw a stack of papers at him. "Once again, the dowager princess has been ill advised and acted upon it." His manservant reached down to pick up the scattered papers and quickly scanned them. By now, Henry had stomped his way up the dais and had settled on his throne beneath a scarlet canopy. "Katherine informs me that, since the new year, she is forbidden from giving me anything. Giving me! They are not hers to give. They belonged to my lady mother and shall soon adorn my lawful queen."

"How would you like me to proceed, sire?" the steward asked.

Henry waved his stout hand as if dismissing an idiot. "Tell her I expect the queen's jewels to be in my presence within days or I shall have charges pressed upon her for thievery."

The queen's jewels, soon to be Anne's, quickly arrived. Anne and I went through them together, comparing them with her wardrobe in advance of making suggestions to Henry's jeweler on how to reset some so as to show off her garments, and the woman who wore them, to best advantage.

"You heard that Katherine remarked that she could not allow the jewels to adorn me, the scandal of Christendom?" Anne tried on a ring, too big round for her slender fingers.

"I did," I said.

"And yet, here they are." Anne slipped on a bracelet. "I shall ask Henry to have this refit. And also one made with those rubies." She pointed to an outdated necklace with stunning stones. "It will be good for me to wear them in Boulogne."

She stood up and, a bit regally, swept her hand toward the treasure. "Would you take care of these, then? I'd best get some rest afore tonight's fitting for my gown. 'Twill need to be attended to quickly in order to be ready by September."

"Yes, my lady," I said. I don't think she heard the irony in my subservient voice. Mayhap it was a tone she was growing accustomed to and enjoyed.

I carefully gathered up the queen's jewels and thought about the king's expensive taste—not for rings and bracelets, but for stubborn women.

There were only days before the ceremony at Windsor to invest Anne as Marquess of Pembroke, and trouble to sort out afore it began.

FIFTEEN

Year of Our Lord 1532
Windsor Castle
Calais
Whitehall Palace

At the end of August we made our way to Windsor Castle, which had been prepared for Anne's investment ceremony. She was to be made Marquess of Pembroke, a rank that not only prepared her to be a royal consort but would befit her to meet with others of great rank while in France. We readied her in her rooms. Her aunt, the Duchess of Norfolk, had been selected to carry Anne's mantle of ermine and her coronet. This was a great honor, but the arrogant duchess found it not so. She dithered back and forth but finally, on the day itself, sent her lady-in-waiting to deliver the news.

"My lady the Duchess of Norfolk sends her regrets, madam. She must decline the honor of serving you during today's ceremony."

Anne turned toward her. I watched the woman through narrow eyes: it had been she I'd seen at the reformer meetings. "Why *must* she decline?"

"She did not tell me, my lady." The woman held herself with a haughtiness equal to her mistress's.

All knew it was a deep insult and I hoped Anne would address it directly. She did not disappoint.

"Then I shall inform you why," Anne said. Her black eyes flashed and her mouth tightened. "Though the king required her father's head but a few years back as payment for treason, the duchess feels that her dignity, and rank, preclude her from serving a Boleyn, even one about to be the queen."

The ladies in the room gasped. All knew it to be true but none had yet said the word "queen" aloud when connected with Anne. Unspoken also was the knowledge that the duchess was one of Katherine of Aragon's staunchest friends.

Anne, for once, seemed at a loss. I felt for her. She was stuck. The Countesses of Derby and Rutland were already serving her but she needed another highborn woman of sufficient rank to carry her mantle and coronet in order to keep her head high among the nobility. This was one dilemma Henry could not get her out of.

Please help her, I prayed, startling myself that I did.

Then the Duchess of Norfolk's own daughter quietly spoke up. "I shall be pleased and privileged to carry your mantle and coronet, my lady, if you'll permit me."

Dear, dear Mary Howard. However did she spring from the loins of Elizabeth Howard and that hellhound duke?

Anne walked over and hugged Mary. "Thank you, Cousin. I would be honored to have your service. And here"—she reached over to her box of jewels—"let us find something that shall catch the Duke of Richmond's attention, besides the lady who will wear it, of course."

Mary laughed; all knew that she and the king's son were in love. Her mother opposed the match. Mary now had a more powerful ally than her mother.

That morning Anne was conducted into the king's presence with her ladies all round her. Her shining hair tumbled over her shoulders like a black river in the sunshine; my arms ached with the hundreds of brushstrokes I'd given it so it would appear thusly. Her olive-tinted skin was warm with the crimson velvet of her gown. The jewels had been quickly reset and now shimmered in the morning sunlight streaming in through the high clerestory windows.

Henry was flanked by the Duke of Norfolk, whose daughter carried Anne's mantle, and the Duke of Suffolk, who looked as though he'd eaten spoilt meat. Anne knelt before the king and Bishop Gardiner, yea, he who had just months before argued with Henry for the church's supremacy over the king, read out her patent. "This patent confers to you, and all your offspring, the title of Marquess of Pembroke, and all the attendant honor and income which comes with such title."

The title was notable. It not only permanently placed Anne in the nobility, it made her rich. It had once belonged to Henry's beloved uncle Jasper Tudor and was worth one thousand pounds per year income, a fortune, but one that would not go far. Like all nobility, Anne would be expected to spend, give, employ, and dress according to her rank. No other woman had ever been given the rank of marquess before. It had been solely an honor for men.

I watched Gardiner's face as he spoke. He showed not a trace of hypocrisy. There were some at court who believed that the pope was the ultimate law for both church and state in England and some who felt that both were rightly vested in the king. A few, like Gardiner, seemed to know not whether they were fish or fowl and, for that, were respected not by either.

Mary Howard stepped forward and Henry took the crimson velvet mantle, trimmed in royal ermine, and the gold coronet of a marquess from her small hands. He gave her a reassuring look. "Thank you, mistress," he said with especial kindness. Mary curtseyed and stepped back. Anne remained kneeling as the king draped her with the mantle and crowned her with the coronet. Their eyes met and locked at that precise moment and I knew, instinctively, what they were both thinking.

The next time this happens it will be at a coronation.

Henry had ordered a sumptuous meal of roast oxen and stewed fruit and creamy syllabubs lightly curdled with wine to celebrate the occasion. He and Anne both sat on the dais up front. I sat nearby and, after eating richly and dancing with a few friends, prepared to return to my rooms.

"My lady?" A voice came from behind me. "A dance?"

'Twas the man who'd given me his pew on Easter Sunday. "Sir Anthony," I said, delighted.

"Just Anthony, to my friends." He smiled at me and I smiled back afore I could stop myself.

"Anthony, then. How do you fare?"

"I fare well, mistress." He called me by an unmarried maid's title, and, though I was a widow, I did not correct him. "Happy to be here to celebrate this occasion with the marquess." He nodded toward Anne, who was flushed with success and the love of a powerful man. "Would you like to dance?" I was about to beg off when he held up his hand. "Please, help an old man whose joints grow stiff with lack of use."

"Old man?" I laughed. "You're hardly of an age with the king." Realizing that I may have just insulted the sovereign, I clapped my hand over my mouth. Anthony grinned. Now that we shared a secret I supposed I owed him a dance.

I danced with him more than once, more than twice, mayhap nigh on five or six times, though I danced with other partners as well. Afterward, he took me aside and we sat and drank a cup of wine to cool down and talked.

"Where is your wife?" I asked, though just after I said it I wished I hadn't. It sounded like a personal inquiry! Anthony, a gentleman, did not press an advantage of my impulsive comment.

"I am not yet married. My father is completing my marriage negotiations even now."

"Congratulations," I said.

He wrinkled his nose. "Thank you. Methinks. I expect to be married after the court returns from Boulogne and France. Will you be going, to serve the marquess?"

I nodded. "Yes. And I expect that my own marriage will be settled shortly after we return. My brother has indicated that I'm given leave to attend Anne in France but that he will finish settling my own marriage matter shortly afterward. I'm to marry my former husband's nephew and heir."

"Congratulations are due to you, too, then," Anthony said.

"Thank you. Methinks." I set my tone and expression to indicate my distaste as well. I had so few friends. Anne was ever occupied, Lady Zouche newly wed. It was enjoyable to spend an evening with him.

"Then let us not waste time, lady. The musicians strike up again." He led me to the dance and shared the latest news from the king's privy chamber, funny tidbits about a courtier who cried when he lost a tennis match with the king and one who never paid his gambling debts but came up with feeble excuses such as the need to care for packs of sick greyhounds. When I returned to my chamber that evening I was lighter of heart than I had been for a long while.

On October the eleventh we set sail in the *Swallow*, leaving Dover for Calais. I leaned over the side of the ship, not sick, as others were, but giddy with excitement.

"I've never been anywhere but England!" I exclaimed. The wind ran wild through my hair and the sea salt sprinkled both skin and garments. I cared not. It was exhilarating. And, for a little while longer, I was free like the swallow we sailed on.

Anne laughed at me. "You'll arrive in England again shortly. At Calais. But from there, *nous irons à la France!*"

Henry had spared no expense on this, her bridal trip. He knew he was safe now that he and Francis had become firm allies and his realm was under his control.

"Ten years ago you returned from France, lady. And now you return hence to become queen!"

She smiled. "I am hoping that Jean du Bellay, the bishop of Paris, will marry us," she said. "With Marguerite to stand in for me. I feel as if I became a woman in France, and Marguerite is more a sister to me than Mary ever was. She first introduced me to true faith."

"I wish that for you then, too," I said. "Are you certain, about the king, I mean? That he is being completely forthright with you?"

"Yes," she said. She did not chide me for asking yet again. It was my duty as her dearest friend, and she knew it. "I have looked into his eyes and he told me the truth of the matter with Katherine. Who besides a man, the woman, and our Lord would know if the woman was a maid or not? I am nobody's fool," she reminded me, and I stood reassured.

More than two thousand nobles and knights escorted Anne and Henry to Calais. Some of the most important Englishwomen were missing— Henry's sister Mary, who loathed Anne, and the Duchess of Norfolk, who was as welcome as a persistent itch. But it mattered not. The Boleyn contingent was there in full force. Henry had even allowed my brother Thomas to accompany Edmund and me. Edmund speculated that it was because, as we were so close to Anne, our family had risen with the tide. I agreed that might be a part of it but I also suspected that the king wanted Thomas to witness the wedding for himself. Thomas had lost. Henry had won. Match over.

Although Anne had separate chambers, she lodged at the Exchequer with the king. I, and twenty or so of her other ladies, were nearby to attend to her needs, of course. We dined and danced every night; though Calais was English, French musicians and performers came from all over France to delight Henry and his bride-to-be. Anthony was among the men's contingent and often sought me as a dance or conversation partner, which made the trip more pleasurable yet.

However, there was still no word from Father du Bellay about the wedding. On the fifteenth of October Francis sent a delegation of notables to Henry. They arrived in the room he'd commandeered for a receiving chamber.

"Sire." The ambassador bowed low. "I am come to invite you to France. My noble master, King Francis, has planned a, how do you English say, a *par-tee, une célébration*, for your final days as a man unmarried, in advance of your wedding. There will be hunting and bowls and wrestling and all sorts of diversions suitable for Your Majesty. *C'est ça!*"

"Marvelous!" Henry boomed. "Have preparations been made for the marquess to attend as well?"

The room grew quiet. The ambassador wiped his hands on the sides of his breeches. "I am sorry, sire, but as the Princess Marguerite has taken ill there would be no *femme* of appropriate rank to meet your most gracious lady. My master does not wish to display any disrespect in that matter. He has, though, left instructions that the marquess and all her party are to be well entertained and taken care of in your absence. And *le roi*, King Francis, has made the arrangements *pour retourner* with you after the ten days, to visit his friend *la marquise*."

Anne sat quietly, looking first at Henry, then back at the ambassador. It was a slap to her and she knew it. But what could Henry do? He could not decline Francis's hospitality without endangering their alliance. And Francis had given a respectable reason for Anne's dismissal. Anne herself came to Henry's aid.

"*Merci, monsieur*," she said in perfect lilting, sensual French. "Please thank your master, *le roi* Francis, for his thoughtfulness on my behalf, and tell him that I shall look forward to claiming the first dance with him when he arrives at Calais."

A look of relief refreshed the ambassador's face and the king became genial once more. Henry was always happy when someone eased him out of a pinch.

"*Tu es vraiment une reine*," Henry whispered to her in familiar French on the way back to their lodging. *You are truly a queen.* She had handled it magnificently. I couldn't have been the only person who viewed the gloating smirks exchanged between Sir Nicolas Carewe and the Duke of Suffolk.

In her quarters with her ladies, though, Anne

wept hotly. "This is Eleanor's doing, for certes. She prevented the bishop from coming to perform the marriage. She prevented me from going to France, and she prevented Marguerite from meeting with me."

I made soothing murmurs to agree and reassure. Anne had been close to Queen Claude, Francis's first wife, in whose court she had come of age. His second wife, Eleanor, was the sister of Charles the Fifth—niece, therefore, to Katherine of Aragon, incentive, therefore, to degrade Anne whenever possible.

An hour passed and then Anne dried her tears and looked in the mirror. Then she glanced up, a firm look upon her countenance. "This shall not stop me. *Je suis vraiment une reine.*"

True to his word, Francis had arranged for delightful entertainment, singers and mimes and jugglers and puppet masters, for the ladies who remained in Calais. And on October 24, I began to prepare Anne's clothing and jewelry for the arrival of the men the following day.

My brothers arrived back from Boulogne arm in arm, which was an unexpected and worrisome sight. They soon parted ways, though, Thomas to the alehouse, Edmund to Cromwell's offices. Henry had arranged for a three-thousand-shot salute to be fired as Francis arrived at Calais, and Francis bowed graciously in recognition of the honor. Francis sent a box to

Anne, and I was with her when she opened it.

"*Mon Dieu.*" She lifted a stunning diamond out of a satin-encased box of gold. It was huge, an egg, and it held the attention of all in the room. "*C'est magnifique.*"

"'Tis worth thirty-five hundred pounds," Lady Zouche declared, and we broke into fits of giggles.

"Have you been apprenticing with Master Hayes, the king's jeweler?" I teased.

"Mayhap so." Lady Zouche responded with a high-arched brow and we laughed again. "How else should I know if Lord Zouche does right by me of a New Year's gift?"

Anne had her secretary write a note of thanks to Francis and sent it with an expensive illuminated manuscript, embossed in gold, with delicate, intricate designs and in blue ink made of carefully crushed stone. But Anne would not see Francis herself, not yet. That she had reserved for Henry's great banquet a few days hence.

The banqueting hall had been magnificently decorated with finely woven Turkish tapestries as well as with cloth of tissue and cloth of silver. At each table were gold wreaths encrusted with precious stones and pearls and the room was lit by dozens of candleholders wrought finely by English silversmiths. Hundreds of beeswax tapers were lit and replaced as needed to keep the room in a warm hum.

We were but fifty courses into the night on two hundred French and English dishes that had been prepared before my dining companion excused himself. I glanced at Mary Howard and we hid our smiles. The good people of Calais did not pace themselves as courtiers knew to do for Henry's many courses and often took sick partway through. The room was discontented, though, because Anne was nowhere to be seen. Of course I knew why.

Someone slipped in next to me. "I see your dining companion has abandoned you. I came to remedy that, if I am welcome." It was Anthony.

"You are most welcome," I replied warmly.

After the final course was cleared the trumpeter blew his horn. Anne and six of her ladies entered. Anne was finely dressed in cloth of gold with a shimmering, lacelike cloth of gold loosely draped over her gown. They were all masked, of course, I had seen to that; it was part of the tableaux. Anne's sister, Mary Carey, was by her side, as was her sister-in-law, Lady Rochford; both women knew their fortunes now lay like gown and kirtle with Anne's. Each lady chose a French man to dance with. Anne, of course, chose King Francis and stayed close with him all night, to Henry's obvious envy.

I felt sorry, then, for the Duchesse d'Etampes, Francis's official mistress, who was also present. For the look upon his face during that dance proved that Francis, too, found Anne irresistible, though she acted with perfect decorum.

After Anne had opened the dance floor the musicians struck up again and the rest of the guests danced in the great dance chamber. Henry immediately reclaimed Anne from Francis and unmasked her. I smiled at that. It was hard to keep my eyes off of Mary Howard and the Duke of Richmond as they were obviously besotted with one another. It recalled to mind my young love with Will Ogilvy.

Anthony claimed many dances with me and I even saw Anne and Lady Zouche take notice of this. We talked and laughed and though the conversations never went deep, I enjoyed his presence and humor. He was not classically handsome but the lightness of his face and the sprinkle of freckles across his pale skin were sweet.

We rested for a moment and he said, "I have fair lodgings here in the Exchequer. A warm fireplace, and I room alone."

There was no question mark, and yet a question had been asked.

I held his gaze. He was a kind friend, a gentle man, soon to be married, who wanted nothing more than to share a few nights in the heated atmosphere of Calais. He assumed, wrongly, that I was no longer a maid, having been married for a number of years. For certes a mood of romance had been set these past weeks.

I felt the ache of my skin, which longed to be caressed. I tired of awakening in cool, lonely linens by myself. I had no one to share my midnight secrets with. I had never known the intimate pleasures that my sister, Alice, had promised awaited the bride of a good man.

And yet I could not. I would not. It was not right and, in truth, I did not want it. Not with Anthony.

I took his hand in mine. "I have fine rooms, too, Sir Anthony. But I am glad to know you are well lodged."

He kissed my hand graciously and didn't immediately slip away as a lesser man would have done, to find more willing arms, but kept company with me till the close of the evening.

By the time the night ended, all present had been convinced that there was no woman in our realm better suited than Anne to be the consort of our King Hal. She had grace, poise, wit, and a profound intelligence. And it had long been clear that Henry was willing to stake his kingdom for her.

One night shortly after Francis had returned to France, Anne had her chamber set up with fresh linens and flowers, had spiced wine and fine wafers brought in, and provoked a roaring fire. She gathered me and the Countess of Derby to her but dismissed all others. Shortly thereafter the king arrived with his groom of the stool and close friend of nearly twenty years, Henry Norris, along with a priest whom Anne had pointed out as having been a strong supporter of Luther.

I looked at Anne. She smiled and said nothing. Instead, Henry spoke.

"As all are aware, I am a legally unmarried man and the marquess is a legally unmarried woman. She and I, of our own accord, wish to become husband and wife. The good father here"—he indicated the priest—"has agreed to both perform the ceremony and to keep it secret till such time as I see fit to reveal it at court. I trust you'll do the same."

His eyes, wet and beady like a crayfish's, bore into us. Which of us had the inner fortitude to disagree? It wasn't I. I nodded my assent, as Anne knew I would.

The priest performed a short service. We witnessed it. Norris and the priest took their leave, as did the countess. I stayed for a moment to make sure that Anne's robes were fit for her wedding night and just after.

" 'Tis all satisfactory," she said, steering me toward the door. The air crackled between them. "Thank you, My Lady." It was not unkind, but Henry was not a patient man and he'd already waited nigh on six years.

I kissed her cheek and returned to my cold bed.

The next morning I arrived later than normal, expecting, rightly, that the king would be loath to take his leave. I helped a love-flushed and exultant

Anne into the dressing chamber and then said, "I myself will look after your bedding, madam." It was hard not to be envious of her just then, she having enjoyed the physical warmth and love the night before that I had denied myself.

I pulled the coverlet back and spied what I knew I would find. A large blot of blood from the loss of her maidenhood. I called the countess, also a witness to the wedding, to my side and chatted about some pretense. I ensured that she saw the bloodstained sheets. She looked in my eyes, and I looked back at her before speaking to Anne's laundress. "Please see that these linens are changed immediately."

I wanted them to see the blood. Henry's marriage to Katherine was being dismantled because he claimed she had not come to his bed a maiden. Not one of Katherine's servants or ladies had rushed to confirm stained sheets the night after her marriage with Henry. Mayhap there had been no stain to confirm. Prince Arthur, after all, had claimed to be lusty and amorous as the court performed the bedding ceremony the night of his wedding to Katherine and afterward had called for water, saying that the previous night he had been in Spain and that being a husband was thirsty work.

I found it hard to believe that Katherine, raised by royal parents, would not have known that her marriage was not valid till it was consummated and would not have been coached to achieve that of haste.

I wanted no such talk about the court for Anne. Within hours, I knew, news of the secret wedding and then consummation would travel in a few high and low circles. Anne had been a virgin till the previous night. In recent years whilst Henry and Katherine had wrangled over her maiden-hood there had been no proof of her virginity. I wanted to make sure there was no such question where Anne was concerned.

Yes, my lady Anne, my queen, my friend, there are others who may know if a bride is a maiden at her wedding, besides the man, the woman, and our Lord. And I've just ensured that news of your chastity will be reliably established.

Anne came to me later, eyes flashing. She pulled my bedchamber door closed behind me and before I could speak said, "You pointedly showed the Countess of Derby my sheets. And my laundress."

"Yes . . . ," I began.

"Word has already reached my mother, and through her, me. His Majesty wanted this wedding a secret for now. If it gets back to him, he'll be livid. With me."

I tried to explain to her my motives, that it was for her protection, for her reputation, for the legitimacy of whatever child may soon come. But she waved her hand in my face and bade me stop speaking.

"I understand your intentions and affections. But do not implement your own ideas henceforth without discussing them with me."

She gave me a grim smile and left the room before I could speak again. Apparently, my friend had been replaced by the queen. Or mayhap she had had her first inkling of fear of her most beloved husband.

A week later we returned to London, where my betrothed awaited.

Sixteen

Year of Our Lord 1533
Greenwich Palace
Whitehall Palace

His Highness had decided to start the new year off with a bearbaiting. As his bear garden was not quite finished at Whitehall, he traveled the court to Southwark, in the midst of the stews south of London. We boarded a dozen or more finely appointed barges, I along with Anne in Henry's fine boat, and graciously sailed our way up the river to enjoy the brutality.

Henry and Anne sat in the royal seats, I next to Anne, and, curiously enough, an empty seat remained next to Henry. I raised my eyebrows and looked in the direction but Anne shook her head to discourage me from asking any questions. Though he were married to my dearest friend, Henry was still king and had not a word for me. I do not think he noticed me at all, truth be told. I was content with that. Like the hare, I had no desire to attract the eye of the hawk.

The bear was already chained when we arrived. "I like it best when they are chained by the leg and not by the neck," one of Anne's lesser ladies said to me. " 'Tis better sport when they can reach out to smack the dogs." Many placed bets on the outcome of the baiting. I noticed that the future Countess of Blenheim, Will's sister, Rose, was a particularly enthusiastic gambler.

Women could be partial to blood sport too.

Afore the dogs were set loose someone slid into the seat next to Henry—Cranmer, the priest whom Henry had appointed to be the next archbishop of Canterbury. The old archbishop had passed on some months before and Henry, Anne told me, was eager to replace him with someone who would be sympathetic to His Highness's philosophies.

Cranmer was a learned man, a good man, an admired priest, and, of course, a reformer who had been convicted to *sola scriptura.* He'd also been chaplain to the Boleyns and I knew Anne had a firm hand in his appointment.

The bear caller shouted out, "Tha dogs'll be loose soon, set about ta worry the great beast in fronta ya." He glanced up at the king and, as he did, seemed worried a bit himself at his royal patron. "I baited 'im with blood meself afore the evenin' came so's he's as heated as one a th' old bawds in the stews!"

Henry guffawed at the lewd joke before turning to the priest. "Cranmer!" he boomed. " 'Tis a good sight to see you. I've a mind to settle our discourse on the archbishopric."

"As you wish, sire," Cranmer said.

Was there ever a phrase that Henry found more dear?

We all kept our eyes on the bear as well as the dogs now loosed to attack it, but our ears belonged to the king.

"You can plan to celebrate Easter Mass and, uh"—Henry fumbled, uncharacteristically, for a moment—"Whitsunday as archbishop."

Cranmer noted. " 'Tis as good as done, then, sire?"

" 'Tis as good as done."

The dogs challenged the bear, who lashed out at them, barking, biting, baiting. Chained, the bear could not reach them when they backed away from him. "I can like as feel his breath steam my neck when he roars," I whispered to Anne. She nodded, but I could tell she was mainly concerned with what Henry was saying.

"I shall prepare my thoughts to be read aloud after being invested," Cranmer said. It was getting harder to overhear them now, as the crowd roared along with the bear and barked out encouragement of its own.

"You are, of course, sovereign in all ways now, in your own realm. Parliament shall pass that quickly as well. But, Your Majesty, if any should protest?" Cranmer asked.

Henry didn't answer him; instead, he stood to cheer, for at that very moment the great blond bear broke his chain and roared at the dogs, one after another, violently felling each with a mighty swipe of his paw.

We were rowed home late, and after helping Anne I returned to my room and let Edithe help me undress. I would need my sleep. The next night I would entertain my brothers, Edmund and Thomas, in my apartments, for dinner.

"Welcome, Brothers." I opened the door to my chambers myself. Edithe had helped me to get dressed and Anne had her chef prepare a rich meal to be delivered and had also kindly loaned me one of her menservants.

Thomas breezed in, hugged me tightly, and gave me two kisses on each cheek and one on the top of my head. After popping a sugared plum in his mouth he sat down at my table and poured himself a cup of spiced wine.

Edmund, always more reserved, took my hand, but he, too, looked to be in high spirits.

Edithe glanced at him and they held a gaze of a moment. She looked frightened. Edmund looked confused as to why she was looking at him at all. She quickly curtseyed to me and then left the room. The look that went between them was odd; I could not judge what it meant but I knew it wasn't natural.

Anne's manservant relit a candle that had blown out and then served the oxen and light manchet. Thomas ate hungrily, Edmund sparingly. He mostly talked.

"Baron Blackston is here," he said. "He'll be at the masque tomorrow night, looking for you."

"Of course," I said. "Is everything . . . settled?"

Edmund nodded. "Simon shall discuss it with you himself but yes, as your brothers, we wanted to let you know that 'tis all settled. I handled the financial matters, of course."

"Of course," I said. I was sure he would be oblivious to my irony.

"And Thomas, as eldest brother, of course made the final decision that 'twould be best if you married. 'Tis his right, of course, as Father is . . . unwell."

I looked at Thomas, who would not meet my gaze. "Certainly." My voice was stony. We made small talk of Allington and Edmund seemed of a lighter mood, even talking about perhaps bringing a bride home soon and that the place could use the warmth of a woman's touch.

I pity the woman who must warm you with her caresses, I thought. But I'd learnt to keep my tongue better disciplined.

After an hour or so they made their departure. I tried to get Thomas alone so I could speak with him privately but he stayed well out of my reach. Edmund ensured that Thomas left afore him and closed the door behind them both.

As soon as Anne's serving man cleared the plate and left, Edithe came rushing out into the large chamber. She fell on her knees and clung to my dress.

"Mistress, I must repent. Can you forgive me?"

"Rise, Edithe. Whatever do you mean?" I'd never seen her distraught; rather, 'twas usually I who was distraught and she of a firm mind.

"He came today. He were asking questions, he were. About those letters from Master Will, to you."

I sat her down in a chair by the fire and then pulled another one alongside her. "Who did? Who asked for my letters?"

" 'Twas Master Simon, 'twas. He said Miss Rose, I mean, the countess, told him that there were letters betwixt you and her brother Will and that she herself had delivered many and found them to be . . . indelicate."

Indelicate? Hardly. Mayhap expressive. But not indelicate.

"The letters are long gone," I reassured her.

" 'Tis nothing to worry about. They have been gone for years."

She began to cry again. "He asked me if I knew where they was, lady. He said he'd hurt my Roger and see to it that he never worked again if'n I didn't confess exactly as it was."

Now I was shaking. "But you don't know where they are. Do you, Edithe?"

She nodded. "I do. I took them from you when you were a young girl and had to marry old Baron Blackston. Thought I was doing you a favor, putting Will out of your mind if not out of your heart. I brought the letters to Hever Castle and hid them 'hind a slat in the barn. Thought it not right to destroy them, they not being my property and all."

I stood up. "Did you tell this to Simon?"

She nodded. "I'm sorry, lady. But I was right vexed for my Roger." I turned to gaze out the dark window and think. After a moment she added, quietly, "I didn't tell him about your copy of Master Tyndale's Bible, though. He didn't ask."

I turned to her. "You've found that?"

"I'm your lady maid, mistress. I know everything about you."

Well, at least my calm, plainspoken Edithe was back. I sighed. " 'Tis good."

"I suppose now that I've, now that I've sinned awful against you I shan't be able to read Holy Writ anymore. But 'twas in reading it for meself

241

that I learnt to come and beg forgiveness. I canna understand Latin, course, so mostly I canna understand what 'tis the priest says at Mass."

I tried to keep the look of shock off my face. "You can read?" As soon as I'd said it I was sorry I had. "I mean, you have read it?"

She smiled. "I can read, mistress. Once I found that you had that copy, well, I traded favors with one of the seamstresses who can read. I would work on her sleeves of an evening after you'd gone to bed and she'd teach me how to read. I learnt right quick! And oh, how I've loved hearing from our blessed Lord meself. Who could have thought it? 'Tis as if He's here right aside me!"

The lightness of her face reminded me of Will's when he'd given the Bible to me. I felt some shame for the carelessness with which I'd treated Tyndale's work, God's word, seeking my own comfort within its pages but not the writer Himself. Bilney could be burnt and Edithe spent from lack of sleep and yet I read not but selfishly for my own relief.

I reached my arm out to her. "You may, of course, read it at any time. But I will tell you now. 'Tis not my copy. Do you understand?"

She looked confused but agreed with me. "Yes, my lady, if you say so."

"If I don't own a copy, and someone should come looking for it, you can rightly tell them that I do not own one."

She smiled then. "I understand. But . . . what shall you do about Master Simon?"

"I do not know, Edithe. I do not know. I shall pray."

I sent her to bed and then undressed myself in the chill and quickly crawled under my coverlet. I brought Master Tyndale's translation with me and left one solitary candle lit in the wrought iron candelabra beside my bed. I paged through the Gospel According to Saint Matthew again and saw nothing to spark me. I closed my eyes. I wasn't used to praying without a book of hours to guide me. I missed its reassuring direction.

I freely admit that I come seeking only an answer and comfort, though I wish 'twere not so. I am weak and I am sorry, but I need assistance. What shall I say when Simon asks me of the letters? In the name of the Father, the Son, and the Holy Spirit. Amen.

I crossed myself and then flipped back to the Epistle of Saint Paul to the Romans, chapter 8, and lightly touched the daisy wreath, the one remaining symbol of my love for Will and his for me, the love, as it were, that placed me in this pinch.

I read, *What shall we then say unto these things? If God be on our side: who can be against us?*

I blew out the light and then, in the darkness, whispered, "Please be on my side."

• • •

Now that Henry was married, and it had been consummated, he was ever in a festive mood. I did not understand why, but from mid-January on he grew even more benevolent in his manner and entertainment. A masque celebrating the seasons, though we were in the grip of icy January, was to be held that night. Anne went dressed as summer, her gown a becoming green and her rubies having been set as apples, a badge of fertility.

Henry went "disguised" as the sun.

I helped Anne dress, and as I did, I leaned over and whispered in her ear about the letters Simon had found. She dismissed her other ladies for a moment.

"Were they intimate?" she asked.

"Not unbecomingly so," I answered. "But there would be no room for misunderstanding where our hearts lay."

She nodded and took my hand. "Mayhap you tell him they were a childish infatuation?"

I looked down.

"I know you do not like to misspeak," she said. "But you needn't tell him that your affections persist. For your safety's sake," she said, and I nodded. All knew that women, as chattel, had as many rights as a horse or a plow. We were ever dependent upon the good graces of the men placed over us.

"Well spoken," I said.

"Although Henry and court business take up more and more of my time, my concern and affections for you are ever constant," she said, reaching out to squeeze my hand. She recalled the other ladies and we set about the finishing touches of her preparation.

I sat near Anne at a table with her other ladies-in-waiting, dressed in a gown of russet with layers of mauve, gowns slashed becomingly to reveal the gold kirtle underneath. Though it may have been more popular to appear as spring or summer I knew my looks did better with the warm colors of autumn. I saw Anthony; he met my gaze and looked at me appreciatively but spent the evening admirably concentrating on the wisp of a girl destined, I supposed, to be his wife. Shortly after the music began, Simon, in magnificent winter gray, swooped in and compelled me to dance.

"My bride," he said, yet there was no softness in his voice. His cold hands had grown stronger since the last time I'd seen him, and his face harder. I suspected that the title, and the power and money that went with it, had given him courage. And conceit.

"Sir," I said. " 'Tis good to see you again. When did you arrive?"

"A few days hence," he said. "With only a small retinue of servants to attend to my needs." A volta was struck up, the most intimate of dances,

245

and Simon took the occasion to hold me even closer, tighter, for certes, than was comfortable.

"Not Meredith?" It had seemed to me that, though she had formally been Baron Blackston's maid, she had spent much of her time abiding with Simon.

He fairly spat on the dance floor. "Harlot. She became with child from, who knows, some stable boy, I suppose. I turned her out in her shift. No, I'll leave it to the next baroness to choose the women servants from now on."

I noticed that he hadn't said he'd leave it to me. The music changed to something softer, slower. He drew me near as a lover and nestled his mouth near my neck. I felt near to suffocation but pressed forward. "Since we speak of serving maids, my own lady maid, Edithe, said you had come to pay her a call."

He pulled away, angry, I saw, that I had raised the topic afore he could. "Shall we sit and talk, my lady?"

I nodded and he led me to a vacant table. After sipping some small beer he began the conversation. "The future Countess of Blenheim had suggested to me, upon my arrival, that there were some correspondence I may want to be aware of. She has deep-seated feelings of family loyalty but felt compelled by her noble sense of honor to share with me that you and her brother, the priest, William, had been writing to one another. I went to inquire of you and, as you were out, asked your lady maid for her assistance."

"Edithe indicated to me that you threatened her, not asked for her help," I responded.

He snorted contemptuously. "You believe a lowborn serving girl over the titled man you hope to marry?"

I did not respond.

"I had my man ride out to Hever and, ah, acquire the letters. I've read them. They please me not."

"Your man must have had to race to Kent and back without stopping. And 'tis not often pleasing to read mail intended for another. Thievery begets bad sentiments all round," I said.

" 'Tis not thievery for a man to investigate whether or not his bride has been compromised. So, here is my thought, *my love*. There are no dates on the letters. Mayhap they were written when you were a child, a child who had been wayward and mayhap not well disciplined or brought up to know that this kind of discourse between a man and a maid is unseemly. Or mayhap, as the countess has intimated to me, some of these letters are more recent, between a priest and a woman who is intended for another."

He grew quiet as a servant came to refill his mug and mine. I glanced up and saw Rose's gaze fixed upon me. Her brother Walter had not come, but their ward, Charlotte, danced in the arms of my brother Edmund. The servant left and Simon picked up the malevolent thought he'd left off with.

"Your brother Thomas, all know, married a whore who makes her way round the realm like a coin. I've no intention of doing that, nor risking my son's bloodline with a woman who has an easy shift. Think on this tonight. I shall visit your apartment tomorrow afore the evening meal and you can tell me if these letters, and the sentiments within them, are from long ago or mayhap are still fresh in hand and heart. I bid you a good evening, my lady."

He stood up and took his leave, and as he did, I noticed that others remarked of it. 'Twas common knowledge that we were to be married and his rude dismissal would be noted.

I made my apologies and went back to my room. I did not share my concerns with Edithe as it would only vex her further.

After she helped me to bed I blew out the candle and lay there under the grimace of a cold January moon. I would not sleep all night, and that reminded me of Simon and his physic draughts, ones certain to keep the baron from being intimate with me and therefore from producing an heir to undo Simon. Of feeble-minded Meredith, pregnant more likely by Simon or one of his boon companions than by a stable boy. Of Simon's threat to Roger. Was this a man I could trust with my life or the lives of my future children?

And yet, I had few choices. Edmund would be livid if this did not come to pass. Indeed, he'd like as not been plotting this very outcome with Simon from the beginning. I was not exactly the village old maid but even Anthony, who was older, had been partnered with a much younger and supposedly more fertile bride. My niece was years younger than I and newly wed. And I'd been well trained to understand living with a tyrant.

Anne would not turn me out, this I knew. Perhaps she could help find me a husband.

And strangely, the option I had so long ago dismissed out of hand grew more welcome. *Mayhap I could serve You in an abbey, eventually.*

I allowed myself to sleep, then, to rest my bones for the winter storm I'd face on the morrow. One thing still troubled me. What benefit did this hold for Rose, and why had she approached Simon?

SEVENTEEN

Year of Our Lord 1533
Greenwich Palace
The Tower of London

Simon appeared early the next afternoon. I met him in the greeting room of my apartments.

"You are right," I said. "My sentiments remain as they are expressed in the letters."

"I knew it!" he screamed. "You've been betraying me, and my uncle, all along. Your family's contemptible morals are never better displayed than in these debauched letters."

"Come now. Debauched? Hardly. I do not act upon those feelings. Nor does the man in question, if he even holds them at present."

Simon's face was still twisted. "So you say, though I do not believe you, nor am I certain that you had not acted on them afore and may well again in the future. I have no desire to share my wife, neither her affections nor her caresses, with another. I would likely take you to wife only to find that you are not a maid."

I looked him in the eye and kept my voice low. "Why ever would you expect to find me a maid, Baron? I am a widow, you recall."

He returned my gaze, malevolently, then blinked like a lizard. "I leave, immediately, to inform your brothers that my offer of betrothal has been withdrawn."

Within an hour Edmund burst through my door and took me by the hair. "For what means, Sister, do you speak to Lord Blackston of lies? You have had no correspondence with Will Ogilvy. I'd know."

Mayhap he had spies?

"I have not claimed that," I choked out, my neck bent backward. "Simon stole old letters and made of it what he would."

He let go of my hair and shoved me into a chair. "They should have been burned long ago. They should never have been written. I myself would not marry a woman so compromised. So you've ruined your life. Fool! Then where will you go?" he taunted. "Because of your imprudence you have set aside years of planning and negotiations. I've already paid a dowry for you with the highest titled position you could hope for. I will not allow Father to pay another, bankrupting us for your lack of judgment."

I knew this was coming, because it always came down to money and position with Edmund, and yet still took chill. There was no honorable way for me to marry any man above a serf without a dowry, and no good family would take on that shame. "I can serve Her Grace forever. Or the king will provide a dowry for me. Or I'll go to an abbey."

Edmund laughed. "There will be no abbeys left when the king is done dismantling the Church's properties. And he will not be willing to pay a dowry for a disobedient wench. Cromwell keeps a good hand on the king's money, as I know. Even *Lady Anne,*" he said with contempt, "must pay expenses of her own pocket or beg the king to cover her debts."

There had been rumors that the king was considering reclaiming the monasteries from the Church in Rome for the Church in England.

Anne's plan was to use them to provide income for the poor, traditionally the responsibility of the Church, which would now become the king's purview and which she had hoped to administer for the good of the needy. Could Henry really be planning to empty them into his own coffers?

If 'twere so . . . there might be no abbeys left where unmarried highborn women may live out their lives in a gentle manner. Deep in thought, I was distracted and didn't see him swing.

He hit me with a closed fist. From experience, I knew it would bruise and I'd need to remain in my rooms for days. "Do not come looking to me for assistance. You are on your own. And if I should hear any rumors that call my own reputation in question over this matter or any other I will put word about of your indecency, embellished, if necessary, which will make you unfit for royal service to a queen."

I had Edithe send for Anne and she came as soon as she could. Edithe let her in and she found me in my bedchamber, where I lay, quietly, on my bed. *Forgive me, Lord. I now imbibe too often of a convenient mistruth.* And yet, I had feared for my life.

When Anne came into the room I rose to approach her and she settled me back onto my bed.

"No, no, do not disturb yourself," she said. She ran a finger around the bruise on my face. " 'Tis not a trivial wound." She sent Edithe to her rooms to instruct her lady maid to ask the king's physician for some ointment. "What happened, dearest?"

I poured out my story to her, holding nothing back. "Was I wrong? Wrong to admit to it? Wrong to do so knowing he would refuse me?"

She held me in her arms. "It matters not now, either way. 'Tis done and your conscience intact." After a moment she continued. "The king and I steal away to be married—again. This time in front of a court priest, Rowland Lee. Henry Norris will witness as well as Sir Heneage. I'd wanted you to come, but I think it best be Lady Berkeley."

I nodded. "I shan't be able to be seen for a bit. Mayhap when the swelling goes down the gossip will too." Of course all would know that I had been repudiated.

"No one will speak against you," she promised, "for fear of me." I took comfort in that, for I knew it to be true. "And when my son is born, I shall ask the king, as an especial favor to me, to give you a dowry so you may marry a kind man of the gentry or a second-born son."

"Thank you, madam," I said. Even she knew that she could only push Henry's purse so far. Then it struck me. "A son is to be born? *Your* son?"

She nodded and laughed. " 'Tis why we go to be married anew. I am with child and Henry wants to ensure there is no question can be raised of his legality."

I held her in my arms. "A son! A son, Your Grace!" I joined her in laughter. "I am sorry I cannot serve you in this matter. Lady Berkeley will do well by you, I know."

"Hush now," she said maternally. I'd not seen her that way. Mayhap it was the child within her made her so. "I've already asked her," she said. So she'd asked Lady Berkeley before she knew of my bruises. For a brief moment I wondered if asking Lady Berkeley to be a witness was to punish me for the linens at her first wedding. But I pushed the thought away.

She took her leave shortly thereafter, and she and Henry were married, quietly, at York Place. Whilst few had been privy to the knowledge of the first marriage, which had been performed mainly to set Anne at ease, the king made sure all knew of this one, upon which rode the legitimacy of his son.

I healed, of a time, and the pitiful looks stopped coming my way. *Surely,* I thought, *Henry will be so overjoyed at the birth of his prince that he will indeed give Anne whatever she wants, including a dowry for me, mistress of the robes, faithful friend of a lifetime.*

And if not, mayhap there would be abbeys remaining. Cromwell could not dismantle them *all,* for certes. There were hundreds. *I am willing now to thus serve You, of my own free will. If indeed I have been called of purpose.*

In the dark months of Lent I quietly attended reformer meetings held at court. Anne was not the only one nurturing new life. Within the quiet, nourishing womb of the meetings my tiny faith began to grow.

Just before Easter Thomas Cromwell unveiled the next stage of his legal masterpiece, the Statute in Restraint of Appeals, before Parliament.

"What does this mean?" I asked Anne. We were in her chambers fitting her for the magnificent pleated cloth-of-gold gown she would wear to Easter Mass, the first time she would be publicly prayed for as queen. I carefully buffed the jewels encrusting her gold crown.

"His Grace read me the documents," she said, caring not at all that others were in the room to listen. "It means that the king is the final legal authority in all matters involving England, Wales, and indeed anywhere that is an English possession."

The seamstress hadn't pulled the waist tight enough and Anne adjusted it for her before continuing. "Cromwell has built an unshakable case proving that England is an independent empire. Which means that the English crown is actually an imperial crown. The title 'pope' was originally assigned to the ruling Roman caesars, *pontifex maximus*, and not to religious leaders; the case is proved both by Scripture and by tradition that Henry is ruler over all things in his own land."

Jane Rochford snorted and Anne silenced her with a look. I had to admit, though I agreed with the logic, I thought Anne's lecture a bit tiresome too. It troubled my pride that she felt the need to educate me on Latin, in which I had always excelled. Truth be told, she'd been lecturing all a bit more often since her wedding.

"So when Parliament passes this act," I said, and it was a foregone conclusion that it would, "no one can appeal beyond him, not to another ruler, not to the pope, on any matter."

"Exactly," Anne said. "Henry will be subject to no power, temporal or spiritual, on earth." She turned and looked at me, smoothing her hands over her slightly bulging belly. "Does this do?"

I smiled. "All will recognize your position now, Your Grace."

And Henry's.

After Mass at Easter my brother Thomas came to my rooms. "Thomas!" I looked behind him to see if Edmund had come with him. Thomas blushed, apparently aware of what I was doing.

"I come alone," he reassured me. "Would you like to walk in the gardens?"

"Indeed." I let my lady maid know where I was going—I had given Edithe leave to spend

Easter at Hever—and then took my brother's arm. The tulips bloomed and the bees buzzed merrily about the dew-tipped grass, throbbing with a green so pure that it hurt the eyes to look at for long. Thomas took my hand and led me to a great stone bench by the river. A swan and its mate glided slowly toward us.

"They mate for life, you know," I said. "Once given they never retreat."

"Admirable," Thomas said. "Mayhap we can learn something from them." He took my hand in his. "Meg, I've come to apologize. I had no idea how your betrothal with the baron was going to work out. Edmund had led me to believe that Simon was a good man and that was best for you."

I nodded. "Why didn't you speak with me?"

"'Tis shameful to admit it, but Edmund paid my debts for me and increased the money I get from Father each month. And, well, I own that he made me feel important. All know that, in practice, he is the elder brother and I the wastrel. He played upon my pride to get me to agree. In reality, I fear it was only to bully you by a show of force."

I rested my head on his shoulder. "It is well and good, Thomas. You are not a wastrel. You are a gifted poet, a writer, a gentleman, a tender heart, a loving father. 'Tis how God made you. And Edmund cannot take Allington from you."

"No, but Father has given him leave of the

finances to run it and all other properties and interests," Thomas admitted. I confess, my heart sank at the news.

"I cannot take back my actions," he said. "But I wanted you to know I repent of them. And anyway, Edmund has been paid back in full, for certes."

I lifted my head and looked in his eyes. "What do you mean?"

"You haven't heard? The Earl of Blenheim's ward, Mistress Charlotte, the one that Edmund was keen to marry, is now betrothed to Simon instead. His title, and fortune, are both greater than Edmund's. Marriage negotiations are already under way."

"Which is why Rose was so interested in ensuring I did not marry the baron," I said.

"I'd wager," Thomas said. "Edmund was in a murderous rage for weeks. He avoided court so as not to see them together. I hear from Master Cromwell, though, that he may have found another bride."

"I pity her," I said. "And Charlotte. Rose was no friend to her to hand her over to Simon."

Thomas nodded and then replied, "I leave for Essex tomorrow but will be back, along with my wife and son, for Anne's coronation in May. I am to serve as her ewer, in Father's place, as he is too unwell to attend. The king has not forgotten Father's friendship with his own father." He looked at the mated swans, now slipping past us. "Will Ogilvy will be here too. I hear from our nephew John Rogers that Ogilvy does not do well."

On the twenty-ninth of May, Anne was sumptuously conveyed from Greenwich Palace to her quarters at the Tower of London, which Master Cromwell had refurbished in advance. I and many of her other ladies would be quartered nearby, of course, to provide comfort and amusement and assistance. It was the zenith of her life and she shimmered like a mirage on a hot summer day. There was much merriment in the ladies' chamber for two days, with minstrels and mimes and jugglers, and then, on Saturday, the procession to Westminster, climaxing on Whitsunday, when Anne was to be crowned.

I found it poignant that her coronation would be held on Whitsunday, celebrating the Day of Pentecost, when our Lord sent the Holy Ghost to give us wisdom to learn how to live in this world afore we joined Him, to lend comfort in the distress we oft found in the walls in which we lived. I stood next to the archbishop of Canterbury as Anne alighted into her litter. She had on a brilliant gown made of white cloth of gold, which were, for the moment, hidden by her thick royal coronation robes of purple velvet furred with ermine. The gold coronet on her head signaled her royalty while her bare feet signaled her humility to serve—Christ first, and then husband, and then subjects. As mistress of her robes I had acquired that material specially for this day, bartering like a furious fishwife with the royal cloth merchants to make it affordable within her Pembroke moneys and promising harsh retaliations should they foresell the same fabric to anyone else.

It was worth it, to see her on that day. Twelve ladies dressed in crimson cloth of gold would ride beside her, followed by carriage after carriage of serving nobility and visiting dignitaries.

"She is magnificent," Cranmer said, staring at her admiringly, as did all along the way who serenaded her and read aloud poems and scriptures lauding her.

Not all brought praise. On the way to Westminster Abbey, there had lined some women who stood back far enough not to be seen but certainly within range to be heard, and to throw evil-smelling things.

"Bawd!" one shouted, and threw a ball of muck at her carriage.

"Schemer!" another cried. Several more orbs of refuse were lobbed at the carriage afore the king's men put a stop to it. I, in a carriage several behind the queen, saw the hate in their faces. And, mayhap, fear. They had not the time, nor the ability, nor the inclination to reason with the legal omniscience that was Cromwell's *Collectanea*, nor consider the future of the realm. They did not know, as I did, that Anne had saved herself for her marriage, a marriage the king had assured her was moral and just as his first one was not. These lowly women simply saw that if 'twas legal for the king to set aside his aging wife and marry again, what would stop their husbands from doing the same?

I took my seat at the abbey along with my niece, Alice's daughter Margaret, nicknamed Margery, who had recently married Sir Anthony Lee. "Dowager Baroness," the knight who showed us to our seats said, calling me by my proper title.

There, next to my young, newlywed niece, waiting for my beautiful, fertile friend to be crowned, I felt the weight of the age that the word "dowager" implied, though I was but a few clock dials past thirty. Margery must have caught my cheerless look.

"Do you ever wish 'twas you?" she whispered to me, feeling safe, I suspect, because of the cover of the music.

"As queen?" I answered. "No, never."

"And yet," she pressed on in curiosity, "you who were her friend and equal now must serve her instead and have no family nor husband of your own. 'Tis not so beguiling."

I did not chide her. I rather recognized myself in her, as a younger woman, asking impertinent questions of my sister, her mother, the lady Alice.

"A lady-in-waiting is a noble post," I said. "A

lady's value is not vested in the work that she is called to do, but rather in the rank and position of the one she is called to serve."

Margery nodded and returned to ogling the fine gowns and crowns around her.

I, though, was drawn to look at the crucifix with our Lord upon it, vaunted near the flying buttresses that quietly held up the abbey. As the trumpeters and minstrels came forth I knew I had an answer to the question I'd pressed upon our Lord again and again since coming to the passage in Master Tyndale's translation of the Epistle of Saint Paul to the Romans, chapter 8. Had I been called of purpose?

In a moment as quick as lightning striking a stump I understood that my call was to serve them both. Margery was right. It was not so beguiling. For that flashing moment, I abided the pain of ever going unheralded. *Always the setting,* I'd said of myself as a child. *Never the stone.* And yet a stone wanted for a setting to vaunt its purpose and beauty, did it not? 'Twas the call of the setting not to draw attention to itself but to the stone. My eyes drew back to that stone.

Anne walked forward, majestically, regally, along the railed route of seven hundred yards between the dais of the hall and the high altar of the abbey. Over her head was carried a gold canopy and she was preceded by a scepter of gold and rod of ivory topped with the dove.

After High Mass was sung Cranmer prayed over her and Anne prostrated herself before the altar, where he anointed her and then led her to St. Edward's chair, where she was crowned.

I looked up as my dearest friend was crowned queen of England by the archbishop of Canterbury. Her years of patience, of obedience, of political savvy and personal achievement, her enduring affection, yea, even true love for the king had all been invested for this moment. And the fruit of it was the prince who grew within her.

Henry had planned days of celebration. I admit to it: I hadn't bargained with the cloth merchant only on Anne's behalf. I had purchased some fine materials for myself, my favorite a vibrant green taffeta to put all in mind of spring and new life with tiny pears embroidered with gold thread around the slightly daring neckline. I'd have gowns sewn which I hoped would entirely dismiss the "dowager" in my title from all who set eyes upon me.

EIGHTEEN

Year of Our Lord 1533
The Palace at Whitehall

The king had ordered jousts for June 2 that were full of shouting and sweat and spectacle, to be followed by a grand ball for the evening. Every person of consequence from the Welsh marches to the border with Scotland and even far-flung Calais arrived at the court, which gasped for air, it was so overburdened, to celebrate Anne's coronation and the forthcoming birth of the Prince of Wales. I took care to ready Anne first and then stopped back at her apartments to check on her after being dressed myself in a gown that shimmered now azure, now jade, depending on the light and my own movement. My neckline was just north of daring, and though I'd privately bemoaned my childless state, it had allowed me to keep my figure intact. I wore a single large emerald set in gold round my neck and its accompanying bracelet, a gift from Anne the Christmas before. Edithe had becomingly twisted my golden-red hair and woven a thread of gold throughout it.

"You look like a peacock," Jane Rochford pronounced as I arrived. The rest of the room laughed at her and I pursed my lips modestly to hold back a grin, for I knew she was wrong.

" 'Tis in no way true," Mary Howard said. "Her dress is second only to Her Majesty's and you, Jane Rochford, are as jealous as an alehouse on Sunday morn."

'Twas a pity, really. Anne sought to do well by her friends and 'twould not have taken too much for Jane to befriend Anne, who'd wanted that, for George's sake, all along. Anne's mother, as mistress of the privy chamber, took Jane aside for, presumably, a private instruction on decorum. Lady Boleyn was fighting a battle that could never be won.

We followed Anne down the long stone halls from her apartments to the Banqueting Hall and thence to the Long Chamber, which had been set up to accommodate dancing, celebrations, and conviviality all evening. Anne was lifted onto a dais near the king, and after we'd helped to serve her, we partook of the feast ourselves.

After the banquet the king had the musicians strike up to play and, to my surprise, danced first with some of Anne's ladies. Including myself!

He held out his hand to me. "My lady?"

I curtseyed and took his hand. He swept me into his arms. Yea, his eyes were still a bit beady and his face was reddened under his great beard due to the effort of a day of jousting and an evening of dance. But his power and his wealth and his self-confidence and even his still-handsome face bonded together in an alchemy of presence that was visceral and undeniable and took even my breath away. He looked down at me and smiled. He knew he still had the genius of charm.

"You do not look of a dowager to me," he teased, and I blushed. Did he truly know all? How could he have guessed what my intent was in dressing myself thusly? He seemed to repent of the tease. "But 'tis the prerogative of a beautiful lady and I would have it no other way at my court," he said. "You have been a constant and true companion to the queen. I thank you for your friendship to her."

" 'Tis my pleasure, sire," I said. And then he, like any other man present and yet not like any other man present, for certes, made pleasant conversation till the song was over. He bowed gallantly and went to sweep a young blond lady-in-waiting into his arms.

I had no lack of other dance partners waiting. Anthony Litton was there and we passed a friendly hour; Henry Percy danced with me. There were plenty of others. But there was only one I'd really come looking for.

I'd spied him across the room, of course. I knew that he would be the first person I would seek out with mine eyes, but neither my pride nor my reputation would allow me to approach him first, especially with the trace of gossip after Simon had refuted me still scenting the air. I caught his eyes upon me several times but his look was different from the last time he had looked upon me thus. It was not filled with repressed desire and emotional longing. It was somehow unsettling, though I could not clearly see how. My heart sank. Was my fine dress to catch the attention of all men, including the king, save the one I had it in mind to impress? And yet, mayhap he had moved on in heart and mind, as was well and right and as it should be.

I'd not been able to do likewise.

He finally came to me. "Would you care to take a respite of your continuous merrymaking, my lady?" he teased. Though I should have to repent of it later, I was well pleased to hear a suggestion of possessiveness in his voice.

"I would rest a spell and keep company with you, Will Ogilvy," I said, having not a care for the Jane Rochfords of this world, who were certainly training their eyes upon us. I was safe within Anne's, and the king's, circlet of protection.

Will smiled, his eyelids crinkling with real pleasure, throwing off for a moment the shadows that dogged them. He took my hand, and I melted with the familiar, most welcome touch of it as he led me to a table well within the public gaze but without the focus of attention.

We made merry talk for a while and I shared, quietly, how he had pleased me through the gift of the New Testament, and how I had grown and changed because of it. " 'Tis a good thing you are not often here," I said. "I may be prepared to spar with you again—and win!" I brought up a passage I found, mayhap cumbersomely translated, and wondered of his opinion. He smiled and shared a thought, but his heart seemed heavy. I knew why.

I thought mayhap he would suggest meeting me in the gardens on the morrow. Instead, he said, "I would like to speak with you privately too. Can you come to my chambers later this night?"

My face must have shown my surprise.

" 'Tis all honorable," he was quick to reassure me.

At that, I laughed. "I do not think that you have ever had a dishonorable intent, Will Ogilvy, however much I should have liked to have disovered one and held it against you for blackmail or to make my own mixed motives appear more seemly."

He smiled back. "Oh, lady, then mayhap you do not know me as well as you think." His eyes drew me in with their sense of familiarity and I blushed. "I am thus trapped and cannot decide whether to disabuse you of your false, but flattering, notions or let you continue to entertain them and envision me as heroic." He leaned closer to me and whispered, "In any case, I shall stay here for another hour, and if you can disentangle yourself without being noticed, meet me in my quarters." He explained to me where he would be chambered and that he would leave a small slip of paper peeping out from under his door so I would know that it was the right one.

I made light conversation with some others, danced a few songs, and then slipped away. Although my gown was tight enough to bruise my rib cage and my feet begged to escape their tight slippers, pride won, and I remained in my fine dress. I soon found his chambers and, after looking about me to ensure that I had not been followed, knocked lightly.

He opened the door and allowed me in. Although we'd already greeted one another earlier he drew near to me and gently kissed each cheek. Though his family was highborn his rooms were only two, a sleeping chamber and a greeting chamber, where we sat. He had modestly closed the door to the sleeping chamber. "Please," he said, pointing to the most comfortable chair next to the fire, and then handed me a small cup of wine. He sat down next to me and I couldn't help but let my thoughts wander to what it might have been like had we been able to sit together of an evening, every evening, and exchange thoughts on the day and other pleasantries.

"Will, I must confess something," I said. "I spoke indiscreetly about you. My brother wanted me to marry Baron Blackston, Simon, and I was about to. But there were things that frightened me." I explained to him about the sleeping draughts, and the temper, and my fear that I myself could end up at the mercy of Simon's London physic should I become inconvenient someday. "And so I admitted to still . . . caring for you. Though I assured him nothing improper was between us he was disinclined to believe it. I fear it may call your reputation into question."

He nodded. "I know of the matter. Rose told me in an effort to blacken your name because she wanted the baron for Charlotte. You've done nothing wrong. I am glad you are out of his grasp."

Relief swelled within me and I let a few tears slip down my face. "I could not have lived with your ill opinion of me."

He reached over and tenderly wiped the tears from my cheek. "There is nothing and no one who could ever compel me to hold an ill opinion of you, Meg," he said. His voice was rough and he took a care to keep a distance between us. "And now, there is something I'd like to speak of to you."

I nodded and sipped my wine.

"As you well know, I've been serving the merchants in Antwerp as chaplain. But I've also done some translating, and have been of late helping to get Tyndale's copy of the New Testament printed in England, to save shipping fees and the danger of import, so it might be more widely distributed."

I nodded. " 'Tis noble work."

He hung his head. "I am afraid I am not so noble. Because of my father's rank and title I felt that I was well able to prevail upon those who are better funded to provide money for the presses here in London. I also felt myself to be a fine judge of good character. Only I was mistaken. Lord Abney had indicated an interest in our work and, blinded by pride, I invited him to a meeting. I wanted to show all that I had powerful connections as well as bring good to the cause."

"I thought Abney was a strong conservative," I said. "He has no use for English Bibles."

" 'Tis true," Will said. "Only he professed otherwise and I was so eager to get his goodwill and fortune that I disclosed too much to him. He arrived at the meeting, took note of all who were there, and reported back to Cromwell."

"Oh," I said, horrified. "But surely Cromwell, as a reformer, took their case."

"Cromwell may be a reformer, but he is also the holder of the king's purse strings and a lawyer, a man building his own fortunes. 'Tis illegal to run the presses for Scripture in English. 'Tis illegal to print without paying tax, but how can one pay tax on that which is illegal?"

I nodded and sipped my wine. "What happened?"

He let his head drop into his hands. "Cromwell savagely enforced the law. All lost their positions, and Chelsey's presses were confiscated, as were all of his materials and receipts, leaving his family penniless and without means to support themselves." His voice broke at the end.

" 'Tis not your fault," I said, reaching over to take hold of his arm. "We are all righteous and yet still sinners." I quoted Luther's famous saying, heard often at reformist meetings.

Will took his head from his hands and looked at me. "I suspect I am more sinner than righteous. A good man has lost his means because of me. His family is broken. As I have taken vows of poverty and have little means, I have asked my father to reimburse Chelsey. My father has refused."

"I'm sorry," I said quietly. "What can I do?"

He looked me in the eye. "You can advise me if I should leave the priesthood or not. I fear that I am more man than priest, more proud than humble"—he looked away and finished—"more flesh than spirit, sometimes. I tire with the struggle and yet know not what to do. I trust you. I value your opinion. I need your counsel. I have no one else to ask who considers both my needs and our Lord's. My other friends will invariably favor one side or the other. Not you."

My head and heart throbbed. Was he really asking me to tell him whether or not to leave the priesthood? Sitting here, alone, in his chambers? I, unmarried and in favor with the king, and Anne ripe with the son who would not only deliver the kingdom but my dowry in just a few months?

"That's not a decision I can make," I said. *Though I'd like to.*

"I ask you not to make the decision. I ask you to offer counsel," he said. "Will you pray about it and meet me tomorrow night and share your thoughts?"

I nodded. He leaned over and rested his head heavily on my shoulder. I looked wistfully at the beckoning thick brown locks but obediently kept my hands at my sides. It put me in mind of Saint Paul's letter to the Galatians wherein he exhorts Christians to bear one another's burdens. *I would gladly do so if 'twere Will's burdens I could carry.*

Shortly after, I slipped back to my room and the next morn I thought through my dilemma. Anne's coronation was too public of an event for me to miss anything at all, and she was always surrounded by ladies, or His Majesty, so there was no way for me to even talk with her about my situation. I loved my sister, Alice, but she would not be a help here because, I knew, she would always take our Lord's part, but I had to consider both. Afore dinner I rested in my room and took out the New Testament. I opened it up and it fell open to Romans 8 because of the wreath. I glanced down at the verse I'd looked at so many times, lately with fulfillment and joy; my eye was drawn directly to it. This time, though, the verse brought me not comfort but pain. I sat there till I was certain I had an answer that did right by our Lord and Will. 'Twas just as well he hadn't asked me to consider my own needs along with theirs or my answer might have been quite different. Once certain, I gathered the dried wreath of daisies into a small silken pouch and went to meet Will.

I passed the Duchess of Norfolk in the hallway. "My lady Duchess," I said politely. She grunted at me, chewed out a command to her lady servant, and swished away. Not yet dinnertime and she smelt of soured wine.

When I was certain the hallway was empty I knocked quietly on Will's door. He opened it up and let me in. He was casually dressed in a dark brown riding outfit and never, ever looked finer to mine eyes. The injustice of it all screamed inside me and I held my inner tongue lest I lash out at God and undo what years of tight weaving of faith and circumstance had accomplished to close the breach between us.

"Meg." He took one look at my face and knew. "You cannot advise me to leave the priesthood," he said, closing the door behind him.

We sat, side by side, nearly leg by leg, in front of the fire. "I must rather ask you questions," I said. "Not advise."

"Go on," he replied.

"What will you do if you return to Antwerp?"

"Miles Coverdale is completing a copy of the entire Bible in English. Not just the New Testament! He draws from Tyndale, of course, who drew from Wycliffe, but also from the Latin Vulgate, and, well, he has asked me to be of assistance to him. De Keyser will publish it," Will said. "Another bit of information is that de Keyser's young sister-in-law, Adriana, is keen for your nephew, John Rogers."

"No!" I said. I had heard nothing of it. "Poor girl." I understood.

Will shook his head. "I don't know. Mayhap John will leave the priesthood for her."

I was tempted to ask what further complication could arise to make this conversation more difficult for me but, lest I entice some eavesdropping demon to creative action, I did not.

We remained quiet for a moment longer, our breathing in rhythm. I finally asked the question I knew I must. "When you chose this course of action so many years ago and told me, in the garden at Hever, you said you were called. Are you still? Or have you been released from that call?"

He closed his eyes and I waited, hoping with everything within me that he would say that he had run his race and was now released.

"I am not released," he said.

I nodded. "I knew it as I said it." I looked in his

275

eyes, aching not only for himself but also for me.

" 'Tis not always so beguiling to serve, is it?" I echoed Margery's comment to me.

He smiled at the girlish phrasing. "No, 'tis not." He looked at me for a moment longer. "And yet God is worthy of service we may deem as unlovely. As Christ demonstrated Himself."

I nodded my agreement and let my tears fill my eyes afore blinking them away.

"Your eyes are deeper green when you cry." He took my hand.

I smiled and then stood and kissed him on one cheek, and then on the other. "I'd best take my leave." I handed him the silk bag with the daisy chain in it. "To remember me by," I said.

He took it with his left hand but didn't open it. He took my right hand into his own and kissed the back of it. "*Nihilo quo tui meminerim mihi opus est.*"

I need nothing to remember you by.

He returned to Antwerp, and I remained at the court, which was feverishly preparing for the birth of a prince.

NINETEEN

Years of Our Lord 1533 and 1534
Hampton Court Palace
Greenwich Palace
Whitehall Palace

We spent the summer at Hampton Court, cool and refreshed in Wolsey's well-designed gardens of knots and herbs whilst mother ducks escorted their ducklings to the muddy Thames and the great wide-open. Anne was nigh on ready to deliver the babe and though she never indicated to anyone, not even to me, that she was concerned lest the baby not be a prince, I knew it was heavy upon her because I knew her mind.

One evening after dinner Anne retired to her rooms to rest and when she returned to the king's chambers, where we'd all gathered of an evening to play cards, she found the king laughing and flirting with a pretty lady-in-waiting, the one he had partnered at dance immediately after me at Anne's coronation banquet. I believe she was the niece of Lady Daughtry, who had fairly pushed her into the king's view. The young woman didn't seem to mind and didn't seem to be as innocent as her laughter.

"What goes on here?" Anne said loudly enough

for all present to hear. "I take my leave for a moment, to rest with your child, and when I return I find this strumpet"—she pointed at the young woman in question—"having taken my rightful place?"

Oh, Anne. No. No, dearest. Having grown up with a reasonable father she'd not had to learn to temper her tongue. I'd heard her argue with His Majesty in times past, but ever with an ear to her tone, to win him as a partner or spar with him as a friend. And in private. Henry was not a man to lightly brook being rebuked in public by his wife.

"Madam, you will contain yourself. And if I choose to dally of an hour with a *young* maiden, you shall shut your eyes and endure as your betters have done." His face was mottled like an ale drinker's nose and as red. "You ought to know that it is in my power to humble you again in a moment more than I have exalted you."

Anne stood, mouth open and seemingly stunned. Then she wisely closed her mouth and said nothing further. She was not a woman to run from the room in a tantrum. Instead, by her manner, she dismissed the young woman, curtseyed to the king, and took her leave to sulk. In spite of my pleading, she refused to talk to him for a day, for two days. After the third, I'd convinced her to approach him soothingly, and she, finally seeing the wisdom in this, approached him to repent. He took her in his open arms. I hoped that she had learnt that lesson once and well. But I knew her better.

We moved to Greenwich, where the king and his beloved lady mother, Queen Elizabeth, had both been born, at the end of August. Henry set about making preparations for celebrations for the arrival of the prince, including jousts to observe the arrival of a new member to royal manhood. He had banners printed proclaiming the arrival of the prince. Edward was in favor for the prince's name, and the date, of course, was unknown till the night of September 6, when Anne felt the first pains. We were cloistered with women, of course, as Anne had withdrawn for her lying and thus from male company till well after the birth. She was holding a reading, arguing spiritedly with dear Lady Zouche and me, and then of a sudden she grew quiet.

" 'Tis time," she said. " 'Tis time."

We hastily cleared the tables and helped her to her chamber, which was well prepared and waiting. After undoing her stays I helped her into the gown we'd chosen for the birthing and brought round thick stacks of linens needed for the birth. The midwife was there with her knives. By midnight we'd stoked the fire higher to bring the room to a fever, which would forestall one in the queen. Anne moaned lightly in pain as the contractions came and went.

Lady Boleyn took her daughter by the arm to attempt to comfort her and ease the pain. At dawn

Anne's waters streamed forth and I helped her walk about the room whilst the linens were changed, then helped her back to bed. By midday Anne was panting, sweating, calling out in long, drawn-out moans that clearly indicated her anguish but remained, nevertheless, in her control.

"Lord, Lord," she cried out. "Assist me. And the prince!"

At three o'clock in the afternoon the midwife urged her, "Push, madam. Push again. There ya go, 'e's coming now, 'e is. Push!" I prayed and willed the baby into the rank, stuffy room diffused with blood and tears and sweat.

As the baby's head crowned I felt profoundly happy for Anne, and deeply sad for myself. A visceral ache heated my own legs and womanhood; I yearned with the desire to birth a child myself, something even the lowest-born woman could do but that seemed to have been denied me. I was drawn back to the moment, though, by a sharp cry. The baby's cry. I looked as the midwife scooped the baby into linens and then handed him to me whilst she helped Anne expel the afterbirth and Lady Boleyn dabbed Anne's brow. I wiped the blood from the baby's face and limbs. I peeled the linen back long enough to look.

'Twas a girl.

Lord Jesus, no. Lord Jesus, please do not do this to Anne. She has been your champion.

Both Lady Boleyn and Anne glanced at me and

I shook my head, just a little, to indicate that it was not the hoped-for prince after all. Anne fell back into her bedding; her black eyes sank deeper yet into their sockets. I handed the baby over to Lady Boleyn to be cleaned and went to comfort my friend. The look on Anne's mother's face was one of dread.

His Majesty came in later, presumably to fawn over his daughter and encourage his wife. He did neither. Although both king and queen put a good show on for observers, all knew that it had not been for another daughter that Henry had challenged the world. Although he commented politely on the babe's coloring—his coloring—the celebratory jousts were canceled.

Three days hence the baby was christened Elizabeth after both Anne's and Henry's mothers. Every noble in the realm save Anne, who was recovering, was present. The Dowager Duchess of Norfolk bore the baby into the hall, in the center of which stood the great silver baptismal font which had been specially brought from Canterbury and filled with warm water. The church blazed with light: five hundred torches carried by the king's guards were lit as it was proclaimed, "God, of His infinite goodness, send prosperous life and long to the high and mighty Princess of England, Elizabeth."

I was vexed. This was not the son Anne needed. What would God offer through this tiny pink princess with Anne's slender fingers and Henry's red hair?

And yet, I loved her deeply from first sight.

Most of the courtiers kept their heads down and their comments pleasing. But I saw the glance that coursed from Sir Carewe to Suffolk and back again. It was one of delight, and mayhap victory.

In December the princess Elizabeth was moved to her own household at nearby Hatfield, to protect her health and demonstrate her status. I encouraged Anne, who missed the princess's daily visits, to cheer herself for the Christmas court.

"Why?" she asked, her voice laced with melancholy.

Recalling our vow to honesty, I replied, "The king already has a daughter, lady. Your well-being depends upon your ability to bring forth life again, and quickly, dearest. A son."

In February we went to visit Princess Elizabeth, who was sharing a household with Henry's older daughter, Mary. Our royal entourage, large and befitting of the newborn princess, arrived at the redbrick residence, which was tall and stout in the middle and yet had wings flung on either side like open arms. Henry had permanently separated Mary from her mother, Katherine of Aragon. After having a daughter of her own Anne said to me, " 'Tis a sorrowful thing for a mother to be separated from her daughter. I shall try to make a peace between us so Mary has a place at court, which may, at least, soften things a little."

Lady Bryan, who was Anne's cousin, had been Mary's governess and was in charge of the princess Elizabeth's household now. As she cared for both girls she could, mayhap, see a way to bring peace.

"If Mary will only acknowledge me as queen and Elizabeth as princess," Anne told Lady Bryan, "I shall see to it that all goes well for her. That she is well married, well provided for; I shall bridge a peace between Mary and His Majesty. 'Tis so little to ask." We had only rare contact with Mary and did not know what to expect. The look on Lady Bryan's face told us what we could expect, though: we would not be warmly received. She came back shortly thereafter. Her face looked as though she now regarded this royal appointment with regret.

"Mary refuses to leave her chambers but has sent a message." She looked directly at Anne. "She shall not call Elizabeth 'princess,' as she claims there is only one princess, herself. But out of courtesy, she calls the Duke of Richmond, her father's bastard son, 'brother,' and as her father acknowledges Elizabeth as his own she is prepared to address her as 'sister.'"

Anne said nothing but sat down in the nicest of the nearby chairs. "And me?" Anne asked in a tight but quiet voice.

"She will not see you. She knows no queen in England save her mother. She refers to you as 'my lady Pembroke,' " Lady Bryan said.

The next day after a bracing, refreshing ride out in the forest park around Hatfield, Anne tried again. "I understand that Mary may reserve some ill will for me, but mayhap we shall find peace if we each yield some to one another."

Lady Bryan returned. "She will not see you, madam."

"Then I shall not seek her goodwill again, nor offer mine!" Anne shouted, her voice shrilly bouncing off the stone walls, as of yet unhung with royal tapestry. "Rather I shall work to bring down the pride of this unbridled Spanish blood!"

We remained for another day or two, Anne holding and rocking Elizabeth and leaving instructions for her wardrobe, her household, and her diet. I mainly swaddled the baby close to me and breathed deeply of her tiny, perfect head and little mouth, puckered like a purse. My sorrow over my childlessness was provoked anew at least twice a day; a tide of grief flowed forward, then resignation pulled it back.

Sir Nicolas Carewe did not participate in the dining celebrations Anne had planned for Elizabeth. Notably, he took his meal in Mary's chambers.

As we rode home to Greenwich in the fine chariot King Francis had sent in advance to celebrate the birth of Henry's prince, I asked her, "My lady, I understand that Mary is right vexing and I commend you for not demanding her presence. But you were of a temper that is mayhap not becoming of a queen. Is it because you are ill?" I'd noticed that she'd eaten little and lightly and was often at the close stool.

She sighed. "I know. I am ill but 'tis for a good cause. I am with child."

I reached to pull her near. " 'Tis marvelous news! Mary will come round," I said, hoping to keep her calm till the child was born, which would be a sizable task indeed.

"No," Anne said. "No, she won't. She's her mother's daughter."

In spite of her ill health and weariness in carrying the child and her distress over the spat with Mary, Anne entertained her ladies that night. The courses were delivered to her apartments and we spent the evening passing time with court chatter and games of dice. Anne took an especial interest in the new Duchess of Suffolk, the naive fourteen-year-old bride of the Duke of Suffolk, who had, indeed, right quickly married his son's betrothed afore his old wife, the king's sister Mary Rose, was in her grave a week.

Mary Rose, once the celebrated Queen of France, once married to her dashing lover, Suffolk, was now gone. Her bed was warmed by the girl her husband had lusted after afore his wife was even dead. How much this world offered, how little it surrendered. I prayed fervently and often for my lady to be delivered of a son.

Late May was a delightful time for a picnic and Anne sought to bring some merriment to the court and to Henry. Henry, always at his happiest with his friends about him and good times pressing in on him, was delighted with the picnic Anne had planned in the park near St. James Palace, home of the future Prince of Wales.

"Come, Majesty, let us walk," she said as she tucked her arm into Henry's, and they strolled the grounds, which had been carefully groomed to look natural and untouched. I busied myself with her other ladies and then took part in a tournament of rook with several of Anne's ladies and some of the gentlemen of the privy chamber.

"Do you have a partner, lady?" one of them charmingly asked me, the double entendre caus-ing a spray of laughter among the listeners. It had been a bit tense at court, awaiting the birth of the babe, and I welcomed the change and courtly flirtation.

"Not presently, Sir Thomas," I responded. "I find myself quite unpartnered at the moment. And you?"

"Alas, I remain happily unmatched," he said, blinking his deep blue eyes in my direction. Thomas Seymour was a few years younger and just approaching the power and charm of a man come into his own. "Though as I should not care to see a woman as beautiful as you without a rook partner, mayhap I could advise your moves."

I laughed aloud. "I have done quite well at rook without your advice, sir, but your company would be most welcome."

He pulled up a chair beside me and kept pleasant company whilst I beat Lord Lisle handily. I turned around—Madge Shelton, the queen's cousin, was to be the next partner in the game, but she was not to be seen. Earlier I had watched as she cornered Sir Henry Norris, a handsome, titled man in want of a wife. He had respectfully disengaged himself from her. Mayhap she was looking for him again?

"Looking for Mistress Shelton?" Jane Rochford's voice was in my ear ere I even saw her approach.

"Indeed I am," I said. "We were to be partnered at rook next. Have you seen her?"

Jane nodded in the direction of the king, who sat beneath the spreading canopy of a contorted oak tree. On his lap—his lap!—sat Madge Shelton.

"Where is the queen?" I hissed to Jane.

"She went for a walk with her father, but look, she approaches now." Jane pointed toward the wooded area on the outskirts of the park, where the queen had suddenly appeared.

I watched her as she watched them. I held my

breath, expecting an angry outburst or a slap to Madge. Neither happened. Anne smiled serenely and nodded to Madge. "Cousin?"

Madge bowed her head. "My queen."

"Yes, she is your cousin, sweetheart, I'd near forgotten," Henry said in what seemed to be an effort to make light conversation. "She does resemble your sister, Mary."

Anne smiled. "The resemblance is in all ways remarkable." And then she joined Henry Norris and the others at the rook tables.

She had learnt. I watched the king, and whilst he made as though he were happy to toy with Mistress Shelton, his eyes were upon Norris and Anne, laughing with the others at play.

Later that night as I helped her undress she told me, "He's bedded her."

She said naught else, and her tone warned me not to ask.

By late June Madge was an irritant to all in Anne's chambers. She wore the king's favor like a gaudy set of paste pearls and lorded her position over all.

"The king tells me that he is, of a time, not inclined to play cards, having lost to the queen too many times," she said one day.

"The king is exceptionally tired these days, having worked all day and night on matters of state," she said another morning as she idled on a chair whilst Jane Rochford and I repleated

Anne's dresses. "You forgot a crease, Lady Rochford," Madge pointed out.

"And you forget your manners, mistress," Jane snapped. "Be glad the queen suffers your presence. You are a nothing and a nobody without a brain in her head nor a thought worth sharing. So please don't spread them like the plague upon the sensibilities that they are. Mayhap you think being the king's doxy raises you to a position of knowledge and authority."

"It did for . . ." Madge let her voice trail off and she caught the sharp look that passed between myself and Lady Rochford. She said nothing more but took her leave. By that afternoon Anne walked into my chambers as I prepared myself for that evening's dinner.

"What transpired between Mistress Shelton and Lady Rochford today?" she asked.

I told her everything that had transpired, including the fact that Jane Rochford had, uncharacteristically, subtly come to Anne's defense when Madge had been about to slander her. "Why?"

"The king has summoned me to discuss it. Seems Mistress Shelton went to him in great distress and said that Lady Rochford, and I, had harassed her."

"You were not even present!"

Anne nodded. "I shall, delicately, put an end to this, I hope."

That night after dinner there was a pounding on my door. When Edithe opened it there stood Jane

Rochford, blustering in fury. "I am exiled from court for a month. Because of you! And Anne!"

"What are you speaking of?" I asked, indicating a chair where she might be seated. She waved me away with a wild hand.

"Mistress Shelton complained that I had been badgering and teasing her for weeks and then finally told her today that she was worthless and was poxy."

"You said no such thing," I exclaimed. "You called her a doxy."

"Her vocabulary, like her morals, is sadly lacking. But that's not all. Seems that the queen allowed him to believe that while I defended her. You heard me!"

I nodded. "And I told her so."

Jane snorted. "For naught. I understand what is happening here. Anne wants me banished—so she can have George for herself!"

"Hush, Lady Rochford, 'tis in no way true, you work yourself up," I said. I tried to put my hand on her arm but she swirled it away from me.

"You remain loyal, but 'tis for naught. She'll turn on you one day. And, like me, you shan't forgive her either."

She turned and slammed the door behind her. Edithe came back into the room, clearly shaken. "Good riddance, my lady," she said to me. "Shall I help you with your gown?"

I nodded and then, after I was prepared for bed,

went to my chamber and closed the door. I opened up my copy of Holy Writ and read for comfort and companionship, and afterward spoke with the Lord Jesus about the situation. I sought peace, but instead, He forewarned me. I knew somehow that this situation with Jane had lit a small pile of kindling that, I knew not how, would blaze into a conflagration that would burn down the house.

Also, against my will, Jane had sown a seed of doubt in my heart about Anne's loyalty toward me.

I recalled to mind one of King Solomon's proverbs that Master Fulham had insisted that Anne, Rose Ogilvy, and I memorize as girls. *These six things doth the LORD hate: yea, seven are an abomination unto Him: a proud look, a lying tongue, and hands that shed innocent blood, a heart that deviseth wicked imaginations, feet that be swift in running to mischief, a false witness that speaketh lies, and he that soweth discord among brethren.*

'Twas Jane Rochford, clearer than any Holbein portrait could want to be.

In early July, I went to Anne's chambers one morn to help her dress for an audience with the Venetian ambassador, but she was still in bed, her beautiful hair matted like a tangle of dark thread on the underside of a tapestry, her skin sickly and taut.

Jane Rochford, just returned from exile, was

already there. "She has pains," she announced in a voice tinted with triumph. "Mayhap I should send for her mother."

I nodded. "Indeed."

"And our sister, Mary Stafford?" she insisted.

"Be gone!" I hissed loudly enough for her to hear but not, I hoped, for Anne. Jane laughed quietly and went to find Lady Boleyn. After her banishment she no longer even pretended to false affection for Anne.

Mary Boleyn Carey had married a lowborn soldier from Calais named William Stafford a few months before and, because she hadn't asked either Anne's or the king's permission, she had been exiled from court for months. I knew the real reason that Anne could not tolerate Mary's presence, though, and it had nothing at all to do with her lowborn husband nor her maddening manner. Rather, it had everything to do with the fact that unlike Anne, Mary had both a daughter and a son by the king. Baseborn, but healthy and alive. Anne, superior in nearly every way to Mary, was inferior in this one critical matter.

"She's not going to call Mary to court," Anne said. "I shan't allow it."

"She has no intention of recalling Mary," I said. "Now, just lie back and we shall pray together that these pains will subside and all will be well."

Anne clutched my hand and eased back. She

rolled on her side like a tiny rowboat listing on the Thames and I prayed aloud.

"Lord, if it be your pleasure, please spare this child, for his sake and for my lady's sake and for His Grace's sake. Please stop the pains and soothe her womb and have a care to assist the child within." All knew the pains were too early; a child born now could not survive.

Lady Boleyn arrived and we sat on either side of Anne, and, for a time, she seemed comforted. I sent word by Anne's secretary to tell the Venetian ambassador that the queen was unwell. By noon, the chamber had grown as quiet as the Kentish fields in the dead of a summer day. Anne rolled from her side and looked at me.

" 'Tis no use. I bleed." We called the midwife and Anne travailed to deliver the babe, present in body and yet in spirit already with our Lord. It was just possible to see that the child had been a boy. I folded him in a small linen and prayed over the body as the midwife took care of the queen.

"Was it a boy?" Anne asked.

I nodded. She remained quiet for many minutes and then, as we eased her into a clean dressing gown, she said, "Mayhap the God I thought I knew I know not at all."

I had the bloodstained sheets burnt.

His Majesty did not visit. He sent word that he was overoccupied with Master Cromwell but would keep her in his prayers and hoped for a swift return to health. It sounded like the fond but disinterested sentiments one would send to a worthy courtier, not to a wife.

She sent him a sweet letter apologizing that her ill health inconvenienced him and finished it by saying, "I look forward to the day when we, together, celebrate the birth of our son. I shall hasten to recover in order to hasten that day."

Her atypical gentle manner had won a reprieve. A day later the king visited my lady's chamber, bringing dates, a bracelet of diamonds, and sweet kisses and gentle words which I had not heard from him in some time. They gladdened her heart and gave her hope. "I believe he repents of his lack of attention," she said to me as she called for Lady Zouche to bring her washbasin. "Meg, please find a suitable gown for tomorrow night's dinner. The king is eager for my attendance."

While Anne had not been able to deliver to His Grace what he wanted, Master Cromwell had.

That autumn, in the king's mighty presence chamber, Master Cromwell announced in front of all gathered courtiers, politicians, gentry, and visiting notables that Parliament had passed the Act of Succession, which made Mary a bastard and the male issue of Anne and Henry, followed by Princess Elizabeth, the only legal successors to the crown.

Though she'd not authored the act, it seemed that Anne had indeed triumphed over Mary's unbridled Spanish blood.

Cromwell then read out the Act of Supremacy, also passed by Parliament. "Parliament herein reaffirms the king of England as the only supreme head on earth of the Church in England. The English crown shall enjoy all honors, dignities, preeminences, jurisdictions, privileges, authorities, immunities, profits, and commodities to the said dignity. This is a recognized and inalienable right."

The room grew warm with the sweat and fast breathing of hundreds of anxious listeners. The traditionalists, lead by Nicolas Carewe, appeared unseated. Sir Thomas More quietly left the room: Henry saw him leave, yet still appeared pleased, under the canopy of state crowning his great throne. Anne looked pleased for him, and indeed, for the reformist cause. Parliament had firmly declared that the pope had no jurisdiction in England, in fact, never had.

Finally, Cromwell read the last parliamentary act, the Treasons Act. All knew that treason was the worst charge to be laid against man or maid, with the exception of excommunication, which was, thankfully, no longer a valid threat. Cromwell, splendidly attired in his mighty robes of black, power draped about him like legal ermine, called out in a voice loud enough for all to hear.

"This very act prohibits all who maliciously wish, will, or desire by words or writing, or by craft imagine, invent, practice, or attempt any bodily harm to be done or committed to the king's most royal person . . . or to deprive him of any of their dignity, title, or name of their royal estates, or slanderously and maliciously publish and pronounce, by express writing or words, that the king should be heretic, schismatic, tyrant, infidel, or usurper of the crown . . ."

Cromwell read on for another five minutes, but none save the king and Anne were listening any longer. What this meant was that all were legally prohibited from speaking against anything the king had done or might do. Parliament, or rather Cromwell, had just given Henry unbridled power, and nothing and no one could stop him.

Later, at a reform meeting in Lady Carlyle's sumptuous apartments, there was a glow of happiness that the Church in England was now autonomous. I knew by furtive look and discomfort-able manners that several realized that giving absolute power to anyone save God was dangerous, foolish, and shortsighted. None of us dared say anything, of course; there were spies all round and today's speech made it plain what dissenters earned for their honesty.

'Twas troubling, though. Had the brilliant Cromwell not seen the Achilles heel he'd firmly embedded in his own document, believing it to advance England and reform but placing them both in bloody hands? Or had he drunk deeply of power's nectar and could not now see soberly the effects this document might have?

I suspected it was the latter, and Cromwell had unwittingly placed a very large bundle of sticks on the smoldering embers of destruction.

TWENTY

Year of Our Lord 1535
Whitehall Palace
Templeman Castle
Greenwich Palace

In January of 1535 Henry saw to it that Cromwell was well rewarded for his loyalty as chief henchman. Cromwell was appointed vice-regent, vicar, and special commissary, which made him not only the highest civil authority in England, save for His Majesty, but also the highest religious authority in England, save for His Majesty.

Henry, of course, remained head of the Church of England. Though he sometimes listened intently as the truly godly and learned bishops Anne had angled into place spoke and exhorted, His Grace also spent chapel time reading over accounts and jotting poesies and notes in the permanent copy of Holy Writ placed in the royal box afore handing it over to Anne, who oft replied in the same manner. Out of compulsion or desire, I know not. But it vexed me some, I'll admit. As for me, I flourished under the teaching of men who taught, in English, and plainly, from God's word.

One afternoon in early spring Anne instructed me to get her riding outfit ready and then called for her chamberlain to have her horsemen prepare some steeds for riding. "I feel the need to ride out," she said.

"Is it . . . safe?" I asked her.

She nodded solemnly. "I began to bleed this morning."

Ah. I, like all of her ladies who cared for her future, knew exactly when her flow should come and prayed that it would not. But it had. Another month with no promise of a son. I, always eager to ride, prepared her clothing and then went to change into my own riding habit. We had servants attend to us, of course, but they knew well enough to stay a comfortable distance behind us.

We galloped out and across the parkland next to the palace before cantering and then walking. "We've got better steeds, thanks to His Majesty, than we had as girls, don't we?" I asked.

She grinned. "Yes, he can be a generous benefactor. He's just arranged for several more horses of spirited blood to be delivered for me. He said he wants the steed to match his mare."

Coming from another man, that sentiment may have been a denigration, but when it had been said, all knew that Henry was signaling to a faithless court ready to shift loyalties within a moon phase that Anne was queen, his wife, and still held his affections in her elegant hands. Seeing her now, her color high and her spirit restored by his renewed affection, it was not difficult to see why.

"You look well," I said. "And I am pleased."

"The air does you good, too, Meg," Anne said. "You are lovelier than when we rode as girls. I see why Sir Thomas was so taken with you at the masque last week; indeed, I believe he first trained his charm on you at a picnic a year earlier."

"Your memory astonishes me," I said, laughing, but thankful for the compliment. Anne was aware of her own effect on men but never begrudged another woman beauty or attention. She was jealous only for the affection and attention of her husband; 'twas reasonable, for certes. "I suspect Seymour trains his charm on any who eschew hose for gowns."

Anne smiled but then turned to the sound of an approaching rider. None should ride toward us unless there was trouble. " 'Tis George," she said a bit distractedly.

Her brother shortly arrived but did not dismount. He did bow his head. "Ladies," he said before raising it again. "I wanted you to know afore you returned to your chambers," he said. "This day, the king has begun to enforce the Treasons Act. I was in the privy council yesterday when it was announced. Today the sentences were carried out."

Anne nodded but the high color drained from her cheeks.

"His Majesty had four Catholic monks of good repute hanged, drawn, and quartered, their entrails burned in front of them before beheading them for denying that he, not the pope, was the head of the Church in England. And then, to show that he is just, he had fourteen of the reformers who had fled here seeking sanctuary burnt at the stake for refuting infant baptism."

This was the man my lifelong friend succored in the bosom of her heart.

The look on Anne's face was somber and she remained quiet for some time before responding. "I cannot do anything to help them. I cannot cross His Majesty and even I have learnt when I can offer counsel and when I must hold my peace." She looked toward the castle, the west wing, where Henry was constructing a massive addition. "What I may do is bring English Scripture into places that it has been forbidden and allow all to read. I can place firm beams, load-bearing beams, men of goodness and godliness, committed to reform, on the altars and in the chaplaincy and hope that they can stand. I cannot do more."

She lightly dug her heels into her mount and rode back alone, George and I trailing her. By evening, when Henry expected her to entertain some guests from Francis's court, she had recovered her gaiety and drew near to the king. What other could she do? She, a beam, had to bear up too.

Within the month, Anne had Matthew Parker, a reformer of calm and patient temperament and dedication to the Scriptures, and a friend of Will and John Rogers, appointed to an important position in Stoke-by-Claire. She also named him as her personal chaplain.

It seems our king had whetted his taste for living without consequence. In June, he had Cardinal Fisher, Katherine of Aragon's champion, hung for a day before being beheaded; his head was placed on a pike just outside for all to see.

A few weeks hence Anne came to my rooms, dismissed Edithe, and sat on my bed, head in hands.

I joined her. "What is it?" Anne was not given to fits of sadness or displays of weakness.

"Henry has had Sir Thomas More condemned to death. He refused to affirm the king as head of the Church in England, holding to his belief that the pope is the rightful head of the Church everywhere. More is to be beheaded as well."

"I'd heard," I said. The news had blown through court like an ill wind. "But why does this sadden you, dearest? Sir Thomas was for certes no friend to you."

She nodded and twisted her emerald wedding

ring about her finger. "I admit I am not a generous enough person to grieve his death, though I do not believe he dies justly. However"—she looked at me and I saw, for the first time, fear in her eyes —"Henry loved Thomas More. He thought of him as a father, a brother, a counselor, a friend, of many decades. Does Cromwell not see that if Henry can change his affections, of an instant, for one well-beloved counselor he can do that for another in like manner?"

I took her hand in my own, soothing her without a word. Because the words we did not, could not, say were: if Henry set aside one wife, a well-beloved wife, in an instant, could he not do that of another in like manner? That was the heart of the matter. We both knew it.

Fisher's head was taken from its pike, pitched into the Thames, and replaced with More's.

England was as restless as an unwell child, and the king restless along with her. His answer was to take Anne, and the court, on a long progress throughout his own properties, the properties of his nobles, and even to the west country. We started at Windsor, moved to Reading, and then planned to go through Oxfordshire to Templeman Castle and Sudeley Castle in Gloucestershire. We'd progress through Wiltshire, Southampton, then Portsmouth, followed by Winchester, feasting and bankrupting his hosts all the way.

Henry wanted to see his people face-to-face, judge their loyalty, and affirm his sovereignty. We left as soon as More's pulse stilled.

Endless hunting and dancing and dining kept the king at peace for months, happy, his heart and hand interlaced with Anne's, which was, I supposed, best for all. Still, there was no sign of a child and she'd gone many months now without a pregnancy. So when she pulled me aside to speak in private I thought mayhap she had good news. But it was other news she wanted to share.

"The king has told me that we leave, on the morrow, for Templeman Castle," she said. "The Earl of Blenheim has erected a great jousting stadium in honor of His Majesty, has arranged for a pageant and a masque. I expect the Ogilvy family will all attend."

I nodded. "But Will is in Antwerp, with Miles Coverdale."

"I wanted you to be forewarned," Anne said. "And I want you to take one of the gowns you've just had made for me—that one of garnet sarcenet with gold shot throughout—and keep it for yourself. I shan't have you showing up at Rose's home looking any less fashionable than she."

I squeezed her hand in silent thanks.

"I have not forgotten my promise to ask the king for a dowry for you," she said. "I shall, next time I am with child. My brother, George, can find a good man for you, a noble knight or other kindly person in high gentry. Or mayhap you prefer Thomas Seymour?"

I laughed. We both knew Thomas Seymour was out of my grasp even if I wanted him, and I didn't. "I have no wish to partner Master Seymour for anything other than the briefest of dances, Your Grace. But thank you."

We arrived at Templeman, I in Anne's litter, which meant that Rose would have to remain in a curtsy while I alighted because she knew not whether it would be me or Anne who would come out first. I hid a smile. I was not beyond enjoying the poke but I had no wish to cause further ill will.

"Lady Blenheim," I said. Her father-in-law had passed away; her husband was now completely vested in his title, as was Rose.

"Dowager Baroness," she said, emphasizing "dowager." I minded it not. The years had not been kind to her and her self-righteous spirit had soured her within as well. Her eyes looked unwelcoming, as always, but also deeply smudged.

Once the court had settled in their rooms—new ones had been prepared for the king and for Anne, whom Rose continued to refer to as "my dear, dear childhood friend the queen"—the earl called us into his gardens, where he held an enchanting pageant. I looked about me. Where was Will's father . . . and brother? Neither were here when the king was being entertained? I set

Edithe to make inquiries from the servants, so as not to draw attention to my queries, and was shocked at what she reported back.

"Seems Master Walter has passed on, my lady, only a few weeks ere the progress. His father and mother are putting things to right at their estate and 'tis too soon after the death to be at a masque an' all."

Walter. Dead. Dear, sweet Walter. The heir.

I purposed in my heart to approach Rose that evening with my condolences. Her card table was full, but I found an open spot at one nearby so that I could approach her with my sympathy at the right moment. She caught my eye but didn't wave me over. It did seem to me that she spoke more loudly, though. Mayhap so I could hear?

Lady Lisle offered pity and comfort and then asked Rose, "Will your father recall your brother Will home, then? He's your father's heir now, is that not right?"

Rose spoke up. "Thank you for your gentle wishes, my lady. My brother Will has already returned home and performed Walter's funeral, a private family matter. As he is a priest, and told my father only last year that he was called to remain a priest, I shan't expect him to be named my father's heir. That honor will go to my eldest son, Philip." She caught my eye, smiled, and turned back to her table.

It grew clear to me that she did not want my

good wishes, so I finished my game of trump, thinking that Rose had already trumped me and we were not even at the same table, and took my leave.

Walter was dead. Philip, a spoilt little man given to fits of temper any time I'd seen him and overindulged by Rose's unmanned husband, now heir to two great estates. But even more startling, Will was here.

The next evening, our last afore moving on, I attended to Anne's needs in an unusual haste. As I brushed out her hair I tugged at a knot.

"Have a care!" She quickly put her hand to her head. "If I didn't know better, madam, I would say you were in an unseemly hurry to dress yourself at risk of service to your queen."

"I'm sorry," I said, but then I caught the gleam in her eye. She knew Will was here, mayhap had known all along.

"You may be sorry but 'tis clear you cannot focus on the task." She waved me away. "I'd prefer the patient hands of Nan Zouche tonight. Be gone!"

I hurried to my own chambers and dressed myself in the garnet gown that shimmered like deep flames when it caught the light, threads of gold running through it like an unspoken promise. I knew how much the fabric had cost—I'd procured it on the queen's behalf. If all the earnings from each person in the village surrounding Allington

Castle were pooled together for one year, 'twould be enough to commission the dress. I masqued myself with a gold and black feather headdress.

The great hall at Templeman was magnificent. Rose's husband was bound as ivy and oak with Cromwell, who had appointed him to several lucrative positions. Indeed, Cromwell himself had joined us on progress. My brother Edmund was there with his new bride, an untested girl who spoke little and seemed to be currently avoiding Katherine Willoughby, the Duke of Suffolk's young wife, who had a lively spirit and quick tongue. I'd had several words with Edmund's wife during the weeks she'd been on progress with us, tried to befriend her, but it soon became clear that Edmund had poisoned the air between us and she was reluctant to offer anything but the most proper and perfunctory greetings. I'd not seen her smile since their smallish wedding. I suspected he'd kept it low-key because it was rushed after Charlotte had married Simon.

"Are you enjoying the progress, Tilda?" I asked her.

" 'Tis fine. And you, Margaret?" she offered meekly.

"Do not call her Margaret, 'twas my mother's name. My sister's name," Edmund spat out, "is Meg."

I bade them good evening and, sighing, took my leave. I should have to ask Alice, also present, if she'd had better luck with our sister-in-law.

Of course Baron Blackston was there. His wife, Charlotte, was an especial favorite of Rose's. Simon asked me to dance and I had little choice but to agree.

"How are you, Meg?" His voice clearly showed that he couldn't be less interested in my well-being.

"I do well," I answered. "I see that your wife is with child. Congratulations."

He smiled and steeled his gaze before the thrust. "You know young ladies. So often with child so quick after a wedding. And many times thereafter. Like your friend, the Countess of Blenheim, our hostess."

Yes, Simon, I am aware of my age and lack of fecundity. "I wish you goodwill with your child," I said, and then added a little barb from which he could draw his own meaning. "I shall certainly keep your child in my prayers." Simon looked ready to say something further when someone tapped on his shoulder.

"May I?" he asked. It was Will. His being near family with Simon made it difficult for Simon to do anything other than graciously agree.

"From the arms of a fallen angel into the arms of a priest," I teased. I noticed Will did not wear vestments but was dressed in typical courtly attire. Mayhap it was because it was a masque.

Though he was masqued, as was I, it was still

possible to lock eyes and we did, he showing more open interest in me than he had the last time, which confused me. The music seemed far away, as did all others. I was only aware of one person.

"I may not be a priest for long," he said, and I nearly pulled away from him at the shock of that. *Beatissima!*

He held me close to keep things looking normal all round. "I will find you to speak of that in a short while." He kept his tone even and quiet and disturbingly unemotional following that kind of revelation. "For now, I must tell you something of great import, and quickly. Our friend may be in trouble."

I leaned in and whispered, "Anne?"

He nodded. "I must speak quickly as I am promised elsewhere shortly. The smith's son," he said, "whom our friend considers as one of her own, may not be so trustworthy after all."

Cromwell! Cromwell was a smith's son; in fact, there had long been petty murmurs among nobility about his being raised too high from the floors of the smithy. "There must be a certain danger if you are reluctant to name the man," I said.

Will nodded. "He's said that he has a goal in mind—reform, for certes, and the wealth of the realm, and his own coffer. Like any smith he will pick up or cast aside tools as required for the task."

"Our friend?"

"Maybe," Will said. "The king's eye wanders, his interest wanders. Carewe and other courtiers unfavorable to the queen comment time and again on her bewildering inability to bring forth a son from such a virile man as the king. 'Twas a time he would not have listened. But Rose's husband, thick with Cromwell, says the king listens now. I understand that he may be asking Cromwell to investigate Anne."

"To find?"

"Whatever he may."

The song drew to an end. "I will be wary and do what I can," I promised. "And . . . your other news?"

"I shall seek you tonight. Soon," he promised, but his air seemed reserved. He let me go and then slipped into the crowd of hundreds.

In spite of the attention my dress, and my nearness to the queen, drew to me that night I left early so Will could speak with me at his pleasure.

I dismissed Edithe early—her husband had accompanied the Boleyns—and remained in my rooms alone. Shortly a knock came at my door. I opened it with great expectation only to be let down.

"Oh. Come in," I said to my sister, Alice. She stooped down and picked up a slip of paper that I'd left peeping out from under the door so Will could find my chamber in the hallway where Anne's women were housed.

"This was in the hallway," she said. I took it in hand and closed the door behind her. "May I have a seat?" she asked after a moment went by without my offering.

"Oh yes, yes of course." I indicated a plumply cushioned chair next to the window and pulled one alongside her. As it were the height of summer it was not yet black outside.

"I was concerned when I saw you leave," she said. "Are you all right?"

I nodded and grinned. "Perfectly. I, ah, well, had been going to share my condolences with Will, at the loss of his brother. Later."

Alice drew near me and took my hands in her own. "I knew he'd be here tonight, but only just. My son John told me that Walter had passed on and that Will's father had recalled him from Antwerp. John arrived just ahead of Will. John also shared with me that, well, that Earl Asquith has named Will as his heir."

"His heir? But Rose felt that her son Philip would be named heir."

"I suppose that may have been true had Will chosen to remain in the priesthood. But it seems he has not. His father is, even now, searching for an heiress to marry him to, to increase both their holdings and status and . . . family members. John believes the earl may have found such a young woman and, indeed, has already spoken to Will of the matter."

311

It didn't need to be said that I was not a great heiress, had, in fact, no dowry at all, no great title to offer, and at this age, even my ability to add to a family was in doubt. He would have been a suitable match for me as a second son. But not as an heir.

"I'm sorry," Alice said. " 'Tis better to hear it from me, though I suspect he will tell you on his own as well."

I nodded. "Thank you, Sister," I said. Then I stood. "Would you mind if I had some time on my own to pray?"

"Of course not." She drew me to her, kissed my cheeks, and squeezed my hands before taking her leave. I would not replace the paper under the door.

As she left, I spied Will coming down the hall. I had no time to shut the door; he'd seen me.

'Twas a pity that I'd not had time to pray, as I'd indicated I would, ere Will reached me. I stood in the doorway.

"Meg, can we speak together?" he asked.

Twenty-One

Year of Our Lord 1535
Wolf Hall
Hampton Court Palace
Whitehall Palace
Windsor Castle
Greenwich Palace

Though I desperately wanted to take him into my arms, I shook my head no. 'Twas useless now. I recalled how, as a girl, I'd noticed a robin in a nest outside of my bedchamber window. When the light shone upon the window the robin could not see that it was a plate of glass; instead, it kept flying into the window over and over again, uselessly banging its head trying to get somewhere it would never be allowed entrance. I'd had one of my father's menservants relocate the nest so that the bird might, though unhappily, live.

I unbridled my tongue. " 'Tis clear to me that when your father bade you become a priest you obeyed, though you said it was because you were called, and I believed you. And now, now when he wants you for an heir, and when a dowry is out of my reach, as it had not been when we last met and you reaffirmed your call, he summons you forth out of the priesthood and you obey."

I stepped back inside my door. "Your call is subject to your father's will, but not to the desires of my own heart, nor your own, and never has been. I will pray for you, Will, and for your marriage and for your heir. I bid you good evening."

I shut the door and slid to the floor. He stood on the other side of the door for a long while but did not knock nor call my name, though I silently willed him to. After some time I heard his footsteps retreat and then I let myself cry.

In September we made our last stop on progress before returning to Hampton Court Palace and picking up the king's, and Cromwell's, business of state. His Majesty's courtiers had, unusually, chosen Wolf Hall, the estate of the Seymour family, to cap off the summer's journey.

Our first night there found us enjoying a musical performance. "Sir John has commissioned the musicians to play an evening of music that was composed by, or inspired by the compositions of, His Majesty," Anne explained, admiration for her husband clear in her eyes. "There is no sovereign in the world who could have an evening of musical entertainment claimed to his talents other than His Grace."

It was true, the king had composed many songs in his younger days, and, even now, would pick up a lute or stringed instrument and play with a deft hand.

As I'd told my sister I would, I partnered a dance with Thomas Seymour, as did nearly every other lady present, but he was most interested in the pretty young daughter of a nearby nobleman and it was fine with me. I had resigned myself to a monastic life serving my God and my queen. Madge Shelton, cast off by the king, had not devised a like plan for her life.

"Why does Henry Norris partner the queen at dance, again?" she complained. "I have danced with him once, but he has now thrice danced with the queen, and that after having twice danced with Lady Lisle. And now, look," she said. "Thomas Seymour is besotted with young Lady Latimer though she be twice married herself."

"Mayhap they prefer to dance with married women who see them as friends and not as men in desperate need of wives, as some are wont to see them," Nan Zouche replied tartly. Madge turned up her lip, but I agreed. Anne's cousin Madge had been the favorite of many men but the wife of none, and others, of course, had taken note. Men were reluctant to take to wife a woman who had already been taken to bed many times over.

Though the evening was led by a song that the king had composed in honor of Anne, 'twas clear early on that Mistress Jane Seymour, Sir John's daughter, was the night's real presentation.

Jane had served in Anne's household off and on, of course, as had most every girl and woman of gentle birth. So she was not a stranger to us, but she had spoken rarely, offered few opinions, had not played cards or enjoyed the lighthearted banter about learning or religion or anything else so often discussed in Anne's rooms. I'd oft thought it was not so much that she was unwilling as unable. So 'twas hard to know wherein Henry found her charm, unless it be in her constant downcast gaze or prudently folded hands. His eye and his conversation were oft drawn in her direction. And when they didn't turn there naturally, her brother Edward or Sir Nicolas Carewe gently steered her back into his path. Soon enough she guided herself there.

"I like not the looks of that," I told Anne, remembering Will's warning.

Anne made no comment, of course. But I knew she was paying attention and recognized a new level of danger. Mistress Seymour had, of the king's accord, rejoined Anne's ladies. In early October, one night after we'd returned to court, I was halfway through reassembling the queen's gowns and putting away her Scriptures and prayer books when Jane Rochford entered the room.

"My lady," Jane said. "I have some information for you." She looked in my direction and then back at Anne.

"That will be all for this evening, Meg," Anne said, not unkindly, but it was a definite dismissal. I curtseyed coolly and took my leave.

Within the hour Anne sent her lady maid to recall me back to her chambers. When I arrived I was shocked to find her dressed plainly, in garb of lower quality than even her lady maid would wear.

"What is this?" I asked. She'd already dismissed the rest of her maids and her rooms were eerily empty.

"Sit with me." She indicated the gilded chairs near the fireplace, which was already roaring on this cold autumn night. I did as I was bade.

"Jane had approached me with . . . concern . . . over my lack of a child."

"Jane has concern for you?" I asked with incredulity. "As of which date? I remember not."

Anne smiled wanly. " 'Tis hard to believe, but then recall to mind that as my fortunes go, so do George's, and therefore Jane's. She asked me if there were a problem with my, ah, ability to hold on to a child. I replied that I knew not, but that sometimes, well, the king were tired and had trouble doing the man's part in the matter, which is understandable, for certes, when you consider his responsibilities to the kingdom." She looked down at her rough boots at that and didn't look me in the eye. No woman wanted to divulge difficulties with her husband's manliness. But this was not a problem to remain between man and wife. It was a crisis for the realm.

"And how does Jane Rochford propose she help in this delicate matter?"

"She knows a woman . . . an herbalist . . . in nearby Aldwych. She mixes draughts and ointments and concoctions that can assist a man in this matter, and some which, when the mother drinks of them, help her retain a child."

"A witch?!"

Anne shook her head. "No, 'tis not a witch. 'Tis an herbalist. But many confuse the two just as you do. Which is why I am thusly garbed to ride out and fetch these potions. I cannot risk sending someone for them and mayhap gossiping that I frequent a witch. Jane Rochford says she is too frightened to go herself."

I took her hands in my own. "No, dearest, you cannot go. There must be another way. And your bleeding has not started this month, so it may be that you are already with child. Can you risk that with a nighttime ride into Aldwych? Can you risk being seen visiting a woman who some may, mistakenly, claim as a witch? Surely there is no one in the land who will not know your face."

She stood up and raised her voice. "Can I risk losing another child when the king visits me irregularly and even then may not be able to consummate? Can I risk having the stone-stupid Jane Seymour insinuate herself into my bed and onto my throne?"

Again, I recalled Will's warning. He was not a man given to intemperate speculation, so the risk to Anne was real.

"Then I shall go in your stead," I said. "Tell me where to go."

She shook her head. "No."

I reached over and took off her humble cloak. "Yes, lady. We made a vow, in Hever garden, friends to the end, never leaving one another's side, loyalty firmly pledged, come what may. I shall serve you in this matter."

"I do not deserve your friendship, Meg," she said.

"No, you do not. But alas, there it lies," I teased her as she let me unbutton her. I noticed a twitch near her left eye and her hands trembled. I believe it was the first time I had actually seen anxiety overcome her to any degree.

I helped her undress and then I put the servant's clothing on myself. It was a harsh fabric and irritated my skin. I suspected fleas nested in the cloak as I felt the pinprick of bites on my arms and the nape of my neck and Anne scratched an irritation on her own collarbone.

"Roger, the husband to your maid Edithe, and one lady from Hever will ride with you to the street of the physic but not beyond, and wait for you there. I trust them to ride, but not, mayhap, to keep a secret if pressed by someone high-born," Anne said. I recalled how Simon had intimidated Edithe and agreed with her. "I told Jane Rochford that I would ride a lowly steed so as not to call attention to myself." Anne handed me a pouch of coins. "For the draughts and poultice."

I pulled the cloak around me as I slunk down the hall. I passed by several who knew me and none looked my way nor nodded; rather, they kept a distance. Fear of the fleas, I suspected, glad that I went unrecognized.

I pulled the hood even closer as I crept through the servants' quarters, where no guards were posted, and out toward the stable. A light rain fell but the tight wool kept me dry. I arrived at the stable and, as Anne had promised, Roger and a lady servant were there. Roger caught my eye, recognized me, but said nothing. He called for three horses to be brought. When my steed was brought I sent him back. "I prefer that mount," I said, pointing out my own horse. If I were going to be riding through the night into London, I did not want to be bedeviled by a horse I was unfamiliar with. As my horse was not caparisoned with royal garb it should not matter.

We rode out of the stables and through the courtyards; through the gate, which Roger had arranged with the gate servant to be opened; and into the city. It was not so far up the beat-dirt roads to Aldwych, where my lady said the physic practiced. "Remain here," I said to Roger and the lady, and they idled in the dark outside of an ale-house, holding my steed, whilst I made my way up the dark street. I arrived at the small building with stars painted across the door and knocked.

The door was opened not by a haggard old crone, as I'd expected, but by a beautiful young woman. "How can I help you?" she asked, her accent indicating that she were not lowborn.

"I've come for some potions to help my mistress hold her baby," I said. "And, mayhap, give her husband . . . strength to make another child . . . if he needs it."

She nodded warily, looked behind me, then indicated I could come in. I was as wary, or perhaps more wary, than she, but there was no turning back now. "Sit here," she told me. She went into another room and I could hear bottles clanking, There were physic jars on a small shelf in the next room. Several of them looked suspiciously like Simon's sleeping draughts. I wondered where Jane Rochford had got her herbalist information. The maiden came back into the room and handed me two pouches. I paid her and, before I left, tied the pouches inside of my kirtle as Anne had told me to do.

I walked back up the street. I knew the woman wasn't a witch, but I prayed as I left because I felt unclean after the visit, filled with foreboding of some kind. Should I simply throw the potions away and tell Anne I was unable to get them? And yet, mayhap, like burn ointment or herbs to ward off a fever, they could help.

Roger led us back to the castle, and just afore we reached the gates to enter I heard a swoosh of air and then a scream. 'Twas Anne's lady servant. Her horse had been shot with an arrow, and then, shockingly, one hit her clear through the temple. Her eyes registered surprise and then locked with mine in a mute cry for help.

"I come!" I reined in my horse to turn to help the woman but was prevented from doing so by the manservant.

"Go on, my lady, ride on!" Roger urged me forward as I saw a dark figure rearm a bow. Roger leaned over and slapped the side of my horse, which then took off and headed directly for the stable. Roger galloped alongside me to urge my horse on. We left the serving woman in the street, though Roger said he would send a guard to assist her after I was safely inside. I knew he said it to comfort me and force me forward. There was no assistance that could be offered that would help.

I ran down the hallway, seedy cloak pulled around me, and into my empty rooms. Once on my bed I began to shake. I quickly undressed myself and crawled under the linens, shivering and praying that Anne's serving girl might live.

But she did not. Anne told me the next day that the girl had died, as had the lowly steed that Anne had been expected to ride. My fine horse had most likely saved me. It could not have been an accident—who besides Jane Rochford and her collaborators had known of Anne's mission on an ignoble mount?

"Methinks that arrow was intended for me, and mayhap that they would expect to see herbs on me when the body was found, and charge me with witchcraft," Anne said. She pulled me close. "I pity the girl who died, but selfishly, I am glad it was not you."

I pitied us all: Anne, me, and the poor woman who had died. Would this be the end of the danger?

Jane Rochford did not let her surprise show, indeed, never again brought the topic up. All noticed that she took a special care to tutor Jane Seymour in the ways of the ladies-in-waiting. Anne never drew her near again.

She did drink the draught, though, and her bleeding did not come. By the first of November she was able to announce to the king that she carried his son. His joy in her restored, he drew her near and chose no favorite; they sparred and read aloud and flirted in chapel. All was well.

For now.

Christmas court in 1535 was held, as usual, at Greenwich Palace. 'Twas the favorite of the king, and the queen, too, and as she was with child the mood had been merry. Every reformer in the land prayed for the safe delivery of a son. Surely God would smile down this time and rest the realm in the womb of a woman who had done so much to establish the Church in the land.

Anne herself had given me an overgenerous present of gold and jewels as a Christmas gift.

A new lady had joined the chamber, placed there at the request of Master Cromwell. "Her name is Lady Jamison," Rose, Lady Blenheim, said, introducing her to the other ladies-in-waiting. "My father is even now conducting negotiations for her marriage with my brother here at court over Christmas, and both parties are eager for them to conclude." She turned toward me. "I hadn't expected him to marry, but as he will, I am glad it is to Lady Jamison. Mayhap you could help her find her place at court, Baroness."

I restrained a comment about the place I'd like to find for Rose Ogilvy and instead graciously held out my hand to the young woman intended for Will. "How do you do?" I asked her. She curtseyed prettily and politely and when her gaze met mine I saw that she had not yet earned a single furrow on her brow nor crinkle in her smile. Her fine blond hair was modestly set off by a light blue French hood.

In his epistle unto the Galatians, Saint Paul had written that envying was a deed of the flesh. I regret to admit that deed of the flesh manifested itself at that moment till it near overcame me. I made some kindly small talk and took my leave, praying on my way down the hall back to my chamber. When I arrived, I was met at the door by Edithe.

"I have made it up to you, lady," she said, thrusting a scroll in my hand.

It was inked in Will's hand. "Have made what up to me?" I asked.

"I lost your other letters from Master Will. But his manservant delivered this some hours ago, and I guarded it till you arrived."

"Thank you, dear Edithe," I said. "But you have nothing to make up to me. You have always served me honorably and well and I wish that I could pay you more for your services to me."

She blushed. " 'Tis my honor. I shall take my leave now." She got her wrap and linens and left the room.

I slid my finger under the seal and undid the scroll.

I should like to meet with you and talk in private, about myself, and about our friend. I am not sure if I am welcome, after our last meeting. Please return your sentiments via your lady servant.

Yours, Will.

Twenty-two

Year of Our Lord 1536
Greenwich Palace
Hampton Court Palace

I wrote him a note telling him that I repented of my hasty words and if he'd forgive me I would be glad to speak with him whenever he would. I was then sorry that I had dismissed Edithe for the evening, for I was eager to return the letter to him and set things right between us.

The visitors to court would be leaving anon, I knew, as the Christmas celebrations concluded in early January and all but the customary courtiers returned to their homes and properties. I expected Will to find me soon. And he did.

At Greenwich he was familiar with which were my rooms—well-appointed apartments close to Anne's, because we often cloaked ourselves and went between our rooms late at night to talk over the day's events. Will knocked on the door and I opened it, preparing to offer a friendly greeting of welcome. Instead, he pushed the door closed behind him, took me firmly into his arms, and kissed me for nigh on a minute. My shock turned quickly to response. After a moment he held me far enough out to hold my gaze.

Libido.

"I have wanted to do that since Hever gardens and I gave myself leave to do so now. I'd like to do it again."

I sat in a chair and he joined me nearby. "I too. But . . . I'd told you I did not want you to kiss me thusly until you could make good on the promise behind it. Which would require marriage."

"I can marry you," he said. "I am no longer a priest. And"—he held his hand up—" 'Tis not for the reason you've accused me."

I opened my mouth to repent, in person, of my tongue-lashing but he stilled me with a look.

"When we last talked I told you that I felt called, nay, required, to help Master Coverdale with his translation of the Old Testament, to complete what Tyndale had begun, and therefore present the entire Scripture in the English language. Late in the summer we completed the task. 'Tis done, Meg! The whole counsel of Scripture. In English!"

His eyes shone as they had when he were a boy and I was transported to that time with him. I grinned back.

"Thus my task was completed, and when my father approached me after Walter's death I prayed and did feel a release of my call. Many reformed priests are marrying now anyway—did you know that Archbishop Cranmer has a secret wife?"

My astonishment must have shown. He grinned at me.

"And your nephew John Rogers is soon to marry, though he will remain a priest. Scripture does not enjoin a priest to remain unmarried. As for me, I am called to something else now—I know not what, as He has not disclosed it to me, but I am released from priesthood."

I had longed for those words. Yearned for them. And now that they had come, I felt an unwelcome hesitancy. "In your note you mentioned Anne," I said.

His face turned somber. "Yes. While here at the Christmas court Rose's husband heard Cromwell speaking with the king. The king asked Cromwell if it should be necessary for him to remarry Katherine of Aragon if anything should . . . happen . . . to Anne."

"Happen?" I pressed for more. "If she dies in childbirth?"

"Or any other way, I suspect," Will said. "It was not made clear nor specific. Cromwell told him no, he would not be required to remarry Katherine—in fact, 'twould further free him. The king is not fearful of making whatever changes he requires to meet his desires. I would not be surprised if he set Cromwell's fine legal mind to figuring out how to disentangle himself from Anne. His love for her seems to have run its course."

More's head on a pike appeared in my mind.

"Is she in danger?" I asked.

Will inhaled deeply but didn't flinch. "Not if a prince is born. Then she'll be safe no matter what his feelings. In fact, I suspect his feelings for her will turn on the birth of a prince. Or not. But if a prince is not born . . ."

I grimaced. Neither of us needed to finish the sentence.

"And as for you . . . what of Lady Jamison?" I asked. "It was only a few weeks ago that Rose introduced her to me. Said your father was negotiating your marriage with her. Rose implied that it was a marriage you wanted as well."

He kissed me again, lightly this time. "There is only one woman I have ever wanted to marry, Meg. That is you."

"But your father may not be amenable to that," I said.

"You are right," Will said. "And the negotiations with Lady Jamison continue apace. So I am here to ask you—can you leave court immediately if I were able to convince him?"

"I have no dowry," I said. "Not even a small one."

"I recall. It is a forbidding obstacle, that is true. I do not know a way round that."

I saw one small flicker of hope. "If things go well for Anne and she births a son, Henry will give me a small dowry for her sake. He knows that we are like sisters. The birth of a prince is all that can save her now. I fear that if the child is not a boy, Henry will put her away, mayhap in an abbey. I have heard rumors of his infatuation with Lady Jane and seen his roving affections."

"And if things go poorly for her?" Will asked.

"Then it would be best for you not to be associated with me at all. I am the closest to her and all know it. It may taint you and your house with the king. Your father would never allow shame to fall upon your house and likely would not even accept a small dowry. Mayhap it would be best for us to put aside the passions of youth and face the responsibilities of adulthood with cold resolve."

Will remained silent for a moment before answering. "What if the passions of youth continued into adulthood? And still grow?"

Mine did too. He knew it.

"Could you leave now before Anne's future is decided one way or another? She's had her life, she's made her choices. Now—before my father finalizes the arrangements with Lady Jamison. Which will be soon. Maybe your father—or Edmund—will pay a dowry."

Lord Jesus, is he right? Am I released from my service to Anne? Have I served her well and now, the very last chance I have for a life, and a man, and a child of my own, may I take it?

The answer came immediately to my heart. *No.*

I didn't pull my hands from his but shook my

head. "Neither Edmund nor my father will help me and Thomas is in no position to help though I know he'd like to. And, my love, I have made a promise to Anne. I, too, have a call, to serve. I believe in his first epistle to the Corinthians, Saint Paul exhorts those of us who have been entrusted with a service to be found faithful."

He sighed. "I regret handing Tyndale's book to you."

"No, you do not," I said. "And besides the call to serve, she is my dearest, closest friend. I will not leave her in her hour of need."

"No," he said. "I knew you would not."

"I love you, Will Ogilvy, soon to be Baron Ogilvy. You are the only man I have ever loved and I declare that I will ever love. If I were free, I would give you my oath now. But when my lady was being crowned queen in Westminster Abbey I felt drawn to the buttresses—yes, the buttresses—in that great building. And I know now why. The building is grand and majestic and able to appear thusly because of the buttresses, which remove weight from the load-bearing beams. I have been given a call to serve. 'Tis my duty."

"I understand," he said.

"I know that." I let my tears flow and he did too.

"I will ever only love you," he said.

"I know that too." For the first time I took the initiative to kiss him. "To remember me by."

"*Nihilo quo tui meminerim mihi opus est,*"

he whispered before bowing, courteously, and left my chambers.

I need nothing to remember you by.

The first death came days after my conversation with Will and looked, at first, like something that Anne's friends should rejoice over. Katherine of Aragon had taken ill just after Christmas. With her so near to death, Anne felt compelled to have Lady Shelton, Mary's governess and Anne's own relation, seek a truce between Anne and Mary. She instructed her, via letter, to suspend all pressure on Mary to conform and said that she herself had considered the Word of God's injunction to do good to one's enemy and hoped that Mary would submit to her father quickly whilst it would still do her good.

Mary, surrounded by the mounting strength of conservative courtiers longing for the old days and a return to the True Faith, and hoping for the passing of favor from Anne, refused the offer of friendship as well as the advice.

On January seventh, shortly after having received extreme unction, Katherine of Aragon died, nearly alone, at cold Kimbolton Castle. Henry could not have behaved with less decorum. He dressed in his finest yellow clothes and kissed Anne often and with great passion in front of all. He sent for the princess Elizabeth and showed her off to the court, loudly proclaiming that she would soon be joined by a brother, the prince. He robbed Katherine of what little remained of her earthly goods, setting one of Cromwell's minions to finesse the legalities so that Mary, and Katherine's charities, received naught. She had asked to be buried in a Carthusian monastery, but 'twas not to be; Cromwell had already begun to dismantle as many Church of Rome properties as possible. She was buried at Peterborough Castle, and although he, shockingly, allowed "Queen of England" to be inscribed on her tomb, Henry, for his part, ordered a celebratory joust to be held on the day of her funeral.

"I love Queen Anne with all my heart, but 'tis a shame, Katherine dying alone an all tha'," Edithe said as she prepared me for bed that night.

" 'Tis," I said, wondering if I, too, were destined to die alone.

"My cousin's a maid for Lady Shelton, Mary's gov'ness. She said that Katherine had asked her confessor if she'd done wrong, afore she died. Asked if by her stubbornness in not giving His Grace a divorce, or hieing her to an abbey, she'd brought heresy to England."

I'd not thought of that. "I do suppose that her refusal forced the king to move against the queen," I said, "and toward reform. For that, we may be glad."

"Yes, ma'am. I am, for certes. Also . . . is it wrong, mistress, to pay attention to those who say deaths happen in threes? 'Tis all the maids can talk of these days."

" 'Tis superstitious nonsense, Edithe, and you should know better!" I snapped.

She nodded. "You're right, ma'am," she said. "I'll be taking your mending and leaving now."

"Thank you," I said, my tone softened. She left and I rolled over in the linens and stared at the cold winter moon. I was at least honest enough with myself to recognize why I had snapped. It was myself I was irritated with. I had not been able to exorcise every superstitious thought from my heart, either, and the worry had crossed my mind about death happening in threes too.

Henry's joust had been planned for January 24, and that morn I arrived in my lady's chamber to help her dress for the event. The king would be wearing one of her favors, and I'd had a dress made of similar fabric, fashioned so it was clear to all present whose favor the king rode under.

When I arrived in her apartments, though, she was still in bed. "I am afraid I am unwell," she said.

"But, lady—the king's joust!" I insisted. Nan Zouche looked at me, urging me on. The king did not like to perform without an audience; he played to the ladies, of whom his wife was foremost.

" 'Tis all the activity and chatter round Katherine's death," Anne said. "I shall send my regrets to the king, with a note, and hope to lie here and recover my health before the dinner tonight."

She sent her secretary with the note, and I and many of the other ladies followed to the jousting arena shortly thereafter. The king did not have Anne's favor on his lance. 'Twas not certain whose favor he rode under, but the plain fabric looked distressingly like the light brown gown on Jane Seymour.

He turned back to the field, ready to meet his challenger at the lists, when all of a sudden his great horse stumbled. The crowd let out a collective gasp and then many screamed as both Henry, wearing over one hundred pounds of armor, and his horse fell heavily to the ground. Shockingly, the horse fell partly on top of His Majesty.

"Help us, help now!" one of the noblemen near the field called out. Several men threw off their own armor and ran to the king's side and many others streamed from the arena to the field. They lifted the horse, who was frothing at his bit with his eyes rolling back into his head, and pulled the king out from under him. Tearing off Henry's armor, one checked for a pulse.

"Someone tell the queen!" a call went out, and I saw Norfolk dash back toward the palace. I stood of a moment, looking at His Grace, willing him to stand up, to sit up, to call out. He did none of them, rather continued to lay without consciousness.

"Come." Nan Zouche grabbed my arm. "We must to Anne!"

I picked up my skirts and we ran toward Anne's rooms. We were still well down the hall when we heard her wailing. I pushed open the door to see Norfolk trying to talk sense to her.

"He's dead! Dead!" Anne cried out, and held her hands in her hair, clutching great clumps of it but not tearing it. The tactless Norfolk, always ready to crow bad news, had told her the king was dead!

I took her face in my hands and stared in her eyes. "He is not yet dead, madam. He has lost his senses, but he may yet regain them."

She looked at me, eyes going from wild to guarded. "Is it true?"

"Yes, dearest," I said. "He is fine. Now calm yourself for the babe's sake, if not for your own."

She breathed heavily for another few minutes whilst Lady Zouche rushed Norfolk from the room. Anne settled and within hours someone had sent word that the king was now conscious and speaking but badly bruised.

I spent the night in Anne's chambers, brushing her hair, whispering about light topics to bring a smile to her face. It was first light when she called to me. "Meg."

I awoke from my chair near her bed and came to her side. "Yes, Anne?"

"I feel a trickle of blood down the inside of

my thigh," she whispered. " 'Tis yet only a trickle. I need linen. And prayer."

For whatever reason, it seemed as though the Lord Jesus had stoppered His ears against our many entreaties, because soon thereafter the trickle turned into an ooze and by the fourth day, it was clear that the queen was going to have to do the mighty, sorrowful travail of delivering a child which would not live to take a breath. Our king was delivered from death just afore his child was ushered into it.

The midwife had been called. After the baby's body had been delivered Anne called out, "Was it a boy?"

The midwife looked at the tiny child, crossed herself, and then said, "Yes, madam. A son."

The second death of the new year.

Anne burst out in tears, long jagged sobs from which she would not be pulled back. Four days of weariness and birth work coupled with the certain knowledge of how her husband would take the news fused into an animal-like wail. I sat on one side of her and my sister, Alice, on her other. After some time she looked up at us, composed herself, and said, "I have miscarried of my savior."

Henry was well enough to come to visit her within days. We had her made up to look as lovely as could be, but she was still wan from the delivery. She dismissed us, but I and my sister remained, unseen, in her closet nearby. I wanted to be at hand should she need me when the king took his leave.

He came into the room, dismissed his men, and, from the foot of her bed, said, "I see that God does not wish to give me male children. At least, not by you."

"I am sorry, sire. It was my worry for you, my worry for your well-being when you had been unhorsed."

"You would have done better by me to have kept your peace and nurtured my son rather than let your emotions run untamed and cause his certain death."

I held my breath. *Anne—causing the child's death?* Could he not find it possible to offer her a word of comfort or hope as he had before?

"I do keep my peace, sire. But 'tis hard to do when I see how you favor others with that which rightfully belongs to me."

She spoke of Mistress Seymour, of course, and all the others that had come before her.

"Nothing belongs to you, madam, you understand, except for what I give you. You would do well, as I once warned you, to shut your eyes and ignore, as your betters did."

I could hear Anne sit up in bed. "Katherine shut her eyes because she loved you not. Yea, she may have served you. She was obedient. She did as she was told and as was expected. Because she did not love you, Henry, as I do, she could afford to shut her eyes; it pained her not to shut her eyes. But when I shut my eyes I see my husband in bed with another woman and I cannot bear it!" By now she was shrieking.

Please, Lord Jesus, close her mouth. Close it. Henry hated a scene unless he was throwing it.

She quieted herself and finished softly, "My heart breaks when I see you with others."

Henry stood for a moment, shocked, I was sure, that anyone was speaking to him thusly. If her words moved him, he didn't show it in his response. "I will see you when you are well," was his reply. Within minutes the door to her chamber closed and I went to her. She accepted my arms and words with nary a response.

By March my sister told me that the king had sent a purse of gold to Jane Seymour, along with a sealed letter. An invitation, all were certain, to join him in his chamber.

Mistress Seymour returned the letter to him unopened—thereby deftly sidestepping a direct answer to his invitation—but did reply that as a gentlewoman born of good and honorable parents, and she with an unsullied reputation, she must refuse His Majesty's gift. She would be prepared, however, to accept a gift from him upon her marriage. She withdrew from court to stay at the home of Sir Nicolas Carewe, who had turned into one of Anne's deadliest enemies.

Henry was noted to be moping about at Jane's absence.

And then it was April, not March, that was in like a lamb, out like a lion.

TWENTY-THREE

Year of Our Lord 1536
Greenwich Palace

In early April, afore the Easter celebrations, Anne held a quiet dinner in His Majesty's chambers with some intimate courtiers and noblemen. Subdued laughter and talk wound quietly through the dolorous Lenten evening as we mingled while waiting for the king to arrive; he had been called into a last-minute discussion with his chamberlain. Anne made sure all were comfortable with sugared plums and sweetmeats and wine before seating herself next to Cromwell. 'Twas clear to me that their once-warm friendship had suffered a draft of some sort and I sorrowed it because she needed his protection. I chatted with my brother Thomas, with one ear to Anne in case she needed assistance.

And she did. Though in this matter, I could not help.

"So, Master Cromwell, I understand that the dismantling of the monasteries is well under way. I'd heard that more than half have already been turned over to the crown," she said, ensuring that he knew she was kept informed. Her voice was light and she kept a smile on her face, but all who knew Anne could tell the difference between her light court banter and her prose with a purpose. I admired the fact that she consistently upheld her causes but wondered if, in light of her not-yet-mended relationship with the king, it might not have been wiser to keep the conversation to lighter matters and win some allies.

"Yes, madam, 'tis true," Cromwell replied. "And as we share a faith, for certes you are glad that good English money no longer flows to Italy to support His Majesty's enemies."

"I am very pleased of that indeed," Anne said. "Of course the monasteries and other religious houses were intended to help the poor and educate the people. Am I to understand that will continue to be their purpose under the Church in England? I have of late appointed my chaplain, Matthew Parker, to oversee education at Stoke-by-Claire. I endeavor to see the monies from these houses, as they become available, do good to the people of His Grace's realm."

Cromwell shifted in his seat but he did not retreat from his position. I suspect he knew he had the king's approval for the direction he was taking. "We all seek the best possible outcome for the king, madam. At present, I believe that will be found by shoring up His Majesty's coffers and winning and retaining the goodwill and support of the noblemen—especially those in the north."

"I agree those matters are of great import, but I sharply disagree with using religious houses to achieve them," Anne said, "and I shall actively work to see that the Lord's money is put to benevolent purposes."

Cromwell dipped his head. It seemed as though Anne took that for a capitulation, but actually, it was an acknowledgment of the king, who had entered his chamber. From the look on his face he was in a foul mood.

"Lord Cromwell." Henry clapped Cromwell on the back. "How goes my business?"

"It goes well, sire," Cromwell said after we'd all righted ourselves from prostrate positions. The king took his seat next to Anne and greeted her properly. "I was sharing with your most beloved wife that we are using the monies gained from liquidating properties to enrich Your Majesty, where all good English money should have ended up all along. I shan't let anyone stand in your way."

"Yes, of course," Henry said. "Good work, man." He turned and signaled to one of his menservants. "And now, we are hungry." The first of seventeen fish courses was brought out. I noticed that but for a small slice of carp and a tiny forkful of eel Anne ate nearly nothing. She'd looked particularly wan since the loss of the last baby. Henry did not, as were his usual custom, offer her the best bits from his plate first.

Master Cromwell never looked in her direction again that night. Anne had alienated a powerful man. Like Katherine before her, did she not realize that in a battle of wills with His Majesty the challenger would always lose? I suspected that she would not give up, though, as she, too, had a call and remained faithful to it. She pleaded with the king on behalf of the wealth of the abbeys for days afterward to little avail, except to irritate him further.

If she didn't understand where things stood between them at the beginning of the month, for certes, she did at the end.

Late in Easter week my brother Thomas slipped into my room after quickly knocking. I was already in my dressing gown for the night and Edithe had left.

"Thomas!" It was unusual for him to appear at my chamber at nighttime.

"I have overheard something that you must pass on to Anne," he said. He drank down an entire cup of ale and then told me. "Nicolas Carewe is planning to bring Anne down. He's got Cromwell on his side now—told Cromwell that his plans for the abbey and monastery money would never be approved by Anne and that all knew when Anne was in favor things went the way she directed the king. That Cromwell couldn't take a chance on Anne becoming pregnant again and winning His Majesty to her side."

"And Cromwell believed him?" I pulled my robe around me.

"He did," Thomas said. "He has risen a long way from the smithy and seems, in his own eyes, anyway, invincible. He likes that noblemen such as Carewe play to his ego. Carewe has promised that if Lady Jane Seymour is made queen she will be pliable to the will of Carewe, who will remain pliable to Cromwell's. Carewe also reminded Cromwell of the fate that Anne had wrought on Wolsey, who had, as you know, been in Crom-well's position for many years."

"Henry wrought that on Wolsey, not Anne." I sat down in my chair. "Exactly how do they expect to get Anne out of the way so Mistress Seymour can poach her stag?"

Thomas looked at me. "I know not for sure, because as they approached this juncture in the conversation they noticed I was about them, and all know, of course, my feelings for Anne. I do know that Carewe whispered 'adultery' to Crom-well."

"And adultery against the king, under the new acts, is treason."

"A capital offense," Thomas agreed.

Capitalis. My Latin rushed back to me. Of the head.

"I must keep a low profile myself now, and, sickeningly, ingratiate myself with Cromwell so I myself am not suspect. But warn Anne to have a care where other men are concerned."

He slipped out as quietly as he arrived. I could not go to Anne that night without drawing undue attention, but I did ensure an early arrival at her apartments the next day. The news didn't seem to surprise her but did further aggravate her uneven nerves.

A week or more hence a young musician, Mark Smeaton, was mooning about Anne's chambers, flirting with one woman or the next in between the songs that he played on his lute. He was a young lad, not yet twenty, and unschooled in the ways of the court though quick to pick up on courtly flirtation. When he tried it on Anne, however, she batted him down and he moped around playing melancholy songs. Finally, she could take it no more.

"Why are you so sad, Master Smeaton?" she asked.

He sighed, looked longingly in her direction, and replied, "Ah. 'Tis no matter." He mooned after her in a distressingly familiar way and she needed to put it to rights.

"You may not look to have me speak to you as I should do to a nobleman," she said, "because you be an inferior person."

Truly, a man with any manners at all would

not have placed her in such a position.

"No, no, madam," he replied. "A look sufficed me; and thus fare you well." He took his lute, and his charms, to Mistress Shelton, who received him as coldly as Anne did or worse.

Where Sir Henry Norris was concerned, though, Madge Shelton was not so ready to forgive nor forget an offense. It seems she had not forgotten being snubbed at Wolf Hall, and rather than blame her own loose shift for a lack of suitors she had decided to blame Anne.

"Tell us, Sir Norris, why have you not yet taken a wife?" Madge asked in her pretty voice one evening over cards.

"I would tarry for a time," Norris said.

Madge laughed loudly, as did some of her friends. "Sir, a time? By your age many a man would now have sons and daughters ready to be placed at court."

I held back a tart retort that many women her age would, too, because of course it could be directed back at me.

"Mayhap you prefer a woman who is already taken?" Madge badgered, looking at Anne. "A queen, mayhap?" Norris and Anne had enjoyed one another's company, but only as friends; she played cards or engaged in light banter with him, as she, and all of us, did with many courtiers.

There was an audible gasp in the room. I recalled to mind that Madge's mother was the governess to Mary, Katherine of Aragon's daughter, whom many hoped to restore to the succession. Was she pushing Anne?

"Then you look for dead men's shoes!" Anne snapped. "For if aught were to come to the king but good you would look to have me? Foolishness!"

The room grew silent. Naught had been charged afore Anne spoke, but under the new laws, by thus speaking of the king as dead, trying to forestall an accusation, Anne had rather stepped into a previously nonexistent trap. Norris knew it.

"If he should have any such thought," he said, "I wish my head were off."

"Begone!" Anne said, clearly shaken by the direction of the conversation. Norris fled from the room and one by one the ladies and gentlemen dispersed as well, leaving only Nan Zouche; my sister, Alice; and me to serve Anne.

Madge Shelton was one of the first to leave, of course, arm in arm with Jane Rochford. It was not difficult to guess where they were going. Sir Nicolas Carewe.

On April 30, Master Smeaton was arrested. No one spoke of it, but rumor filtered back that he was being racked in order to force a confession of adultery with the queen. As the king prepared for a week of celebrations, including a May Day joust, he introduced Anne to some visiting ambassadors as "my entirely beloved wife."

His eyes, though, were dead. For the first time I felt that mayhap all was truly lost.

That night, Anne and I were in her rooms. "What shall I do?" she asked me. Her long, tapered fingers were clenched into fists. She was too thin, and there were ash smudges under her eyes.

"Can you go to him quietly, speak of your love?" I asked.

"He will not see me privately. In public, he acts as though all is well but he knows, and I know, that there is a wall between us. A wall he has placed."

"Does he see Elizabeth?" I asked. We had previously judged the king's affections for Katherine by his willingness to see and act kindly toward Princess Mary.

Anne's face came to life. "Yes! Go fetch Elizabeth." She was already in her quarters, having been brought from Hatfield for the celebration. I went to the princess's chambers and brought her back to her mother, singing little songs to her along the way. Anne clung to the toddler when she arrived and Elizabeth entwined her little fingers in her mother's hair. Anne kissed Elizabeth's pretty pink cheeks a dozen times or more and cooed to her in French, and her daughter responded with uninhibited joy and love. Shortly thereafter, Anne sent for

Elizabeth's finest outfit, her carefully fitted hat, silk hose, and shoes.

"Where we go, *maman?*" Elizabeth asked prettily.

"To see Papa," Anne replied. I tried to lighten the mood by teasing Anne that she was making Elizabeth a slave to fashion as she was herself, but she was now in no mood for joking. Already, I suspect, she knew what the stakes were and that she must use every tool at her disposal to save her life.

She scooped Elizabeth up and brought her outside of Greenwich proper, expecting the king to ride in from a hunt. When he did, he drew his horse near to them but did not dismount. I watched from the window as Anne pleaded with him, held their daughter to him, curtseyed to him, and cried. It seemed for naught. He slapped his horse's flank with his gloves and headed back to the stable. Sir Nicolas Carewe, Anne's traitorous cousin, had just been given the Order of the Garter promised to the now-overlooked George Boleyn. There were no surer sign for the courtiers who watched, unseen, from every window, that the king's affections for Anne and her daughter had passed.

In my chambers, I cried for both them, forsaken and forlorn on the castle green.

The next day, May Day, found the king in an unusually jovial mood. He had all of his favorites around him, both men and women. Anne's brother was there, of course, as was Sir Henry Norris, who had well served the king for nigh on two decades. Afore that they had been brought up together. When Sir Norris's charger stumbled, Henry graciously offered him the use of his own. Nicolas Carewe was there, and he'd brought along Jane Seymour.

Anne was regal in the queen's box but she was thinner than ever and her dresses, though I'd had a care to have them taken in, still hung a bit about her. Her eyes, lovely jewels of black like the deep obsidian brought back from the Holy Land, still shone.

Lord, have a care for my friend through this treacherous passage.

After the match, Henry uncharacteristically asked six men to join him on a ride back to Whitehall. He had no intention of returning to Greenwich Palace, where we would. Henry Norris and George Boleyn were two of the six. The king slipped away without a word to Anne.

By midnight word had raced back to Greenwich. Lord Zouche had told his wife, Nan, what had transpired, and she ran to the queen's chambers to wake and to tell us. Jane Rochford and Madge Shelton had been notably absent from the ladies since the afternoon.

"You have been accused of adultery with Mark

Smeaton, Your Grace," Nan told Anne. Anne sat on her bed.

"Smeaton? That whelp of a lute player? Surely Henry cannot believe—"

Nan held up her hand and then took Anne in her arms. "Not only Smeaton, lady, but Henry Norris. It seems that your cousin Madge Shelton had run to Carewe with the details of your disagreement of a few weeks back, claiming that it had been a lover's spat centered about a hope for the king's death."

"And Henry believed her," Anne said, her voice dull. "Where is Norris?"

"To be conducted to the Tower upon the morning tide, madam." Lady Zouche indicated that I should sit on the other side of Anne. "The worst, my lady, is that they have accused you of adultery and incest with your brother."

"George?" Anne stood up. "They have accused me of carnal knowledge of my brother, George? What evil fool brings this charge that it may even be considered?"

"His wife, Jane Rochford," Nan whispered. Anne stood, turned her back to us, and then vomited on the floor.

TWENTY-FOUR

Year of Our Lord 1536
Greenwich Palace

The next morning guards were sent to take Anne to be interrogated before the council at Greenwich. I dressed her quickly in a gown that was both somber and regal and pulled her hair under one of her famous French hoods.

"I hear my uncle Norfolk will be on council," she said. "Mayhap he will bring some reason to the questions. 'Tis not so long ago he were an official at my coronation and the birth of Elizabeth."

"Yes, Your Majesty, we may pray 'tis so," I said, but held little hope in the constancy of Norfolk's affections.

"Fitzwilliam will be there too," Nan Zouche said. "Have a care. Have a care." Fitzwilliam had been an especial friend to Wolsey and had always held Anne responsible for his death. For which among us could serve a master we believed to order the slaughter of innocents? No, no, 'twas far better to scapegoat someone to the side so that we might continue to shut our eyes and serve in peace.

With the hour news came back to us that while

Anne had not been condemned, yet she would be taken by boat to the Tower. I quickly packed several of her gowns, and her prayer books, Bible, and letter-writing materials. Her hair combs. I left the royal jewels in her box but took her personal items out, some strings of pearls and a dual locket ring, afore racing down to my own rooms.

"Edithe!" I handed the jewels over to her. "Quickly. I want you to leave Greenwich and go to Hever. Find Roger and get him, and your son still at home, and leave Hever. Go to My Lord Asquith's home, however you may get there. I do not know what will happen at Hever but you need to find safe employment and 'twill not be here nor there."

I handed the bundle to her. "Do not open this, stash it in your saddle bag, and be gone. Give it to Will when you reach him. He will find service for you in his household, with his lady, or in his family. Go! Now!"

"What has happened to the queen, my lady? Where is Anne?" she asked me, wringing her red hands.

"She is to be taken to the Tower."

"Oh no. No!" Edithe cried. "And you, mistress. Where will you go?"

"I shall stay here until I am allowed to join the queen. My place is to be with my friend and offer her whatever comfort and love I may."

"No, ma'am, please. You must to your sister's

house. Or Allington. Edmund will take you, given the circumstances."

"Go," I said to her firmly. I held her to me, hugged her one last time, and left for Anne's rooms.

She was there when I arrived. "It went poorly. My uncle Norfolk was no help at all. He simply said 'tut tut' and shook his finger at me. In a haste to return to his rooms and dally with his mistress, I suppose."

"We shall not need his help," I said defiantly. "There are surely others."

"You're not to come with me, Meg," she said. "Lady Kingston, the wife of the lieutenant of the Tower, will be in charge of the four ladies I may take with me. Mrs. Stonor, the mother of the maid who has 'witnessed' much of my illicit goings-on, will come. My aunt Lady Boleyn, favorite of Katherine of Aragon, is come to twist the sword. As is Jane Rochford."

"Jane?"

"I suspect to keep me from talking," Anne said. Her eyes were red and rimmed but she'd regained her dignity and I would not do or say anything to unsettle it. "Thank you for packing my things, dearest. And, and should I not see you again . . ."

I ran to her and held her tightly in my arms. "I shall follow anon. I shall find a way to get to you. I will not leave you in any manner. I will be there shortly. Depend upon it."

She nodded and said no more, nor did I. We both needed to believe that it would happen.

That night word filtered back to Greenwich that Henry, still at York Place, alternated wandering about the palace bemoaning his bad luck to all who would hear with festive, flirtatious merriment with Jane Seymour. He'd taken to carrying a small book in which he had written down all of the ways Anne had tricked and bewitched him, pressing it upon all who would read it and agree. His capacity at table was surpassed only by his appetite for self-pity. His maudlin moaning drew silent disgust from all listeners, even those who wished to see his daughter Mary reinstated in the succession. If he'd stuck simply with Anne's perhaps having had one lover, some may have believed him. But when he claimed that she had had more than one hundred secret lovers in three years, including her brother, even her enemies knew to disbelieve him.

That night, afore his baseborn son the Duke of Richmond went to sleep, he stopped by his father's chambers. Word came that Henry kissed his son violently on each cheek and told him, weeping, "You and your sister Mary owe God a great debt for having escaped the hands of that cursed and poisoning whore who had planned to poison you both." One can only imagine what Richmond, whose wife, Mary Fitzroy, was an especial favorite of Anne, thought of this rant.

Greenwich was in a silent panic. No one knew

whether to go, to stay, who would be next, or what was happening at the Tower. I moved in with my sister, Alice, and shared her lady maid, who, because of her long affiliation with the Rogers family, would not be tainted by us Wyatts. It was a good thing Alice and I were together because on May 8 our brother Thomas was conducted to the Tower under suspicion of adultery with Anne.

I allowed myself the indulgence of letting my mind wander for a moment to consider what life would have been like had Anne married Thomas and I married Will. I ached with the wishing of it and turned my thoughts away.

"I had not a chance to bid Thomas good-bye!" I wailed in her chambers. This time I let myself cry and Alice did too. Even Edmund, mayhap with an eye to our family name if not for fraternal devotion, tried to get Cromwell to speak on Thomas's behalf. It was no use. The king's blood-lust had been stirred beyond restraint, and, I fear, he viewed this as a chance to rid himself of all who may have irritated him for any reason at all.

My father had been told of Thomas's arrest and aroused himself from stupor long enough to say, "If he be a true man, as I trust he is, his truth will him deliver." Then he fell asleep. Edmund said he would prevail upon Father to write a letter on Thomas's behalf to the king.

I sat down one night, after Alice had gone to bed, and prayed. *Lord Jesus, please let me go to*

Anne. Her trial, if there even be one, will happen quickly. She needs comfort and love and that means me. And surely, Lord, of all the bishops she has placed on Your behalf in England, one could be spared to soothe and console her?

A picture came to mind. Lambeth Palace. I would speak, if I could, to Archbishop Cranmer.

I confess it was not easy to find Cranmer, but now that I had no duties to Anne I was free to make my way. I took my steed and rode to Lambeth Palace. I'm sure I looked a sight when I arrived, and his servants were loath to let me in.

"Wait—'tis Lady Blackston," one of them pointed out. I was glad to be recognized and nodded as I shook off my hood. They let me in and I pleaded for a moment with Cranmer.

When I was ushered into his chamber he greeted me kindly but coolly. None of us knew whom to trust and whom to keep at arm's length.

"Archbishop," I said, "thank you for seeing me."

"Gladly, my lady," he said. "I know you are the aunt of John Rogers, devoted to the cause. And, of course, great friend to the queen. I am, even now, writing to the king on her behalf."

I could barely stop the sobs from coming forth. "So you will champion her, then?" I asked.

I saw the look on his face and knew that he would not go as far as she needed him to, and my voice grew pointed. "She needs your assistance, sir, as she readily offered it to you in placing you to this position. Have you no shame or sense of honor?"

"I do what I can, my lady. I offer the king a letter in which I explain that I have never had a better opinion of a woman than I did in her, which makes me think that she should not be culpable. But," he added to me, "of course His Highness would not have gone so far except she surely had been culpable."

"You cannot think that!" I said. "You know that is untrue."

He flinched. He was a man conflicted in the job he never wanted; I suspected he would like nothing more than to retreat to a small country home with his secret wife. But it was not to be.

"None of us chose to be here but, Bishop Cranmer, as we find ourselves in this time and in this place, you must play the man and do your part."

"You shall not scold me, madam," he said. "I tell the king, herein"—he tapped the letter—"that I love her not a little, for the love which I judge her to bear toward God and His gospel. But if she be culpable of these things, then no one should but hate her because of the way she has mistreated the gospel."

"I understand now. You are going to allow Anne to take a fall to save the reform." He did not deny it. "How does your letter finish, sir?"

He looked down upon it. "I tell him that I trust His Grace will bear no less entire favor to the gospel because he was not led to it by affection to her but by zeal unto the truth."

"If there is one thing made plain, Archbishop, in this entire matter, it is not that His Majesty has zeal unto the truth."

He looked at me, stricken, as I said that, realizing that by my saying it and his hearing it we could both be judged guilty of treason. "Is there anything further I can do for you, madam?"

"Yes." I drew my cloak about my riding habit. "You can convince Master Cromwell to replace Anne's ladies with friends who love her and will bring her care and comfort in her last days. 'Tis the least you can do. Find a way to get me to the Tower."

He nodded. I expected that he would not act upon it. But he did.

Within days the council began to break up Anne's household. It would be disbanded by the thirteenth of May. Anne had not yet had her trial. Would she have one at all? The fact that her household was being broken up indicated that the king had already concluded that she would not be coming back to court. The courtiers who gained so much by her favor now fled and, like Saint Peter, denied in every manner possible knowledge of her at all.

The king, for his part, made several romantic rendezvous to Beddington, wherein Mistress Seymour lodged with Sir Nicolas Carewe, chief perpetrator of the case against Anne. Even the fishwives of London, we'd heard, the same stout matrons who had hurled dung and insults at her carriage three years past, now stood by her in righteous indignation. The king had not a care for their, or anyone else's, opinion of the matter.

"My lady," said a messenger come from Crom-well's. I had been packing my things, supposing that Edmund would, compelled by duty or at least not wanting to shame the Wyatt name, take me in for a short while if I could not lodge with Alice for a spell.

"Yes?" I said.

" 'Tis orders." He handed a scroll to me. "You, your sister, and Lady Zouche are commanded to the Tower. These men"—he indicated four burly guards standing behind him—"are to escort you on the tide."

"Do we go as . . . prisoners?" I swallowed back my fear.

"You go first to serve the queen," he said tautly. "After that, I know not."

TWENTY-FIVE

Year of Our Lord 1536
The Tower of London

There are many ways to arrive at the Tower of London, though there are few ways out. Kings and queens ride in before a coronation, retinue trailing like a train of ermine. Prisoners, however, arrive on foot, shoved through one cavernous gate or another by the wardens, who live, as all do, at the mercy of a merciless king. Some unfortunate few are delivered to the Tower by water.

The Thames lapped against our boat as it stopped to allow for the entry gate to be raised. The metal teeth lifted high enough for the oarsmen to row us into the Tower's maw, called Traitor's Gate. This beast never ate its fill and, like all beasts of prey, ate only flesh. It brought to mind the words of King David: *My soul is among lions: I lie even among them that are set on fire, even the sons of men, whose teeth are spears and arrows, and their tongue a sharp sword.*

I glanced up as Lady Zouche caught a sob in her handkerchief. I then looked to my older sister, Alice, for comfort. She held my gaze with a somber shake of her head. Our falsely accused brother was even now waiting, being digested in the belly within. For the first time Alice had no comfort to offer me, no tonic of hope.

Momentarily we bumped up against the stone stairways leading out of the water and were commanded to quickly disembark.

I had half expected Henry to quarter her in some kind of dungeon, but no, Sir William Kingston informed us upon our arrival that Anne was staying at the Queen's Lodging, which had been refurbished to her tastes just three years past, in advance of her coronation. We walked up the green and to the doors that led to her apartments. Four armed burly guards stood in front of the door. When we arrived, they parted like the Red Sea and let us through.

I opened the door and went in first. Her receiving room was simpler than when we were last there: one bed and several pallets, now pushed up against the wall. A study desk. Cold stone walls—no tapestries to warm nor cheer had been sent. A pitcher of water sat on a basin. There was a privy pot squatting under her bed. Then I saw Anne, in the corner of the receiving room, sitting on her bed, her hair pulled back but not done, her shoulders back, not wilting in defeat. Her aunt, Lady Norfolk, gossiped in a corner with Jane Rochford. Clearly neither was there to serve.

"We've come, darling," I said, rushing to her bed and taking her into my arms. She fell into them for a moment, then regained her composure.

"I'm so glad you've arrived," she said. Her voice and her hands tremored slightly. "The ladies here will want a break from their strenuous service, for certes." At that she began to laugh, not the low, husky laugh I was accustomed to hearing from her but one with the high pitch of hysteria hiding just behind the jollity. "If you're allowed to me then it must be done and over with. What of the king's council? Why have they not questioned me to see if there needs be a trial?"

"The king's men told us on the way to the Tower that the trial has already been scheduled, Your Grace," I said. "The gentlemen of the privy chamber will be tried today. You and George are to be tried on Monday next."

"On what have they based these charges?" she asked. "When they bring them to me, I can but say nay."

"On hearsay, Anne."

Jane Rochford kept her distance. While my sister, Alice, unpacked some new garments for Anne, and Lady Zouche brought her copy of Tyndale's Scriptures, I addressed myself to the ladies taking leave. Lady Norfolk turned her back on me afore I could speak.

But Jane pulled herself up into an arrogant stance and shot me a buttery grin. "If you're kind to me, Mistress Wyatt, I shall see to it that Jane Seymour offers you a place in her privy chamber, along with me."

"I am not surprised that you sold yourself so cheaply. But to sell your husband too?" I said. "Even Judas held out for thirty pieces of silver." I drew near to her, near enough to see the bloodshot veins in her eyes and to inhale her putrid breath, which smelt of her many black teeth. "Recall you this, Jane Parker. He who lives by the sword shall die by the sword."

She recoiled from me at that and crossed herself.

"You needn't cross yourself, madam," I said. " 'Tis a promise from the Lord Jesus Christ Himself."

She, Mrs. Cousins, and Lady Norfolk took their leave; the king had sent a litter to carry them back to court so they need not suffer the indignity of the waterway. I was glad to be rid of them. Nan Zouche kept herself busy unpacking some things we'd brought for Anne and my sister went to visit my brother Thomas, lodged nearby in the Bell Tower. Anne seemed deeply grieved to learn that he'd been imprisoned too. I did not share with her that our final fate had not yet been clarified.

I attended to Anne. "How do you fare?" I asked quietly. Now that Jane and the others were gone she settled in.

"As well as I may," she said. "How does my mother? My father? My daughter?"

"They grieve, and the babe, of course, knows naught. Lady Bryan shall be loving to her, as ever. I, I took your pearls and your locket ring and hid them. I shall ensure she receives them if . . ."

"If I cannot," Anne finished. I nodded.

When Alice returned to the Queen's Lodging she whispered to me that all of the men of the privy chamber had been found guilty of adultery with the queen, though none save Smeaton would admit anything at all, nor malign Anne, even when promised leniency if they'd admit.

"Speak up, Lady," Anne called from her chair. "I wish to hear the details. You've naught to spare me from."

"The jury was packed with noblemen sympathetic to Katherine and Mary, madam, as well as those who favor Jane Seymour."

"Who has, I suppose, taken up residence in my bed?"

I shook my head. "She says she will not partner with the king till after they are married."

Anne laughed. "She's only just clever enough to imitate but has not the wit to generate an idea of her own nor the morals to hold to them if she had." She quieted some. "And the men tried today?"

"Have been returned to the Tower to await traitors' deaths, my queen," Alice said. No one needed to elaborate on what that meant.

"Even Ambassador Chapuys, a Spaniard whom you know to be no friend to you nor to your faction, stated, 'They were condemned upon presumption and certain indications without proof of confession.' "

"Methinks he will not repeat that to the king," Anne said bitterly.

"No, my lady," Alice said. "I think not."

When Anne dozed off for a moment Alice and I clung to one another and grieved for our brother Thomas, whose fate was still undecided. When I stepped outside of Anne's chambers for some air I could see the tower in which he languished.

Some time passed and Sir William came to check on us and deliver the evening meal. Anne took it graciously and then asked, "If these men have already been convicted of fornicating with me, then there is no hope that I shall be found innocent, is there?"

"The poorest subject the king has will see justice," he replied.

Anne laughed again, but it was controlled.

We quieted her with food and wine and spent the weekend at prayer. I did everything within my power and beseeched God, on her behalf, to do what was in His, to help her remain calm and dignified on Monday.

Although the men of the privy chamber had been tried at Westminster, Anne and George were to be tried within the Tower itself. Special stands were constructed within the King's Hall, as if for a great sporting event; we could hear them building all weekend long.

I chose a somber yet royal dress of purple for

her to wear, modest and yet becoming. She wore a cloak trimmed with ermine, as was her right.

"Thank you, Meg," she said to me. Her voice was steady, as were her hands.

" 'Tis my pleasure to dress and prepare you for whatever your needs are, Anne," I said.

She leaned over and kissed my cheek. "Your friendship is a constant reminder to me of God's goodness."

I turned away then, so she could not see my tears, and prayed that I, too, would find God's goodness in these spiderwebbed corners of life.

Nearly two thousand spectators sweated and grunted and leaned a ready ear in the great hall when we entered. 'Twas like a baiting—all seated round watching the prodding in hopes of provok-ing a response to bring the crowd to their feet. As it was summer, no candles were needed in support of the light streaming through the great, veined windows. Anne's uncle, the faithless Lord Norfolk, presiding as lord high steward for the day, was seated at the center of a large planked table in front. A chair, comfortable but certainly no throne, was placed for Anne. As the Scripture exhorting me not to return evil for evil came to mind, I repented of my wish that there would be a warm corner in hell for Norfolk someday soon and instead prayed for his eyes to be opened this day and justice to be served.

Sitting on the panel of peers was Henry Percy,

Lord Northumberland, Anne's first love. What, I wondered, would her life have been like had she married him? Would Wolsey, now with plenty of time in eternity to consider his life anew and again, wish himself back in time and offer his assistance to the marriage rather than blocking it and making way for the king?

"Madam," Norfolk began, "you are principally charged with having cohabited with your brother, George, Lord Rochford, and other accomplices. You are charged with having promised to marry Henry, Lord Norris, upon the king's death, which you both hoped for. You are charged with having favorites in the court, men and boys, and plying them with gifts so they could slake your lusts. You are charged with witchcraft. To these charges, what do you plead?"

Anne stood, waited till all eyes were upon her, and answered. "I plead not guilty to each offense, My Lord of Norfolk."

Norfolk read off the dates of the supposed adulteries. I was exultant as I heard them. In many of them, Anne was in a completely different place than the accused spot of rendezvous. A simple review of the king's books could affirm that. Or the men charged were elsewhere. Or she had been recovering from childbirth, surrounded at all hours by her ladies, and still bleeding.

Anne refuted each charge. The spectators, all

two thousand of them, seemed with her. I heard some cheers on her behalf from the crowd, which Lord William's men quickly quieted.

"It may be so that you can lay claim for these dates, but the document specifically claims that there were divers other dates and places, both before and after," Norfolk boomed out.

"Unless specific times and places are named I cannot answer the charges," Anne said. To that, there was no reply. I knew then that she was done. One look at Anne's face and I knew she knew, had long known, that guilty was the foregone conclusion of the "trial."

"Do you admit to nothing at all, madam?" Norfolk said, after being prodded by Anne's longtime nemesis the Duke of Suffolk.

"I do not say that I have always borne toward the king the humility which I owed him, considering his kindness and the great honor he showed me, and the great respect he always paid me. I admit, too, that often I have taken it into my head to be jealous of him where other maidens were concerned. But may God be my witness if I have done him any other wrong."

'Twas not a wife in the world who could not confess likewise. The crowds in the stands made it plain that they were now on Anne's side. Alas, the peers summoned by His Majesty's council were not.

"Gentlemen? Your verdict?"

One by one they stood and declared, "Guilty." And then sat down. To a man.

Anne stared directly at Henry Percy as he choked out the word "guilty." She had been right. It was not good to pledge yourself to a weak man. Mayhap, she'd learnt to her distress, not to one overly strong, either.

Norfolk now stood and declared the sentence. All knew that the typical method of death for a traitoress was burning alive, and that was what we all expected. I stiffened my back so I should not let my friend down at her hour of need.

"Because you are queen," Norfolk said, "we declare that you should be burned, or beheaded, at the king's pleasure. His judgment will be sent for."

Anne swayed slightly but did not fail. "I am resigned to die, but I regret that so many others, innocent and ever loyal to the king, would die with me." She waited in the silence. No one responded. "I would ask a short space for shrift, to settle my accounts and make things right with God," she finished. It was always possible that the king would have her slain the next morning or even afore.

"You will be notified of the king's response," was Norfolk's reply. At that, the peers turned and left. The guards held back the crowd while Anne, and we ladies, returned to Queen's Lodging to prepare her for her death, by burning, or beheading, we knew not which.

• • •

Later that day George Boleyn was tried. All expected him to be acquitted but, alas, what did him in was a letter from his wife stating that her husband had certainly had a sexual relationship with his sister, the queen. The queen herself had told her, Jane Rochford went on to state, that the king was unable to perform as a man. Mayhap that is why the queen sought comfort often with other men, including her brother.

Anne hung her head when she heard the news. "I am filled with regret," she said. "I recall, of a moment, advice that Margaret of Austria gave to me and the other maids of honor when we were but young girls serving in her court. 'Trust in those who offer you service, and in the end, my maidens, you will find yourself in the ranks of those who have been deceived.' For Jane Rochford deceived me, and now she has deceived all. I trusted in her, once, to my peril and to George's."

The next day the king allowed Archbishop Cranmer to visit with Anne, to offer spiritual comfort and hope, and we ladies took our leave to walk and offer her some privacy. But Cranmer brought ill tidings as well as comfort. I should not have thought that things could have grown worse. But they had.

When we returned Anne sat, motionless, in her chair. "What is it, my lady?" I asked.

371

"Cranmer has just told me that my marriage has been annulled," she said.

"Wonderful!" I cried. "Then you cannot have been adulterous to the king—if you had no marriage at all. Is that not true?"

Anne turned to me and smiled wanly. "Seems sensible, Meg, but alas, while I have had no valid marriage, my charges still stand."

Would no one speak up against this nonsensical offense? But who could, and retain his head?

"By what charge has your marriage been voided?" Nan Zouche asked.

"By the king's carnal knowledge of my sister, Mary," Anne said quietly. "It seems his conscience has now quickened inside him and he is taken with regret that he allowed me to 'bewitch' him when he knew all along that it was not right to marry me, his having been with my sister. Cranmer has agreed, in form, anyway, and annulled our marriage."

Naught could be said.

"Elizabeth has been made a bastard," Anne said, her voice growing dull as the wash water in her basin, which had not been refreshed.

She stood, walked to the window, and stared out. I joined her.

"The princess will be all right, dearest," I said, rubbing her back lightly for comfort. "Mayhap as the king's bastard she will be safer than as his heir."

"Mayhap," Anne said. "I have written to Master Parker and sent the letter with Cranmer. Cranmer did for me what he could, I know, but he is not as strong as I would have hoped. I have therefore given Matthew Parker charge over my daughter, her spiritual life and well-being. With Henry as sire and me as a mother I trust Elizabeth will need a quiet mind and a steady wit to guide her. I believe Bishop Parker will see that she comes to the truth of our Lord."

"Parker is trustworthy. And I will ensure that Elizabeth receives your jewels. When I have occasion to speak to her I will speak of you."

Anne drew near to me. "I heard some in the crowd afore my trial whisper that this is justice served. That I forced Henry to set aside Katherine, now I am being set aside for Jane."

"You did not force the king to do anything, Anne," I said. "And Katherine was not foully charged as an adulteress and a witch, nor set to die by public beheading or burning."

She looked me full in the face. "I truly believed him. That his marriage to Katherine had been dead for years, all knew. He said his marriage had been invalid, cursed, because of Arthur. That God had told him he must marry anew and get him a son for the realm. I trusted in him and carried forth with honest intent certain in the knowledge that Henry would not lie to me."

"Do you still believe he told you the truth?" I

asked her. It was plain to me that His Majesty was not only willing to lie, but that he convinced himself that the lies were truth and therefore had full confidence in them.

Anne did not directly respond. Instead, she said, "Mayhap he has convinced Mistress Seymour that our marriage was invalid, cursed, due to his knowledge of my sister. And that I am a witch. And she, as I did, carries on with honest intent."

"You're more charitable than I, dearest," I said.

"Meg, I must confess to you." She drew me back toward the window. "I did perhaps have a nagging suspicion that all was not as he said. But I was desperately in love. I wanted to believe him. I wanted to be married. I wanted to be queen. Mayhap I did wrong by Katherine because I wanted her to be a shrew who was not a maid at her marriage. I am not invulnerable to self-deceit."

"None of us is. Let your soul be easy, Anne," I said. "God will sort it out. And you acted upon the words spoken to you by the king, whose word is law." She nodded weakly so I took her by the hands to steady them and led her to table to partake of a cold meal of cheese, meat, and bread. Whatever self-deceit she had allowed herself would be paid for a hundred times over at Tower Green.

We stayed up late that evening; Lord Kingston

was kind enough to give us extra candles. We talked and, yea, even laughed over some of our girlhood adventures and discussed which gowns had been particular favorites. Even till the end, Anne cared about her clothes. She remained true to herself and I loved her for it.

The next morning we heard the scaffolding being built, early, on Tower Hill. By noon on the seventeenth of May each man falsely accused of adultery with Anne was beheaded.

My brother Thomas was able to watch from the Bell Tower, and he copied down George's last words so I might bring them to Anne for comfort. She read them over. He confessed his sins, spoke his regret that he was more often a hearer of the gospel than a doer, and entreated his listeners to do the opposite. I saw both the keening grief at his loss and her pride that he died strong in his faith in her face, etched already beyond its age with fatigue.

The king rested from his midnight festivities and rendezvous long enough to declare that Anne would die by beheading on Friday, May 19. Sir William told us that a French swordsman had been sent for and that it should be no pain, it was so subtle. No one commented that in order for the executioner to arrive from France in time he would have had to have been sent for well in advance of Anne's "trial."

As Anne heard Lord Kingston out I heard

the note of hysteria creep into her voice for a moment. "I have heard say the executioner was very good, and I have a little neck." She put her hand round it and laughed. Sir William backed away and out the door.

We stayed up with her, and her almoner, all night afore and she grew calm again. She asked me to read aloud in the first epistle of Saint Peter the Apostle.

Submit yourselves unto all manner ordinance of man for the Lord's sake, whether it be unto the king as unto the chief head: or unto rulers, as unto them that are sent of him . . . for so it is the will of God, that ye put to slander the ignorance of foolish men . . . for it is thankworthy if a man for conscience toward God endure grief, suffering, wrongfully . . . For Christ also suffered, leaving us an example that ye should follow his steps, which did no sin, neither was their guile found in his mouth: which when he was reviled, reviled not again, when he suffered, he threatened not: but committed the cause to him that judgeth righteously.

I closed the book.
"You have lived a good life, my dearest, loveliest friend. You have borne the weight of England's Reformation on your shoulders. You

have used your influence to place men who stand solely on Scripture"—I looked at her almoner—"throughout the Church of England and they will stand, and lead others, long after you are gone. You have borne a good daughter. You have been a most excellent wife and loyal friend. The rest is now to faith."

Anne nodded. "Saint Peter reminds me that I am called to suffer wrong and take it patiently and without rebuke."

"And Saint Paul writes to the Romans, 'Dearly beloved, avenge not yourselves, but give room unto the wrath of God, for it is written: vengeance is mine, I will reward, saith the Lord.' I admit to an unseemly eagerness to see what vengeance our Lord has in mind for Henry."

Anne allowed herself a little smile. "Dear Meg. You are always constant."

"Well, 'tis in Holy Writ!" I exclaimed. That brought a fuller smile from her, and it was lovely to behold.

"You are right," she said. " 'Tis easier to be meek when you know false charges will not go unanswered. I shall follow in the path of my Master. To do otherwise would be a burden on my soul—and a weapon for Henry to use against my daughter." Her black eyes grew sharp again. Her mind had lost nothing to grief.

We prayed for a time and then, nigh on daybreak, she awoke me. When I looked at her, I saw she was firmly in control of her emotions. Her hands did not tremble. Her smile was steady. Queen Anne was back.

"Rise, Meg. We must dress."

TWENTY-SIX

Year of Our Lord 1536
The Tower of London

In my final duty as mistress of robes I dressed Anne in a modest gown of gray damask, which had been lined with fur against the morning chill. It was good English fabric for a good English queen. She insisted on wearing an English gable, for modesty, and not the French hood for which she was so well known. "I was born an English girl, and I shall die an English woman," she said. I brushed her long, beautiful hair one last time, so it would glisten, and for her comfort, and for memory of our long friendship, before tucking it into the gable and draping her with royal ermine.

"Here." Anne handed something to me in her gloved hand.

"What is this?" I asked, taking it from her.

"It's my jeweled prayer book. I no longer need it," Anne said with a smile. "Do you remember how, on the night Will Ogilvy declared that he would become a priest, you handed me your prayer book? Said you had no use for it, nor for Will, nor for God any longer?"

I smiled and laughed with her. "Yes, Anne, I recall it well. 'Tis not a night I am likely to forget!"

"I read from it, your beautifully rendered Latin, your thoughtful notes, whilst I served Queen Claude."

I took it from her hand. "I shall think of you each time I read it." I opened it up and on the front page she had written, *Remember me, when you do pray, that hope doth lead from day to day.*

"To remember me by," she said.

I took her in my arms and we clung to one another as we had when one of us had tumbled from a steed as girls. "*Nihilo quo tui meminerim mihi opus est,*" I said.

I need nothing to remember you by.

I opened the door to the Queen's Lodging and let my lady lead ahead of us. It was a short walk past the great hall, where she had once celebrated her coronation and then, recently, defended her innocence, along the west side of the White Tower, built five hundred years past by William the Conqueror. We passed by it and we caught the first glimpse of the scaffolding upon which she must stand.

There were nigh on one thousand people come to watch—the king had decreed that only Englishmen and Englishwomen might view the beheading, no foreigners of any rank. There were some catcalls and some jeering and nary a word of encouragement. We passed by my lord the Duke of Suffolk and his young bride, Katherine Willoughby. We passed by the Duke of Richmond, the king's bastard and Anne's stepson, who bowed his head just enough for the crowd to notice. I silently thanked him for it. Anne's cousin, his wife, Mary Fitzroy, was not there.

We stopped at the bottom of the scaffold and she turned to me and put her mouth close to my ear. "You know why I say what I will say and I do it willingly. But if you ever have occasion, do not be reluctant to commend me to His Grace and tell him that he hath ever been constant in his career of advancing me; from private gentle-woman he made me marquess, from marquess a queen, and now that he hath left no higher degree of honor he gives my innocence the crown of martyrdom." She wanted to have the last word, our Anne, up to the last day. I was gladdened to see the spark had not left her.

She kissed my cheek and looked me in the eye. I nodded my agreement, knowing I could say no such thing if I wished to retain my head. I let the tears slide freely down my face and I could hear Nan Zouche sob in the background.

The constable took Anne's arm and helped her up the hastily built wooden stairway and I alone followed. She walked to the edge of the platform and addressed the crowd, voice firm, face bold.

"According to the law and by the law I am judged to die, and therefore I will speak nothing against it. I am come hither to accuse no man, nor to speak of that whereof I am accused and condemned to die, but I pray God save the king and send him long to reign over you, for a gentler nor a more merciful prince was there never, and to me he was ever a good, gentle, and sovereign lord."

She did not admit guilt nor make a false confession. I knew upon what she stayed her mind: the Henry of nearly a decade, who had wooed and won her, who sent her sweet letters and fine jewels and argued points of religion with her and offered her the choice bits off of his plate. If 'twere to be that which she chose to hold in her last moments, and not the tyrant the man had of late turned into, I should not begrudge her, nor anyone, fine memories at the end of her life.

"And thus I take my leave of the world, and of you all, and I heartily desire you all to pray for me," she finished.

The crowd, of a sudden, turned and grew respectfully silent. "God bless you, Your Grace," one called out loudly, and there was a wave of hums of approval and agreement.

Anne returned to the center of the platform. I gave her an encouraging look and removed her ermine mantle, leaving her gracious white neck unencumbered. She stayed me from lifting off her headdress; instead, she took it off herself, first shaking free her magnificent black hair one last time afore tucking it under a modest white cap.

"Jesu, receive my soul; O Lord God, have pity on my soul," she spoke as she knelt. I knelt near her to tie a blindfold around her eyes—she, unlike many others led to this place, needed nothing and no one to restrain her in her place. I had scarce stepped back from tying the blindfold when the sword of Calais sliced through the air and through her neck, severing her head in one clean blow. I heard gasps and sighs from the crowd and then nothing.

Her head rolled but a little way from her body, and I could see her lips still moving in silent prayer for a few moments while the blood pumped outward from the body and from the head. I was stuck firm in my place by the horror of it, jarred loose only by the clattering of Nan Zouche and Alice as they ran up the stairs with linen. I quickly leaned down and picked up her head, eyes still open and aware as the linen slipped from them, as they looked at me. I willed the bile back down my throat and forced myself to look into those eyes with love for the few moments before awareness dimmed from them.

Within seconds, she slipped away. I took the head into the smallest and finest of the linens and carefully wrapped it, her blood running thickly between my fingers, under my nails, and staining my forearms as I sought to save her from any indignity. Gorge rose in my throat but I swallowed it back every few seconds and tried not to feel the spidery trickle of blood running down my arms. Nan and Alice quickly wrapped the body and, while the guards held back the crowds, we made our way the hundred or so feet toward the chapel of St. Peter ad Vincula. On the way we passed the freshly dug graves of the men of the privy chamber, so recently laid to rest.

Do not waver. Do not stumble. Do not faint. Keep walking.

Once inside the church we removed her outer garments: much like the Roman soldiers casting lots for Christ's clothing, Anne's clothing were required to be parceled out to those who worked in the Tower keep, though she was allowed to keep her shift for modesty. We placed head and body together in a hastily emptied elm chest. It would be buried, and guarded, immediately.

"Good-bye, dearest," I whispered afore they closed the lid. "Till we meet again."

Sir William's men escorted us back to the Queen's Lodging. Nan Zouche was sick on the green along the way. "Get moving, and get your things," one guard roughly commanded.

"Where are we to go?" Alice asked. She looked wan and ill.

"You"—he pointed at her—"will go to the household of your son. You"—he pointed at Lady Zouche—"will go to the keep of your husband.

And you"—he pointed at me—"will be escorted back to Greenwich Palace, where you shall await your brother, who is now your guardian. He shall come to collect you shortly."

We were to keep our lives. But mine would be enslaved to Edmund. I looked up to where my brother Thomas was still imprisoned and sent a prayer his way. I had no strength to do more.

Before we left Anne's quarters I was sick over and over again in her privy basin.

As we left the Tower my anger grew. The man charged with delivering us back to our quarters carried on, either out of ill will or stupidity, about how the king was now free to marry Jane Seymour, and he would do so, anon, at York Place, and then present her as queen after Mass at Greenwich on Whitsunday, June 4. She was, I'd heard, at that moment being fitted for her wedding gown! *Have a care, Mistress Seymour,* I thought. *You know not whom you marry. Or mayhap you do.*

I knew Anne had been required by our times, by our God, and by her hopes for her daughter to speak well of the king. And I knew she was at peace. But it did not seem right that His Grace —the man who had not a sense of the meaning of the word yet carried the title—should be frolicking with Jane Seymour.

"Commend me to His Grace . . ." Anne's words came floating back to me.

I would. I would do exactly that. I knew not how but afore I was banished from the palace I would do it. With a life with Edmund ahead of me I risked little, if anything at all.

Once at the castle, I packed my items and sat in my small quarters, wondering when Edmund would arrive. I did not leave my room at first. I closed my eyes and I saw Anne—her eyes staring at me, last bits of life being snuffed out. They had looked at peace and yet I was not. The next time I closed my eyes I saw the two of us dancing together as girls, learning under the steady gaze of the dance master. I willed myself to read Scripture till I was tired, and then I tried to sleep again. This time, I saw Anne as she was on her Calais wedding night, the air crackling between her and Henry. She was so happy. I saw her snapping her fingers at a servant. She was certainly born to be royal. I heard her witty ripostes to Suffolk, unmanning her lifelong enemy to the bemusement of the king. I opened my eyes to stop the pictures and words.

Mayhap sleep would elude me. I wandered the hallway, toward the kitchen, and as I passed the great hall I could see her, dancing, for many years past. Unwell now, I returned to my room without eating. I felt my own head; 'twas feverish, and yet I had no lady servant to assist me.

That night I put my own dressing gown on afore bed. Hours later, I woke up screaming and clawing at my arms. I'd been dreaming that her blood was still running down my arms and I could not get it off. When I awoke I saw that I had scratched deep streaks into each forearm. They bled now, with my blood, along the same rivulets that Anne's had. I wiped them off with a linen.

Someone kindly sent a servant with food the next day; I knew not whom, but I suspected it was someone sympathetic to Anne, of course. Afraid to sleep, I spent the second night trying to think of a way to speak with the king, but of course, he was already at York Place with Mistress Seymour. Late that night I left my things in my traveling chest and made my way in the blackness down the hall to the chapel. I pushed open the door—it squeaked but a little—and made my way to a pew, wherein I looked up at the Lord on the cross and prayed. After an hour or so I began to make my way back toward the door out of the chapel and stopped, of a moment, at the royal box. In a feverish moment, I knew how to convey Anne's final message to Henry, to superstitious Henry, in a way he would never forget and would, I hoped, haunt him forever.

I crept back to my chambers and dug through my chest till I found what I was looking for—a quill and ink. I pulled a plain cloak about me so that if I should be seen in the hallway I should not be recognized. As the court was mainly with Henry at York Place there was little likelihood of being found out. And then I snuck back into the royal box at the chapel and opened the Scriptures to Acts of the Apostles, chapter 2, which should surely be read at the celebration of Pentecost, Whitsunday, when His Grace should be in this very place with his new bride.

In the margins next to the Scripture I disguised my hand as best I could and wrote, *You hath ever been constant in your career of advancing me; from private gentlewoman you made me marquess, from marquess a queen, and now that you hath left no higher degree of honor you give my innocence the crown of martyrdom. Your beloved wife, Anne.*

Once done, hand shaking, I blew on it till 'twere dry and then raced back to my rooms and finally, in the dead of night, allowed myself to sob aloud and collapse into fevered sleep.

When I awoke, it was not Edmund come to collect me.

"Thomas!" I leapt up and hugged him. "You are freed!"

He smiled at me. "I am freed. Father had written to Cromwell and Cromwell had me let go. The king is too distracted with Mistress Seymour of a moment to have a care for those he'd worried had once dallied with Anne."

I let the tears slide again. "I know not what to do." I gulped back my sobs. "Am I to remain with

Edmund, who may not have me? Or burden Alice on her widow's portion? Or you?"

He sent his manservant to take my case. "I have not always been the brother you needed, but as your appointed guardian, I believe that I can be of assistance now."

He led me to the litter and I, still in a fever and exhausted, stumbled along behind him. Once in the litter I let it jostle me to sleep till Thomas put his hand on my leg. "Meg. We arrive."

I woke myself and looked out the window.

" 'Tis not Allington," I said.

He smiled broadly. "No indeed, Mistress Wyatt, 'tis not."

I watched in wonder as Will Ogilvy came forth from the door of the great hunting lodge and strode toward the litter and I stepped out into his arms. My legs, still weak from the events just passed as well as from the ride, buckled and he scooped me up into his arms and carried me into the lodge. He set me down on a long seat and when I made as if to speak he put his finger on my lips.

"Hush, it will be time for talking later. You are safe now, and you must eat and sleep and become well."

He leaned over and kissed my brow. When I next awoke I found Edithe standing over me.

"You were right, lady, Master Will found employment for me and for my Roger. Come

388

now"—she helped me to my feet—"I will take you into your chamber and I will help you bathe and bring you some broth and meat."

I slept on and off for a day or two, and when my fever abated I let Edithe dress me in one of the fine dresses Anne had given me and pull back my still-thick hair into a twist, and then I joined Will for dinner. My brother Thomas had ridden off to hunt nearby, cleansing himself of memories, I supposed, and would shortly rejoin us.

I sat across from Will at a small wooden table. "Thank you for bringing me here, and allowing me to regain my senses and health," I said after we'd eaten.

"Do you want to tell me what happened?" he said.

I nodded and told the whole story—with the exception of my writing in His Grace's copy of Holy Writ. That secret would remain with me as it would risk the hearer as well as myself should it become known. "You will have to thank your wife for your kind hospitality," I said. He moved his chair uncomfortably close to me for a married man.

"You shall thank her yourself," he said.

"Is she here?" I looked about me and caught a smile on Edithe's face afore she disappeared into the kitchens.

"A man can hope, for certes," he said. "My father was required to call off my engagement with Lady Jamison. I am not a married man. Mayhap you can remedy that."

I let my look express my shock, certain I had misheard in my fever. "Call it off? Upon what grounds?"

He reached out and took my hand and then laced his fingers through mine. "Precontract."

"Precontract? With . . . oh . . . ," I said. "You told him you and I were precontracted."

"Yes," Will said. "Because, Meg Wyatt, in my heart, in every other way, and near in word itself, I have been promised and pledged to you forever."

"Was he angry?"

Will nodded. "He sent me from him for a time, here. I have not yet been recalled."

"Will your father then approve of our marriage?"

"I care not," he said. "In spite of your misguided judgments I do not always heed his hark."

I blushed deeply at the memory of that accusation and he laughed aloud and kissed my hand.

In order to regain my dignity I said, "Well, you must care some because we can hardly wander from town to town and beg our bread."

"Leave those details to me, mistress," he said. "If my father will not see to keep me as his heir after we are married then we shall go to Antwerp and I will work with printers I know. Printing Scriptures and other works is what I am called to.

I know it now. I can put my family's fortune to good use, if I remain heir."

"And will you so remain if you have me? I have no dowry." I hung my head. "I know 'tis a shameful thing."

He took my face in his hands. "I will gladly take your shame upon me when I let him know what we have done. And now, my lady, you have not yet answered me."

I looked up at Will, for the first time in many years, feeling hope, and the love of my man, and the love of my God, all at once.

I leaned forward and kissed him softly on the lips. "Yes, Will Ogilvy, I shall be your wife."

Oh blessed Lord Jesus. Thank You.

The next night Will invited a friend, a priest of Reform persuasion, as well as my brother Thomas, who had not yet returned to his wife, and two members of the nearby nobility to witness our vows. As I dressed in my gown, I took the portrait of my mother out of my chest and looked at it, tracing my finger over her face.

"I have not let you down, lady mother," I said afore returning it to its wraps.

I took Anne's prayer book in my hand and closed my eyes. "You will always be a part of me, my dearest friend. You wished this for me, I know. Be at peace."

After the short service all took their leave. It was just Edithe and I in Will's chamber.

"I have never had a more joyful occasion in serving you, lady." She helped me into a loose, lovely white dressing gown. She brushed my long hair, which hung halfway down my back and around my shoulders.

"And I am ever thankful to have you here," I said. She curtseyed politely, made sure the wafers and cheese and wine were set, and took her leave. Shortly thereafter Will came in. He stood looking at me, and I at him, for a full minute. The years of our lives, the many years I thought all was lost, and indeed it was, had been reclaimed and returned to us.

"You are beautiful, My Lady," he said quietly. He drew me to him and then drew us both to the foot of the bed, where we sat side by side. He opened my palm and in it put a small silk bag which I recognized as having once been my own.

"I had this made long ago. Open it," he urged me.

I undid the strings and poured the contents into my open hand. A hammered gold necklace, a daisy chain. "There is no gift that could mean more," I said softly.

"May I?"

I nodded and he took the chain into his hand and then fastened it about my neck. When he was finished, he leaned in to kiss me once, twice more, the sweet and then urgent kisses I'd waited for all my life. The kisses of my husband.

"*Te amo*," he whispered to me later as we lay together and watched the moon rise outside the window.

"*Te amo*," I whispered back.

It was good to speak Latin again.

Five months hence, before the Christmas celebrations began, Will's father recalled him. Will insisted that I accompany him. "Do not worry," he said. "My father cannot abide Rose's husband, and though he should like young Philip, he does not, and does not care to suffer him to be the heir to two fortunes. Including his own." He squeezed my hand for comfort.

I was shown to my rooms, and later that night, after dinner, his father called me forward in his study. "Well, Mistress Wyatt," he said. "We meet again."

I held my tongue and did not correct my title. "Yes, sir. Thank you for your hospitality."

"I understand that my son has married you, rather than the great heiress I had chosen for him. You have no remaining dowry and no fortune. Do you bring anything at all to this union, My Lady?"

I stood fast and said nothing, but smoothed my hands over the sides and front of my thin gown, chosen specially for this reason and worn without stays. As I did, his eyes were drawn to the growing swell of my stomach. His heir.

He said nothing at all but, for the first time ever, I saw the smallest of smiles twitch on Baron Asquith's stern face. I allowed myself a small smile in return. We had come to an understanding.

What I had once so easily dismissed, a simple life as a wife and a mother, had now become my greatest pleasure. I mourned Anne, who had not had the mighty love of a good man, but rather the uncertain affections of a mighty man.

She will never be forgotten, for certes.

Author's Note

I stood in front of Anne Boleyn on Easter Sunday, or I should say, I stood in front of her portrait at the National Portrait Gallery in London. Because I wanted to reflect on her life but not inhibit others from viewing the painting, I stood a few feet back and let others pass in front of me. Two women of a certain age did just that.

"Floozy!" one sputtered.

"Schemer!" her friend hissed as she moved quickly past Anne, who stared, calmly, back.

I felt as though someone had just spat on a friend.

Throughout the ages Anne has been portrayed as a man-eater, the woman who used her feminine wiles to woo Henry away from his faithful, aging wife. And while it's true that Henry sought to divorce Katherine of Aragon and marry Anne Boleyn, the woman, and her story, is much deeper, purer, and more complicated than that. Historian Dr. Eric Ives, perhaps the world's most respected biographer of Anne Boleyn, says, "Historians see through a glass darkly; they know in part and they pronounce in part." Maybe there has been more pronouncing than knowing where Anne has been concerned.

While this is a work of historical fiction, I've

sought to remain as true to the history as to the fiction. Ives says that Anne "would remain a remarkable woman in a century that produced many of great note. There were few others who rose from such beginnings to a crown and none contributed to a revolution as far reaching as the English Reformation."

Anne really was lifelong friends with the sisters of Thomas Wyatt, and they are believed to have accompanied her to the scaffold. The son of the eldest Wyatt sister did have a son named John Rogers who became a priest, and then a Reformer, and was commonly believed to be the first Protestant martyred under Bloody Mary, Henry's eldest daughter. In my story and genealogy chart, I have switched the names of Meg and her mother and Henry Wyatt's eldest daughter and her mother for this story so that two "Annes" wouldn't confuse the reader. Many believe Margaret, Lady Lee, to have been the Margaret in my story, but the birth dates of Henry Wyatt's children, as well as his first marriage and the birth date of Lady Lee, suggested something else to me, as seen on my genealogy charts and in the story within. Many of the things said and done in the book are actual recorded history, and some, like making Henry and Katherine Carey the illegitimate offspring of Henry VIII and Mary Boleyn, are theories I have adopted based on what I feel is good history. This is true, too, of the private commitment of Anne and Henry in November 1532, *espousals de praesenti*, formalized by intercourse, which, according to Eric Ives in his biography *The Life and Death of Anne Boleyn* is a plausible alternative scenario put forth not only by Anne's and Elizabeth's supporters but also by those who had no personal stake, and even by some who had potential motivation to undermine.

In 1540, just five years after the king made Thomas Cromwell the highest civil and religious authority in the land, after himself, he had him beheaded because he did not like Anne of Cleves, procured for the king by Cromwell. And, perhaps, Henry felt that Cromwell had risen too high, always a danger in Henry's courts. Henry married his fifth wife, Catherine Howard, that very same day. The king seems to have made a practice of tying together murder and marriage.

Jane Rochford, George's wife, did die by the sword just six years after Meg had said she might. Jane was found guilty of assisting in arranging clandestine meetings between Henry's fifth wife, Anne's cousin Catherine Howard, and Queen Catherine's lover. Jane was imprisoned in the Tower, declared insane, and finally executed by a single blow of the ax in 1542.

Meg's fuller story, of course, is mainly fictional but drawn from the time. Many women, then as now, give their lives to the call of service that goes unrecorded except by the One who notes all and never forgets.

To learn more about the Tudors and Sandra's books, please visit www.sandrabyrd.com.

HISTORICAL BIBLIOGRAPHY

Over the course of my life I have eagerly devoured hundreds of books, fiction and non-fiction, set in Tudor times and all have influenced and delighted me, but there are several books I hold in highest esteem and referred to time and again while writing this book. I've listed them below. In addition I was blessed with the resource of living historians. Principal among them was Lauren Mackay, Tudor researcher, scholar, and master of history/Ph.D. candidate in Sydney, Australia. Lauren, you are a stealth weapon and I can't express the fullness of my gratitude. Thanks to Professor Matt Panciera, Latinist at Gustavus Adolphus College, for his critical assistance with Latin. I would also like to thank the aptly named Memory Gargiulo for her Tudor historical insight and ready knowledge and Maureen Benfer, Tudor seamstress extraordinaire.

Principal Works of Reference

Ives, Eric. *The Life and Death of Anne Boleyn.* 2005.

Starkey, David. *Six Wives: The Queens of Henry the Eighth.* 2004.

Tyndale's New Testament. Translated by William Tyndale. A modern-spelling edition of the 1534 translation with an introduction by David Daniell. 1989.

Hamer, Colin. *Anne Boleyn: One Short Life That Changed the English-Speaking World.* 2007.

The Love Letters of Henry the Eighth, To Anne Boleyn: And Two Letters from Anne Boleyn to Cardinal Wolsey: With her last letter to Henry the Eighth, and the king's love-letter to Jane Seymour. Reprinted from the Harleian Miscellany, with an introduction by Ladbroke Black. London: 1933.

Somerset, Anne. *Ladies in Waiting: From the Tudors to the Present Day.* 2004.

Thompson, Patricia. *Sir Thomas Wyatt and His Background.* 1964.

Zahl, Paul F. M. *Five Women of the English Reformation.* 2001.

Starkey, David, and Susan Doran. *Henry the Eighth: Man and Monarch.* 2009.

Worcester, Sir Robert, KBE DL, Chancellor, University of Kent, *History of Allington Castle.* 2007.

To Die For
Reading Group Guide

1. The book opens with a glimpse of the friendship between Meg and Anne as teenagers and follows them through courtship and marriage, treachery and setbacks, childbearing and childlessness, immense riches, and a final difficult plummet to death. How is the evolution of women's friendships in the twenty-first century similar to, and different from, women's friendships in the sixteenth century?

2. A major theme in the book is the balance of love versus duty. Each has its own rewards and costs. In which situations must the women in the book balance love and duty? Does one character have a better grasp on the balance than the other? What kinds of love-versus-duty conflicts do women today face?

3. Tudor women, even and perhaps especially the highborn, had extreme social limits on their autonomy, and yet they did have some personal and community power. How is that illustrated in the book? Which characters use their power only for personal gain, and which use their power for the good of others, and how? Did/do women

have certain types of power that were/are unavailable to men?

4. Discuss the concept of small personal sacrifices for the greater gain of a group. Cranmer, in particular, would have felt that he was sacrificing Anne for a greater good. Do the ends ever justify the means?

5.Readers often have clear preferences on first- vs. third-person narration. Did the first-person narration of *To Die For* influence your feelings about the book, about Meg, about Anne? Since the author made a clear choice to present this in the first person, what would have been gained or lost by a third-person point of view?

6. Although the book is set nearly five hundred years ago, how are the women and men in it like people you know—your sister, your mother, a person who knifes you in the back at work? How are the men and women in this book different from people in your world? Which is better . . . and why?

7. There is a quality-control concept that says you never know the temper of a metal until it is tested. Testing alone proves strength—and character. How is that played out for Meg? For Anne? For George Boleyn and Jane Rochford as

well as others in the book? How has testing improved the quality of your relationships and your life?

8. Early in the book Meg laments that she is always the setting, never the stone. Later, at Westminster Abbey, she has an epiphany that while that is still true, she has been viewing it all wrong. In which arenas in life are you the stone, and in which the setting? Do you prefer one over another?

9. Books written about the Tudor court seem to be perennial favorites. Why do you think this period, more than many others, captures readers' hearts? What does that say about human nature?

10. During the Tudor years, and many years thereafter, a person's position in his or her family dictated affection, career, marriage, and financial well-being. Is that still true in any way? How?

11. Is Anne Boleyn, as depicted in this book, anything like the Anne Boleyn of common knowledge? Has reading this book informed or changed your opinion on Anne Boleyn in any way, and if so, how?

Author Q&A

1. Though many men in this novel are conniving and cruel, Meg's father is particularly vicious and abusive. In your mind, why is he so angry? What prompted you to imagine him this way?

Very little is known about the real Henry Wyatt. We do know that he was imprisoned, and most likely tortured, for two years during the reign of Richard III for his support of Henry VII in an early revolt. Some research indicates he had a daughter the year he was released, in 1485 to 1486, with his first wife, who presumably died. He did not remarry or have another child for nearly fifteen more years.

Men were certainly allowed to beat their wives and children during this time period. It's a possible application of the phrase "rule of thumb"; a man could beat them with a stick no thicker than his thumb. I wanted to show a common threat to women. Although it was abusive and harmful, most women developed the resilience to prevail and cope to the best of their abilities and resources. Meg certainly did.

Although he cherished his second, younger wife, I believe that Henry Wyatt's cruelty manifested itself as a result of his own torture in the Tower. Some people overcome poor treatment and become better people because of newfound empathy and resilience; others absorb the cruelty into their spirit and it becomes a part of them. In my rendition, Henry Wyatt represented the latter, as did his second son, Edmund.

2. Many books and movie scripts have been written about the rise and fall of Anne Boleyn and the Church of England. What drew you to this historical period and to these characters?

Books and movies are condensed drama; therefore, the most engaging stories take place during extraordinary times. Because the stakes were so high during the Tudor years, there is always excitement and change. Love, lust, hatred, murder, good versus evil, self-sacrifice, gluttony and greed, envy, spiritual birth or renewal, spiritual deception, friendship and betrayal, family that remains true and family who backstabs you out of selfishness—these are all elements of human life. The Tudor Court had them in abundance. Everything we undergo today they underwent too, only writ large, with bigger stakes than most of us have. So we both identify with them and are, maybe, a little in awe too.

Amazing gowns, huge castles, and precious jewelry don't hurt to write and read about, either! The time period is, simply, enchanting on all levels.

3. After Will declares his intentions to become a priest, Meg gives Anne her book of hours, claiming that she has no use of it, or of God. This scene feels as though it could take place at any point in history, including the present. What do you think is so relatable about this scene?

There's a point in each person's spiritual journey where he or she has to cross from immaturity (Why are you doing this to me?) to maturity (Not my will, but yours be done).

When we reject God because He is not forcing things to work out the way we want, we're acting out of a sense of entitlement common to everyone in the human race. Each of us, on the way to spiritual adulthood, eventually has to acquiesce to God's greater knowledge and better purpose.

Meg voices the frustration and hurt we each feel from time to time. Hopefully, by reading about someone just like us, we can see that while it doesn't always happen on our timetable, as life unfolds, it eventually make sense.

4. Meg often worries how living at court will change her. Indeed, the royal court of Henry VIII is a bizarre contradiction, full of people so religious and yet so wicked and deceitful. Does this remind you of any modern equivalents? Do you think a moral person can truly survive such an environment and escape with his or her morals fully intact?

Bad company corrupts good character, of course. The trick, then as now, is to become discerning about who is truly motivated by good, though they be fallible, and who is in it for politics or personal gain and will harm any who stand in their way, no matter if they claim piety or not.

I do believe that people can tangle with evil and corruption and come out with their morals intact and perhaps with stronger resolve. But I believe all such will be permanently changed by seeing people as they really are, good and bad and a blend of both. Naïveté is not an option anymore; with much wisdom comes much sorrow. But wisdom is to be sought after and is necessary for a purposeful life.

5. On page 84, Anne argues with Meg, "You blame God for the deeds of men, I blame the men themselves." In *To Die For*, there seems to be a delicate balance between believing that God is all-powerful and that men have the free will to do good or evil. We often struggle to understand why God allows bad things to happen. Did you use your characters to work through some of your own conflicting feelings on this subject?

Yes. I, like everyone else, have had misfortune knock at my door from time to time. Mostly it was nothing I'd anticipated: the situations were shocking and unsettling to my worldview and faith. When we're surprised by hardship or calamity, it knocks us off of our feet, and I wanted someone to "fix" it and questioned how a loving parent could even allow that to happen.

There are those who blame God for every trial, trouble, or adversity, and then there are those who call upon Him as their best resource during a crisis or loss. I learned from the latter and grew as I unclenched my tight grasp on life. Meg did, too. In Tudor times, as now, that which doesn't kill you makes you stronger. Anne was a strong woman, and as far as my research goes, she never questioned God's justice. God is in the business of producing adults to "be strong and courageous," not mollycoddling our weaknesses. But He is always a very present help in times of trouble.

6. Though he eventually goes on to reveal his capricious nature and disregard for true godliness, Henry at first makes a valid argument: since Scripture dictates a man shouldn't marry his brother's wife, the pope himself doesn't have the authority to permit the marriage. Do you think the whole situation began with a good intention, or was it an exercise in twisting religion to fit the will of man from the get-go with Henry?

Henry was well educated in both secular and spiritual matters and was able to intelligently grapple with and argue both—which made him believable no matter his motivation. I think he zeroed in on a point of contention that was bubbling up at the time, *sola scriptura*, and figured out how he could capitalize on it for his own intentions. It was a valid argument and an important part of the Reformation. But had the pope granted Henry his divorce, Henry's conscience would not have been troubled by this Scripture. It certainly wasn't when he sought dispensation for having slept with Mary Boleyn before marry-ing Anne.

As I said in the book, God often uses the strongest beast, not the gentlest beast, to plow the hardest fields. Henry was indubitably strong. The changes that came about as a result of those turbulent years encouraged healthy refinement within the Roman Catholic Church besides founding the English Reformation and the Church of England, providing accessibility to Scripture for the common man, and birthing whole branches of Protestantism, which still thrive today. What might have been intended for selfishness or evil, and certainly did cause considerable pain to those involved, eventually yielded a harvest of goodness.

7. The latest research argues that Henry seemed very sincere in his belief that he and Katherine were wrongly married and thus God cursed them by denying him an heir. In *To Die For*, he also

seems very convinced of this truth. On page 153, Meg ponders the situation: "If a queen could not lie, could God's anointed king? Surely one of them must have." What do you think?

Through my research I came to believe that Henry had narcissistic personality disorder. It can be mild early in life, but grows to become darker, more controlling, more punishing, and capricious as life goes on and the narcissist senses that his good looks, charm, and powers are fading. Henry was worried about his legacy. This may explain why Henry grew from a golden prince to a "tyrant," the label assigned by historian David Starkey.

Like all narcissists, Henry was unable to ever admit, even to himself, that he was wrong. So he constantly rewrote history to his benefit and interpreted circumstances to support his self-righteousness and self-pity, both of which he had in spades. Narcissists change things first in their own minds, overwriting the file of what actually transpired. And then they place unshakable faith in the new rendition; the old version exists no more. This allowed Henry to believe, without a doubt, that how he saw and remembered events was black-and-white certainty. Narcissists then convince others, by their unwavering belief and genuineness, that they are telling the truth. We want to believe them. Till we can't.

8. There's a wealth of information available about Tudor England and Anne Boleyn and dozens of versions of the story in print and film. What kind of research did you do in preparation for writing this novel? Do you have any favorite resources, either in the academic or entertainment arenas?

Eric Ives is the most famous of Anne's biographers, and justifiably so for his impeccable, credible research and thoroughness. I am certainly a fan. I read perhaps another dozen nonfiction books that covered Anne's life and the English and French courts during her interactions with them. I read, and am still reading, Tyndale's translation of the New Testament. Although I whetted my love of Anne on historical fiction, I avoided it for several years before writing this book and throughout the writing of this series, so as not to commingle someone else's historical fiction extrapolations with my own. When I finish writing my own Tudor books, I will dive right back into the genre and begin happily reading Tudor fiction again.

I also engaged a historical researcher, Lauren Mackay, who has a degree in Tudor study and is also a lifelong Tudorphile. She was not only an invaluable source of historical truths but helped me to discern whether motives, dialogue, and consequences as I'd envisioned them were true to the characters and the time.

Of course, I visited England. I stood in Anne and Mary's bedroom at Hever, and prayed in front of Anne's book of hours. I wandered Hampton Court to gather a sense of her life there, too. I stood in front of Whitehall and imagined Meg there. It was to die for.

9. When Meg finds God again, it's because of a passage from Isaiah that she finds written in Henry and Anne's shared book of hours: "He was a man of sorrows, acquainted with grief." Meg feels she hears God speaking directly to her, telling her that He also has suffered and thus knows her suffering. What does this Bible passage mean to you? Do you have a favorite piece of Scripture as well?

My favorite piece of Scripture at any given time is whichever one God is using to speak to me at the moment, because when He does, I know He is attentive to my concerns and hears and loves me in both hopeful and ashen circumstances. He has already prepared a plan and a way.

I think this is why that passage was so effective for Meg. She felt like she had undergone a lot—beatings by her father, loss of the love of her life, putting aside her own hopes and dreams for a life of meaning and serving her friend, who seemed to have it all. When she sees Christ suffering, she understands that He relates in every way to her sorrow on a human level and she opens up to Him. She also sees Him as God, knowing that He has already prepared a plan and a way, and she begins to trust. When she does, her life of excitement truly begins.

10. The first epistle of Saint Peter the Apostle, as Meg reads it aloud to Anne in her Tower prison, instructs men to submit to their kings and other rulers as they are sent by God Himself. Throughout this story, however, we're shown the evils a ruler can visit upon his people when he believes he is, and is treated by all as, God's anointed sovereign. Do you think this belief gives the power hungry a terrible license? At what point do you think a person must violate this instruction? Or do you agree with the rest of the epistle that encourages the faithful to endure wrongful suffering?

I don't think the power-hungry need a license from others; they ascribe it to themselves and eventually are beyond all correction from the voice of reason. What we as individuals must do at any given time is discern what our role is in "such a time as this." Are we to stand up to evil, publicly, as Bonhoeffer did? Or are we to keep a low cover and do good under the surface, as the Ten Booms did? Both responded to Nazi power in appropriate ways for the paths their lives were to take and the good they were to do while on them. One thing we do know for certain: it's never God's will to call evil good or good evil, so we are not to, either.

11. As you say in your Author's Note, Anne Boleyn has been portrayed and perceived as a harlot, witch, schemer, brilliant strategist, friend to the Reformation, and singularly intelligent and strong woman. After writing this book, what is your opinion of her? Why do you think she still evokes such controversy?

I think Anne was a complex woman who has, for too long, been denied the shading of any mortal life. She was certainly groomed and encouraged to push herself and her family as far along the road to success as she could take them and did so willingly, even sought out those opportunities. And yet that is no different from the expectation any family of that time would have had for their daughters and sons. She was witty but could be sharp, too. She had charm and allure and wasn't afraid to use them on her own behalf, but she was also a loyal friend who used her power, almost without fail, to help others and especially the nascent reformed church in England.

It's easy to pick up a touchy fact that makes all of us married women a bit angry—she was the other woman in a divorce case—without realizing the complexity of the times. Many believed Henry's marriage to his brother's wife had been wrong; it had indeed required the pope to dispense of that fact. They believed that England could come to ruin, or be gobbled by the Spanish, without a male heir. They understood that other queens had quietly retired to abbeys when they'd been unable to "do their duty." Normally, royal marriages were not love matches. They existed to purpose and that purpose must be fulfilled.

Anne evokes emotion because she was, and always will remain, larger than life. And because she died in such a great and terrible way at the hand of the man pledged to love and protect her.

12. Besides the fascinating machinations of Henry VIII and his noble contemporaries, Henry's reign was an important period in the history and evolution of Christianity. In your opinion, what are some of the most profound, lasting changes that resulted from the Henry/Anne/Katherine triangle?

It was the time when men truly began to reason from Scripture itself for themselves—as Henry and those he employed did to ascertain the validity of his marriage. By the end of Henry's reign there were Bibles in English in every church in England. God was now on His way to being at home in both the cathedral and the croft.

Center Point Publishing
600 Brooks Road ● PO Box 1
Thorndike ME 04986-0001 USA

(207) 568-3717

US & Canada:
1 800 929-9108
www.centerpointlargeprint.com